VANESSA NELSON

THE
SEARCHING

THE HUNDRED - BOOK 5

THE SEARCHING

The Hundred - Book 5

Vanessa Nelson

Copyright © 2020 Vanessa Nelson

All rights reserved. This is a work of fiction.

All characters and events in this publication are fictitious and any resemblance to any real person, living or dead, is purely coincidental.

Reproduction in whole or in part of this publication without express written consent is strictly prohibited.

To find out more about Vanessa Nelson or her books, please visit: www.taellaneth.com

For my four-legged house mates, who make me laugh every single day.

Contents

1. CHAPTER ONE — 1
2. CHAPTER TWO — 8
3. CHAPTER THREE — 14
4. CHAPTER FOUR — 25
5. CHAPTER FIVE — 31
6. CHAPTER SIX — 37
7. CHAPTER SEVEN — 45
8. CHAPTER EIGHT — 52
9. CHAPTER NINE — 61
10. CHAPTER TEN — 67
11. CHAPTER ELEVEN — 77
12. CHAPTER TWELVE — 87
13. CHAPTER THIRTEEN — 92
14. CHAPTER FOURTEEN — 102
15. CHAPTER FIFTEEN — 114
16. CHAPTER SIXTEEN — 121
17. CHAPTER SEVENTEEN — 132
18. CHAPTER EIGHTEEN — 138
19. CHAPTER NINETEEN — 146

20.	CHAPTER TWENTY	151
21.	CHAPTER TWENTY-ONE	159
22.	CHAPTER TWENTY-TWO	164
23.	CHAPTER TWENTY-THREE	169
24.	CHAPTER TWENTY-FOUR	180
25.	CHAPTER TWENTY-FIVE	187
26.	CHAPTER TWENTY-SIX	195
27.	CHAPTER TWENTY-SEVEN	210
28.	CHAPTER TWENTY-EIGHT	217
29.	CHAPTER TWENTY-NINE	224
30.	CHAPTER THIRTY	232
31.	CHAPTER THIRTY-ONE	247
32.	CHAPTER THIRTY-TWO	263
	THANK YOU	268
	CHARACTER LIST	269
	PLACES	271
	ALSO BY THE AUTHOR	272
	ABOUT THE AUTHOR	274

Chapter One

Yvonne finished the last mouthful of food on her plate and set her cutlery down. She could sit for a while. There was nothing requiring her attention just now.

A sharp contrast to the hectic pace of the past few days. She and Guise had arrived in the Royal City, the jewel of the Valland kingdom, only two days before, and had barely had time to draw breath since. A confrontation with the court's most senior Circle Mage, who had turned out to be a sorcerer steeped in blood magic, had been swiftly followed by a treasury full of deadly magical creatures. Then there had been the discovery of the murder of the court's treasurer. And the Circle Mage had brought himself back from the dead, killing a good number of the King's soldiers to make his escape.

The Circle Mage was still missing. Every resource of the Valland court was engaged in searching for him. And all the effort had yielded nothing so far. Hiram was as skilled at hiding as he was at forbidden magic.

She shivered slightly in the morning sun, and shoved thoughts of the blood sorcerer aside for now, seeking distraction. It was easy to find.

"The food here is almost as good as Modig's," Yvonne said, leaning back in her chair, tea cup held between her hands. Along with her empty plate, a range of beautifully-made porcelain dishes, still holding enough food for at least one more full meal, almost entirely hid the pristine white tablecloth. The scents curling into the air were almost tempting her to another helping, even though she was sure she could not eat another bite.

"The staff here would be delighted to hear you say so, mristrian," Guise said, tone quite serious.

"They have heard of Modig?" she asked, raising an eyebrow. They were sitting at one of the few tables on the roof terrace of one of the Royal City's finest hotels, with unrivalled views of the great city around them. The Royal City was the centre of the Valland kingdom, and one of the most law-abiding places in all the known lands. It was a far cry from Three Falls, the city of criminals, where Modig's hotel had been. And the staff here were all entirely human, as far as she could tell, unlike the part-goblin Modig.

"The best hotels keep an eye on each other," Guise answered, mouth lifting in a smile, a gleam in his eyes, which were bright green in the morning light.

If the food, and her surroundings, had not been enough to hold her attention, Guise was a potent distraction. His voice was one of the most beautiful sounds in the world, even after the many years she had known him. He tilted his head, the sunlight catching on his long, silky black hair, turning his grey skin even paler, looking like exactly what he was, a high-ranking lord of the Karoan'shae, used to the finer things in life.

"The manager here has already asked me if I know how to find Modig, and if he might be looking for a new kitchen," he said.

Yvonne laughed, shaking her head slightly, glad to be able to laugh after the past few days.

The search for Hiram had been fast-paced and fruitless. They were all exhausted. The King, his General, the supposedly retired soldier, Sarra, who seemed to be second only to the General in the court, Guise and Yvonne. And so, Sarra had decreed a day off. They would reconvene the next day to decide on next steps.

Yvonne had been tempted to argue, and was glad now that she had not done so.

A good night's sleep, a long bath, an excellent breakfast, and the faint scents of the flowering plants twining around the roof terrace had relaxed her shoulders, making her realise just how fraught the last few days had been. She was slightly annoyed that Sarra had been the one to recognise that they needed rest, even though Sarra was an old, experienced warrior, used to managing soldiers.

Nothing was normal now. The Stone Walls had been destroyed. The valley behind the walls, which had provided a safe haven for those with nowhere else to turn, was in ruins. Most of the inhabitants of the Sisters' valley were dead, including Adira, whose loss still made Yvonne's heart ache. As if that pain was not enough, a sorcerer skilled in forbidden magic had been at the heart of one of the most powerful royal courts in all the lands. Yvonne had tried to kill him once, and failed.

"We will find him," Guise said, breaking through her thoughts.

She blinked, bringing herself back to the here and now, the faint breeze brushing across her face, the fading warmth of the tea in the cup she still held, the teasing scents of the food on the table. Even with a goblin and a hungry human, they had not managed to finish the hotel's breakfast.

"I have enquiries I can make," Guise continued, not waiting for her response. He was a master at gathering information, loving secrets as much as he loved his fine tailoring.

"Good," she answered, putting the tea cup down.

He hesitated and her mouth curved into a smile again.

"You don't want me to come with you," she guessed, laughing softly when he inclined his head, a faint line between his brows. "Now, who might you know in the Royal City that would not want to speak to a Hunar?" she asked, voice light.

His lips curved. "People with no taste at all, mristrian."

She should be getting used to compliments from him, yet they still took her by surprise, heat rising in her face.

"I have plenty to do," she told him. "I need to send a message to Pieris, apart from anything else." There were always tasks to do, even while travelling. Mundane matters like laundry, tending to her horse, checking on the supplies she carried. She had found some time, in a few brief moments, to replace some of the spells she carried in the pouch at her waist. More were needed. And she should also write some letters. Long overdue. Not least to Joel and Mariah, letting her children know that she was safe and well.

The old, familiar stab of guilt passed through her chest. She took a breath in, waiting for the worst of it to fade. Her children were used to her absences. They had, somehow, grown into fine young people. Guilt was replaced by the equally familiar pain of missing her children. She blinked, the sting in her eyes fading. Letters. She could, at least, send them letters.

And, if she had the time, she needed to replace her small knife. She had thrown it at Hiram and not recovered it. And was not sure, now, that she would want it back.

"The hotel will provide you with whatever you need," Guise told her, with the quiet assurance of someone born to wealth and privilege. He had never had to negotiate for a room in his life. And she was quite sure that he had never been turned away from a tavern in the dead of night, in the pouring rain, soaked to his skin, or told, at the only other tavern in the village, that he could sleep in the horse barn and pay handsomely for the uncomfortable night. She could still remember the straw poking through her clothes, scratching her skin.

"Thank you," she said.

He inclined his head a fraction, although his lips were pressed into a line. She lifted her brows, asking a silent question. Anyone who did not know him might find his expressions hard to read. She had a strong sense that there was something more he wanted to say. Something important. And yet, he was holding back.

He reached into a pocket and brought out a piece of heavy parchment, folded over to make an envelope, sealed with wax and a spark of magic she recognised as his own.

"Would you keep this for me, mristrian?" he asked, stretching forward and putting it on the tablecloth next to her plate.

There was no writing on the parchment, it was just sealed over.

She picked it up, feeling a slight weight inside the folded parchment. Not much, though. The spark of magic that he had used to seal it also hid its contents. She tucked it into a pocket and nodded once.

"I'll hold it for you."

He hesitated again, looking away, across the rooftops of the city, to the green hills beyond. He was not looking at the scenery, she thought. Rather, he was trying to find a way of phrasing whatever he had to say next.

"I will not open it unless I need to," she added.

Everyone had secrets. Guise more than most. And she had discovered, not that long ago, that he had made a promise, quite some time ago, that he could not talk about. A promise that had brought her to the edge of her patience, as angry as she had ever been with him. He held information that could have helped them track down the sorcerer behind the attack on the Stone Walls far more quickly than they had.

And she guessed, by the way he was not meeting her eyes, that whatever was in the folded and sealed parchment had something to do with that promise.

She remembered wondering, not that long ago, if he did trust her. And realised now that he did. He had given this item into her care. Trusted that she would hold it. And not open it, unless necessary.

"Thank you, mristrian." He lifted his eyes, and her breath caught for a moment at the gold swirling through the green. She did not think she would ever get used to that, or the effect it had on her, now that she knew what it meant.

Before she could say anything, or react, his gaze went past her. His mouth turned up in a rare smile, gold fading from his eyes.

Yvonne did not need to turn to know who was joining them. A pair of goblin warriors she knew. Brea and Thort.

When she and Guise had arrived at the hotel the first night, she had been surprised to find the goblin couple already there, and rooms arranged for all of them, along with stables for their horses. Yvonne was still not quite sure why Guise had found it necessary to ask a pair of his oldest friends to join them, but was glad of their company. They were resourceful, and had been carrying out searches of their own for the past two days looking for the blood sorcerer, with no good results, either.

She glanced up now, in the morning sun, to find the goblins approaching. They were dressed for combat, in the close-fitting black greatcoats, trousers and knee-high boots that Yvonne had first seen in the Karoan'shae palace, what seemed half a lifetime ago. Of almost equal height, with the pale grey skin, green eyes, and long, silky black hair of high-ranking members of the Karoan'shae, they each moved with the easy grace of a master predator. Goblin warriors. Who had been living a quiet life, dressed in loose desert clothing, when she had first met them and their daughter, Jesset. Yvonne could not help but think that the black uniforms suited them better.

The table had been set for four, although Guise had insisted that they start breakfast without the couple. Now that they were here, Yvonne was glad. Goblins had appetites as large as wulfkin, and there would not have been enough food for all of them.

"Did you leave any food for us?" Brea asked, inspecting the contents of the dishes across the table as she took her place, Thort opposite.

"A little," Guise answered, still smiling. The goblin pair were among his closest friends, Yvonne still slightly surprised to realise that Guise, a master of secrets, had friends. He knew a great many people, and before she had met Brea and Thort, she would not have said that any of them were his friends.

"What do you recommend, Yvonne?" Brea asked.

"Everything," Yvonne answered, the first thing that came into her head. She laughed. "It was all excellent. I particularly liked that, though," she said, and pointed to a dish of fried mushrooms. She had managed not to take all of it. Just. It had been tempting, though. Fresh mushrooms, fried in butter and a mix of herbs that still sang on her tongue. She laughed again as both Brea and Thort reached for it at the same time, forestalled when a shadow appeared. One of the silent-footed, efficient waiting staff. Guise murmured a few words and the waiter left. Yvonne had a feeling that the table would soon have more food. More than enough for two hungry goblins.

Thort handed his lady the rest of the mushroom dish, and Brea deferred. At first, Yvonne thought Thort was being polite, realising she was wrong as Brea lifted a brow.

"Do you think I don't know what you're doing? You're trying to give me this so you can have the whole plate when more is brought."

Thort grinned, unabashed, and split the remaining mushrooms equally between his and his wife's plate. "Satisfied?" he asked, voice full of a warmth and love that had endured for years.

Brea sniffed slightly, an affectation more suited to a goblin lady than a warrior, and inclined her head. But her eyes were shimmering with gold as she looked at her husband.

Yvonne picked up her now cold tea, ducking her head to the liquid for a moment, not wanting to intrude on a private moment. She could not help making a face as she put the cup down. She could drink cold tea. She preferred not to.

Before she could do or say anything, a waiter appeared at her elbow with a fresh pot of tea and a clean cup, while another waiter appeared at her other side and cleared away her plate and cold tea.

"This is good," Brea said, waving a mushroom in front of her, speared by her fork.

"What are your plans for the day?" Yvonne asked, pouring herself more tea.

Thort exchanged glances with Guise, who tilted his head.

"I am making enquiries," Guise said.

"The Karoan'shae doesn't have a formal presence here, but there are usually a few goblins around. We're going to see what they have to say," Thort told Yvonne. The Karoan'shae, and goblins in general, did not concern themselves with human affairs. Not normally. But a blood sorcerer was not normal. Yvonne thought that the Karoan'shae would be keen to help hunt for Hiram, if they could.

And that had been decided upon long before this breakfast, Yvonne knew. She should not be upset by it. The three of them had known each other a very long time, and were used to working together. Still, she was unsettled by it.

"I am going to have a day off," Yvonne declared, cradling the tea cup in her hands, letting the warmth chase away the stupid sting of hurt.

"There is a quite excellent market in one of the squares near here," Brea commented, eyes gleaming. "Crafts from all over the lands."

"Is that so?" Yvonne asked, interested. She rarely had time to browse market stalls. A little time spent there would be welcome. She might be able to replace her knife. And she might find some gifts for her children, too. There had rarely been time, or money, to buy gifts over the years. And today, unusually, she had both.

"The hotel can arrange shipping back to your home, if you wish," Guise added.

She took a sip of hot tea, let the flavours fill her senses, and smiled. Now, that was a good idea. And would keep her nicely distracted, for a little while, from thoughts of the blood sorcerer they were all hunting.

Chapter Two

The market was one of the most diverse she had ever seen, and it made her sorry she had taken so long to carry out her self-appointed, mundane tasks.

She had spent the rest of the morning making a fuss of her horse, Baldur glad of the attention, insisting on many scratches behind his ears as she checked over him and his harness. Going through her saddlebags and belongings had not taken long at all, and she had a short list of items she needed, her bags left ready for travel out of long-ingrained habit. She had paused for what she had intended to be a light lunch while she considered the letters she needed to write, and the message she should send to Pieris. Her fellow Hunar was somewhere on the road to the Royal City, but he would be glad of news before he reached the gates.

Except that the hotel had provided her with a three-course feast that she had thought would be impossible after the hearty breakfast, but which she had found she had managed quite well, even the dessert which had been something as light as air, citrus and fresh in her mouth.

So it was mid-afternoon before she had left the hotel and made her way to the market, taking her time wandering here and there. She had her cloak around her, the Hunar's symbol covered, wanting to remain anonymous for the moment. Oath-sworn to help those in need, a Hunar would find work, even in the Royal City. As it was, wrapped in the plain cloth of her cloak, she blended into the crowd, her pale skin and dark hair common in Valland. The scars around her neck and shoulders that might have drawn attention were hidden as always by the scarf she wore.

The merchants were delighted to gossip with her, sharing information about happenings along the Great River, and to haggle over prices.

Word of the fall of the Stone Walls had reached the market, and even with the lively chatter around, she saw the shadow of grief on some of the merchants' faces. Some of them might have spent time in the Stone Walls themselves. Or known people who had. The Sisters had made a point of not taking sides, of accepting anyone who came through the gates and needed their help. A refuge like no other.

In between the gossip, and the haggling, and the moments of sadness, Yvonne managed to spend a considerable amount of money. Not only did she find a replacement knife, she also found several items that she thought would make excellent gifts for her children and Guise, as well as buying some cloth in a deep blue that she could not resist. She needed another shirt, she told herself, giving the merchant the hotel's name to send the cloth to.

She was about to make her way along the next side of the market square, slightly dismayed to realise that she had only been along two edges so far, when rapid movement at the corner of her eye drew her attention.

She turned, automatically reaching for her spell pouch and sword, a reflex ingrained after years of training, only to move her hands away as soon as she saw who it was.

A familiar girl with blond hair loose around her shoulders was sprinting along the street towards her.

Yvonne moved to meet her, and braced herself just in time. Priss hurled herself at Yvonne, wrapping her arms around her waist, clinging tight.

"I knew that was you. I knew it. I could sense you."

"Good day to you, Priss," Yvonne said, unable to stop a smile.

She was a far cry from the frightened, determined nine-year-old that Yvonne had first met in an abandoned tower in the Forbidden Lands only a few months before. Kidnapped by the Ashnassan, sold to the ancient enemy, used by him for her blood, and her power. But not destroyed. Not in the least. Priss, and the other girls that had been rescued, had survived their ordeal.

Priss' grip was strong, her face full of life and laughter as she looked up.

"Are you here to see the King?" Priss asked.

"Priscilla." A man's voice cut through whatever else Priss might have asked. The slightly exasperated tone was one Yvonne knew well. She had used it often when Mariah and Joel were growing up.

"But I want to know," Priss protested, letting Yvonne go and stepping back. Yvonne blinked as she took in Priss' clothes for the first time. She was wearing a riot of colour. A red blouse, a purple skirt, with a brilliant green scarf tied around her slim waist. All the clothes were of excellent quality, naturally, but it was a remarkable ensemble.

"I am sorry for my daughter's haste," the man continued.

Yvonne looked beyond Priss to find a couple there. Perhaps around her own age, dressed with the understated elegance of wealth and power. They were both blond, with blue eyes, and she would know them as Priss' parents anywhere.

"It's no trouble," Yvonne answered. "It's good to see Priss again."

"You must be the Hunar," the lady said, half-reaching forward with one hand. "Who rescued our daughter. I'm Hannah. This is my husband Edmond. We wanted to send our thanks before, but were not sure how to find you. Thank you. For finding our daughter. For returning her to us."

"It was my honour," Yvonne said, inclining her head slightly and ignoring her natural instinct to protest that she had not done so alone. Over the years she had learned that accepting thanks helped a Hunar's supplicants. The task they had set for her was done. And it seemed to ease their minds to offer thanks for it.

Priss' parents had not asked for her help, though. It had been a task she had set for herself and, seeing Priss tuck herself between her parents, sure of their welcome, was reward enough. The girl had always been confident. Precocious, even. This was a softer side, standing between two people who loved her, both parents with a hand on their daughter, as though wanting to reassure themselves that she was real.

"She said it was the best adventure," Hannah added, shaking her head slightly, a fond smile at her mouth as she glanced down at her daughter. Priss looked up, a broad smile on her face, and Yvonne saw the lady's eyes brighten with unshed tears. Not the first time, she suspected.

"It was more adventurous than I would have liked," Yvonne said.

"I think she wants to be Hunar when she grows," Edmond said. His expression was harder to read, but Yvonne thought she saw regret in his face. He and his wife lived a life of privilege, and doubtless knew it. The life of a Hunar was often hard.

"She will need some training, in her powers," Yvonne said, not directly answering him. From the slight nods from each parent, she saw that they had realised that, perhaps some time ago.

"They wanted me to go to court and learn from Hiram," Priss said, nose wrinkling. "But I didn't want to. He was all wrong."

"He was indeed," Yvonne agreed, not wanting to think about just how corrupt Hiram was, not in this sunlit afternoon. However, the court was not all corrupt. Not by a long way. "If you can find him, you might like to spend some time with Ewan," she suggested. The younger Mage, an apprentice at the court, was steeped in the same kind of clean power that ran through the Hundred. He would make a good tutor for Priss, Yvonne thought. It would get them both out of the court, and keep Priss' sharp mind engaged.

"The young one?" the lady asked, brows lifting. "He was always in the background. We've never really got to know him."

"We were going to ask Dundac if he could help," the father added, a shadow crossing his face. "But Priscilla tells us he won't be coming back."

And had not told them everything, Yvonne noticed. She met Priss' eyes and saw an oddly grown-up expression there. A touch of determination in the set jaw, and vulnerability around her eyes. Holding on to secrets. Not wanting to tell them. Perhaps afraid of hurting her parents. Perhaps afraid of what they might do. From the careful hold her parents had on her just now, Yvonne would guess that they had been keeping their daughter close since she had been back.

"No, Dundac will not be back," Yvonne agreed, her voice even despite the sorrow in her chest. Another Hunar, and a friend, lost. And there had always been too few of the Hundred.

The parents guessed he was dead. They didn't want to speak it aloud for fear of upsetting their daughter. And their daughter did not want to tell them everything for fear of upsetting them. Yvonne half-opened her mouth and closed it again. It was not her place to interfere, and she understood the impulse to hold secrets inside. She had rarely, if ever, told her children everything.

"Ewan, though," Edmond said, glancing across to his wife.

In that glance, Yvonne saw their mutual concern, and the relief of having someone to turn to. An intensely private moment, in a public street.

"He does good work," Yvonne said, remembering the bright, clean magic that Ewan had carried with him. She did not need to push the lady or the lord further, she saw. They trusted her word, as Hunar, and as one of the people who had rescued their daughter.

"So, are you going to see the King?" Priss asked, impatient with the conversation over her head.

"I have seen him. A few times."

"We heard about the Stone Walls," the lady said, cutting across whatever Priss might have asked next. "A tragedy."

"Yes," Yvonne agreed, her throat closing. "Roa is alright, though," she told Priss, seeing the girl's face pale. The Stone Walls might be an abstract idea for her parents. For Priss, it was where some of her fellow captives, and friends, had gone when they had all been rescued from the Forbidden Lands.

"Oh, good. Where is she?"

"I think she is staying with my children," Yvonne answered, "along with a few other people from the valley."

"I didn't think anyone had survived?" the father asked, startled.

"A few did. Not many," Yvonne said, throat tight. She could still remember the feel of Adira's hand in hers, the Sister's skin too cold, her breathing harsh. Adira had held on to life long enough to pass on vital information about the attack on the Stone Walls. And had died under a warrior's grace, rather than the long, lingering and painful end she would otherwise have endured.

"Why don't you take Priscilla to the stalls?" Hannah suggested to her husband.

Priss did not want to leave but said a polite goodbye to Yvonne, far more measured than her greeting, and went with her father, holding his hand.

Her mother stared after her daughter, hands clasped together in front of her tightly enough that her knuckles were white.

"We are being very lenient with her," she said, voice low, words coming out in a rush. "She picked the outfit. She wants to wear colour every day, she says. And it does no harm."

"She is a remarkable young lady," Yvonne said, mouth curving up. "She is going to be a force to be reckoned with when she grows."

Hannah laughed softly, eyes bright. "She already is." She paused, eyes still staring past Yvonne to look at her daughter, then dragged her attention back to Yvonne. "I cannot tell you what it means, Hunar, to have my daughter back. To have her safe. We do not know how to repay you."

"There is no need. I am glad to have found her, and that she is back with people who love her."

The lady stared at Yvonne for a long moment, unblinking, tension around her eyes and mouth, then her lips curved up. "You really mean that."

"Yes."

"Extraordinary. It is a rare thing, in my world."

Yvonne did not know what to say to that. The lady's world, and her own, were so very different.

"If you ever have need of anything, and we might be able to help, let us know," the lady said, the tension gone from her. "It would be our pleasure to help the person who found our daughter."

"Thank you," Yvonne said, recognising a sincere and heartfelt offer. And a powerful one. She might think of them as Priss' parents, grateful for their daughter's return, but Edmond and Hannah were Lord and Lady Grace, among the highest nobility in the Valland kingdom.

"And now, I had best rescue my husband. Priss will have bought half the market if we are not careful."

Yvonne laughed, thinking of the many purchases she had already made.

"It was a pleasure to meet you, Hunar."

"And you, my lady."

Yvonne turned to watch as the lady joined her husband and daughter, Priss standing out among the crowd with her vibrant colour choices. The parents kept to either side of their daughter, one of them with a hand on her at all times. Not wanting to lose her again. Priss looked up at them both from time to time. Yvonne was too far away to see her expression clearly, but thought it was a mixture of exasperation and fondness. Indulging her parents. For now.

Chapter Three

With her purchases packed and on their way to the house at Fir Tree Crossing, that was the first place she had owned but which did not quite feel like home, not yet, and her own supplies refilled, Yvonne made her way back to the hotel terrace as night was falling. The season was turning. The warm summer giving way to a cooler autumn. Even so, it was still possible to sit on the terrace, helped by the braziers that the staff kept stoked, and the blankets that were offered to everyone.

Yvonne found a seat near the edge of the terrace, with a view of the city, and sank into the luxury of cushions under her and a warm blanket of soft wool over her, a glass of wine and tray of savouries nearby. The hotel staff seemed convinced that if they did not keep supplying her with food, she would fade away. Or perhaps they were just always this attentive to those they considered to be important guests. Perhaps this was what it was like to be very wealthy, or very powerful. The sort of attention that made Yvonne's skin itch slightly was simply something that the wealthy and powerful, like Guise, would take as their due.

She was not used to it, never having had worldly wealth or power, and knew that the attention now was because of her association with Guise. The hotel staff probably did not know about the bond between them, that made them more than husband and wife. But the hotel staff did understand that she was important to Guise, and treated her with the same attention. She wondered if she would ever get used to any of it.

She was mulling that over, her wine glass still mostly full, when one of the staff approached her, bowing slightly to catch her attention.

"Hunar, your pardon. A palace messenger left this for you."

He was holding out a silver tray with a folded and sealed bit of parchment on it. A seal that anyone in this city, or the kingdom, would know. The stylised V for the Valland kings. And, in this case, also the King's name.

"Thank you." She set down her wine, took the parchment and waited until the staff member had moved away before breaking the seal.

Hunar. I have found something we need to discuss. Come at once. Victor.

She was on her feet almost before she had finished reading. She could not imagine what the King needed to discuss with her, but whatever it was she was curious to hear it. They had been getting nowhere in their search for Hiram, the former Circle Mage at the heart of the Valland court. Any news would be welcome.

The evening had enough chill in the air that she stopped to gather her cloak on her way out of the hotel, pausing again at the reception desk to ask if Guise had returned. He had not. And Brea and Thort were still absent, too.

It was unusual, but not concerning. If they had been able to gather any information in their hunt for Hiram, they would stay out as long as they needed.

"If they get back before me, will you let them know that I've gone to the palace?" she asked. The night manager assured her that he would do so, and she headed out into the night.

The palace was a short distance away, uphill, the streets quiet as most people returned home for the night, the few shops she could see closing. She passed a pair of soldiers on one of the regular patrols that made their way through the streets, and exchanged a brief nod with them. She recognised their faces from her visits to the palace over the past few days.

Unlike her first visit to the palace, no one stood in her way or questioned her business as she went through the main entrance in the walls, past the armed soldiers on watch and towards the main doors of the palace building.

Inside the entrance hall the torches set on the walls had been lit against the darkness and there was the usual collection of people. Another pair of guards. A pair of messenger boys, dressed in the bright blue uniforms that let them stand out in a crowd, making faces at each other. And one of the palace staff, an elderly man with a rounded belly, thinning hair and bright, intelligent eyes, who was senior assistant to the Steward. It was all perfectly normal. Nothing seemed out of place. Nothing to warrant the hasty message from the King.

The normality should have soothed her, and did the opposite. She kept her face and movement calm, looking around again, trying to work out what was making her uneasy. There was nothing she could see.

The Steward's assistant stepped forward, eyebrows raised, as Yvonne came inside.

"Hunar. We did not expect you today."

"I'm here to see the King," Yvonne said. Clearly, King Victor had not told his staff that he had asked for her to visit. She and Guise had been in and out of the palace almost more times than she could count over the past few days, visiting the King, his General and Sarra, all of them sharing what little information they had been able to gather about Hiram's possible whereabouts.

The assistant's eyes sharpened with interest, but he simply inclined his head. "Of course. He's in his study. I'll take you to him."

Yvonne followed the older man through the palace, in a route that had become familiar over the past few days. There was an audience chamber on the palace's ground floor, but Victor preferred to conduct the real business of his court in his own private study, which was a large room on the upper floor.

She matched her pace to the Steward's assistant as he led her upstairs, past another pair of palace staff, arms full of what looked like bedclothes, and they approached the quartet of King's Guard that accompanied the King everywhere. The quartet stepped aside from the King's door, inclining their heads to her. They were all familiar with each other.

As with the entrance hall, it was all perfectly ordinary. Nothing seemed out of place. And yet, her skin was prickling with unease, and she had to check her fingers before she could move for her sword and spell pouch.

The assistant knocked on the door and waited a moment. There was no reply from inside.

"Go ahead. He'll be glad of the break. He's been reading reports all afternoon," one of the guards said. She recognised him as one of the guards who had been in the treasury when the chests had exploded with the traps set by Hiram.

The assistant knocked again, and entered the room without waiting for a reply, Yvonne following.

The room inside was darker than it should have been, and cold enough that Yvonne could see her breath, with no fire lit in the great fireplace.

The door swung closed behind them, as most of the King's doors were designed to do, shutting out the guards.

"Sire?" the assistant said, stepping forward. "The Hunar is here to see you."

He was moving towards the great desk that was set near the windows on the other side of the room. Normally piled high with papers, in the uncertain light all Yvonne could be sure of was that the surface was clear, wood gleaming in the faint light coming from the windows.

"Stop a moment," she said to the assistant, and pulled a light spell from her pouch, sending the miniature candles into the air around her so that they could finally see.

Chaos met her eyes. The chairs that were normally arranged around the fireplace were out of place, some overturned. The papers from the desk were strewn across the floor, in a haphazard pile, and amid the tumbled chairs and papers lay a familiar form. A tall man barely a few years older than she was, plainly dressed, his dark hair tousled, the Valland King lay on his back, sightless eyes staring up at the ceiling high above, the end of a dagger poking out from under his ribs.

Her breath rushed out of her, her body locking in place for a moment. The King had been full of life and energy, never still in the short time she had known him. Seeing him motionless was almost as much of a shock as the weapon in his chest.

"Sire!" The assistant's voice rose to a shriek which must have carried to the guards outside, and he rushed forward to the desk.

"Wait," Yvonne said, moving forward. Nothing in the room made sense. The chaos suggested there had been a fight, which none of the guards outside had heard. And the King was a trained swordsman. He would not have simply stood and waited while someone stabbed him in the chest.

Even as she stepped away from the door, she sensed movement behind her. Instinct and training had her stepping aside, hands going to her sword and spells. A masked figure moved past her, at speed, heading for the dead King and assistant.

Yvonne turned to follow the movement and saw another masked figure emerge from behind the King's desk, naked blade in hand.

She called out a warning, knowing it was too late even as she spoke, and watched as the figure who had been behind the desk killed the assistant Steward with one smooth, practised sweep of a long blade, slicing through the older man's neck, sending a gush of blood across the papers and the King's body.

The first masked figure launched at the second, and they fell back, crashing into the King's desk with a sound that should have alerted the guards outside, if nothing else had.

The door remained closed.

Yvonne looked back at it and saw the faintest outline of a spell drawn on the back of it. A spell for silence. It looked like it had been there for a while. She stared at it, sure that it had not been there the last time she had been in this room, barely a day before, trying to think who might have had access to the King's chambers, and the skill to draw such a spell.

Movement and muffled sounds behind her made her turn again. The two dark-clad, masked figures were wrestling with each other, neither seeming to have the upper hand, and with them so close, Yvonne could no longer tell which was which. Which one had killed the assistant. Which one had been hiding behind the door.

One of the figures delivered an elbow to the face of the other, prompting a soft cry of pain that sounded feminine. The attacker pulled back, glanced across at Yvonne, standing with her mouth open, hands at her weapons, and then ran out of the room through a hidden door near the fireplace that clicked shut behind him.

Leaving the other masked figure leaning back against the desk, one hand to her face. The cry of pain had given her away. Yvonne knew this particular assassin.

"Ulla, what are you doing here?" Yvonne asked.

"I didn't do this," the assassin answered, straightening.

"No, I didn't imagine so. Who did?" Yvonne asked, hearing the slight tremor in her own voice. Standing in the King's study, two dead men at her feet. The King was dead. A shiver ran through her.

Silence from the assassin.

"He killed the King," Yvonne prompted. "And the assistant Steward."

"It's worse than that. He made it look like you did it," Ulla told her, voice clipped, and pointed to the King's body.

"That's ridiculous," Yvonne said, moving forward to the King's side. She crouched beside him, staring at his still face. He had been a good ruler, and a decent man, from what she had learned over the past few days. Used to ruling his kingdom. Used to having people obey him. But someone who seemed to care about his people, and their well-being.

His sightless eyes troubled her, face frozen in an expression of shock.

Then she looked down at the knife buried in his chest and drew a breath.

"That's my knife," she said. The one she had lost, when she had thrown it at the blood-crazed sorcerer. She had not retrieved it.

"Is it?" Ulla asked, crouching at the King's other side. She sounded genuinely curious.

Yvonne glanced up, mouth half-open to ask Ulla what the assassin had meant, that the killer had made it look like Yvonne's work, and stilled before the question could leave her mouth.

There was a crude symbol etched into the bare wooden floorboards near the King's body. One that was familiar. She had the mirror of it at her shoulder. The Firebird's symbol, the great bird with her wings outstretched.

Someone had drawn the Firebird's symbol next to the dead King. And killed him with her knife.

Looking back down at the body, she saw one of the King's fists was clenched, a scrap of fabric in his fingers. It looked like part of a shirt sleeve. Hard-wearing fabric, similar to the sort Yvonne wore every day. So similar, in fact, that she glanced down at her own shirt sleeve, seeing no tears or rips.

"You know who did this," Yvonne said, looking up at Ulla's masked face, not even her eyes visible.

"I can't discuss it," Ulla answered, sounding tense. "Assassin's business."

"The King is dead. And the assassin left evidence against me," Yvonne said, not backing down.

"You want to talk about this now?" Ulla asked. "There are guards on their way."

"How –"

Yvonne did not have time to finish her question, as Ulla was moving away, and the door behind them, the one Yvonne and the assistant had used to enter the room, opened.

"Sire," the General said, coming into the room. The King's closest confidant and friend, the elderly man was as upright now as any soldier in his army, the grey at his temples one of the few signs of his age.

Yvonne looked back at him over her shoulder, realising at once how it might look. She was crouched next to the dead King, in a room full of chaos, with the assistant Steward dead beside her.

"General," Yvonne said, voice higher than it should have been. "Someone has killed the King."

The General stopped in his tracks, colour draining from his face as he looked around the room. Yvonne rose to her feet, and saw his gaze travel past her to the assistant Steward's body and the crude carving on the floor.

"A Hunar did this," the General hissed.

"No," Yvonne said, quite certain.

"I don't believe you," the General said, voice low and rough. "The Hundred have lied before," he added, drawing his sword.

Yvonne opened her mouth to argue, but no sound came out, all her words choked by the knowledge that he was right. Members of the Hundred had lied. Had killed. Had proved to be unworthy of the title of Hunar. He had no reason to believe her. She took a step away from him.

"Stay where you are," he ordered. "You have questions to answer."

She hesitated. She was Hunar. Her oaths bound her to help others. And she had not done this. Still, she glanced aside at the body, at the symbol on the floor, the dagger in the King's chest, and the scrap of cloth in his fingers. And took another step back, the bottom of her stomach falling away. She knew she had not done this. But it would be so easy to blame her.

"Stay there," the General ordered, taking a step forward. "Answer for your crimes."

"I did not do this," Yvonne said.

"I do not believe you," the General said. "Guards!" he called, and rushed forward.

"This way," Ulla hissed.

Yvonne glanced back to find Ulla in the secret doorway that the first assassin had used.

Yvonne was across the room before she had time to think. Whoever had killed the King had meant for her to be accused. And the General would not listen to her just now.

The door clicked shut behind her, cutting off the General's cry of fury.

Yvonne found herself in a narrow passageway, one of the servants' tunnels that must cross through the entire palace. The floor under her feet was made of wood, worn from years of use, the walls, when she touched them, trying to get her bearing, made of plain plaster, rough against her hand. It was almost pitch dark, all the light having been left in the room behind them.

Ulla reached past her, the assassin crowding close to her, pressing something over the door latch. Something that had an acrid smell that burned Yvonne's nose.

"That will hold them a while. Come on," Ulla said, and took off into the dark.

"Wait!" Yvonne called. "What about the other one?" The other assassin, who had, in fact, killed the King.

"Long gone," Ulla said over her shoulder, voice sounding further away. "Come quickly."

Yvonne spared a moment to use a spell to enhance her senses, then followed.

Ulla navigated her way through the palace servants' tunnels with ease, never pausing or hesitating when she reached a crossing point or alternate path. The assassin was clearly well versed in using such tunnels.

Yvonne was not. The walls pressed around her. The ceiling was too low. Her breathing was too fast, heart thudding in her ears. Every time they passed one of the doors built into the tunnel walls she expected the door to open, and reaching hands to take hold of her, pull her out of the tunnels and into the waiting grip of the King's Guard. Or for another black-clad figure to magically appear out of the walls, another naked blade in its hand, despite Ulla's assurance that the other assassin was long gone.

No one found them. They did not come across any servants.

At length, the tunnel dropped sharply. There were no stairs, but the wooden planks turned to packed earth, telling Yvonne they were underground.

She tried not to panic, to focus instead on Ulla's back, still running ahead of her, keeping her focus on the assassin. Ulla would know a way out.

And the assassin did. At length, when Yvonne was drenched with sweat, and the edges of her sight were fading as the spell wore off, the assassin drew to a halt, waiting for Yvonne to catch up before she opened a door.

They stepped into an empty cellar, well-maintained with stone walls and floor. Ulla shut the door behind them and Yvonne blinked. It was invisible from this side.

"You need to leave the city," Ulla said, moving towards the crude wooden steps up to the next level of the building. "No one is going to believe you are innocent."

"That's ridiculous," Yvonne said, out of breath, muscles protesting as she went up the steps. The first shock of the King's death and the General's arrival had worn off and now, aching with effort, she wondered if she should have stayed, tried to reason with the old soldier. "I am Hunar."

"This is not the first time someone has been wrongly accused," Ulla said, voice dark. "Do you think they will listen to you?"

Yvonne stared up at the assassin, mouth open in instinctive protest, and could not speak. The General had seen her crouched next to the King's body, with the assistant Steward dead nearby. And when the General called in the local cerro and his range to try and track her, they would find her scent all over the room, and particularly on the knife. Her knife. Used to kill the King.

The King had been betrayed by one of the longest-serving members of his court only a handful of days before. The Circle Mage Hiram had turned out to be a blood sorcerer. Hiram had been someone the court trusted, and had known for years.

Yvonne was an unknown quantity. Recently arrived. The General, and the King's court, had no reason to trust her beyond the symbol at her shoulder.

She closed her mouth, lips in a thin line, and followed Ulla to the stairs.

"Do you know another way out of the city?" the assassin asked.

"Yes," Yvonne said. She had never been to the Royal City before, but the Hundred had shared the information they had. There were many ways out of the city. Both open and secret. There was at least one secret way not that far from the hotel. "I need Baldur. My pack."

"You get your pack. I'll get Baldur," Ulla said. "I'll leave him by the old mill tower. You know it?"

"The red one? With the round window? Yes." It was perhaps a block away from the hotel. Yvonne did not know how Ulla planned to steal into the hotel's stables and remove Baldur, but if anyone could manage it, it was her.

"I'll meet you in a few days," Ulla said, opening the building's door and disappearing into the night, leaving Yvonne open-mouthed, questions jammed in her throat. Not least, how the assassin would find her in a few days.

Voices nearby startled her and she pressed herself back against the wall on instinct. Ulla had shut the door behind her, though, and no one could see Yvonne, hidden in the darkness of the unused building.

A pair of men walked past the house, leaning on each other, one of them giggling helplessly. Doubtless on their way back home from one of the city's taverns. Yvonne envied them their carefree existence. They had probably never had to deal with a blood sorcerer. Or been suspected of killing a king.

And never had to sneak out of one of the safest, most law-abiding cities in the known lands in the mid of night, before the King's Guard caught up with her. The world spun for a moment, her mind refusing to accept everything that had happened, despite her tired body and the faint smell of stale earth on her clothes, picked up from the tunnel.

The thought that soldiers would be on their way to the hotel had her moving away from the wall and out of the door, careful to close it behind her.

The abandoned house was not that far from the hotel. Yvonne made her way down a pair of alleyways, keeping to the shadows, the bright symbol of the Hunar hidden under her cloak, and crept into the hotel through one of the servants' entrances, startling one of the junior maids and what looked like a stable boy who were keeping each other company in the shadows outside the hotel's walls. Yvonne ignored them. They would both recognise her, but it could not be helped, and she suspected the pair were absent from their duties, so would not be eager to tell the manager they had seen her.

She found the servants' stairwell and made her way up to the floor that her and Guise's rooms were on, pausing to check his room first, opening the door without knocking. It was empty, perfectly ordered and neat, with a candle set by the fireplace providing a little light. That was something that the hotel staff did. It did not look as if he had been back to the hotel since morning, although it was hard to tell.

She went into her own room and paused as she crossed the threshold. The hotel's staff had left a tall candle burning at her fireside, too, which showed her that someone else had been in her room. There was a pile of pale cloth carelessly discarded on the bed. She crossed over to it, using her cloak to cover her hand as she turned it over. It looked like one of her shirts, even if she knew it was not, and there was a tear in the sleeve. Another piece of evidence against her.

Her first impulse was to throw it into the fire. But she would have to pause to light the fire first, and she did not have time. She could all too easily imagine that there were soldiers approaching the hotel already. There was no time. And she could not bring herself to touch it, to take it with her, skin crawling at the idea. So, she left the shirt where it was and grabbed her saddlebags, already packed for travel from the afternoon, taking a precious moment to look around the room to make sure nothing else had been left, heart in her throat. Satisfied that all her belongings were there, she turned and headed for the door.

Chapter Four

S HE HAD NOT GONE more than a pace towards the door before it opened, two familiar figures stepping through.

Brea lifted a brow when she saw Yvonne's hand on her sword hilt, the other brow lifting when she saw the saddlebags across Yvonne's shoulder.

"Trouble?" the goblin asked.

"Bad," Yvonne said. "Where's Guise?"

Brea exchanged a glance with her husband, both of them tight-lipped.

"What is it?"

"We can't find him," Brea admitted, something in her voice sending a prickle across Yvonne's skin.

"What?" Yvonne asked.

"You first," Thort said, before Brea could speak. "Bad trouble?"

"The King is dead," Yvonne told them, and had to lock her knees as the shock of that ran through her. The Valland King, central to the peace of the known lands, was dead. Killed in his own study. "There was an assassin in the room. Two, actually. One was Ulla. She didn't kill him."

She was speaking too fast, voice high, words tumbling out, making almost no sense to her ears.

"Sit," Thort said, coming forward.

"No time. It was my dagger. And a piece of shirt left in the King's hand." Yvonne tilted her chin towards the bed, and the shirt there.

Brea and Thort looked from her to the shirt and back, expressions grim.

"Someone wants you accused of murder," Brea said, voice tight. "Were you seen in the palace?"

"Yes. I went in the front door. And the General came into the room while I was there. With the King."

"There's been no alarm," Thort said. "How did you get out?"

"Ulla. Servants' passages. She's getting Baldur for me. I need to go," Yvonne said, voice rising at the last.

"Yes. Now," Brea agreed.

"But, Guise," Yvonne said, halting in her move towards the door.

"We'll see to Guise," Brea promised. "You get yourself out of the city and safe."

"Yvonne, go," Thort said. "Guise would never forgive us if something happened to you. We'll find him," he said, echoing his wife's promise.

"And then we'll find you," Brea added, giving Yvonne a little push in the small of her back, making Yvonne realise that she had been simply standing, staring at the pair of them, rather than moving.

She drew a breath, settled the saddlebags more securely over her shoulder, and nodded to them both. If anyone could find Guise in this city, it was Brea and Thort. And they were not accused of murder.

And Guise could more than look after himself, Yvonne knew. Goblins learned the arts of war from their cradles. He was likely to be far more successful at keeping himself safe than she was in finding a way out of the city.

She managed to leave the hotel through a servants' entrance, into a narrow alleyway that separated the hotel from the next building, startling one of the cleaning maids and what looked like another one of the stable boys, who had been wrapped up in each other against the wall of the hotel as she passed. The girl gave a muffled cry of surprise, which turned into giggles as the boy murmured something in her ear. Yvonne wondered if it was the same pair she had passed on the way into the hotel, or if this was simply a favourite spot for lovers to meet, and envied them their innocence.

Yvonne kept moving, saddlebags across her shoulder, cloak gathered around her, hiding the Hunar's symbol. She had drawn the hood of her cloak part-way up, casting the lower part of her face into shadow. No one in the Royal City walked about with their hoods fully drawn up. It would call too much attention.

She paused at the end of the alleyway where it led into a wider street, the open space in front of the hotel visible to one side, breathing too hard and too fast from the short walk. The ground felt unsteady under her feet. After the headlong rush here, and giving Brea and Thort the news, she was shaky with reaction. The King dead. And his killer had planted evidence that pointed to her. She had fled the scene rather than try to explain. And now she needed to get out of the city. Alone. With Guise missing, and Brea and Thort on his trail.

Even as she caught her breath, the rapid footsteps of boots marching in concert sounded. The streets here were cobblestones, well maintained, footsteps startling and loud in the otherwise quiet night.

She stayed as still as she could in the shadows and saw, across the street, a group of soldiers, led by a familiar figure, making their way to the hotel. Sarra. Allegedly retired from the King's Guard. She was leading eight soldiers and even from the distance, Yvonne could see the tension in the soldier's body and the hard lines her face was set into. Something was very wrong.

The King was dead. The man Sarra had sworn fealty to. And Sarra took her oaths of loyalty very seriously indeed. If Sarra was here, with soldiers, it meant that she did believe Yvonne was involved with the King's death. Yvonne's stomach twisted. She liked the old soldier.

The soldiers went into the hotel, and Yvonne slid away, along the street away from the hotel, sticking to the shadowed side as much as possible, trying not to walk too fast or too slow, imagining herself a citizen of this city, on her way home from an innocuous errand. Not running away from the King's Guard.

Baldur was waiting, cloaked in the shadows of an overhanging roof near the mill tower, his dull, dapple grey coat blending into the dark so well that she would not have seen him if she had not known where to look. The mill itself was little more than a facade now, long since out of use, the buildings around it shops and workshops, empty at this hour, making this a quiet and convenient spot to leave a horse for an escapee.

He made no sound when she set the saddlebags across his shoulder, perhaps sensing the need for stealth. She gave him a pat on his neck, checked his harness quickly, then took his reins and began leading him through the city streets. Whoever had saddled him had also muffled his hooves with the cloths she kept with his saddle, and he made as little sound as she did walking across the cobbles.

As they walked, she went over the city maps in her mind. The Hundred had collected many over the years, sharing information, including the old ways in and out of the city, from days before there had been peace in these lands, when sneaking in and out of the city was useful.

She could only hope that the vigilant soldiers were not watching every escape route. And that no one was nearby as she paused in the next group of shadows to cast a spell to enhance her senses, then another spell, drawing invisibility over Baldur and herself. It was a camouflage of sorts, a spell to encourage others to look away, which should stop anyone from seeing them. Providing they did not come across anyone with magic sensitivity. And providing Baldur did not make too much noise.

The grey horse followed her like a ghost through the quiet streets. There were no alarm cries that she could hear. The palace had managed to keep the death quiet. For now. There were no more soldiers. No patrols. Not one person on the route she had chosen.

A knot of tension grew between her shoulder blades. This seemed too easy. Almost as if someone had cleared a path for her.

She found herself moving more and more slowly, Baldur's nose nudging the small of her back more than once as she paused, straining her ears to listen.

She found another patch of shadow near a corner and stopped, Baldur silent behind her. She put her head, carefully, around the next corner. The exit from the city should be close by. A false wall that was actually built in sections she and Baldur could weave their way through.

The alleyway ahead seemed deserted, the wall tantalisingly close. There was nothing that she could see, and yet her instincts were telling her to be wary.

And then there was movement in the shadows. The tiniest shift.

Someone was there. Waiting.

She held herself still, barely breathing.

Another movement. And another.

At least four people were ahead of her, concealed in shadows.

"How much longer?"

The whisper was loud in the dark, and she almost jumped, holding herself still against the wall with effort. The invisibility spell was still close around her, and Baldur. They could not see her.

"It's been hours," another whisper. Different to the first. A higher pitch.

"Quiet," another voice hissed.

"I hear something," another voice murmured.

Yvonne tensed, Baldur motionless behind her.

Before she could reach for her sword, she heard something, too. The faint sounds of footsteps. Coming from the wall ahead of her. She stayed where she was.

A group of people, four in all, moved out of the wall, carrying heavy packs, which they set down on the ground. Relieved of their burdens, they turned and made their way back through the wall without speaking.

The four people who had been waiting in the shadows moved forward, each of them reaching for a pack.

Smugglers.

Yvonne had to lock her knees to remain upright, relief making her lightheaded for a moment.

Not soldiers. Not a patrol sent to wait for her.

Simple smugglers.

She held herself still as the four people shouldered the packs, grunting under the weight of them, then moved off through the streets.

Only when she was sure the alleyway was deserted did she creep forward, Baldur behind her, and approach the wall.

It was an extraordinary design. It looked absolutely solid as she approached it, and yet she had watched four people walk through it.

She was almost touching the wall before she saw the gap. A slender, dark fissure ahead of her. She turned, keeping Baldur close behind her, and a narrow passageway opened up in front of them. It would be a tight fit for her horse, but she was not leaving him behind.

They made their way through the narrow gaps between the stones, Yvonne expecting to hear a cry of alarm, or discovery, at any moment.

And then they were at the other side, the ground dropping away in front of them, a slope of uneven grass, brightly lit by the full moon and cloudless sky overhead. There was no ground cover, not for her, or her horse. She took a moment to renew the invisibility spell, feeling her energy fading. Using magic for her own purposes was exhausting, part of the price for being Hunar. Their spells were meant to help other people.

Somehow, they made it down the slope without being seen, if indeed anyone was looking for them, Yvonne's heart pounding, her mouth dry, every step an exercise in concentration as she tried not to make any noise.

Then they were standing at the side of a narrow road. Not the King's Highway, but a well-worn track that might lead to one or other of the country estates or farms around the Royal City.

She looked back the way they had come, seeing the high wall of the Royal City, apparently impenetrable, rising high above them. The whole city seemed to still be asleep. Word of the King's death had not spread. Not yet.

And she needed to be as far away from the city as possible when the alarm cry went up.

Chapter Five

Baldur huffed in disgust at his surroundings. Another thicket of shrubs, among great, ancient trees. A far cry from the comfortable stables, and stable hands, he had become used to. A few heavy drops of rain splashed across his face and neck and he snorted again.

Yvonne scratched behind his ears, murmuring an apology, sound almost lost in the driving rain around them. She did not like being wet, either. The only saving grace was that the rain would make their trail harder to follow, and hopefully impossible, with the measures she had taken along the way.

They were both worn out. Baldur looked like he was wearing mud socks, coated up to his knees, his belly liberally splattered with the stuff. There was even some in his mane, the end of his tail stuck together, with bits of twig and leaves mixed in. She was just as filthy, bits of bark and leaves sticking to her clothes, the hem of her cloak heavy with more mud, boots covered in it as well. Her skin was crawling under her clothes, itching for a bath, or a cleansing spell. The feeling of dirt on her skin brought back old memories. Things she did not want to remember. Pain and fear. And the chill of air across her scalp and neck.

Huddled against the base of a tree, she put a hand up to her head, needing the reassurance of the weight of her hair. It was as filthy as the rest of her, but it was there. Real under her fingers. There was no quarrel. No feral wulfkin. No other terrified girls.

Just an exhausted woman and her horse, hiding, hoping that they would not be discovered.

She clenched her fingers to stop herself reaching for her spell pouch. It would be so easy to use one, or two, and then she and her horse would be clean again. Not dry, but at least clean. The memories would fade.

And she could not risk it. The Valland Court had more than one Mage at their disposal, who would be able to trace the use of magic. They might have found the trail she had left, out of the city, with the invisibility spell she had used.

She had stopped using magic once that spell had worn off, not wanting to risk discovery, or the further drain on her energy.

Then she had resorted to the tricks she knew for deceiving anyone trying to follow her. Picking strong-smelling plants to use as a basic hunter's foil, scattering them, along with some of the pungent herbs from her saddlebags, crossing as many different water sources as they could.

Baldur had spent much of that first night up to his belly in water, ploughing through rivers and ponds, uncomplaining, with Yvonne balanced on his back.

She hoped she had done enough to leave dead ends for any wulfkin using their nose, and any of the King's soldiers that could track people by footprints and other traces.

Only when she thought she had obscured their trail enough did she turn them towards the nearest wild forest, that stretched south from the Royal City. Once they were deep enough inside that, they should be able to make their way south, out of Valland.

It was not a perfect plan. Or even a good one. But it was the only one she had just now, the only thing her panicked and tired mind had been able to come up with, that first night leaving the Royal City.

Several days later, she had not come up with a better plan, or even any alternative at all. She could not remember the last time she had slept properly, or stopped for more than a few moments to let Baldur drink and graze.

Ulla had said she would find her, but Yvonne did not know how the assassin would manage that. And Brea and Thort had promised to find Guise. She had no doubt that the goblins were all together, and in a far better state than she was. Between them, they could probably take on an army.

She could not wait for any of them. She might have escaped the King's soldiers so far, but she was out of energy and knew she could not outrun them forever, particularly not within the Valland kingdom's borders where anyone she might come across would be another witness, leaving another trail to follow.

The edges of her sight were hazy with fatigue, limbs heavy. She needed to stop for a bit longer. And Baldur, despite his great endurance, needed a better rest, too.

The onset of this driving, relentless rain had given her an excuse. It would make them harder to track, and obscure any trail they had left, too. They could afford a few hours' rest.

She woke with a gasp of fright, on her feet before she was fully alert, one hand on her sword hilt, looking around for the threat.

It was daylight, the space around her cast into bright greens and dull browns with splashes of white as the sun shone through the shrubs and trees around her.

Nothing.

No threat.

No attacker waiting to strike, or forest predator assessing her potential for its next meal.

Just her, and her horse.

Baldur was dozing, one foot resting, but now he opened his eyes, ears sweeping forward. He made a soft, sighing noise, shifted his weight to rest another foot, and closed his eyes again. Not worried or disturbed.

Whatever had woken her had been in her mind.

She had a tearing pain in her chest, as though something had been ripped out, and sank back to the ground, settling against the tree trunk she had been sleeping against. Nothing was wrong here.

But somewhere, out in the world, something was badly wrong.

The tear twisted, and a hint of darkness slid through her mind. Darkness she had experienced before, when the Stone Walls had been brought down. Endless, pitch black. It seemed to grow as she noticed it, the void pulling her forward.

The rending, Pieris had called it. Her fellow Hunar was a far more dedicated student than she had ever been. The rending happened when someone managed to breach the boundary of life and death. It had happened before, Pieris had said. And nearly destroyed the world.

And now, it was happening again.

She shivered, teeth clattering together, the yawning dark pulling her towards it.

And then it was gone. As if it had never been. Leaving her gasping for air, huddled against the tree, becoming aware that she was cold and damp.

The rain had let up sometime during the night, the occasional drop making its way through the shrubs they were hiding in. But everything was wet. The leaves, the bark she had her head against, the ground she was sitting on.

She made herself get up again, making it to her feet far more slowly than before, the weight of her cloak dragging as she stood.

It was not really the weight of sodden cloth, she knew. It was several days without proper rest, or food, and the constant fear of discovery. She had never been on the run before. She did not like it.

A frantic journey, and Baldur's great stamina, her horse moving forward as long as she asked him to, had brought them here. Somewhere in the wild forest that stretched across the lower mountain ranges between the Royal City and Three Falls. Days' travel from anywhere. And, she could only hope, far enough from the Royal City and any obvious travel routes that no one would be looking for her here.

She was more certain that Brea and Thort had found Guise and were safely out of the city as well, or perhaps still in the hotel. After all, no one had accused them of murder.

She missed Guise. More than she would have thought possible. Most of her journeys over the past year had been taken in his company. She missed having someone else to share the basic day-to-day tasks while travelling. And she missed his presence. A companion who treated her like an equal, who would happily ride in silence, or exchange idle conversation. The only person in the world that made everything sharper, more alive and more vivid.

A fat drop of rainwater landed on her face, startling her out of her melancholy.

She and Baldur could not stay here. Someone had killed the King. And that someone had managed to implicate Yvonne. And she still had the nagging sensation of a Hunar's unfulfilled promise inside her. She had promised Adira to find the attackers of the Stone Walls, find them and stop them. Most of them were dead, but the mastermind was not. Not yet.

So, hiding was not an answer. She needed to move.

For a moment she was tempted to continue south, follow the Great River, and return to Fir Tree Crossing, and Mariah and Joel, to hug her children. Her eyes stung as she remembered their laughter. The temptation twisted her heart. Still, she did not move. She had long ago made a promise to keep her children safe. So, she could not go to them. Not yet. Not while she was accused of murder.

Her stomach growled, reminding her it had been a while since she had eaten. A new itch started across her forearm, dirty fabric clinging to her skin. She needed food. And a bath.

She opened her saddlebags and pulled out the last of her travel rations. She could hunt, if she needed to, and forage. She knew from past experience that both were better done with something in her stomach. Hunting and foraging required patience, which was difficult when she was hungry.

When she had eaten, and taken a drink from the waterskin, she opened her small supply of horse feed. Not much left there, either. Her saddlebags were designed to tide her over for a day or two, not much more than that, and it had been several days now.

Baldur accepted the handful of grain with as much dignity as possible when he was damp and coated with mud, turning his attention to some of the leaves around him as she pulled out her map, spreading it open against his side. Not for the first time, she wished she had a map like the one Pieris had made, combining goblin and Hunar magic. The old, waxed parchment map she carried was frayed around the edges and did not have a great deal of detail.

Still, she tried to trace the course they had taken, one finger moving across the map. Away from the Royal City, avoiding the King's Highways and the Great River. Into the forest. Somewhere.

And there, on the map, tantalisingly close, was a familiar spot. Somewhere she knew well. Willowton. A few days' journey. Perhaps.

There was dirt under her fingernails, she noted, as she stared at the map. Her skin prickled with disgust. She hated to be unclean. And yet, she could not help it.

She had no energy to spare for cleansing. She and Baldur would need to be filthy a little while longer.

Willowton.

Elinor was gone, her house burned. There was no safety there. But there was someone. A connection of Guise's, who liked secrets almost as much as he did. The cloth merchant, Lita. She might have information, know how to find Guise, or perhaps Brea and Thort.

And Lita would be able to get messages to Fir Tree Crossing, to let Mariah and Joel know that Yvonne was safe, at least for now.

Yvonne stared at the point on the map a little while longer. It was risky. Her connection with Elinor was well-known. As was the fact that Elinor was dead.

But she had no food left and almost no money, thanks to the shopping she had done the day the King had been killed. There were finance offices in Willowton that she could visit. And taverns that she had never visited, that would have baths.

The thought of warm, clean water almost made her cry, fingers reaching for her spell pouch before she knew what she was doing, a cleansing spell between her fingers, parchment smooth against her skin. She forced herself to let go. No. Not now.

Willowton.

The destination settled in her mind, she folded the map away and checked over Baldur's harness. They had another long journey ahead, and she needed to find food to keep them going.

Chapter Six

THE CLOTH MERCHANT'S HOUSE was exactly as she remembered it. Vibrant blue, proclaiming its owner's wealth to anyone who saw it. There was a hive of activity on the floor above the ground and a much calmer but no less business-like activity on the ground floor, with the showroom displaying the same astonishing array of fabrics she remembered from her previous visit.

There was a back door, of course. Yvonne had risked the extra energy for an invisibility spell to slip through the door while it was open for a delivery, making her way as silently as she could through the building to the cloth merchant's office.

The door was open when she got there, the room empty.

She took a step to one side out of caution, still shielded from view, and stared at the empty chair behind the enormous desk. It had never occurred to her that Lita might be away. She had been so focused on getting here.

Baldur was safely hidden in an abandoned building not that far away, happily nibbling on the plant life that had taken over the interior of the building when the roof had caved in.

Her whole body was aching with exhaustion, from her feet to the top of her head, and every part of her skin itched. There had been no time for baths.

Even as she stood, wondering what to do next, a rustle of skirts from outside preceded Lita's arrival into the room. The cloth merchant had a heavy ledger in her hand, a slight frown between her brows. She nudged the door shut behind her as an almost absent movement, the click of the latch loud in the quiet room, then paused, lifting her head, and sniffing the air, nose wrinkling.

Before Yvonne could say anything, Lita moved across to her desk, put the ledger down and reached into one of her desk drawers, bringing out a loaded crossbow and pointing it more or less in Yvonne's direction.

"If you're going to sneak into someone's office, you should at least have a bath first," the cloth merchant said, voice clipped.

"I would love a bath," Yvonne answered, cancelling the invisibility spell so that Lita could see her.

Lita's eyes widened, mouth opening, a shocked gasp emerging. She also twitched, pulling the trigger on her crossbow.

The bolt flew across the room, thudding into the wall a few paces away from where Yvonne was.

"Dammit," Lita said, "that wasn't even close."

"I'm quite glad of that," Yvonne answered.

Lita glared at her, setting another bolt into the crossbow before she returned it to her desk drawer, then looking back at Yvonne, eyes travelling across the beautifully made chairs around the room, hesitating. Torn between politely asking Yvonne to sit, and concern for her furniture, Yvonne thought. She could not blame Lita.

"What is that smell?" the cloth merchant asked.

"About two weeks of travel," Yvonne answered, nose wrinkling. "You should see my horse."

"No," Lita said, emphatically, "I do not wish to. You are quite enough." She stared at Yvonne for a long moment. "I suppose this explains the odd message I had from Brea the other day. She asked me to look out for Guise's friend, and keep them safe."

"That's not very specific," Yvonne commented, staying where she was against the wall of the room. Lita did not seem particularly welcoming, the crossbow bolt still quivering where it had struck the wall.

"No," Lita agreed, shoulders slumping slightly. "I suppose I should ask you to sit, and offer you refreshment."

Yvonne choked on a laugh, drawing a glare from the other woman.

"It's alright," Yvonne said. "What I really need is a safe place to rest for the night. Perhaps with running water."

"Oh." Lita's expression lifted, eyes brightening. "That, I can do. I have a guest house you can use. There's room for your horse, too." She reached into another drawer, producing a pair of keys which drew Yvonne's immediate attention.

Those were not standard keys, but the complicated sort often used for treasuries or safe boxes. Very difficult to pick, or force open. Lita didn't notice Yvonne's stare, too busy writing something on a scrap of parchment. She came around the desk and held out the keys and parchment, nose wrinkling as she got closer to Yvonne. "That's the address. Go through the gate at the side, not the front door. The small key opens the gate. The big key opens the door at the back. There should be some feed in the outbuilding and room for your horse."

Yvonne took the keys and parchment, amused again when Lita took a hasty step back. She read the address and her brows lifted. It was in one of the more affluent neighbourhoods, where she had rarely ventured.

"I have the house next door," Lita added. "Perhaps you would join me for supper this evening?"

"Thank you," Yvonne said. She really wanted to just sleep until morning, but a few hours' rest would help. And a bath. She had used most of the few coins she had left to get some food from one of the market stalls on the way here, the stallholder eyeing her, and her tired, filthy horse, with great suspicion.

"Until later, then," Lita said, then hesitated. "How are you going to get out of here?"

"The same way I came in," Yvonne said, drawing a breath, bracing herself for the drain of energy from another spell. "Until this evening."

She pulled the invisibility spell around her and watched as Lita's eyes widened again before heading over to the door, opening it, and leaving the building the same way she had come in.

Being clean was one of the best feelings in the world. She was onto her third round of bath water. The first bath had been horrifying, seeing the dirt that had come off her skin and her hair. The second bath had been much better. And this third was a luxury. Just to make absolutely sure she was clean.

Lita's guest house had turned out to be a small, beautifully furnished cottage near the ornate gates of a much larger house and grounds. Possibly a servants' cottage in times past. Yvonne did not care. It had a large outbuilding and, more importantly, the luxury of a bathing room next to the single bedroom.

The outbuilding had already been supplied with clean hay for bedding, a feed store that was half-full, along with water and feed buckets. Far from the first time someone had stabled a horse in the building. Baldur's ears had swept forward at the smell and sight of feed, although he had graciously stood while she used a cleansing spell on him before she gave him food and water, brushing her horse while he ate, until his coat gleamed and her arms were trembling with the effort. He had accepted the attention as his due, and had been half-asleep before she had left him.

With her horse settled and content, she had turned her entire focus on the bath. She had broken one of her usual customs, bringing food into the bathing room with her, needing the energy as much as she needed to be clean, and now rested in the enormous bath, pleasantly warm, clean from head to toe, full of food, limbs heavy with tiredness. She had managed a cleansing spell for her belongings between the second and third baths so she had clean clothes to get into once she had got out of the bath. Which she did not want to do. She wanted to stay here forever.

And could not. Not just the nagging, unfulfilled promise pulled her out of the bath, but the knowledge that there was much still to be done. She hoped Lita would have information to share. And then Yvonne had to decide what to do next, and how she might find Guise.

There had not been much time to sleep, after taking three baths, before she was due at Lita's house for supper. She had fallen into a dreamless sleep in the guest cottage, and was thick-headed as she made her way from the guest house across to the main house. Night had fallen, and the gardens were lit here and there with candles carefully placed in glass jars. There must be at least one gardener about the place.

As she came up to the front door of the house, she realised she had no idea who else might be in the house, whether Lita had a family living with her, or perhaps more guests.

The door opened as she approached, Lita herself waiting for her.

"You smell much better," the cloth merchant said. She had changed from her earlier formal dress and was now clad in a floor-length brocade robe that would have cost as much as Baldur.

"I think I used most of the soap in the guest house," Yvonne confessed, stepping into the house.

"It was worth it," Lita responded, closing the door behind her guest.

Yvonne took a breath in, smelling the subtle, fresh scent of the house. Beeswax and lemon. Expensive house-cleaning products. There was no other adornment, no overpowering scents. The house was two storeys tall and about as large as the house Yvonne had bought for her family. All resemblance ended there.

This house was, like Lita herself, beautifully presented, not a speck of dust to be seen, gleaming wooden floors stretching away from them, the staircase that rose from the ground floor to the upper storey likewise spotless. The floors were covered here and there with what Yvonne recognised as luxurious rugs from the southern realms, with brilliant colours and intricate designs. The walls of the house were plain, the better to display the occasional piece of artwork. Lita had expensive tastes, and the means to indulge them. The art and the rugs that Yvonne could see would cost more than her own house. "You have a beautiful home," Yvonne said, realising she had been staring for a while.

"Thank you," Lita said, sounding like she meant it. "Would you believe I won it in a game of cards?" Her face was full of mischief as she said it, looking around her home with a fond look that Yvonne thought would be on her own face when she looked at her horse.

"Yes," Yvonne said, laughing. "I am surprised you didn't get half the town."

"That would be greedy," Lita said, mischief still in her face. She could have had half the town, Yvonne suspected. She could not help wondering how many people had underestimated Lita. Not anymore, Yvonne thought, not with the bold, blue trading house. Or with this magnificent home. But, before Lita had painted her business premises cobalt blue. Or set up home here. She would have been dismissed easily by the older merchants.

"Do come through," Lita said. "We're the only people in the house. The housekeeper made enough to feed an army, but she's gone home now."

"You live here alone?" Yvonne asked, following Lita through the house's entrance hall and a set of open double doors to a large room with an impressive fireplace, a great mirror over the fireplace reflecting the light of a few candles set in front of it, and a vast dining table, that had spaces for half a dozen people along each side, with one more at each end. The table had only two places set, opposite each other at one end, the rest of the table's surface covered with dishes.

"Most of the time," Lita answered, more mischief crossing her face, along with another fond look that Yvonne had seen from time to time on Elinor's face, when her mentor had been recalling her lovers. Lita was a beautiful woman. Yvonne could well imagine that she would have company from time to time.

The softer look vanished as Lita glanced at the heavy curtains across what must be windows to the outside. "I do still have to have guards, though I make sure they stay at the perimeter."

"That sounds risky," Yvonne commented. The last time she had been in Willowton, when she had first met Lita, the cloth merchant had been accompanied by hired guards. Some dispute with the other merchants, Yvonne remembered.

"The house is protected," Lita said, sounding quite confident.

Before Yvonne could ask more, some instinct of danger made her turn and she froze to the spot.

There was a cat behind her, about knee-high, with great yellow eyes staring at her, tufted ears swept forward, its fur a mottled blend of sand and darker tones. It looked like a slightly large house cat, apart from the tufted ears. And yet she stayed quite still as it settled back on its haunches and yawned, showing a set of blinding white teeth. It looked back at Yvonne with the flat eyes of a master predator, lip curling.

"Interesting," Lita said. "Most people try to pet him. But you know what he is."

Protected, Lita had said. And had said they were the only people in the house, a curious turn of phrase that Yvonne had missed. No wonder Lita had seemed confident in her security here. Southern wild cats were renowned for their hunting prowess and aggression if they felt their territory was under threat.

"I saw a pair of these cats take down a man once," Yvonne said, shivering slightly at the memory. The man had survived only because three of his companions had joined the fray, tearing the cats off him and dragging him away from the cat's nest, and the tiny kitten that had been hissing at his would-be kidnapper. The man had been scarred for life, and lucky to be alive. One of the cats had been tearing at his throat, unable to reach his skin through the scarf he had tied around his neck.

The man, and his friends, had been less than pleased when Yvonne had reported them to the nearest law keepers. The native wild cats were near-sacred creatures to the rulers of Abar al Endell, and Sir, the current ruler of the southern lands, had long ago given orders they were to remain undisturbed.

"Not something you easily forget," Yvonne added.

"I imagine not," Lita agreed.

The cat looked between them both and made a soft, chirping sound. Almost an enquiry. There was a great deal of wildness in it, though.

"Now, now," Lita scolded. It took Yvonne a moment to realise she was speaking to the cat. "Be nice. Yvonne is my guest. Why don't you go and find your mate and prowl about the grounds for a while?"

The cat tilted its head, transferring its flat gaze to Lita, the eyes changing somehow, a subtle shift into what would be affection on a human face. It made a low purring sound and turned, padding away through the house as silently as it had arrived, leaving Yvonne weak-kneed, heart thumping.

"Sorry," Lita said, sounding anything but apologetic. "I am so used to them now."

"Protected," Yvonne repeated Lita's word, sinking onto the chair in front of her. "I see." Her voice was faint. She could not imagine how a cloth merchant in Willowton would have come to have a pair of southern wild cats. "Did you win them as well?"

"No." Lita poured two glasses of wine, set one beside Yvonne, and moved around the table to her own place. "They were a gift. I've had them since they were cubs."

A gift. Yvonne's brows lifted. The only people permitted to give the cats as gifts were members of the ruling household. Then she shook her head slightly, not sure why she was surprised. Of course Lita would know someone, or more than one person, in Sir's household.

"A mated pair?" Yvonne asked, shifting to face Lita.

"Yes. They seem to think I'm their cub. Or something like that," Lita said, frowning. "It's very sweet, until they decide to bring me gifts."

Yvonne choked on an unexpected laugh. She could well imagine the sorts of gifts that wild cats might bring their mistress. "My children used to bring me their hunting kills. When they first started hunting." She shook her head, staring into her wine. "Fortunately, after the first occasion, they left them in the kitchen rather than bringing them to my bedroom."

Lita laughed, and waved her hand at the table. "Please, help yourself. My housekeeper is a competent cook. And you look like you could use some food," she added.

For such a grand house, the dishes of food were relatively plain, but all of them well-cooked, and full of flavour. Two different main courses of meat, with a variety of vegetable dishes, some of which made Yvonne's brows lift. The wildcats were not the only things in this house that had come from the southern lands.

Lita kept the conversation light, commenting on some of the latest fashion trends in the town, equal parts disgusted and amused, until they had finished their main course and had some dessert sitting in front of them.

"The Stone Walls are down," the cloth merchant said, sitting back from her plate, staring at Yvonne across the table. "Is that what brings you here?"

"In a way," Yvonne answered, eyes focused on her wine. She had not drunk much, and was tempted to swallow the rest in one great gulp. She set the glass aside. It would not help. "King Victor is dead."

Lita frowned, tilting her head, looking like she was trying to make the connection.

"Victor was killed," a new voice said.

Chapter Seven

Yvonne came to her feet, her chair falling to the floor, one hand on her sword-hilt before she recognised the voice. Ulla.

The assassin had slipped into the room from behind one of the heavy curtains, still clad head to toe in black.

"Have you been there the whole time?" Yvonne demanded, keeping her hand on the sword hilt. She had not heard the window open, or felt any breeze from the outside air.

"No. I arrived just as you were getting dessert," Ulla said, coming across the room to stand next to the chair at the head of the table.

"What did you do to my cats?" Lita demanded. She was still sitting, looking less than pleased to see her newest guest.

"They were delighted to see me," Ulla answered, taking a seat in the chair. "Aren't you going to offer me some food and wine?"

"I'm more likely to offer you the door," Lita snapped back.

They knew each other, Yvonne realised. Of course they did. She picked up her fallen chair and took her seat again.

"It's been a long journey here, and something to eat and drink would be helpful," Ulla said, sounding as if she were keeping her calm with some effort. "I have much to tell you. And you, Hunar. I was not expecting to find you here."

"Where did you expect to find me?" Yvonne asked, with a bite in her voice. "You told me to get out of the city."

"I was not sure you could," Ulla said frankly. "The Hundred are not known for their cunning."

Yvonne clamped her jaw shut before she could say something unwise. After all, the assassin had helped her escape from the General, the King's Guard and indeed the city.

"If you didn't expect to find her here, where did you think to find her?" Lita asked, echoing Yvonne's question.

"In the Valland dungeons, perhaps. Or on their executioner's block. They seem quite convinced you killed Victor."

Lita drew a short, sharp breath.

"Food. Drink," Ulla reminded her.

Lita glared at Ulla's covered head and rose to her feet, going to one of the wooden cabinets at the side of the room and bringing back a plate, cutlery and a wine glass, making a place for Ulla at the head of the table, between Lita and Yvonne. Then the cloth merchant refilled hers and Yvonne's glasses, taking her seat again and waiting, arms folded across her stomach, while Ulla served herself from the food on the table, poured herself a glass of wine and settled into her chair as if she was perfectly at home in Lita's house.

Yvonne forced herself to remain still, and quiet. The assassin would not be rushed. And if Ulla had made the effort to come here, she probably had good information to pass on. Besides, Yvonne was curious as to how Ulla would manage to eat and drink with her face covered.

That mystery was easily solved, Ulla simply reaching up and unfastening the covering across her face so that the fine black fabric fell in a drape to one side of her face, trailing across her shoulder.

Yvonne had a momentary shock, seeing Ulla's face. The assassin was beautiful. Bronzed skin, finely arched black eyebrows over large, dark eyes, the sort of bone structure that artists loved to paint. She did not look dangerous. And yet, she was. Bad assassins tended to die quickly, if they graduated at all.

A previous conversation with Guise, where she had asked him if he had any male friends, came to mind and she ducked her head to her wine glass to hide the smile. She should have asked him if all his female friends were beautiful, as well. And suspected she knew the answer.

"That's better," Ulla said a few moments later. She had cleared half her plate in moments, her table manners at least as good as Guise's, or Yvonne's. "I have been travelling a long time," she told them both.

Now that her face was revealed, it was easier to read her moods, and see the weariness on her face, dark shadows under her eyes, a touch of strain showing in tension at the sides of her mouth.

"You have not come directly from the Royal City," Yvonne guessed, and Ulla inclined her head. "From Abar al Endell?"

"I had no idea my travel plans were so interesting to you," Ulla said and took a sip of wine, careful and controlled, in a way that suggested she wanted to down the whole glass. Yvonne's attention sharpened. Something had troubled the assassin. "Someone tried to put a contract on the Hundred."

Yvonne was glad she was sitting down, eyes widening in shock, heart and breath stopping. Someone wanted the Hundred dead. So badly that they had offered a contract to the assassins of Abar al Endell. And when an assassin from that school took a contract, the target ended up dead. Always. Yvonne's stomach twisted as her breath rushed back into her lungs. No wonder the assassin was tense.

"It failed," Ulla added, into the silence in the room, perhaps thinking that was what held Yvonne quiet. "Sir's ancestors long ago decreed that the Hundred were not to be touched. No one from the school would take such an assignment."

"The whole of the Hundred?" Yvonne asked, hearing her voice calm and measured. As if it were not her life, and those of her friends, under discussion.

"Even so."

"That's ..." Lita began, voice trailing off as she seemed to struggle for a strong enough word. "Remarkable," she said at length.

Ulla had finished her plate, and reached for more food, her sleeve sliding back a fraction to show the tattoo on her inner wrist. The same one that all assassins received on their graduation. A stylised dagger.

"Did the contract list the names of the Hundred?" Yvonne asked, curious. Hunar were rare. They always had been, even when the first Hunar and the so-called Hundred that followed him, had been alive. And yet, somehow, most people seemed to believe that there were, indeed, a hundred of them.

"No." Ulla paused, fork halfway to her mouth, narrowing her eyes slightly. "An interesting omission. I had not considered that before."

"How could you fulfil a commission not knowing your targets?" Lita asked, sounding genuinely curious. Yvonne bit the inside of her lip to hide a smile. Another one who loved information, and secrets. Her smile faded. She wished Guise were here.

"It's been done before. It's up to us to do the research," Ulla said, putting her fork down.

"But you are not here because the school turned down a contract," Yvonne said, sitting back and eyeing the assassin.

Ulla looked up and met her eyes, a hint of surprise crossing her face. "The sums offered were enormous. Tempting, even with the ancestors' decree in place."

"Do tell me what my life is worth?" Yvonne asked, voice light.

"You don't seem surprised," Lita said, before Ulla could answer. "And very calm."

"It is hardly the first time someone has tried to kill me, or have me killed. Some people do not like the Hundred at all. Believe we interfere in matters which do not concern us."

"A thousand golden crowns. For each one of the Hundred," Ulla said, before Lita could ask more questions.

Yvonne's breath rushed out of her again, room spinning for a moment, shock holding her still. A thousand golden crowns would keep anyone in comfort for life. The total pay offered would buy a kingdom. Then her eyes narrowed. The currency was not a coincidence.

"Definitely golden crowns?"

"Most assuredly. The agent brought a hundred of them to demonstrate good faith. Quite genuine."

"You said someone tried to put out the contract. And they used an agent. The patron remained anonymous?"

"Yes." Ulla's face tightened, an expression that Yvonne had not expected crossing her face. Fear. The assassin looked like she had seen a ghost. "Investigations were put underway. Enquiries made. Two of the school's best people." She blinked, eyes brighter than they had been, and looked up to meet Yvonne's eyes again. "We found their bodies two days later. Drained of blood. No message. There was no need of one. The head of the school told the agent we would not take the contract, and that was the end of the matter."

Drained of blood. Yvonne's breath caught. It might be a coincidence. Draining of blood was an unpleasant way to kill someone. But Hiram was alive. And he liked blood.

"Someone killed two assassins?" Lita asked, voice rising in pitch.

"More than two, I'm guessing, or you would not be so worried," Yvonne said.

Ulla's lips pressed together in a thin line and she nodded, once. "After the head of school made his decision, one of the trainees decided to try and take the contract himself. Too full of theory. Thought he knew everything. He was returned to us in pieces."

"Someone you were training," Yvonne guessed, her voice soft. There had been heart-felt pain in Ulla's words.

"Yes. He could have made a good assassin, if he had only learned a little humility."

"I've met youngsters like that," Yvonne said. "A lot of them, actually. Never believe that there's any danger until it's too late." Sometimes with terrible results. Sometimes the lesson was learned, and not repeated, like the time Mariah had tried to make friends with a wasp and had her finger stung.

Ulla dipped her chin, acknowledging the point, staring into her almost untouched wine.

"So, you came to tell me that someone tried to hire the school to kill the Hundred," Lita said. "Why me?"

"I went to the Royal City first," Ulla answered, face and voice tight. "To ask some questions of the King. Only someone was there before me. And then I had to leave." She flicked a glance in Yvonne's direction.

"So, the contract had already been offered, and turned down, when we were in the Royal City?" Yvonne asked, frowning slightly. "You could have mentioned it."

"We were otherwise occupied," Ulla said, voice sharp. "If we had stopped to gossip we both might have been captured. As it was, I had to leave the city before I got anything useful."

"I am sorry that helping me escape ruined your plans to gather information," Yvonne said. "But I am grateful for the assistance."

"I was going to catch up with you on the road, but you kept yourself well hidden," Ulla said.

"Thank you." Yvonne inclined her head, accepting what she recognised as a great compliment.

"To your question," Ulla said, turning back to Lita. "I came to ask you where to find Guise, so that I could warn the Hunar," Ulla corrected, taking a hearty drink of wine. "We turned him down. Others might not."

Lita's expression was blank for a moment.

"The assassins have a code," Yvonne said, keeping her voice gentle. "But there are killers out there who will just look at the money offered and not care what they are being asked to do."

"I see." Lita swallowed, hard.

"It cannot come as a surprise to you that there are paid killers," Ulla said, a touch of acid in her tone.

"No, of course not. But. The Hundred." Lita sounded unsettled. "Who would want to kill them?"

"Not everyone likes us," Yvonne reminded her, trying for a lighter tone. The Hundred could cross borders, enter courts, and generally move unchallenged through the lands. It was a courtesy they had long been granted. The people who needed a Hunar's help welcomed them. The rulers of the lands that the Hundred moved through were often less delighted to see them. The Hundred answered to no one but their oaths, and a number of rulers over the years had found that both baffling and dangerous.

"And you have some idea of who it might be. The one who tried to make the contract," Ulla said, eyes narrowed.

Yvonne did not speak, staring into her wine, a memory of Hiram's face rising in her mind as she had first seen him, handsome and confident in his power, before he had revealed his true nature. A blood sorcerer, half crazed with power. He had raised himself from death once already. She frowned as she thought of something.

"The agent. He would have needed to meet his master," she said, looking up, distracted by the slight movement of the curtains at the edge of the room.

"Not necessarily. Sometimes there are intermediaries," Ulla answered, her gaze following Yvonne's.

"That's interesting," Yvonne said, setting down her wine, reaching into her spell pouch for a reveal spell as the curtain rippled again. Almost as if someone were standing behind it.

"Get down," Ulla shouted, moving forward, grabbing Lita's arm and dragging the cloth merchant under the table.

Chapter Eight

Yvonne ducked out of her chair, under the table, as something heavy struck the table over her head, splitting the polished surface, sending plates and glasses and dishes and cutlery to the floor around her, something striking her shoulder as it fell. A dinner knife had fallen beside her. She grabbed it, twisted the reveal spell around it, and flung the spell across the room to the curtains, activating it as it flew.

The spell cascaded over the curtains, revealing nothing. There was no concealment there. But figures were coming into the room from behind the heavy curtains. A half dozen at least. Clad in close-fitting clothes, a motley collection of colours, their faces partly concealed by cloth across their lower faces.

Not assassins, then.

But skilled enough to make their way through Lita's grounds and find a way into the house, past the wild cats. And throw something that had broken Lita's table.

Yvonne flung a concussive spell at the nearest attackers, knocking them off their feet, and took a step forward, her sword in her hand, meeting the next attacker.

Dimly, she was aware of a high-pitched scream of alarm. Lita, she thought. A low-voiced command. Ulla.

But the attackers were focused on Yvonne. She was not wearing a cloak, and the Hunar's symbol blazed green in the candlelit room, drawing the attention of all the intruders.

She drew her long dagger and kept her back to the ruined table, kicking her chair out of her way, into the path of another attacker.

They were working as a unit, co-ordinated and deadly. They might not be assassins. They were still lethal.

She blocked the next sword strike with the flat of her blade, sweeping her long dagger forward and striking home, the man grunting in pain, staggering back.

She moved sideways, kicking another chair in front of her, blocking the path of the next attacker, and hacked at the arm of the next man with little finesse but as much power as she could bring to bear.

Her sword, honed to a fine edge and bound with spells, sliced through the man's arm, severing it, a cascade of blood pouring out of the wound. He yelled, staggered back, his place taken by another attacker. She kicked the chair forward, catching his shins, but he moved around the chair, sword in one hand, length of rope in another.

He threw the rope, tangling it around her sword arm. She sliced at the rope with her dagger as he yanked forward, pulling her almost off her feet, towards him and away from the table.

He dropped his sword, putting a hand over her mouth, dragging her back towards him.

She thrust her head back, catching him by surprise, the back of her head connecting with his face, and stamped as hard as she could on one of his feet. She kicked back with the same foot, connecting with something. A knee, she thought.

He stumbled back with a grunt of pain and she turned, kicking out again, catching something softer and more painful this time, doubling him over, sending him to the ground. His head was in reach, so she kicked that, as well, for good measure.

She moved back towards the table, weapons still in hand, shaking the rope off her sword arm, and waited for the next attack.

A pair of men approached her. More careful now. The room was full of the sounds of pain, and the scent of blood.

She sheathed her dagger, grabbed a concussive spell from her pouch and flung it forward.

It caught the nearest man with its full force, hurling him backwards, against the wall, the distinctive snap as he hit telling her that something had broken.

The other man stumbled sideways, righted himself and moved forward, sword raised. She used her free hand and threw another chair at him, catching him in the gut.

He doubled over, still holding on to his sword. She stepped forward, turned her sword, and hit him across the head as hard as she could with the weighted hilt. He fell to the ground.

She stepped back to the table, grabbed her dagger again, and looked around, breathing heavily. She was at the end of the table, no more protection for her back, and no more chairs to fling.

And there had been at least one more attacker.

She moved around the end of the table, facing the curtains that the attackers had used, and sweeping her gaze around the room. There were dead and injured masked men around the side of the table she had been sitting on. And at the other side, another body, Ulla standing over him, her face hidden again.

"He's dead," Ulla said, voice flat.

There were no more threats.

"You can come out now," Ulla added, with barely a change in tone.

Lita's head appeared from under the table, looking around, and she crept forward. She used the table to help her stand, face chalk-white, fingers trembling as she put a hand to her mouth, seeing the devastation of what had been her dining room.

"H-how … W-what …" Lita could not finish her questions, but Yvonne could guess.

She looked around the room, at the bodies and the injured, and her legs trembled. The thing that had hit Lita's table was a great throwing mace, studded with spikes. If it had caught her head she would be dead. As it was, Lita's table was ruined.

There had been no time to think. Just to react. A series of attackers that she had managed to deal with. One at a time. If they had been able to come at her all at once, she would also be dead.

Her stomach twisted and she swallowed, hard. Six attackers. Working as a team. And they had been here for her.

"How did they find you?" Ulla asked.

"H-her?" Lita asked.

"They ignored us. Went straight for the Hunar," Ulla pointed out.

Yvonne looked back at the masked assassin and opened her mouth. No sound came out. She shook her head, becoming aware she was still holding her bloody weapons. A quick, spoken cleansing spell and she put them away.

She was at the far end of the table from where they had been sitting, a dish of small sweet cakes at her feet, almost untouched. She picked it up and took one of the cakes, making her way back around the table towards the injured men.

The one who had lost his arm was dead. Shock and blood loss, probably.

The two she had knocked on the head were alive. The one she had kicked was still doubled over, moaning slightly. The other was completely still. She picked up the bits of rope that had been thrown at her and tied him up. Just in case. Then moved to the groaning man.

"How can you eat?" Lita asked.

"Fighting and spell working takes energy," Ulla answered, before Yvonne could say anything. "You should sit down. You look like you're going to faint."

"I'm fine," Lita answered, sounding anything but calm. She made a startled noise a moment later, a cut-off squeal, and Yvonne turned her head to see Lita sitting on a chair, Ulla's hand on her shoulder.

"Stay there," Ulla told her host, and moved to Yvonne's side on silent feet. "Do you know them?"

"I don't think so," Yvonne answered. She set the nearest chair upright, put the empty dish on it, and turned back to the injured man, who was still groaning.

Ulla had produced a length of slender rope from somewhere about her person and tied his feet and hands together, and was now tugging the cloth away from his face.

"No, I don't know him," Yvonne said, staring at the features revealed. A man, perhaps a few years older than she was, unshaven, with weathered skin and a scar along one side of his jaw, with mid-brown, unkempt hair. She wrinkled her nose. He did not look like an elite assassin.

Ulla was pulling up the man's sleeves, checking for markings. When she didn't find anything, she moved to the next man, and the next, pulling off their face masks as she did so.

They were a motley collection of men who could have come from anywhere from the Rosarch region to Valland. Not northmen, and not from the southern lands. But that still left a huge swathe of land in between.

Yvonne went through their pockets, finding bits and pieces of coins, a whetstone or two, but nothing of any note. No golden crowns. No written instructions.

By the time she and Ulla had finished their searches, the groaning man was alert and furious, twisting against the ropes Ulla had used, spitting curses as he could not break free.

"Who are you and who sent you?" Yvonne asked, settling a chair near his head and taking a seat, slightly amused when Ulla copied her, settling at the man's other side.

"Not telling you anything, bitch. You killed my men."

"Not all of them. And they were trying to kill me," Yvonne said, glancing to one side, wondering if there was more food available. It had been a hard journey to get here, her energy dangerously low, and the brutal fight and magic use had cancelled out the meal.

He glared back at her. "This was supposed to be an easy job."

"Really?" her brows lifted, attention fully on the man. "Someone told you that killing a Hunar would be easy?"

"Said it was all for show. That you can't do anything unless you're asked." The man spat in her direction. It missed, but she wrinkled her nose anyway. Disgusting habit.

"It seems you were misinformed," Ulla said, her voice icily calm. Without being able to see her face, Yvonne could not be sure, but that tone seemed dangerous. For the man. Assassins were taught how to extract information.

The man growled a few curses, wriggling against his bonds again, and muttered something that Yvonne did not quite catch, but which made Ulla go motionless on her chair. The assassin had been still up to that point, but the change was remarkable.

"You spoke with an agent," Ulla said, still in that chilly voice.

The man snarled at her, and made some suggestion about what she could do.

"Anatomically impossible," Yvonne told him. "The lady asked you a question. Tell us about the agent."

"Should have wrung his skinny neck," the man said, making a low sound of frustration as he could not break out of Ulla's rope.

"Do you know that we put poison on our ropes," Ulla told him, still in that frozen tone. "If you keep struggling, you'll start bleeding and the poison will get into your blood."

The man went still.

It was the first time Yvonne had heard about assassins using poisoned ropes. It was possible. More likely, Ulla wanted the man's full attention. Yvonne found that she approved.

"The agent," Yvonne prompted.

The man glared at her, but complied. A short, slender man. Red hair, which was unusual enough that the would-be-assassin remembered it. The agent had worn it slicked back. He'd had fair skin, to go with his red hair, and a strange accent. The man couldn't explain what had been strange about the accent, just that it had been odd. Nice clothes, too, he added.

Yvonne's tracking sense stirred. She had almost enough to be able to find the agent. Enough that she should recognise him if she did come across him. It was more than she had expected.

"Did he give you a name?" Ulla asked. Something in her tone made Yvonne glance across. The assassin was tense.

"Said we could call him Victor."

A name most commonly associated with the Valland kings. Some parents liked to name their children after kings. But Yvonne had a feeling that this particular man had chosen the name himself.

"Where can we find him?" Ulla asked.

"I don't know," the man answered, starting to wriggle against the ropes again, then going motionless, remembering Ulla's threat of poison.

"Where did you meet him?" Yvonne asked, forcing herself to be patient. The longer that they stayed here, in this room, with the corpses, the greater the chance of discovery. And she did not have a happy history with the law keepers in this town. Last time she had been here, an undead lord had tried to kill her using death magic, aided by the Ashnassan tribe. There had been a lot more violence during her visit than the town was used to seeing, and she did not think the law keepers would have forgotten her.

"Three Falls," the man answered, sounding sulky.

Three Falls. Of course. If there was a more appropriate meeting point for agents looking to hire killers, and killers for hire, Yvonne could not think of it. The city was full of criminals and desperate people. Sometimes they were the same people.

"He's not there now, though, is he?" Ulla prompted.

That did not sound like a guess. Yvonne wondered if Ulla had been to Three Falls after she had been in the Royal City, but kept silent, holding her attention on the bound man.

"No," the man answered, sounding even more sulky. "Said he might come here."

"Willowton?" Yvonne asked, brows lifting, her tracking sense stirring. If the agent was in the town, she might be able to find him.

"Dunno."

"He was the agent. Who was he working for?" Yvonne asked.

"Dunno."

One word, in a petulant tone. Yet, she believed him.

"When you had killed me, how were you going to get paid?"

He glared at her, and strained against his ropes again, apparently forgetting that they were supposed to be poisoned.

"Does that matter?" Lita asked, her voice higher than normal. Yvonne looked across at her. The cloth merchant's colour was a little better, although she was staring around the ruins of her dining room with wide eyes, as if she could not believe, or understand, what she was seeing.

"Yes," Ulla answered, before Yvonne could. "It will help us find his paymaster."

"I don't know," the man answered, teeth bared, colour rising. "He knew." He jerked his chin in the general direction of the end of the table where Ulla had been sitting. And the dead attacker. "It's the way we always work," he went on, clenching his jaw for a moment.

"So, you're not the leader," Ulla said, her voice silky soft.

"Clearly not," Yvonne agreed, moving away from the bound man and casting her eyes over the others. They looked like any number of hired killers that she might have seen on the streets of Three Falls, the few times she had been there.

"What I can't understand is where the guards are," Lita said, staring at the door to the room as if expecting an army to rush through it.

Lita's guards. The ones patrolling the perimeter of the property, while the wild cats prowled the grounds.

"They are probably dead," Ulla said.

Yvonne looked back at the bound man and saw the faintest glimmer of a smile on his face.

"That, or they were bribed," she speculated, realising she was right when the man glared at her. "You need better protection," Yvonne told Lita.

"Bribed?" Lita's voice rose in outrage. "After what I've been paying them?"

"No time for that now," Ulla said. "We need to leave."

"Leave?" Lita's voice rose again. "This is my home. It has been violated."

"Fine. Stay here. Explain to the law keepers how you have six dead men in your dining room," Ulla suggested, tone sharp as a blade's edge.

Lita's mouth opened, then she snapped it shut, glaring at the assassin, colour rising on her face.

She might be a cloth merchant with a prosperous business, but she was a controversial figure in the town, Yvonne would guess, and perhaps not on the best terms with the town's law keepers.

"Go and change into clothes for travelling. Pack a bag. Two sets of spare clothes. As plain and tough as you have. Do you have a horse?" Yvonne asked.

"Horse? No. I don't like riding," Lita answered, rising to her feet.

"She can ride with me for a bit," Ulla offered, "if you'll take the supplies?"

"Yes."

"Go get ready," Ulla told Lita. "Hunar, you, too. I'll gather supplies."

Yvonne nodded, leaving the room in Lita's wake. The assassin could manage a commanding tone when she needed to.

It was only while she was saddling Baldur, settling her belongings across his shoulders, that she realised Ulla had said six dead men. Not four.

She brought Baldur to the back entrance of the house and made her way through the rooms to the dining room, drawn by the scent of blood, and found six corpses.

"I didn't mean to kill them all," Yvonne said.

"I know," Ulla said, appearing beside her like a shadow. "But they had heard too much. And they would have killed you."

"I know," Yvonne echoed. She could not look at the assassin, the weight of more dead on her shoulders.

"We need to go," Ulla prompted, turning away and heading back through the house, making her way to the kitchen, Yvonne following.

To Yvonne's surprise, Lita was there, and ready. She was dressed in a beautifully-made split skirt and short jacket, a dainty hat perched on her head, hair tucked into a heavy bun at the nape of her neck, a smaller pack than Yvonne had been expecting at her feet.

"Here. As much food as I could gather that will travel," Ulla said to Yvonne, handing across two cloth sacks strung together with rope. They were heavier than Yvonne had expected when she took hold of them. "Let's go."

"Where?" Lita asked, following Ulla out of the house.

"I know somewhere outside the town," Ulla answered. It was not really an answer, Yvonne thought, but it would have to do for now. Questions could wait. They needed to be out of the house, and out of the town, before anyone alerted the law keepers.

Chapter Nine

The place that Ulla took them to was an abandoned quarry that Yvonne had not known existed, despite the years she had spent in Willowton. The quarry was a short distance from town, remarkably well hidden from view not only by the hills around it, but also by the high, dense shrubs that covered the hillsides. Whoever had started the quarry had tunnelled into the hills, making a large cave, propped up by heavy wooden beams with old, rotting wooden boards holding the soil up over their heads.

Ulla had brought them there, then left to cover their tracks, coming back when dawn was appearing. They should rest, she said.

Yvonne remembered the assassin's need for food and drink when she had arrived at Lita's table. Her own body was heavy with the aftermath of magic and fighting. Rest was an excellent idea.

With Ulla's horse, an inky black mare with fierce intelligence in her eyes, and Baldur keeping watch, they settled in blankets on the ground.

Yvonne woke to find the afternoon sun bright outside the mouth of the man-made cave, and Lita sitting on her blanket not far away, searching through the bags of supplies that Ulla had gathered from her house's kitchen. The assassin was nowhere to be seen, her horse also absent.

"You're awake," Lita said, as Yvonne sat up. "Ulla went into the town. Said she could get in and out unnoticed." Lita's mouth pressed into a thin line. There were dark smudges under her eyes, her skin pale. The events of the night before catching up with her again, Yvonne wondered, or perhaps she simply had not slept well.

"What did she go for?" Yvonne asked, standing up and stretching, slowly and carefully. Her whole body was stiff and still heavy from the fighting. She needed to practice some drills, to ease her muscles.

"She wanted to see if she could find the agent," Lita answered, making a frustrated sound as she got to the bottom of the bag she was searching through.

"What's wrong?"

"There's no tea," Lita said, voice thin.

"Not here, no," Yvonne agreed, keeping her voice gentle. She would guess that Lita had not done much travelling where she had to sleep rough. And she had probably never rushed out of her own home in the middle of the night, away from law keepers who might be pursuing them. "We'll find a better camp soon enough and have some tea then."

Lita looked up, her jaw set, eyes over bright. Yvonne recognised the look. Mariah had worn it on many occasions. Trying to be brave when she didn't understand what was going on around her.

"This is not what I am used to," Lita said at length.

"No. I did not imagine so. It is not what most people are used to," Yvonne said. "I hope it will not be long before you can go home."

Lita nodded, mouth pressed shut, a single tear trailing down her face.

"And you promised me that we would drink wine and mull over Guise's failings," Yvonne reminded her, trying for a lighter tone.

Lita laughed, a small, broken sound, but her mouth curved up. "And you said we would need more than one bottle."

"Indeed," Yvonne agreed, going to pat Baldur. He was taking the chance to doze, resting one leg, and accepted a scratch behind his ears and under his chin with a soft sigh. She fetched a brush from her saddlebags and spent a little time brushing him down. It let her move, loosening her muscles, soothed Baldur and, hopefully, gave Lita something normal and ordinary as a backdrop after the carnage of the night before.

She had swapped the brush for a wide-toothed comb to untangle his mane and tail when he lifted his head, nostrils widening.

"Wait there," she told him, and repeated the command to Lita, putting the comb back into her saddlebags and making her way to the side of the cave, then along to the edge so that she was hidden, but could see out into the sunlight.

A newly-familiar black horse came into view, Ulla settled on her back, a spare horse trailing behind, fitted with saddle and bridle. The assassin slid off her horse and led her towards the cave, Yvonne stepping out to meet her.

"I found him," Ulla said.

"The agent? Where?"

"In one of the hotels. On this side of the town. He's taken the suite on the top floor."

"Did you speak to him?" Yvonne asked.

"He wasn't there. Had been out most of the night, the maid said." Ulla hesitated. Her face was still covered, hiding her expression. "I thought you might have questions, too."

"So, let's go," Lita said, coming into the light.

"What news of Lita's house?" Yvonne asked the assassin.

"The town is buzzing with news that apparently someone tried to kill you in your house, and your wild cats killed them all. Apparently there were ten men. Maybe more."

Yvonne resisted the urge to roll her eyes. Typical exaggeration.

"The cats will be fine," Lita said, with absolute confidence.

Yvonne lifted a brow, curious that was Lita's first reaction. The cloth merchant had an odd smile around her mouth.

"You seem pleased," Yvonne observed.

"I have a certain reputation in this town. And it never does any harm for my competitors to be wary of me," Lita said.

"Still, the law keepers are looking for you. They say they are concerned for your safety," Ulla said, in a tone which suggested she did not believe that story.

"We need to question the agent," Yvonne said.

"Are you telling me I can't go?" Lita asked, chin lifting. "It was my house that was violated."

"The law keepers are looking for you," Yvonne said, in a tone of forced patience.

"And?" Lita asked, brows lifting.

"Do you think the law keepers will listen to you?" Yvonne asked. "Or will they throw you into a cell and forget about you?" There was more she could have said, but Lita was more than intelligent enough to work matters out for herself.

Lita paled further, lips pressed into a thin line. "A lot of people in the town do not like me," she said after a moment's thought, crease between her brows. Powerful people, Yvonne would guess. Other merchants whose businesses had been affected by Lita's success. Perhaps even people she had played cards with. Yvonne suspected that Lita had won more than the house over the years. "So, I cannot go back. Not yet." She did not like the idea. Still, she understood.

"We can't leave her here on her own, either," Ulla said, her masked face moving between the two of them. "Can you swap clothes? Change your hair? That might work."

Yvonne opened her mouth to protest. Lita was at least half a head shorter than she was, and with a fuller figure. It was unlikely their clothes would switch.

"Yes, that might work," Lita agreed, turning a critical gaze to Yvonne. "They will be looking for me in my usual clothes. Not dressed like a man."

Yvonne bit her lip, and moved into the cave. "I have a spare set of clothes."

Changing into Lita's spare clothes did not take long. Thankfully, the cloth merchant had brought another split skirt and jacket so Yvonne could keep her own shirt and scarf. The jacket hid the Hunar's symbol, and although the skirt was a little too short, her boots were long enough that it did not matter.

Lita winced as she inspected Yvonne. The cloth merchant delighted in well-made clothes, and it was evident she did not like seeing her exquisite tailoring fitting so badly.

Lita had fared a little better. Yvonne's shirt and trousers were a close fit, but Lita could still move.

"Hair," Ulla prompted. She had settled on the ground near the cave's entrance, not taking any part in the changeover.

"Do I have to?" Lita asked, wrinkling her nose. Even after a night sleeping rough, her curling hair was beautifully arranged around her head.

"We don't want to attract the law keepers," Ulla answered.

With Lita's hair bound into a single plait that fell between her shoulder blades, she was transformed from the beautifully-dressed, immaculate cloth merchant into an ordinary-looking traveller. She even helped Yvonne arrange her hair, so that rather than its usual single plait, it was piled into a twist around her head.

"Good. You look different enough that anyone who doesn't know you well won't recognise you," Ulla said, getting to her feet. "Here, I brought you a horse," she told Lita, pointing to the new horse, which had been grazing on the shrubs nearby.

"I don't like horses much," Lita protested, nose wrinkling.

"Well, I'm not waiting for you to walk into the town," Ulla told her.

"He's not very pretty," Lita added, walking towards the horse.

"He's a very well-made horse," Yvonne said, going with her. Ulla did not seem interested in helping, beyond providing the horse. "And looks like he'll be calm to ride." She guessed that Ulla had chosen the horse for that reason. It had the look of a steady, reliable mount. Able to travel fair distances and not protest too much.

By the time the change had been completed, and Lita was persuaded onto her new horse's back, it was late in the afternoon. Ulla put their remaining supplies into the back of the cave, well hidden, although she insisted they bring all of their belongings just in case, and they set out into the afternoon.

It was late in the day, the sun falling into the horizon, when they arrived at the hotel where the agent was staying. Ulla had found an empty building for them to leave the horses in, a rare occurrence in this part of the town, and promised to join them in the agent's room.

Which left Yvonne and Lita to make their way into the hotel, Yvonne feeling more exposed than she would have thought possible while she was fully clothed. As well as her clothes, Lita was also carrying Yvonne's weapons and spell pouch. Lita had been horrified at the idea that Yvonne should conceal weapons in the cloth merchant's clothing.

The point between Yvonne's shoulder blades was itching as she ascended the few steps into the hotel's lobby. They had decided to seek a room for the night, which would give them an excuse to get past the reception desk and into the guest areas. Luckily, Lita had a small supply of coins.

The hotel receptionist was unimpressed with Yvonne, even dressed in Lita's beautiful clothes, and only agreed to hire her a room on being shown her money. Yvonne took the key and made her way to the stairs, Lita following, glowering at everyone they saw.

"What are you doing?" Yvonne whispered as they made their way up the first flight of stairs.

"I've decided I look like your bodyguard, so I am trying to look fierce," Lita whispered back.

"Perhaps just try to look bored?" Yvonne suggested, continuing to climb. The room she had been given was on the floor beneath the agent.

There was no one on the upper floors. It was early evening, so most people might still be about their business, or having a drink in the hotel's taproom.

Yvonne made her way up the last flight of stairs, took her sword from Lita, and knocked sharply on the agent's door.

Chapter Ten

"Go away!" a man's voice sounded through the door. Yvonne knocked again.

After a moment there was a muffled protest from the room, then the faint sound of footsteps.

The door opened and Yvonne had the impression of a pale-skinned, red-haired man before she shoved the door back, pushing into the room, resting the point of her sword at the man's throat.

"Anyone else here?" she asked the man as Lita came into the room behind them and shut the door.

"What? Who are you? What do you want?"

"Lady asked you a question," Lita said, in a low tone that was quite unlike her normal voice. Still pretending to be a bodyguard, Yvonne thought, and resisted the urge to roll her eyes for a second time that day.

The man's gaze travelled between them, mouth half-open, giving Yvonne time to cast a quick glance around the room. It was dark, the heavy curtains drawn across the windows, the covers on the bed thrown back as if he had just been disturbed from sleep. The agent was wearing a knee-length nightrobe, barefoot on the hotel's carpet. They had woken him up.

"Is there anyone else here?" she asked again.

The man glared back at her, the tip of her sword against his neck, then ducked away from the steel, dropping into a tumble that an acrobat would have envied, heading for one of the windows.

Yvonne followed him, hampered by the full skirts of Lita's outfit rather than her normal trousers, watching as he twitched back the curtain, grabbed something from behind the fabric, then disappeared.

She pulled back the curtain as she reached it, sword ready, and found that the window was open, a stout length of rope secured into the hotel wall by a heavy metal hook that she was sure had not been put there by the hotel.

Leaning out of the window, she saw pale fabric and pale skin disappearing into the shadows below. They were at the back of the hotel, an alleyway used for deliveries and staff.

"Here, put this away," Yvonne said, handing Lita the sword. "Can you climb?"

"What?" Lita asked, almost stabbing herself as she put the sword away. "No. Of course not. Why would I need to?"

"Then go down the stairs and out to the alleyway. Quick as you can. He's getting away," Yvonne said, settling on the windowsill and grabbing hold of the rope.

"Those are my clothes!" Lita shrieked as Yvonne started going down the rope, as fast as she could, hand over hand.

"He's getting away," Yvonne hissed back, and then needed all her attention for getting down the wall. The agent had left heavy knots in the rope at regular intervals, making the descent easier than she had expected. It also meant that he had been able to get to the ground quickly, and even now was running to the end of the alleyway.

She reached the ground as he turned into one of the side streets, no doubt drawing strange looks.

As she ran to the end of the alleyway she opened her tracking sense. The would-be assassin had given her some information, but she had now seen the man, and even that brief glimpse was enough to be able to follow him.

Lita joined her, flushed and out of breath, as she reached the end of the alleyway.

"He's gone," Lita said.

"I can find him. Come on," Yvonne said, and stalked forward. They were in a commercial area, businesses closing up for the night, and running would attract attention. A purposeful walk, Lita trying to keep up with her, made her just one more person about their lawful business.

As she walked she heard snippets of comments from the shopkeepers and craftsmen closing their businesses for the day. A red-haired man. In his nightshirt. At this hour. And running as if in fear of his life.

Coming to the end of the street, their quarry had turned into a back lane that led between the rear of several properties. The ground underfoot was even, and she spotted what looked like a splash of blood near some sharp-edged stones. He had been barefoot. And had cut himself in his haste to get away.

He was clever, she realised, following the trail he had left them. And had some experience at being chased, she suspected, from the way he tried to escape. She remembered her escape from the Royal City, the heart-stopping moments when she was sure she would be discovered and caught, and felt an unwanted sympathy for the agent. The feeling passed quickly with the knowledge that this was how he had chosen to live his life. It was no wonder he was skilled at escape.

He had made his way in a circuitous route, doubtless hoping to lose anyone following him, and a few times it looked like he had made an effort to disguise his trail with scent, tipping a pair of water buckets across the ground in one place, and throwing down pungent herbs from a window box in another.

Yvonne did not need scent to track, though, and kept going. He might know where Hiram was, or how to get in touch with the sorcerer. And she wanted to know, for certain, who wanted the Hundred dead. She could not afford to lose him.

Determination kept her going through all the twists of his trail.

He had a destination in mind, she was sure of it. The turns and twists he made might seem random, but he was heading in one particular direction, towards the town's large market. The market would be closed, but on this side of the market there were warehouses where merchants stored their goods. A good place to hide, if he could get past the guards.

"We're halfway across the town," Lita said, sounding breathless. "Is he going to stop soon, do you think?"

"I hope so," Yvonne answered. She was out of breath, too. The borrowed clothes kept tangling around her legs, slowing her down, and her hair was slipping out of the style that Lita had created for her.

She stopped in another back lane, looking ahead. The trail stopped somewhere nearby. He was in one of the warehouses around them.

Lita was breathing hard behind her. Not used to moving so fast, Yvonne thought.

The warehouses had pairs of guards at each door. There might also be pairs around the back of each one, too.

The agent had somehow made his way along the street, in full view of the guards, and then around the side of the buildings, heading for the side entrances, perhaps. Her brows lifted. The guards looked alert, and would doubtless have spotted a man running, dressed in a nightshirt.

A moment later and a pair of large wagons, laden with goods, came into view, and she understood how the agent had escaped notice. The wagons were pulled by placid oxen, with a single driver on each. An easy matter to slip alongside the rear wagon, along the street, and then duck into the side of the building.

"Come on," she said to Lita, and set off alongside the wagons, following the route that the agent had taken.

There was a risk, of course, that the guards would see them when they slipped around the side of the building. Except that, as she discovered, the guards were more interested in glaring at each other than in watching their surroundings.

She and Lita made it to the shadow of the warehouse's side without being seen, and she set off again, following the trail. The side entrance of this warehouse was unguarded, and someone had forced the lock, the agent's trail leading inside.

"Sword," she said to Lita.

She could not see Lita's expression in the shadow of the warehouse, but a moment later heard the whisper of her sword leaving its scabbard, and then saw the gleam of steel, Lita holding the sword vertical as she handed it across.

"Wait here," Yvonne told the cloth merchant, then opened the door into the warehouse and slipped inside.

To her surprise, there was light inside. A pair of candles in glass jars had been lit in one area, ahead of her, where the agent's trail led. The rest of the warehouse was dark. She stopped to murmur a quick spell to enhance her senses. As far as she could tell, she and the agent were the only living things in the building.

She made her way forward, between stacks of packing crates, to pause outside the light.

The agent had opened a canvas bag on top of one of the crates, and was searching through the contents. He had managed to find a pair of trousers and shirt on his travels. Perhaps from the bag, as she could see a pair of shoes next to it.

He seemed focused on whatever it was he was looking for, not noticing as she stepped closer to the light.

She pressed as close to the stacked crates as she could, not wanting to be seen, and moved forward again. She had forgotten the extra fabric around her legs. The skirts she was wearing caught on a nearby crate, the slight sound of fabric tearing loud in the quiet space.

The agent stilled, then grabbed something from the surface next to the bag. A sword. He stepped backwards, silent on bare feet, and out of the light, into the shadows of the packing crates.

Yvonne freed her skirts from the crate and took a step back. The crates were stacked in different sized groups, some up to her waist, some just over her head, with space between for people to move about. She made her way, slowly, in the gaps between the crates, round to the other side of the light, where the agent had disappeared. He was human and, as far as she could tell, had no magic. If she could be quiet enough, he might not hear her, or see her.

He was waiting in the dark, between two tall stacks of crates, the pale fabric of his shirt and the steel of his sword gleaming in the poor light. Even with her enhanced sight, details were hard to make out.

Something warned him of her approach. A sense for danger, perhaps.

He turned, sword raised, and then attacked, stabbing forward into the dark.

She turned away his attack with the flat of her sword, his sword arm slamming into the crates nearby. He made a muffled sound of pain but held on to his weapon, stepping away from the crate, towards the light.

She moved with him, until they were close enough to the candles that he could see her.

"You. How did you find me?"

"Why did you run?" she asked.

Instead of answering, he attacked, light glinting off steel as he moved forward.

He was skilled, she realised, countering the attack. And she was hampered by the unfamiliar clothes, the skirts catching on another crate as she moved to one side, avoiding a strike meant for her sword arm. Still, he had run halfway across the town in his nightshirt, his breath quickening as they fought. Being chased was not pleasant, she knew from recent experience.

He backed away from her, into the light cast by the candles, heading for the bag left open on the crate. And the shoes. He was still barefoot. As she glanced down she saw a faint trail of blood. He had cut his foot on the way here. Doubtless it was sore. And hindering his movement.

There was another glass jar, with an unlit candle, near her shoulder. She grabbed it and flung it forward, moving after it, so that he was forced to duck out of the way of the jar, and she was able to slap the flat of her blade against his sword arm, forcing him to drop the weapon.

He slumped back against the nearest crate, the tip of her sword at his throat again.

"This is getting tiresome," she told him. "I have questions. You will give me answers. And then we can go our separate ways."

"Lady, I don't know who you are, but you are out of your depth here." There was a snarl in his voice, lips peeled back. He seemed to believe the threat.

"Doubtful," a new voice said. Yvonne did not turn her head. Ulla had arrived.

The agent's eyes widened, and his skin paled.

"So, you recognise an assassin from Abar al Endell. She has questions for you, too. You will like my questions much better, I assure you," Yvonne said.

"You can't let her have me," the agent whispered. All the anger and the contempt was gone. He looked genuinely terrified.

"Interesting," Yvonne said. "Do you have rope?" she asked, over her shoulder.

"Naturally," Ulla answered, voice dry. She moved level with Yvonne's shoulder, rope ready in her hands. Yvonne stepped back to let Ulla bind the agent's hands and feet. The man did not resist, flinching away from Ulla's touch. If he had not killed the Abar al Endell assassins, then he had some idea of what had happened to them. And what one of their fellow assassins might do to him. The school did not take kindly to its members being killed.

"Is our companion still outside?" Yvonne asked as Ulla finished.

"No," Lita said. Yvonne turned to find Lita standing at the edge of the candlelight, eyes wide as she took in the scene. "You've ripped your skirts," she said, eyes narrowing.

Yvonne glanced down, grimacing as she saw the tears in the fabric, the white underskirt showing through. "They kept getting in the way."

Lita sighed, and looked like she might say more, then held herself silent, wrapping her arms around herself.

"If you answer the lady's questions nicely, I won't hurt you," Ulla told the bound man. She sounded sincere. Yvonne did not believe her.

The agent did not look like he believed her, either, still pale and trembling slightly.

"If you don't answer her questions, I will hurt you a lot," Ulla told him.

Yvonne believed her.

So did the agent, paling further, sweat appearing on his face.

"You tried to arrange a contract with the assassin's school at Abar al Endell to kill all of the Hundred," Yvonne began, and the man swallowed, loud in the quiet space. "Who were you working for?"

"How did you know that?"

"Answer the question," Ulla prompted, snap in her voice.

"I can't tell you," the agent said, slumping back against the crate.

"Really?" Yvonne lifted a brow.

Ulla pulled a knife out from somewhere about her person, turning the blade over in the light as if inspecting its edge.

"I didn't get a name," the agent admitted.

"So, you did meet your employer. Description," Yvonne prompted.

"He will kill me," the agent protested, eyes wide. Yvonne frowned slightly. He looked angry at the prospect of his employer's wrath. But his voice was shaking. Not in fear. Something else. "Did you see what he did to the others?"

"Yes," Ulla said, voice flat. "They were my colleagues. There is an open contract out on you now. And your employer."

The agent tried to swallow, and choked instead, his whole body now trembling.

"Description," Yvonne prompted.

"Rich. Tall. Handsome, I suppose. Dark hair," the agent said, his shaking now causing his teeth to rattle.

"What did you do to him?" Yvonne asked Ulla.

"Me? Nothing. Looks like some kind of poison."

"Step away," Yvonne said, waving the others back.

The agent slumped to the ground, heels drumming against the wooden surface.

"You've killed me," he managed to say.

"Not us. Your master did this," Yvonne said. "Did he mark you?"

"On my arm," the agent said, holding his hands out in front of him, his shirtsleeve falling back. There was a dark mark on his skin. "I fell asleep. Woke up with this. He said I couldn't betray him."

"More death magic," Yvonne said, crouching slightly to get a better look at the marking. "I can't help you," she told the man. "You were dead when he put this on you."

"You know who he is, don't you?" the agent whispered. "The man."

"From your description, he is a Circle Mage. Hiram," Yvonne answered, and saw the agent pale further. He had not known the name, she saw. That had been the truth, at least.

She rose to her feet and went across to Lita, gathering spells from her pouch. Lita was staring wide-eyed at the dying man, and did not move. Yvonne twisted the spells together. Cleansing, unravelling, and fire. She moved back to her former place, facing the agent. "You're going to die," she told him.

"You're Hunar. Help me," the man said.

The magic of the Hundred stirred in response to the man's plea. There was not much she could do, though. He was dying, whatever she did.

"I will find the man who did this. And I will stop him," Yvonne promised, the symbol at her shoulder warming in response. A binding promise of a Hunar.

"He wanted you dead. All of you," the man said, jaw clenched, words trembling with the rest of him. "Not angry. Fear." He gave a cry of pain, and twisted again. The dark mark on his arm had spread, casting long, black tendrils under his skin, the death magic moving through his body. "Help me." The words were almost unrecognisable, but the magic of the Hundred knew them, the Hunar's symbol flaring under the jacket Yvonne wore.

"I will find the man who did this," Yvonne repeated. "This is all I can do for you." She tossed the twisted spells onto the man's body, stepping back as she activated them.

The spells covered the man's body in a blinding shimmer of green light. The same colour as the Hunar's symbol. He made no sound as fire took over, swallowing the green light, swallowing him, burning white hot as it consumed his body, until there was nothing left of the agent but a pile of ash and a scorch mark on the warehouse floor.

"You killed him," Lita said.

"He was already dead," Ulla told her. "Death magic." Her voice was flat, grim.

"I didn't think magic could do that," Lita said, eyes fixed on the ash. She did not move as Yvonne took another cleansing spell from her spell pouch and cast it over the ash. Just to be sure.

"We need to go," Ulla said.

"Let's check his bag first," Yvonne countered, moving towards the packing crate with the open bag and contents spilled across the top.

"No time. I hear footsteps," Ulla said, tilting her head.

Yvonne could not hear anything, but that did not mean much. There was a small leather-bound notebook among the possessions she could see. She grabbed it, and followed the others through the warehouse to the side entrance.

As they moved, she could hear the footsteps Ulla had mentioned. The guards, perhaps. The agent's death had not been quiet.

They made it out of the warehouse and along the street. There were no guards left at the fronts of the warehouses, the main doors standing slightly open. All of them checking their buildings, Yvonne thought. Foolish of them to leave no watchers outside.

She, Lita and Ulla made their way along the street to the next corner, ducking out of sight of the warehouses. It was only when they stopped, all of them breathing hard, that Yvonne realised she had no idea where she was in relation to the hotel where they had first encountered the agent or, more importantly, the place where they had left the horses. She looked around, trying to get her bearings, exhaustion taking hold.

"Which way?" she asked.

"The horses are this way," Ulla said, setting off along the street with swift, sure strides. Yvonne narrowed her eyes but followed the assassin. The assassin's school did not teach, or use, magic in their work. It was one of their core principles. That did not mean that they never used magic. A tracking spell to find the way back to one's horse, for example, would be most useful.

"Stop a moment," Lita said, after they had been walking for a while.

"Do you need a rest?" Yvonne asked.

"Yes. But that's not what I meant. Your hair," Lita said, "you'll get noticed if anyone sees us."

Yvonne became aware that, as well as the tangle of skirts around her legs, she had also been brushing her hair off her face as they walked. Somewhere between the race through the town after the agent and getting here, the pins that Lita had used had slipped, and the whole mass of it had fallen down. When she tried to push it back again, her fingers tangled on a knot, with a pin in the middle of it. She grimaced, trying to pull the pin out and failing.

"Stay still a moment," Lita said, stepping behind Yvonne. A few swift tugs later, and Lita had her hair in a tight twist at the base of Yvonne's neck, secured with the pins she had managed to find. "That will hold a while longer."

"We don't need to be fashionable," Ulla pointed out.

"But any woman walking about with her hair down like that would be remembered," Lita countered, chin lifted.

"Thank you," Yvonne told the cloth merchant. "Lead on," she said to Ulla.

Chapter Eleven

It was early morning by the time they made it back to Ulla's hideout, all of them worn out, the horses with their heads low, Baldur making a soft sigh that sounded like relief when Yvonne slid off his back. She managed to focus enough to send a messenger bird to Pieris, with the urgent warning about the contracts being put out on the Hundred. Pieris was the only one of them with easy access to the messenger birds, and able to get in touch with the rest of the Hundred.

After that, it was all she could do to change back into her normal clothes, leaving her hair in the bun that Lita had fashioned, before settling to sleep.

She woke too few hours later to a snort from Baldur. A gentle warning that had her on her feet before she was fully awake, reaching for weapons, only to find nothing there.

Heart in her throat, she turned to find her belt, with the spell pouch and weapons, next to her sleeping blanket. Lita was wrapped in a blanket of her own, barely stirring as Yvonne gathered her belongings and buckled her belt on. Ulla was nowhere to be seen, her horse missing, too.

"Lita, wake up," Yvonne urged, crouching next to her.

"What is it?" Lita stirred, sitting up, scrubbing her face with her hands. "Where's Ulla?"

"She's not here just now," Yvonne told her, glancing across to Baldur. He was focused on something outside the cave. At first she could not see, or hear, anything, and then felt a slight tremor in the ground under her. Horses. Several of them. Coming their way.

"Get to the back of the cave," she told Lita. "Into the shadows. Stay there. Baldur, guard her." Yvonne moved to where Lita's horse was watching the goings on with bland curiosity, taking the horse by its halter and leading it back to stand next to Lita. Ulla had chosen well, the horse moving without any resistance.

Baldur snorted his disgust at the order he had been given, but moved to put himself between Lita and the cave's entrance as the cloth merchant moved to the back of the cave, where there was no room to stand.

Yvonne crept out of the cave mouth, hiding herself in the thick shrubs that grew on the hillside, careful to stay low and make as little sound or motion as possible, as she crept forward.

There were three, perhaps four horses on the way towards her. The horses seemed to be coming at pace, and in a direct line. Someone knew, or suspected, that they were here. She wondered how many people besides Ulla had known about these caves, stomach tightening. On her own, with nothing solid at her back, three or four people might be more than she could manage. She drew a concussive spell out of her pouch in preparation, drawing in a long, deep breath. Panicking would not help.

The shrubs were high enough that most of the horses were concealed, but she could see the riders' heads as they moved closer, and her brows rose to her hairline in surprise. Familiar faces.

Ulla was in the lead, Brea and Thort riding behind her and, as they drew closer, Yvonne could see that Thort was leading a spare horse that looked like Guise's horse.

She put the spell back, wriggled out of the shrubs and stood up, dusting herself off, as the riders drew to a halt in front of the cave.

"Hunar," Brea said. The warrior was carrying tension in her shoulders, lines around her mouth that had not been there the last time Yvonne had seen her. She also looked worn out. Thort was the same. Both of them were covered in dust from travelling, shoulders too square. Yvonne's eyes travelled past them to Guise's horse and her stomach lurched. The saddle was empty. Guise was not there.

"What happened?"

"We couldn't find him," Brea said, sliding off her horse. "We searched."

"Most of the city," Thort added, joining his wife, and putting a hand on her shoulder.

"We found signs that he'd been taken. A pair of bodies. Signs of a fight." Brea's mouth tightened and she glanced at Thort, before looking back at Yvonne. "Blood. Quite a bit of it. Not all his, we don't think."

"He's been taken?" Yvonne asked, hearing her voice high and thin, feeling the world spin around her. They could not be talking about Guise. They could not. She had seen Guise face down impossible odds, and prevail. He was a far more proficient and formidable warrior than she was, even without using his magic. It was not possible he had been taken.

"That's our guess," Brea confirmed. She blew out a breath, looking away, then back at Yvonne, her eyes dull. "I'm sorry, Hunar."

"You searched most of the city," Yvonne repeated Thort's words. "What happened?" Brea and Thort were among Guise's closest friends. She could not imagine what had stopped them from searching the rest of the city, from continuing the hunt for their friend.

"We were asked to leave," Thort said, voice flat. "Word of the King's death had spread. They could not hold us, but they could send us away."

Her knees hurt.

Why did her knees hurt?

And why was she so close to the ground?

Her palms were flat on the gritty soil around her as she knelt on the ground, head bowed.

Guise was missing.

Taken.

There had been a fight.

Blood.

And Brea and Thort, who would not have rested until they found him, had been evicted from the city.

"We sent a message to the star." Brea's voice was very faint, and a long way away. "But she may not be able to do anything to help."

The star. Helgiarast se'laj Krejefell. The queen of the goblins. Guise's mother. As formidable a woman as Yvonne had ever met.

"I don't understand." Lita's voice sounded as far away as Brea's.

"The Hunar is accused of killing the King," Brea told her, voice flat.

"But she didn't do that," Lita said.

"No. Someone else did, and left evidence pointing to Yvonne," Brea said. "And no one is looking for the actual killer as they are too busy looking for her." Even at the great distance Brea's voice had to travel, Yvonne could hear the edge to the warrior's tone.

"Guise was making enquiries in the city," Yvonne said, her voice as far away as everyone else's. "About the sorcerer. Hiram."

"Yes," Thort agreed.

"Is he still in the city? Guise?" she asked, tilting her head back so that she could see Brea's expression. The goblin warrior's face tightened and she shook her head, once.

"I don't know. He could be. More likely, he's somewhere else."

"We need to find him. I have to find him," Yvonne said, breath catching in her throat. Her chest was so tight she could not breathe.

"In good time," Brea cautioned. "First, we all need some rest. Somewhere safe for a few days."

"We can't go home," Thort commented. "Nor can you."

Home. The children. Mariah and Joel. She had to warn them. And Renard, assuming the older wulfkin was still there. She could not go back. Not now. Not with the Valland court hunting her. Her throat tightened.

Guise was missing. There was a blood-crazed sorcerer loose in the world. One who had hired killers to attack the Hundred. She had to warn them. The world was still spinning, though.

"There's an abandoned town about a half day's ride from here," Lita said, unexpectedly. "There was a plague about twenty years ago. No one goes there anymore. It's not much."

"It would serve us for a few days, though," Thort said.

"Hunar. Yvonne," Brea said, her voice closer, almost real.

Yvonne looked up, finding the warrior crouching in front of her, close enough that she could see the lines of strain and exhaustion on the woman's face, the tiny flecks of red and gold in her eyes along with the green.

"I will do everything that I can to find Guise," Brea said. "I promise." The weight of that promise rang through Yvonne. Goblins rarely made promises.

Guise had made only four in his life, he had told her once. And three of those promises were to her. Rare, precious things. Yvonne blinked, face wet. Brea was absolutely sincere in her words. "For now, we need to be clever. We are all exhausted. We must plan."

"Yes." Yvonne heard herself agreeing. It was not what she wanted to do. It was the most sensible thing to do.

With that agreement, the world came flooding back around her with a roar and she became aware of the sun on her back, the hard stones under her knees, the scent of green from the shrubs around them.

Guise was missing. For the whole length of her journey here. Not travelling with Brea and Thort, as she had believed. Missing. Kidnapped. There had been blood.

Her stomach twisted and she forced herself to draw a breath in. Panic would not help her. Would not help Guise.

There were paid killers trying to find her. The Valland court thought that she had killed their King. And Guise was missing.

There. She had thought it. Now, she had to deal with it.

She drew another breath and got to her feet.

"Let's go."

The abandoned village was eerie. It might have been twenty years, but whoever had built the houses here had meant them to last, so they rode into a village of buildings with blank windows and doors, and no sound of anyone else.

Plants had run riot over the years, taking over the paths and roads around the houses so that the buildings stood as small islands amid greenery. The only exception was the stone-flag stable yard behind the small tavern, that must have been treated with some kind of preservation spell as not one single weed had made its way between the cracks. Spells like that were expensive, as Circle Mages liked gold. Whoever had owned the tavern had possessed ambition for finer things.

Most of the buildings were still weatherproof, including the modest tavern, with a stable block at the back and, to everyone's surprise, fresh water at the pump in the stable yard. It was the only building big enough for them all, so they chose the tavern to stop at.

The building might have been sound. The beds were not. They were infested with vermin and smelled strongly of mould. The benches and tables in the tavern's tap room were still solid, though, and it took Thort and Brea seemingly no time at all to fashion makeshift beds for everyone, using some of the tables, and blankets from the linen presses that had escaped insects over the years, thanks to the cloth bags of pungent herbs tucked in the folds. Even so, Yvonne cast cleansing spells over the blankets before they settled for the night. The horses had been left to roam around the stables, and between the small field at the back of the tavern and the barn. The horses would wake them if anyone approached, Brea said. So no one would need to keep watch.

Both goblins looked exhausted. The weight of worry that they had carried for weeks, and their journey here. Like Ulla, they had come to Willowton looking for Lita, knowing she had a wide network of contacts. Hoping that Lita might know how to get in touch with Yvonne. Brea and Thort had reasoned, as had Ulla, that Yvonne would not risk her children by going back to Fir Tree Crossing. So they needed to try another way to find her.

From the expression on Lita's face, Yvonne was not sure she liked being in the position of messenger. All Lita said, in a mild tone that probably fooled no one, was that she had no better idea of how to get in touch with Yvonne than any of the rest of them. Guise was the one who always knew how to find people.

Yvonne was aching with tiredness by that point, and settled in her makeshift bed, finding that a table top covered in blankets made a fractionally more comfortable bed than sleeping on the ground.

Even though she was exhausted, she lay awake for a while, stomach turning into knots again. Guise was missing.

While she had been making her way out of the Royal City, he had been set upon and kidnapped. Taken. And she had not known. That seemed wrong, somehow, as if she should have known. They were supposed to have formed a bond.

Yet, she had felt nothing.

In her mind's eye she could see Elinor, her old mentor settled at the kitchen table that had been destroyed along with the rest of her house, one eyebrow lifted. Elinor's ghost did not say anything. She did not need to. Yvonne knew that look. It was the one her teacher had used when she was trying not to tell Yvonne she was being a fool.

She had been fleeing the city, trying to get herself, and her horse, to safety. That had required her entire focus. There had been no time to worry about Guise as well. Then, when she was out of the city, she had been focused on staying alive, assuming that Brea and Thort, two of the most capable people she knew, were with Guise, and safe as well.

Guise had been missing for two weeks. He could be almost anywhere in the world by now.

And she had been effectively moved out of the way by the King's death, and the evidence left that pointed to her involvement. One of Ulla's fellow assassins had carried the blade, but the King's killer had been hired by someone. Someone who wanted Yvonne to be blamed. Her mind spun. It was most likely Hiram, but she had no proof of that. Not yet. The agent had told them about the contract on the Hundred, and even then his information had been limited. She remembered the notebook she had taken from the agent's possessions. There had been no time to study it so far. It might have some answers. She was not hopeful.

And then there was Hiram himself. The blood sorcerer who had dragged himself back to life, at the cost of several of the King's soldiers. Who had marked the agent so that the man had died before he had time to tell them much. Who had attacked the Stone Walls, leading the Brotherhood who had slaughtered almost all the inhabitants inside, including most of the Sisters. That slaughter remained unpunished, the nagging sense of a Hunar's unfulfilled promise waking in her as she remembered it. She needed to find Hiram. Destroy him. For the death he had been responsible for, and to make sure there would be no more of it.

Inside her chest the Firebird's wings unfurled, a flutter of feathers and fire. The Firebird was the bringer of justice. She approved the idea of hunting down Hiram.

In Yvonne's mind the bright heat of the Firebird was joined with the quieter, no less intense, presence of another being of myth. The great bear. The unseen Sister, who brought the compassion of the Sisters, and their quiet courage and strength, with her. The Sisters had been caring towards those in need, but no one had ever thought them weak.

The Firebird and the great bear wanted justice for the Stone Walls, and those who had sought refuge behind them, only to be slaughtered in the one place in the world that should have been safe.

Yvonne agreed. Justice was required.

And yet.

Guise was missing. Had been taken. Probably at Hiram's order.

And she wanted to find him.

Not just because he was possibly hurt, and in need of rescue. But also because she missed him. And wanted to know that he was safe. The world would be a much less interesting place if he was not in it. They had barely started to explore the bond between them, what that might mean. Colour rose in her face, her blush unseen in the dark, as she remembered Mariah's decorating proposals. Assuming that Guise would come and live with them.

If it had been one of her children who had been taken, there would have been no hesitation. They were part of her, as if they had been grafted into her bones. Nothing in the world would keep her from finding them.

Guise, though. He had never needed rescuing before. At least, not in the time she had known him.

Healing, yes. Patching up from whatever trouble he had got himself into, yes. But always after he got himself out of the situation.

There had never been a time when he could not free himself.

She could feel the attention of the Firebird and the great bear in her mind. Watching. Waiting. Wondering what decision she would make. Follow the oaths she had taken as Hunar and seek Hiram. Follow what she wanted to do and seek Guise.

She had no idea where to start looking for Hiram. The agent had given them no good information before he died.

She could ask at the Valland court, assuming they would listen and not simply throw her in prison for apparently killing their King.

Even as she turned on her side, restless, trying to find a comfortable position amid the blankets on the hard table top, she remembered the package that Guise had trusted to her care. The bit of sealed parchment.

In the dark, not wanting to wake the others, she drew the folded parchment out of her spell pouch and turned it over in her fingers. She had made a promise not to open it unless she needed to. And although she made promises often, she took every one of them seriously. And yet. This might help her find Guise.

She opened the parchment in the dark, finding it contained a small, round disk. It was cool to the touch. She murmured a spell to enhance her senses and placed it between her palms, focusing.

She had the briefest impression of harsh daylight, Guise walking alongside her. They were at a marketplace and he had just bought this disk from a stallholder. On the edge of the Forbidden Lands.

She knew what this was. It was one of the metal disks that Guise gave to his contacts so that they might recognise each other. It had a trace of his own magic, but nothing more than that. It would not help her find him.

She bit her lip to hold in her disappointment, folded the parchment back over the disk and returned it to her spell pouch. Nothing to help her there.

Her eyes stung, tears leaking out even as she stayed quiet. The tears dried as another realisation stole into her mind.

Hiram was a blood sorcerer. Guise was a powerful goblin. Hiram had seemed drawn to Guise when they had met. Something about goblin blood, perhaps. And goblins were known to experiment with blood magic from time to time.

Hiram would probably try and use Guise's blood.

Before she could give in to the panic that threatened to choke her, the tracking sense, the bit of magic that was hers from birth, woke up.

To find someone, she needed to have a sense of them. An understanding of their essence. She had the barest sense of Hiram. Not enough to follow him. But she knew Guise perhaps as well as she knew anyone alive.

The trail of tracking magic curled through her body, wrapping itself around her from her toes to her chin, letting her know, with a gentle tug, which way she needed to go.

The Firebird and the great bear inclined their heads, unseen by anyone else, accepting her decision.

Guise was missing.

She could find him.

She would find him. And then, together, they would find the blood sorcerer.

Chapter Twelve

There was no bath house at the tavern, naturally, so Yvonne had to make do with a cleansing spell the next day, only slightly refreshed from some unbroken sleep. Everyone else was moving slowly, too. Even Ulla, who rarely showed any signs of weakness. The assassin had left off her face veil, dark smudges under her eyes showing she was under as much strain as the rest of them. The deaths of her fellow assassins, and trainee, were lingering in her mind, Yvonne guessed. It was an odd thing for someone who dealt in death, and warmed Yvonne towards her.

The mundane tasks of seeing to the horses and preparing a simple breakfast kept Yvonne's hands occupied, and loosened her muscles a little, so that when they all sat down together at the remaining table in the tavern, on an odd collection of chairs and a bench, she was feeling mostly awake.

"Has the Valland court made it known they suspect me?" she asked Brea and Thort, once everyone had settled.

"Yes," Brea said, lips tight. "They are not being quiet about it."

"You didn't kill the King, though, did you?" Lita asked. Needing reassurance.

"No," Yvonne confirmed. "I got there too late. Another assassin killed him," she added, staring at Ulla. The assassin did not look up from her food, face drawn. Grief. And something else. Anger, perhaps. Yvonne did not know the woman well enough to tell.

"Another assassin? The school agreed to a contract on the Valland king?" Brea asked, brows lifting in genuine surprise.

"I don't believe so," Ulla said.

"You don't sound very certain," Lita pointed out bluntly, before anyone else could speak. She was picking at the meal in front of her, seeming to have little appetite. Yvonne had some sympathy for her. The cloth merchant's ordered lifestyle had been turned on its head. She had worked hard for the life she had built in Willowton, for the beautiful house, and the expensive offices. And had been forced to flee through no fault of her own.

"I don't know all the contracts that are taken," Ulla answered, a snap in her voice.

"And you can't tell us about the school's business," Yvonne said, remembering her brief conversation with Ulla, the King's body lying between them. "Not unless you've been given permission."

Ulla did not look up, but jerked her head once, agreeing and acknowledging.

Yvonne bit her lip against more questions. Ulla might have told Guise what she knew. If she did, indeed, know anything more. But there was a tangled past there, between Ulla and Guise, that Yvonne was not part of. So, she held her questions in. The assassin would not talk about the King's death, or who might have carried out the killing.

"The King doesn't have any direct or named heirs," Lita said, sitting back from her plate, eyes sharpening. She traded in information as well as fabric. "So, whoever had him killed must want the throne."

"That's my guess," Yvonne agreed. The Valland kingdom had a long and uneasy history when it came to naming heirs. A number of the heirs had tried to overthrow the kings in the past. And King Victor had been even more reluctant than his predecessors. Perhaps he had thought he had time, as he had still been in the prime of his life. She shook her head slightly. "There was a volume of genealogy missing from the treasurer's office when Guise and I were there."

"You thought that Hiram might try and claim the throne," Brea said.

"There would be a revolt," Lita said, shaking her head. "The people wouldn't accept a Circle Mage for a ruler."

Yvonne ducked her eyes to her plate, not saying anything. The people might not have a choice. Hiram seemed crazed enough to take the throne by force, if he wanted it. Yet, he was not the only heir. There was another. A mysterious man who called himself Will and could apparently vanish into thin air.

"He'd have to claim the throne in the Royal City," Brea said. There was speculation in her tone, eyes glinting green as she exchanged a look with Thort. "And fairly quickly, too. The Valland royal family doesn't have many branches, but there are some."

"We can't go to the Royal City just now, though," Lita said. "Not while Yvonne is still accused of murder. And I can't vouch for her," she added, nose wrinkling, doubtless thinking about the half dozen corpses in her dining room.

Brea and Thort looked like they wanted to argue, but could not, frowning at their plates instead.

"I can find Guise," Yvonne said, into the awkward silence that had settled.

All eyes turned to her and she felt colour rise in her face.

"I have some tracking magic. It's given me a trail to follow."

"Do you know how far away he is?" Brea asked, eyes brightening.

"No, I'm sorry, the magic doesn't work like that. It will take me along the trail to the freshest point. It's quite a weak trail, so I think we're still some distance away."

"Makes sense, if he's in Valland," Thort said.

Yvonne was not sure her magic would extend that far, but said nothing. She had never met anyone else with the same magic skill, and had never found any written records of it. It was possible, as she had known Guise for some years, that she would be able to track him all the way to the Royal City.

"Does the trail mean he's still alive?" Lita asked. An excellent question.

"No. It just takes me along his path." Yvonne stared into her tea, trying not to think about the bodies she had found in the past, the tracking magic not caring if its target was alive or dead.

"It's something," Brea said, eyes still bright.

"We should go tomorrow," Ulla said. Everyone turned to look at her. She was staring into her tea, still not meeting anyone's eyes. "We need the rest." It was as close to an admission of weakness as the assassin was ever likely to get.

She was right. Yvonne saw the recognition on the others' faces. As frustrating as it was, they were all at the end of their strength. One night's sleep had not changed that.

By chance, she met Lita's eyes across the table, and saw the weariness and strain in the other woman's face. Of all of them, Lita was not used to hard travel or rough accommodation.

"You would be welcome at my house in Fir Tree Crossing," Yvonne said, the offer out before she knew she was going to make it. Once the words were out, it made sense. She could send messages with Lita, too. Reassurance for Mariah and Joel. And Lita would, at least, have a bed and the security of wulfkin around her.

Lita's jaw set, mouth flat. Determined and stubborn.

"It is likely to be a hard journey," Brea said, voice gentler than her usual tone.

"I want to help," Lita said, voice harsh. Aware of her limitations. Not wanting to be sent away. "And I've never travelled on my own before," she added, voice smaller, a quiver there that Yvonne thought very few people had ever heard.

In any other group of people, that would have been an unremarkable statement, Yvonne realised. Very few people undertook long journeys alone. Merchants travelled in caravans. Mercenaries and soldiers travelled in companies. Even families going to markets would take as many people with them as wanted to go. And Lita had felt vulnerable enough even in her home town to have armed guards. No wonder she did not want to travel alone.

"Very well." Yvonne felt her mouth curve into a smile at Lita's surprise. "But I am not going to play cards with you."

Lita laughed, even as Brea and Thort raised their eyebrows, shaking her head slightly, not answering the silent question.

"I think I saw an orchard on our way in here," Thort said. "We could gather some fruit."

As if by magic, the mood at the table changed. No longer frustration at the delay. Instead, an opportunity to prepare.

"We could search in here, too," Yvonne said. "There might be some preserved food."

"After all this time?" Lita asked, surprised.

"The village seems well made. It's possible they also had some preservation spells," Yvonne speculated.

They didn't find any preserved food, but the orchard that Thort had spotted was full of fruit, enough that even the local bird population had not managed to eat it all. They gathered as much as they could carry on Guise's horse, and Thort cooked some of the over-ripe fruit for an evening meal, folded into sweetened flatbreads. Thort was an excellent cook, making the simple meal full of flavour, and Yvonne went to sleep that night with a full stomach and a little bit of hope.

Chapter Thirteen

The tracking magic led them back into Valland, which was not a great surprise, but then curved away from the Royal City, taking them westwards, across the southern-most region of Valland. A fertile land of sloping hills that provided excellent grazing and growing land, rivers and lakes full of fish. The region had been, at one point, a mighty kingdom in its own right, dotted across with castles and fortified houses jealously guarding the land's riches. The castles and houses had mostly been abandoned, on order of the conquering kings, but many of the buildings were still standing, in various states of ruin.

Guise's trail led them across country, and then on to an overgrown road, green grass rather than packed earth under the horses' feet, nearby trees growing close enough to the road that the riders had to duck underneath branches occasionally. The road had been used recently, Thort pointed out. There were hoof marks ahead of them in the grass. And what looked like the trace of a wagon or cart of some kind, impressions still clear in the soft ground towards the edges of the road. Someone had used this road before them, and not that long ago, if the tracks were still visible.

Yvonne tried to stay calm, riding at the front of the group. Tried to settle the knot in her stomach, the urge to press Baldur to a flat out run ahead. There was no way of telling how far they had to go, or what was ahead of them. Rushing straight ahead was not wise. Even if it was what she wanted to do.

The ground rose steadily, the old road they were following gently curving around a hillside. The trees around them were perhaps a hundred or so years old. They were overshadowed by giants, ancient trees that had been here for much longer. Someone had cut a path for the road through the ancient trees, clearing the way, and the younger trees had seeded themselves, taking over when the road was abandoned.

Through the trees ahead, she caught a glimpse of stone walls. Some kind of building. She pulled Baldur to a halt, waiting for Brea and Thort to join her.

"The trail leads to there," she told them.

"I can look ahead," Ulla offered. She was wearing her face veil again, shoulders square. Trying to present the image of a capable and competent assassin. Except Yvonne did not trust that impression for some reason.

"We'll go with Yvonne," Brea said. "If you and Lita will stay with the horses." The warrior framed it as a suggestion, not a command. Ulla inclined her head, accepting the idea.

So, Yvonne left Baldur with a pat and word of reassurance, Ulla and Lita taking the horses off the overgrown road, away from the building ahead and among the ancient trees, where they could hide more effectively. There was a stream nearby, Ulla said. They would go there.

Brea, Thort and Yvonne left the road, heading towards the building, making their way uphill through the trees. As they got closer to the building, the ancient trees fell away. Like the road, the past inhabitants of this place had cleared a line of sight around it, which had become overgrown.

The building did not look like much. The remains of what had once been a small castle, with high stone walls cut through here and there with narrow windows perfect for firing arrows.

Brea led them along the hillside, careful to keep within the shelter of the trees, catching brief glimpses of the stonework as they went, until they reached the point where the old road met what had been the castle's entrance.

The once mighty doors were down, splintered bits of wood scattered on the ground in front of the walls, overgrown with grass and some flowering plant that Yvonne could not identify from this distance.

The entrance itself was a black hollow, inviting them in. It looked empty.

Brea found them a path up the final bit of hill, to a blind spot on the walls by the entrance, then put her head around the wall, taking a look inside.

"I can't see anyone," she reported back.

"I don't hear anything, either," Thort answered.

Patience, Yvonne told herself, trying to stay still and calm. Rushing in would not help. And it did not mean that Guise was dead.

"He might not be here," Yvonne said, trying not to sound disappointed. He had been here. She knew he had. The tracking magic had never failed her before.

"Only one way to find out," Brea said, moving forward, into the building.

"My beloved," Thort said, a soft smile at his mouth, eyes bright, and headed off after her, Yvonne following in his wake.

The castle might be empty. Or there might be a horde of soldiers waiting for them. Yvonne had no doubt of Brea and Thort's ability to deal with any number of soldiers. But she did not want to compromise Guise's safety. If there were soldiers, the goblins could deal with them while she searched for Guise.

There were no soldiers.

Instead, the hollowed-out interior of the old castle was empty. The floors and roof above had long since disappeared, shattered beams and broken slates scattered across the ground showing the extent of destruction. And a long time ago. Like the broken door outside, everything was becoming overgrown with plants.

"Someone's been here," Thort said, before Yvonne could tell them that, yes, she was sure Guise had been here. He moved across the floor, picking his way between tumbled stone, broken wood and fragmented roof slate, to a corner of the building, Brea following.

Yvonne took another look around, shivering slightly as a breeze curled through the arrow slits above and coiled around her, bringing the promise of winter with it. No one had lived here for quite some time. And the destruction that had been carried out had been deliberate. Calculated. The Valland kings of old had a reputation for being ruthless in eliminating opposition. When they conquered a land, they had made sure that no one there would stand against them. She had always believed the stories. She had just never seen the extent of their power before. It would have taken a great deal of strength to destroy this castle so thoroughly. Or magic.

She shivered again. Perhaps Hiram was not the first power-crazed Circle Mage to be in the service of the Valland kings.

"Yvonne," Brea called, and she shook off the ice crawling across her skin, going to see what the warriors had found.

Thort was crouching by the wall, inspecting what looked like a fresh hole that had been hammered into the stone. It was small, about twice as wide as her thumb, and she could not work out what it was for until Brea spoke.

"Someone put a set of manacles here," Brea told her, pointing. "Hammered them into the stone."

"A prisoner?" Yvonne asked, feeling the first stirring of hope. If Guise was a prisoner, that meant he had value. And would still be alive. He would be. She would not allow herself to think otherwise.

"It seems so. And someone they wanted to keep absolutely safe," Thort added. "This kind of pinning would hold a forest bear."

Having recently encountered the giant creatures, Yvonne swallowed, looking again at the holes.

"So, they brought the manacles with them? And hammered them into the wall?" she asked.

"Yes." Brea's voice was grim, face in stern lines. "They came prepared to hold a prisoner. And used a lot of strength to do so. Hammering those pins into a wall is hard work."

Yvonne crouched in front of one of the holes Thort and Brea had found. All too easy to imagine the heavy metal pins that had been driven into to narrow gaps between the stones, holding a prisoner. Holding Guise.

As she thought that, she had an impression of him here, with his back against the wall, chains hanging from his wrists and ankles. He was exhausted, head down. There was something wrong with his head, but she did not have time to figure it out because he lifted his head, eyes faded green, the weakest she had ever seen them. The faintest spark of gold lit his eyes.

"Mristrian."

"Yes. I will find you," she told him, and saw the gold brighten in his eyes.

"Yvonne?"

Brea's voice called her back to the here and now, and she realised she had moved closer to the wall, her hand on the stone.

"Guise was here. He looked injured. Weak." Yvonne rose to her feet and took a few steps away, the knot of worry that had lifted returning in full force. "I think they have hurt him."

"They would need to, if they wanted to hold him," Thort said, face tight, a spark of red in his eyes. "This sort of thing would not hold us forever."

Yvonne remembered another set of chains, in a dungeon where she and Guise had been put by another madman. Guise, poisoned, at the edge of his control. And the grating sound as the metal pins started to work loose from the stone.

There was no sign of wear here. The pins had been hammered in. It did not look like Guise had tried to fight them. Which was another worry in itself. She could not imagine Guise allowing himself to be held.

"How many more of these stinking prisons do we need to wade through?" Brea snarled, shaking something noxious off her boot.

Brea, Thort and Yvonne were ankle-deep in liquid, searching through what had been the cells of an ancient keep, making sure that nothing had been left behind. The flood in the basement was too thick and smelly to be water. Yvonne did not want to think about what it might actually be made of. Her fingers were itching to reach for one of the cleansing spells in her pouch. Not yet. They still had to get out of the building.

Guise's trail had led them through half a dozen abandoned castles and keeps. All empty. All showing signs of recent use. The now-familiar tracks of a wagon. The evidence of metal pins hammered into a wall, to restrain a prisoner. And nothing else of value.

This latest keep was in the worst shape, the dungeon partly flooded with the awful liquid they were wading through. And, as with the others, it was empty.

"I don't know," Yvonne answered Brea's question. "I am following the trail."

"At least we know we're following something," Thort said.

"Something. That's helpful," Brea snapped at him.

It had been a hard few days, following the trail, with only the three of them to investigate each dungeon. Lita barely knew one end of a sword from the other, assigned to look after the horses. And Ulla had been assigned to keep watch, to alert them of any danger. So it had fallen to the three of them to investigate each time. Each time creeping up to the building, apprehensive of what they might find. Only to be disappointed again. Over and over. Across several days. Stopping to rest briefly when they could. And now, thanks to this latest ruined castle, they were all tired, damp, foul-smelling and, in Brea's case, foul-tempered.

They waded to the broken staircase and picked their way back up to ground level, where they had left Lita, Ulla and the horses.

"Oh, goodness, what is that smell?" Lita said, pinching her nose.

"Don't ask," Yvonne told her, reaching for her cleansing spells. She cast several over Brea, Thort and herself.

"That's better. I'm so glad you made me wait up here," Lita said.

Brea lifted a brow at the cloth merchant, but said nothing.

"Where to next?" Ulla asked. She was tucked into the shadows of the corner of a wall, halfway up what had once been a tower, with a good view of the surrounding land. Like the other places they had searched, younger trees and plants had grown up in the spaces around the buildings that had once been clear lines of sight. To see for any distance at all, height was needed.

For a moment Yvonne could not answer Ulla's question, a wave of exhaustion and despair holding her still and silent. Her tracking magic had never failed her before. It had always led her to the person she was searching for. And this was Guise she was tracking. They should have found him by now. His trail was clear and strong in her mind. With each castle, with each dungeon, she grew more and more worried. Brea and Thort had inspected the ground at each site and confirmed that there were not many people travelling. A few horses. A wagon. Perhaps a half dozen men. No more than that.

It was not enough to hold Guise. Not normally. A half dozen soldiers, no matter how well trained, should be no match for him.

And yet, he had not escaped. His trail continued from dungeon to dungeon, with no sign of struggle at any of the places they had been to so far.

She had not been able to gather any more impressions of him, after that first castle. That did not mean much. She did not fully understand how her tracking magic worked. And they had not found his body. He was still alive. He had to be.

"They probably have him drugged," Brea said, her voice softer than it had been.

Yvonne looked across and saw the warrior's eyes shaded into a soft green, Thort standing at her shoulder.

They were worried, too, she knew. They had known Guise for longer than she had.

"Yes," Yvonne said, the best she could manage just now. She scrubbed her hands across her face and wished for a bath. And while she was wishing for impossible things, she might as well also wish for a comfortable tavern and a good night's sleep.

"We are definitely on the right trail, though?" Lita asked.

This trip had, perhaps, been hardest on her. Confident and assured in her daily life, with a bright and keen intelligence that had served her well, this was very far from her normal life. She was moving far more slowly than she had been, probably carrying bruises from the rough sleeping, her hair tangled, eyes smudged with exhaustion.

Still, she had not complained. Not about the hard travel, or the rough accommodation, or the basic food. From time to time Yvonne had seen Lita look at her hands, the nails rough after the travelling, and seen sadness in her face. This was not what she was used to. Yet, she was enduring it.

As they all were.

"Yes," Yvonne answered Lita. "This is Guise's trail. I don't know why the magic is taking me this way, but this is definitely the way he has gone."

"And we're going the right way along it," Thort added. "The tracks are fresher each time."

"Good," Lita said, pulling her coat around her a little more securely. It was not that cold, but Yvonne understood the need for some comfort.

"Where to?" Ulla asked, still up on her perch.

"We should stop for the night," Brea said, seemingly reluctant. "It will be dark soon."

"This is the best defensive place for miles around," Ulla said, not moving from her position. It was still difficult to tell her moods with just her voice to go by, but Yvonne thought she sounded reluctant.

"Not here," Lita said, nose wrinkling. "Please."

Yvonne looked around the ruined castle, the fallen walls, and thought about the dungeon they had left. She did not want to stay here, either.

"Very well," Brea said, voice heavy. "We'll move on."

"A moment," Ulla said, straightening slightly. "What is that?"

Whatever she had seen was invisible to Yvonne's eyes for a few long moments, even though Brea and Thort seemed to have no difficulty spotting it, either.

Then she could see it, too. A small, dark speck, flying close to the ground, making its way towards them.

"One of Pieris' birds, I think," she said, her heart lifting for the first time in days.

The little creature, built of magic, flew straight to her, hovering in the air in front of her until she put out her hand, braced for the weight of it. The messenger birds were heavy to hold, about the weight of a wine bottle, even though they weighed nothing when she put them into her spell pouch, and must be light enough to fly.

The small bird tilted its head at her, and she gave it the command to release its message, sucking in a breath as Pieris' familiar voice emerged from the bird's mouth.

"We made it to the Royal City a few days after you. The King is dead. The General thinks you killed him and won't hear me when I tell him that's impossible. They can't find you. We were asked to leave." Even through the thin tones of the bird, Yvonne could hear Pieris' outrage. Hunar were generally able to go anywhere, welcomed anywhere. "We tried to find Guise and couldn't. One of the senior Royal Guard, a woman, Sarra, said that she needs to speak to you. Also told us Brea and Thort were here, and forced to leave just before us. We're going to go to Hogsmarthen." There was an odd pause in the bird's speech, perhaps when Pieris himself had paused. "Let me know you're safe and where to find you."

The bird finished its speech, fluttered its wings, and settled into its dormant state.

Hogsmarthen. The trading centre famed throughout the lands. Within the Valland kingdom. It was not Pieris' usual place. Yvonne tucked the bird into her pouch and fetched her map from Baldur's saddle, spreading it open across a fallen wall.

"What is it?" Brea asked.

"Hogsmarthen," Yvonne answered. "It's not Pieris' usual stop. Although I think the rest of the Hundred might be there." Her stomach tightened. She had sent word to Pieris, warning him about the contract someone had tried to put out on the Hundred. He had not mentioned it in his message to her. The messenger birds had never failed her before. Something was wrong, or he was trying to send her some obscure message, a hint that she had missed. "I'm trying to work out why Pieris would go there."

"Because the merchants there gossip more than any old woman I've ever met?" Lita asked, a touch of acid in her voice.

"Because it connects to all the major roads and rivers in the area," Ulla suggested, still up on the wall.

"Because the Sisters are there. Well, the few that remain," Brea suggested.

"All of those," Yvonne agreed, looking at the map again. "We're here, I think?" she asked, pointing to a place on the map. The other side of the Great River from Hogsmarthen, and a little bit north.

"About there," Brea agreed.

"Pieris might think I'm still in Valland," Yvonne said, speculating aloud.

"You are," Brea pointed out.

"True. He's going somewhere with good transport links to the rest of the kingdom. And which is friendly to Hunar."

"What's your usual arrangement when one of you is in trouble?" Ulla asked, sounding genuinely interested.

"None of us have been accused of murdering a king before," Yvonne answered, keeping her eyes on the map. She left unsaid that the Hunar would not summon the others for a personal issue. Only for help with a promise they had made. And this mission she was on just now, looking for Guise, was personal. Pieris would help, if she asked him, of that she had no doubt.

The twist of the unfulfilled promise constricted her chest, catching her breath. The mastermind behind the attack on the Sisters remained at large. The magic of the Hundred pulled, drawing her forward.

She had never ignored a promise before. She had managed competing demands on her attention before, working out what to do first. But had never put her own wishes first. Had never been tempted to do so. Until now. Until Guise was in trouble, and his trail was in front of her.

The oaths a Hunar took were to serve those in need, to put the needs of others ahead of their own, and their own wishes. Setting aside the pull of the unfulfilled promise was a sharp pain in her chest. Perilously close to breaking her oaths. And yet, she could not ignore the trail ahead of her, or Guise.

"You're not going to answer Pieris?" Brea asked, eyes sharp.

"Not just now. We need some rest, and there's the trail to follow. We're getting closer," Yvonne answered, not meeting the warrior's too-perceptive gaze, hoping that they would find Guise before the pressure of her oaths and the unfulfilled promise became too much to bear.

Chapter Fourteen

They were amid the ancient trees on yet another hill, facing yet another fortification.

This was different, though.

The fortified house in front of them was occupied.

Unlike the others they had come across, this one had all of its walls and windows intact. And someone had taken the time, and effort, to clear the ground around the building, so that there were clear lines of sight. The great forest was not quite as far away from the house as it would have been, in years past. Still, it gave the defenders of the house an advantage. Even from this distance, Yvonne could just make out the traces of shapes moving inside. Patrols, perhaps.

This was the place. Guise's trail led straight to it.

The building itself was almost ugly. Squat, only one storey above the ground, and functional. Not the grand house of a rich family but the practical retreat of a leader who needed somewhere safe to sleep. It had been built on the top of a small hill, with a good view of the surrounding lands and, from the way the building sat into the hilltop, Yvonne thought there was most definitely an underground layer. Dungeons were underground.

Behind the house, contained within high, thick stone walls, was a small stable and, in the gap between the house and the stable, they could catch a glimpse of what looked like a plain wagon.

"Finally," Brea murmured.

She was lying next to Yvonne, Thort on her other side, all of them as close to the ground as possible, hidden among the undergrowth that had not been cleared, taking stock of the house in front of them.

"There's no cover. They'll see us coming," Thort said.

"We can go at night," Brea told him, dismissing his concern. Yvonne did not need to see her eyes to know that they would be full of red. Brea had been itching for a fight for several days now, the noxious underground of the last place they had searched only fuelling her temper.

Night was not that far away. The sun was already dipping below the trees. Yvonne remembered that Thort estimated only a few people were travelling in this group. Not enough to watch every window all the time.

"We should watch the patrols. Wait for a gap," she suggested, and saw, by the sideways glances Brea and Thort exchanged, that they had already thought of that. Heat bloomed under her skin, but she did not apologise. Hunar were not soldiers. Hiding in undergrowth. Planning access to a fortified building. These were not skills that she had. She kept silent as Brea and Thort exchanged a few more words, planning their approach.

By the time they had informed Lita and Ulla of their plans, night had fallen. It was time.

They had made it up to the walls of the house without being seen, and around the side, crouching to pass underneath the windows, to the kitchen entrance. One of the horses made a soft, snickering noise. Not alarm. More curiosity. Yvonne shook her head slightly. Not a well-trained war horse. Baldur would have woken the entire forest with his cry of alarm if he had seen strangers creeping up to the house.

Even more careless, the kitchen door was unlocked, and Brea went through on silent feet, weapon ready.

The kitchen, with a fire burning in the grate and an old table and chairs, was empty of people. They were not far away, though, judging by the fire.

Yvonne stayed back, letting Brea and Thort go ahead.

They went through empty, silent rooms, until they reached the main entrance to the building, behind the heavy, fortified doors, before they met anyone else.

The entry hall held a handful of armed men, startled to find intruders coming towards them from inside the house.

With Brea and Thort keeping the guards occupied, Yvonne crept forward, around the edge of the entrance hall. Her tracking sense had woken up, telling her that she needed to go down to find Guise.

It did not take long to find the stairs, in the darkest corner of the hallway. A deep breath in, and she knew that this place was not as toxic as the last place. There should be no liquid underfoot. Still, she moved carefully as she crept downstairs, one hand on her sword hilt, senses straining. It sounded like Brea and Thort were engaged in a lively fight. It was unlikely, though, that the prisoner would have been left unguarded. She was confident that Brea and Thort would win the fight, and hoped that Brea would be in a better mood afterwards.

A soft sound ahead called her full attention forward. There were, indeed, people downstairs. More than one, although she could not tell how many just now.

With her senses enhanced by magic, and a concussive spell twisted between her fingers, she made her way down the last few steps.

The stone steps ended in an open space, with plain wooden doors to one side which, she guessed, were stores of some kind. The other side was more open space, shading into darkness, a pair of men moving towards her out of the shadows, weapons raised. She had a confused impression of what looked like scattered bones behind them, before she threw the concussive spell, knocking them off their feet. Before they could recover, she was moving forward, striking them unconscious with the weighted hilt of her sword, then having to roll forward, rapidly, out of the way of another sword strike. There was a third man. This one was far more wary than his fellows had been, and more skilled. She drew her sword, taking a step back, stumbling as something slid beneath her foot.

There was no time to think as another sword strike came towards her. She blocked it, finding her footing, something crunching under her boots.

She glanced to one side and saw that her initial impression had been correct. There were bones here. There was what looked like a complete skeleton draped against a wall, held by manacles. More bones scattered on the floor. She had no time to inspect them, forced to direct her attention to her attacker as he came at her in earnest. It only took a few sword strikes for her to realise that they were fairly evenly matched as far as skill was concerned. Worse, she was exhausted after the hard journey to get here.

"How did you find us?" the swordsman asked.

"Did you think yourselves well hidden?" she asked, ducking away from his sword, moving sideways.

"He didn't think you'd be able to find us. Or that you would bother."

Yvonne's eyes narrowed and she took another step back. That had not sounded like the speculation of a junior member of the mercenary team. Instead, it had sounded quite well-informed. Someone who knew what they were doing. Who understood who, and what, they had captured, and what his paymaster was capable of.

"Hiram didn't think I would come for my husband?" She kept her tone light and conversational, hoping to draw some more information out of him. By the expression of shock that took over his face, he had not expected her to know who he worked for, or Hiram had not shared all the information with him. "So, he didn't tell you we are married. I wonder what else he did not tell you?" she asked.

"He tells me what I need to know." The soldier snarled, lips pulled back from his teeth. Teeth which were slightly discoloured. Not the blackened taint that Hiram had carried the last time she had seen him, but the faintest suggestion of corruption.

"Is he teaching you, too?" she asked. It was a pure guess, based on what she knew of the blood sorcerer, but she realised she had been right as his eyes widened. "Do you know what happened to his last apprentice? His own son?"

"Joseph? He's away on business."

"Is that what he told you?"

"He tells me what I need to know."

But there was a fraction less conviction in those words.

He had also, whether he realised it or not, stopped trying to kill her, standing a few paces away, with his sword raised, ready, but not actively attacking. In the shadows behind him, she could see the outline of a door, with metal bars, and a glimmer of light beyond, and something in that barred room. Her tracking sense was telling her that was where Guise was, and she wanted to move forward, past this guard with his fanatical convictions, and make sure Guise was all right. But she could not. Not yet. This would-be apprentice had information that could be useful. Information that she needed, and which Guise might need, too. So she had to stay here, and talk a little more.

She waited. She wanted to see if she had said enough to him to sow some doubt, to prompt him to ask questions of his own, or if she would need to prompt him some more.

"What do you think happened to Joseph?" he asked, trying to sneer. It was not very convincing.

"I know what happened to him. I was there when he died."

He had not expected that, clearly, his eyes widening, sword point dipping lower.

"That's impossible. We can't die. He told us."

"When he grafted death magic into your bones?" Yvonne asked, keeping her tone light. That would explain a lot. Hiram had lied to his followers. Hardly surprising. She remembered the dark mark on the agent's arm, branded while he was unconscious. Remembered, too, the curse that had been written into Joseph's bones, and the voice in the ashes when he had died. She wondered if this soldier, and any others like him, knew what it was that Hiram had done.

"Death magic?" He dropped his sword, the metal clattering against the stone floor, pulling up his sleeve, turning his arm. There was a spell grafted onto his inner forearm. One that was all-too-familiar. Joseph, and the agent, had carried the same markings. Death magic. Yvonne was glad that she had not killed the other guards. Releasing Joseph's death curse had been dangerous enough. As it was, with her would-be attacker trying to scrub the markings of his skin, he was distracted enough he did not see her sword hilt coming towards his head, and fell, unconscious, to the ground. Not dead. The magic on his arm remained dormant.

Wishing she had thought to bring some rope to restrain the soldiers, she had to hope that they would stay unconscious for a while. Holding that thought, she crept forward to the barred door. To her surprise, it was unlocked, and opened outward at her tug. A moment later and she saw why no lock had been needed.

The cell beyond had a single occupant, kneeling on the bare stone floor, heavy manacles at his wrists and his ankles attached to chains that were embedded into the wall. The pins that held him looked worn. Doubtless from being hammered in at every new place they had stopped on their way here. The chains and manacles were heavy, well-made. Even at full strength, Guise would have difficulty in escaping those chains.

And he was not at full strength.

The poor light made it hard to see, but he was kneeling with his head down as she approached, sheathing her sword.

"Guise?" She whispered, wondering if her tracking sense had lied. There was something wrong about the shape of his head in the poorer light. She remembered the wrong shape of it in the brief glimpse she had caught of him on the way here, and her heart sped up.

He stirred, lifting his head slightly, and she realised what was wrong.

His hair had been hacked off. The glorious silk of his hair that had fallen below his shoulders, catching the light when he moved. It looked like somebody had taken a blunt knife and chopped it off, as close to his head as possible, leaving it standing up in ragged tufts around his skull.

Worse than that, far worse, was the swelling and bruising around his mouth. His lips curled back instinctively, showing his blunt, white teeth and the edges of his gums. No fangs, though. Goblin fangs were kept tucked away most of the time, allowing them the veneer of civilisation. Just underneath his raised lip she could see traces of old blood where his fangs should be.

Someone had pulled out Guise's fangs.

The shock of it took her breath. A goblin's fangs were precious in ways she did not fully understand. And someone had taken them from Guise.

As if that injury was not enough, he had also been beaten. One side of his face was swollen, his eye almost closed, and she could tell from the way he was holding himself that there was damage elsewhere.

As he moved, and as she crept closer, she could see that he was wearing the remains of a shirt, open at the front. There was no great wound, but there were fresh scars across his chest.

He had been captured and held by a blood sorcerer. Legends of old said that goblin blood was potent.

"Guise. I am sorry it's taken so long to find you."

He stared back at her, mouth half-open, the gleam of his eyes green tinged with red, seeming not to know her.

"Guise," she said again, and knelt in front of him. She was not afraid of him. He would not hurt her. Not ever. Her heart was twisted in her chest with worry, wondering if she was too late. Wondering what Hiram had done to him to make his expression so blank. So uncomprehending.

"Mristrian," he said at length, voice rasping, lips stiff with the swelling, a tremor running through him.

"Yes. Will you stay still for a moment while I get the chains off?"

He didn't answer, slumping slightly towards the ground, turning his head to stare down at the manacles on his wrists.

She remembered another dungeon. When he had been poisoned. Where she had chained him to the wall. Where he had given her the words of the bond that tied them together more surely than any marriage contract.

Unlike the manacles at the other dungeon, these ones required keys. She muttered a curse she had heard a few times at the docks, and went back to the unconscious guards outside, rifling through their pockets until she found the keys. She also used their belts to tie them up, not sure how long they would stay unconscious, then made her way back to the cell.

Guise had not moved, and did not react as she moved to his side, or when she set the key into the lock and freed his wrists. He did move, slowly, stiffly, when she asked him to stand so she could free his ankles.

Once he was free, she stood in front of him. His head was still down, and she could hear his breath, harsh and laboured, and see, now that he had straightened, the extent of damage that had been done to him. Almost every part of his chest and stomach that she could see through the ragged remains of his shirt was covered in small scars. And from the way he was holding his arms, and the faint shadows of old blood on his shirt sleeves, she suspected that his arms were scarred, too.

"He bled you," she said, half-reaching a hand out to touch his face, dropping her hand almost at once, but not before he had made a tiny, almost imperceptible, flinch away from her.

Guise had never flinched from her before.

She clenched her fingers into a fist at her side, forcing herself to remain still. He had been held for a long time. Tortured.

"Brea and Thort are outside," she told him, keeping her voice calm. "We have brought your horse. And your luggage."

That caught his attention. His head lifted a moment. The clothes that he was wearing, as well as being ripped, were also filthy.

"I have healing spells, and cleansing spells," she began, not sure how to phrase the offer. He was so stiff, so remote.

"Yes," he said, the word distorted by his swollen mouth.

"Very well." She pulled the necessary spells out and activated them. The healing washed over him and he hissed out a breath, eyes sparking with red as the healing bit into his skin. "There's food at the horses. Can you walk?"

He did not answer at once, then took a shuffling step forward. It was agonisingly slow compared to his normal pace. And yet, Yvonne had a strong sense that he needed to walk out of here on his own. Brea or Thort could carry him. She could give him some support. But he was a lord of the Karoan'shae, and they did not like to show weakness. Even to their wives.

She stayed behind him as he left the cell and paused outside, eyes travelling around the open space, the collected bones, the three unconscious men.

"Not dead," he said.

"No. One of them has a death curse on him."

His head lifted, startled by the news, then his gaze fixed on the bones again. "There were others."

"He had other prisoners here?" she asked, looking at the collection of bones again, taking a step closer. She had assumed they were old bones, she realised, like the ones on the floor that had snapped under her feet, brittle with age. But these were not. They were fresh. And several of the longer bones she could see had score marks across them. Evidence of cutting.

Rapid footsteps overhead drew her away from the bones, hand on sword hilt, moving forward, in front of Guise, looking up the steps.

She relaxed a moment later when Brea and Thort came into view, weapons ready. They both stilled when they saw Guise, head bowed, in the tatters of his clothes, his hair shorn off.

"You found him," Brea said, a quiver in her voice that Yvonne had never heard before. "We have been looking for you a long time, Guidrishinnal," she added, coming down the final few steps and drawing Guise, stiff and filthy as he was, into a hug. Thort joined them a moment later, and gave Guise a hug of his own.

"You've taken some damage, old friend," Thort said, voice soft, eyes travelling up and down Guise's person. "We found some of your things upstairs."

"There's a bathing room, too," Brea said, nose wrinkling. "I know Yvonne has cleansed you, but a bath would be a good idea."

Guise nodded his head, not speaking. His face was still distorted and swollen with bruising despite the healing spell, and Yvonne could not read his expression.

"Come on, then," Brea said, escorting him towards the stairs, Thort following after Guise. She did not carry him, Yvonne noted, moving at the slow pace Guise could manage. Perhaps understanding, far better than Yvonne ever would, how important it was for Guise to make his own way out of the prison.

Not the first time the pair had helped put Guise back together, Yvonne thought. She had taken Guise to them herself when he had been poisoned.

Still, she had an odd twist in her stomach and a pain in her chest as she watched the three of them go up the stairs together, at Guise's slow, laboured pace. No one looked back to see if she was following them.

There was a long history there. A history that did not include her.

Guise was alive. That was the most important thing. The only thing that mattered, she told herself. And he was not himself. Needed time to heal.

She realised then that she had imagined she would be the one to heal him. That she would take charge of his well-being. It had been a foolish idea. Brea and Thort were far more capable than she was, their long friendship making it natural.

Foolish to think she could do all that herself.

It still stung.

Not wanting to be caught staring if any of them should look, she turned her attention to the three unconscious men, and the bones.

Brea found her a while later, surrounded by miniature candles, examining the bones.

The three men were secure inside the cell. She had managed to drag them in, one at a time, and lock the door behind them. It should hold for a while, at least. They were still unconscious, and she hoped they would stay that way for some time.

"We gave Guise some water to wash, and his clothes," Brea told her, coming to crouch nearby, casting her eyes over the skeleton Yvonne was reassembling. "He hasn't spoken much."

"No," Yvonne agreed, frowning slightly as she looked at the bones in front of her. Basic anatomy was part of a Hunar's training, but there seemed to be something wrong with this skeleton.

"I'm sorry," Brea said, startling Yvonne into looking up. The warrior was staring at the bones, not meeting her eyes. "Thort and I ... Well, we've known Guise most of our lives. And all of his. We started patching his wounds when he was barely walking. I didn't think. Earlier."

When she and Thort had taken Guise into their charge, and led him away.

"We're not used to him having other people who care about him, too," Brea added, voice soft. "The Karoan'shae can be a poisonous place."

Yvonne's breath caught in her throat, thinking about the scope of that admission. "I'm glad he has you and Thort," she said, and meant it, the echo of the pain she had felt earlier fading.

"And we are glad he has you," Brea told her, meeting her eyes, a faint smile on her face. "You are very good for him."

Yvonne blinked, not quite sure what that meant, or what understanding she was supposed to take from it. Luckily, Brea did not require an answer, looking back at the bones.

"Some bones are missing."

That was what was wrong. Yvonne had been trying to make a whole skeleton, and some of the pieces were not there.

"I think this is two people. Although there's only one skull," she said.

"Yes. Both human," Brea added.

"And young, I think, judging from the teeth," Yvonne said. "At least, the one with the skull was young. Full grown, but the teeth aren't that worn."

"These cut marks," Brea said, and then stopped. Yvonne glanced across to find her lips set in a thin line, jaw clenched.

"I think this is Hiram's work," Yvonne confirmed. "And he loves blood. I saw the marks on Guise." Hiram had been more careful with Guise, just slicing into his flesh. None of the wounds Yvonne had seen would have cut down to bone. Not like the marks on the bones in front of her. Earlier victims, she suspected, and felt ice crawl up her spine, wondering just how many people Hiram had bled in his quest for power.

"Yes." Brea bit out that one word and fell silent again, jaw still clamped shut.

"Hiram is responsible for what happened at the Stone Walls. I've made a promise to see him brought to justice," Yvonne said, the symbol at her shoulder glowing in the poor light. "And I will do so."

"And we will help you," Brea said, as firmly and definitely as any promise. "The Sisters were remarkable. Necessary."

"They are not all gone," Yvonne reminded her, her own eyes stinging with renewed grief. The one place of refuge in the world. The place where anyone would be welcomed. And Hiram, and his ambition, had torn it down.

"Are you just going to leave them?" Brea asked, straightening and tilting her head to the unconscious men in the cell.

"Yes. They have been grafted with death magic. The one who spoke to me seemed to think Hiram was training them. Like his son."

"Death magic," Brea said, nose wrinkling in disgust. "Almost as revolting as the idea that any woman would give the blood sorcerer a son."

"He seemed to be a favourite in the court," Yvonne answered, rising to her feet as well. She did not think there was anything more to learn from the bones here.

"The ones upstairs are dead. It's middle night. We have time to rest for a bit before morning. We're going to eat something, and then leave," Brea said, no room for argument in her voice.

Yvonne did not try to argue. Brea was a warrior and commander to her core. They needed a pause, and it was doubtful Guise had been properly fed while he was captive.

Instead, she followed Brea to the stairs, her mind snagging on Hiram's son.

Joseph had been with a group of northmen, hiding at a farm that seemed to be in the middle of nowhere. A farm that had been occupied by a former member of the King's Guard. She had never worked out why Joseph had been there, or what mission his father had sent him on. Now, she wondered if that might be important.

Chapter Fifteen

They came up to the main floor to hear faint noises from the back of the house and made their way through to find a kitchen, the only room Yvonne had seen so far which had furniture. A large table and plenty of chairs sat in the middle of the huge room.

The contents of their food stores had been laid across the worktop, and Lita and Ulla were bickering next to what looked like an enormous oven. Thort was not there, but Guise was sitting in one of the chairs at the end of the table, and once she had seen him, she had no attention for anyone else.

He had washed and dressed in his normal clothes. A pale shirt and a deep green greatcoat, the coat sagging slightly across his shoulders, showing how much weight he had lost. He was not looking at anyone else, staring at the mug of tea that someone had placed in front of him. The light from the candle set on the table highlighted the ragged ends of his hair and the extent of the bruising across his face, particularly around his mouth, which was still swollen.

She took a seat at the corner next to him, not caring that there were other people in the room, and put her hand on the table, palm up.

He stiffened, his entire body going still, as if she had struck him.

She waited, heart thumping in her throat, keeping her hand held out, not saying anything, not paying any attention to the others in the room.

At length, when she was beginning to wonder if she had made a terrible mistake, he put his palm across hers, lacing his fingers through hers. His skin was cooler than she remembered, but the slightly rough texture of calluses was familiar, as was the shape of his hand.

"Did you leave any hot water?" she asked. The first thing that came into her head, as silly as it was.

It startled a half-laugh out of him, and his fingers closed around hers for a moment.

"No. I am sorry. I used all the soap as well."

It was the most he had said since she had found him, and there was the barest hint of dryness in his voice. A tone she was familiar with.

Before she could respond, he lifted his head, meeting her eyes. Only a heartbeat, but it was enough to see the swirl of gold among the green.

"You found me."

"Of course I did," she answered, tightening her hold on him. "I am sorry it took me so long."

"You said that before, didn't you?"

"Yes. I didn't know you were missing for a while. I would not have left the city if I'd known."

"No. You needed to be safe," he told her. His tone was flat, not permitting any argument. She wanted to argue, though. If she had tried to find him. If they had found each other. He would not have been taken, and she would not have been forced to flee the city.

"Yvonne." Brea's voice interrupted.

She turned, startled, and realised that the bickering between Lita and Ulla had turned into a proper argument, the two of them glaring at each other.

"I'm sorry to interrupt," Brea said, "but neither of those two have any idea how to cook. Thort is setting some perimeter traps, otherwise he would cook."

"It's alright," Yvonne said, giving Guise's hand one last squeeze before she disentangled herself and rose to her feet. "Can they go and look after the horses, or something?" she suggested to Brea.

"Good idea," the warrior said, a hint of fang showing at her mouth, and she stalked the few paces to the oven, sending Ulla and Lita out of the room with a few well-chosen words.

Yvonne made her way to the supplies, assessing what they had. Cooking in the kitchen of an abandoned, fortified house, while Guise's guards were either dead or tied together in his former prison downstairs. It did not seem real, and yet her skin had the fresh memory of Guise's hand against hers, the slight roughness of his fingers.

"Can you find a stew pot?" she asked Brea.

"There's not much," the goblin answered, opening a cupboard and showing her.

No stew pot. A pair of large, heavy-bottomed frying pans. That would have to do. She could make flatbread in the oven.

Yvonne busied herself setting up the frying pans, melting butter at the bottom then layering thin slices of potato on the bottom, chopping up their remaining vegetables before adding them, along with beaten egg and herbs and spices from her own supply. Eggs were a luxury when travelling, easily broken. These had been carefully wrapped and carried on Guise's horse, used as a pack horse for the journey, much to its disgust.

"We'll need to find a market soon," she told the room, only then becoming aware of the quiet behind her.

There was an odd quality to the silence. She turned to find that the outside door had been closed, and Brea and Thort were settled at the table near Guise, who was not looking at them.

"What's wrong?" she asked, and immediately felt stupid for the question. A great deal was wrong.

"Come and sit for a moment," Brea suggested.

Apprehension crawling across her skin, Yvonne came back to the seat she had used before. Guise did not look at her either as she took her place, and her brows lifted. He was avoiding them as best he could.

"Do you need another healing spell?" she asked him, half-reaching out a hand and then putting it back in her lap. He did not look like he wanted to be touched.

"No," he said, the one word bitten off, almost angry.

Her eyes narrowed and she assessed him again. This was a mood she had not seen before from him. But then, she had never seen him after he had been kept by a blood sorcerer for weeks, and tortured.

"How did they capture you?" she asked, keeping her voice calm. At the edge of her sight she saw Brea give one sharp nod, approving the question.

Guise did not answer for a while. He had his hands under the table, but from the tension across his shoulders she guessed his fists were clenched.

"Eight men," he said at length. "Poison darts." He shrugged slightly, head still bowed.

"More than one dart?" Yvonne asked.

He nodded, staying silent.

"I see." She sat back in her chair, considering him, and what she knew of him. Arrogant. And almost unaware of it, carrying it as a part of him. "And you think that you should have been able to fight off eight armed men and several rounds of poison?"

His head jerked up, eyes meeting hers for a moment.

"I am damaged," he said, the words torn out of him.

She wanted to hold out her hands, twisting her fingers together to hold them in her lap. He was hurting. Badly.

"You are alive," she told him, voice soft, "and I came to look for you as soon as I knew you were missing." Ignoring the nagging twist of a Hunar's unfulfilled promise that still rose up from time to time. "Do you think I care about your hair or your fangs? You are still you."

His eyes widened slightly, a wash of colour over his face.

"I came to find you," she went on, ignoring Brea and Thort. "You, Guise. Not a lord of the Karoan'shae. Not your wardrobe. Just you."

She remembered taunting the soldier in the crypt downstairs, calling Guise her husband. She had never said the word out loud before, always feeling the push and pull of Guise's presence. Now, though, that word felt right, and true, the weight of it ringing through her. Her heart was beating too fast, and she could not breathe freely. She was not sure she could say any more. Not even to him. She hoped it was enough.

His eyes swirled into gold. "I do not deserve you, mristrian."

"That's true," Brea said, her voice breaking into the space between them.

"And we don't care about your hair or your fangs, either," Thort added.

Guise lifted his head further, gaze travelling around the three of them, eyes bright.

"The fangs are bothering you," Yvonne said to Guise. "A goblin matter?"

"We only have one set," Brea told her. "Once they are gone, they are gone."

"Pulling fangs was a punishment in years past," Thort added. "For traitors and cowards."

Yvonne's brows lifted. "I doubt anyone will think Guise a coward." She was quite sure of that. "Or, indeed, a traitor," she added. He might disagree with his mother, but he had no ambition to rule, that she had seen, far preferring his network of information and secrets.

"Quite so," Brea agreed.

"I do not deserve any of you," Guise said, voice soft, words still slightly distorted by the swelling around his mouth.

"No," Brea agreed, cheerfully, "but you're stuck with us."

Ulla and Lita appeared to have repaired their argument by the time they came in from seeing to the horses, both of them turning unerringly towards the oven, and the food cooking there.

"It's a very simple dish," Yvonne warned them all, bringing the pans to the table. Despite there being some cooking pots, the kitchen did not appear to have much in the way of plates and cups. They were using the metal plates and simple eating utensils that they carried in their packs. She brought the flatbread out of the oven as well, setting it on a clean cloth from her pack.

"This is delicious," Lita said a few moments later. "You are indeed a sorceress."

"No magic involved, I assure you," Yvonne said, feeling her face heat at the compliment. "I like to cook. But, if you want really wondrous food, you should have a meal prepared by Modig."

"Is that so?" Lita asked, eyes sharpening with interest. "Where might I find him?"

"Actually, I don't know just now," Yvonne said, and looked across to Brea, Thort and Guise. "Do you?"

"Last I heard he was going to Fir Tree Crossing. He seemed to think there was a place there for a fancy restaurant," Brea commented, waving her eating utensil around. "This is really good, though."

"Sephenamin would help him, I'm sure," Yvonne agreed.

"Fir Tree Crossing?" Lita asked, still with that gleam in her eyes. "I shall have to visit. You have the most interesting people there."

Yvonne was going to deny it, but then paused, thinking about it. It was perhaps the most peaceful place she had ever lived, thanks in large part to the mayor, who was not a fool and not corrupt, and the law keepers, who were Antonine Rangers, and a cerro who was not a fool or a bully. All three things were unusual. Put together, they were unique.

"It is a good place," she agreed after a moment. "My children are settled there, at least."

No one said anything more until all the food was eaten, including the last crumbs of the flatbread.

Guise seemed a little better, Yvonne saw, looking at him out of the corner of her eye, trying not to be too obvious. She had given him the same share as everyone else, knowing that although he had been half-starved, it took a while to adjust to food again after being deprived.

"We need to be gone from here soon," Brea commented into the comfortable silence of empty plates and full stomachs.

The silence shifted, became hard-edged, apprehension crawling over Yvonne's skin again.

"We're in no shape to deal with Hiram when he comes back," Brea added, perhaps expecting an argument.

No one argued.

"Any ideas where we should go next?" Thort asked, turning to Yvonne.

She felt the weight of all the stares on her, and had a moment of blind panic. She did not know what should be done. What was needed. And then she breathed, and looked at Guise. Wounded, exhausted. He needed time to heal. They all needed a little bit of time to be still, to decide what to do next.

"We need somewhere safe to stay for a little while," she said.

"Good plan. Where?" Brea asked.

Yvonne shook her head, trying to think, mentally reviewing her map, where they were and what was around them. They were in Valland, and they could not go to any of the major towns as the law keepers there would be looking for her.

They might be able to stay in a smaller town. Or a farm. If they could find one. Like a farm that had been occupied by a retired soldier.

"I know where we can go," she said, straightening. Sarra's farm. That they had come across almost by accident on their hunt for the attackers of the Stone Walls. The last place anyone would think to look for someone suspected of killing the King. There was just one problem. The wulfkin had eaten everything in the house, and the nearest markets were at least a day's ride from the farm. They would need to get their own supplies on the way there. She turned to Guise. "I don't suppose you have any money on you?"

Chapter Sixteen

The farm was almost as she remembered it. The well-kept fields. The well-tended livestock. The farmhouse and outbuildings.

There were signs of neglect, though. Weeds beginning to appear in the stable yard. A door in the outbuildings flapping open in the slight breeze. The hungry look from the animals as they rode past.

"If you search the house, I'll see to the animals," Yvonne offered, sliding off Baldur's back in the courtyard.

"Animals?" Brea asked, lifting a brow.

"It seems the least we can do," Yvonne added. This was Sarra's farm. And, judging by the way it had been kept, it had been something she was proud of. No weeds would have been allowed to grow on her watch.

"I don't farm," Ulla said, sounding very certain, even with her face hidden.

Yvonne shook her head slightly. "I did not expect you to."

"I will come with you," Guise told her. He was mending, slowly. Goblins healed almost as fast as wulfkin, she knew from past experience. The bruising across his face was almost gone, although he still moved far more slowly than she was used to. And was far quieter than she was used to, as well.

She accepted his company, taking the horses to the main barn where Baldur's head lifted at the prospect of a comfortable stable. And food.

Sarra had kept her farm well-stocked. There was more than enough food for all the horses, and all of the livestock.

Yvonne took the heaviest sack of feed she could manage and began a round of the fields, making sure that the water troughs were full, scattering the feed in the troughs as she went, almost being trampled by the cows as they shoved each other out of the way in their eagerness to get to the food.

The neighbours who had been looking after this farm had their own livestock and farm to tend. They would not have been able to spare much attention for Sarra's livestock, she guessed.

Lita came back from the neighbouring farm just as Yvonne and Guise were finishing their inspection of the livestock, confirming Yvonne's guess. The neighbours were relieved, happy with Lita's story that Sarra had asked her to look after the farm for a while. Apparently they had been busier than usual, only managing to visit Sarra's farm every second day. The neighbouring farm, nearly a half day's ride away, had also gifted Lita a round of cheese, delighted to be relieved of their stewardship.

By that time, Yvonne was so tired that her bones ached. It had felt like another long journey to get here, and she wanted nothing more than a comfortable bed. And a bath. If possible.

She had found time on the journey here to send a messenger bird to Pieris, letting him know where they were going, urging him to be careful, and to send brief letters to her children to let them know she was safe. With that taken care of, and the animals seen to, she could rest for a moment. Perhaps longer, if she was lucky.

She came into the farmhouse kitchen to find that someone had made efforts to settle in. The foodstuffs they had brought, after the wulfkin's raid on the kitchen, had been put away. The oven fire had been stoked and there was a kettle on the hob, heating water, and the great fire in the hearth had been stirred to life. The whole house had the slightly chilly, damp feel of an unused building. A fire would help.

"We've set up the bedrooms," Brea reported, coming into the kitchen. "You're in the first to the left at the top of the stairs, Yvonne. Guise, you're to the right. Lita, you're at the end, on the left."

"Bedrooms," Lita said, stopping in her stride, the round of cheese still held between her hands. "An actual bed?"

"Yes. They seem well made and comfortable. We've dosed everything with some cleansing," Brea continued, sounding almost cheerful, "and there's a bathing house just to the back. Thort is stoking the furnace."

"Bed and a bath," Lita said, sounding stunned. She sat down abruptly on the nearest chair, the cheese hitting the table surface with a thump, and put her head into her hands, letting loose a long, heartfelt sob.

Not one word of complaint for the entire journey, but it had been hard on her.

"Some food before bed and bath?" Yvonne suggested.

"Good idea," Brea said, politely ignoring Lita's sobbing.

Guise settled at another chair, moving more slowly than he had been. Still in pain. And not wanting to talk about it.

"We'll need to go out for food again in a few days," Brea commented, going to the kettle. She took mugs down from the shelves, making tea as though she were not in a strange kitchen and at the end of a long journey.

"And you're sure no one will look for us here?" Lita asked, lifting her head, brushing her hands across her face.

"I'm not sure," Yvonne said, "but it seems unlikely that anyone would think to look for us here."

"It's an odd place for a former soldier," Brea commented, settling mugs in front of them all, and then taking her own place at the table.

"It is," Yvonne agreed, staring into the tea.

"And it's not the only reason you wanted to come here," Brea added.

Yvonne's mouth lifted in a smile and she looked up to meet Brea's direct gaze. "I thought of it first as a safe place. But you're right, there's more. Hiram's son, Joseph, was here. He was on some errand for his father, and I want to figure out why. And why a former member of the King's Guard would settle here. She said it was her husband's choice. But there were plenty of other farms closer to the Royal City they could have had."

"Is anything ever straightforward?" Lita moaned, her hands curled around the mug of tea. "Can we at least rest for a little while?"

"A little while," Yvonne said. The twist of a Hunar's unfulfilled promise turned in her chest. She had promised to bring Hiram to justice for what he had done at the Stone Walls. For Adira, and for everyone else who had died. She had been able to set that promise aside, with some effort, in her hunt for Guise. Now she had found him, the magic was reminding her of her obligations. Still, she thought there were things here worth exploring. Soon, she told the magic and the promise, and the memory of Adira. Very soon. There was a mystery here that needed solving first.

"It's a farm," Brea said to Lita, breaking across Yvonne's thoughts, the warrior's nose wrinkling slightly, "so I'm not sure there's going to be much resting."

"True," Yvonne agreed, as footsteps sounded outside the door and Thort appeared.

"The bathing house is ready. Ulla has claimed the first bath," he added, coming into the room and taking his own mug of tea. "Is that cheese?"

Two days later, and Yvonne was not sure if Lita would consider the time spent to be a rest. The cloth merchant had initially wrinkled her nose at the idea of tending to the animals, only to then join in with everyone else. The livestock had been rotated to other fields, the water troughs scrubbed clean and refilled, feed left out at least once a day, and Lita had even joined in when Yvonne had decided to make an inspection of the individual animals, checking for wounds. They had left the goblins around the house, tending to the weeds and the odd jobs that needed doing, such as the broken catch in the outbuilding.

Yvonne had also given Guise the agent's journal to study. The agent had, predictably, written it in code, and Guise had a keen interest in secrets. As a side benefit, she thought that studying the journal would give him a purpose, and an excuse to sit from time to time. Guise had been trying to keep up with Brea and Thort, frustrated by the slow pace of his healing.

Ulla had appointed herself as perimeter patrol, and was often not seen for most of the day. It seemed to suit her, and Yvonne had noticed her relaxing more and more in the evenings, when they gathered for a meal.

She came into the kitchen in the late afternoon, to stoke the oven and start getting the evening meal ready, only to find Thort and Guise there already. Guise was in his shirt sleeves, chopping vegetables under Thort's direction. Thort was pummelling something that looked like a bread mix.

"Yvonne," Thort said, by way of greeting. "You've done most of the cooking. We thought we'd give you a rest this evening. Baked vegetables and fresh bread."

"Sounds delicious," Yvonne said. She hesitated a moment. "Is the bath free?"

Thort nodded.

Another bath. It would be a luxury. And she felt slightly guilty leaving others to work. "Do you need me to help?" she asked.

"No," Guise said, looking up, a hint of smile on his face. The first she had seen since they had rescued him. "We will see you later, mristrian."

"Very well."

She fetched a change of clothes, and some soap from Sarra's stores, and headed for the bath house. She must remember to compliment Sarra on this building. It was small, with barely enough room for the furnace, bath and a little bit of floor to get changed on, and plain, the walls painted with whitewash, rather than the tiles more commonly found in high-end bath houses. Yvonne did not care. The bath was large enough, and deep enough, that she could sink into blissfully warm and clean water, and scrub her skin until it was pink, wash out the dust and cow slobber from her hair, and let the work of the day seep out of her into the water around her.

The water was still warm when she was clean, and she stayed still for a few moments more. A pair of days tending the farm had not given her much time to think, but the nagging sense of a Hunar's unfulfilled promise rose up now, along with the questions she had about this farm, why Sarra had chosen it and what Hiram's son had been doing here in the first place.

Sarra was not here to question, of course, and it seemed unlikely that she would simply volunteer the information, so they would have to find out another way.

There was something in the vicinity that the King had thought important enough to keep an eye on. And something had drawn Joseph here, at his father's command.

She tilted her head back, staring up at the plain white ceiling, and frowned, trying to remember where they were on her map, and what stories there were of this part of the world.

For a moment her mind was blank. This was a nondescript part of the Valland kingdom. There were farms, producing a great deal of excellent meat, dairy and grain products. There were a few small towns and villages scattered. No cities.

But.

There had been, once.

Her mind would not bring the details into focus, and she got out of the bath, dressing with a frown on her face, sending a cleansing spell across the empty bath and space around it as an afterthought before heading back to the house.

The bite of autumn in the air made her draw in a breath, the warmth of the bath fading as she made her way back to the house, pausing near the back door to look up at the sky and the few stars that were appearing, bright diamond points against the deep blue span of the early night.

Her eyes searched for familiar patterns, the stars that she knew and could navigate by, and she saw the old Hunter, a little stooped, the arrow he had ready pointing down to the ground far below.

"Food's ready," Guise said, appearing at the door. He stepped out into the night, restored to his usual elegance, coat back on, only the ragged cut of his hair a jarring note. "Stargazing?" he asked.

"Trying to remember why this place is important," she answered. "There's a reason Sarra was here. And Joseph."

"Yes." Guise came to stand beside her, looking up at the stars. "This was not always part of Valland," he said after a while.

"No."

"Food's getting cold," Thort called from the open door, cutting across whatever Guise might have said.

The baked vegetables and fresh bread were delicious, and every scrap of Thort's cooking was finished, everyone sitting in companionable silence around the kitchen table, comfortably full of food, warm and safe.

Brea, Thort and Guise turned their heads at the same time, tension clear, Brea and Thort rising, hands going to weapons, worn even at the dinner table.

"Horses," Guise said. He was still in his seat, shoulders and jaw set. Still hurting from his wounds, Yvonne knew. "A pair of them, I think."

Yvonne went to the door with Brea and Thort, Ulla slipping past them to creep out into the night, the assassin blending with the shadows in moments.

"Yes. Just a pair," Brea said.

"I sent word to Pieris to find us here," Yvonne reminded them, knowing that the warriors would not relax until they knew who was approaching the house. The farm was not easy to find. Whoever was approaching them was doing so deliberately.

Ulla returned, stepping out of the shadows.

"It's Pieris and Jaalam," she confirmed, and slipped back into the house. The night was chilly, and the kitchen was warm.

"They made good time," Brea said, not fully relaxed.

Yvonne moved forward, away from the house, and a few moments later saw the pair of riders approaching, a third horse led behind them. She could not make out details in the poor light, but thought the third horse was carrying packs.

"Lady Yvonne!" Jaalam called into the night, sounding far too cheerful for someone who had been riding most of the day. He was dressed in a similar way to Guise, in the clothes of a gentleman of the Karoan'shae, from the beautifully tailored greatcoat to the knee-high leather boots, his silky hair catching the available light. "It is good to see you again."

"And you, Jaalam," she answered, waiting as they drew to a halt in front of her, then exchanging a brief hug with Pieris when he slid to the ground. She and Pieris were of similar heights. He had more grey in his dark hair, she noticed. "You made good time," she said, repeating Brea's comment.

"Do not remind me," Jaalam shuddered. "We cut across country. We even rode through a hedge."

"He's exaggerating. The birds helped find a shorter route," Pieris told her. "We wanted to get here as soon as we could."

There was no time for more conversation as the horses needed to be unsaddled and brushed down, and Thort promised to put together a snack for the travellers, Jaalam revealing that the third horse was, indeed, being used as a pack horse, laden with foodstuffs that they had thought prudent to bring.

In the midst of the busyness, Yvonne saw Guise step out of the house, exchanging quiet words with his cousin, who seemed to take a long, hard look at him, before folding him into a brief hug. It made Yvonne blink. Apart from Brea and Thort, goblins did not usually hug. But it seemed to be the right thing to do, as Guise was more relaxed when they went back inside.

It was late into the night by the time they were all gathered back inside, Thort setting food on the table. The round of cheese that Lita had brought back from the neighbouring farm, along with some of the fruit Pieris and Jaalam had brought, and flatbreads which took no time to make on the already-warm oven. Jaalam had brought some bottles of wine, along with the plainer foods. Predictably, Sarra's kitchen did not have enough wine glasses, so they ended up drinking from whatever they could find.

Yvonne looked around the table, and had the realisation that, as odd as the gathering was, she was among friends. Even Ulla, and Lita, although she thought that the assassin, at least, would not welcome the term.

The conversation was bright, even Guise smiling, until Pieris turned to Yvonne, sitting next to him.

"I heard from Suanna. Someone tried to get into her bedroom when she was in Hogsmarthen. She's on her way to Fir Tree Crossing. I sent Firon and Mica there, too."

The table quieted. Everyone had been made aware of Ulla's report of the contract being taken out on the Hundred.

Yvonne nodded, the bubble of warmth inside fading. "Good choice," she told Pieris.

"It was the safest place I could think of."

A town on its own, surrounded by farmlands and marshland, bordered by the Great River, patrolled by Antonine Rangers and with a large, well-coordinated wulfkin range. It was the safest place that Yvonne could think of, too.

"What about the others?" Ulla asked.

"Others?" Yvonne lifted her brows.

"The rest of the Hundred. There's only five. There has to be more of you."

Yvonne exchanged glances with Pieris, grief choking her for a moment.

"There have been losses," Guise said, voice soft. He was sitting on Yvonne's other side, around the corner from her, and she had an impulse to take his hand, not sure if that was for her comfort or his.

"Five." Ulla said, voice flat, mouth set in a thin line as she stared across the table at Yvonne. "That is all?"

"For the moment," Yvonne answered, looking into the wine she had in front of her. It was delicious, one of the full-flavoured varieties that goblins seemed to like. It might as well be vinegar for the taste in her mouth.

"We have been too few in number for years now," Pieris added. "We still hold to our oaths."

Yvonne looked up and met his eyes, seeing her own grief and determination reflected.

"Do we know why everyone thinks Yvonne killed Victor?" Jaalam asked into the silence.

It was so incongruous that Yvonne laughed. And once she had started, it was difficult to stop. She saw the sadness on other faces turn to smiles as she laughed.

"Someone set me up," she answered, when the laughter had faded. "Used my knife. Carved a symbol on the floor. Left a piece of shirt in the King's hand, and the rest of the shirt in my hotel room."

Jaalam's brows rose.

"That is certainly comprehensive. I am assuming, my lady, that you did not, in fact, kill the King?" Jaalam asked.

"No. I did not. He seemed a good man. As far as kings go."

That made Jaalam laugh, eyes bright with merriment as he leaned around Pieris.

"Remind me to never get on your bad side, my lady."

"Do you know who did kill him?" Pieris asked. Not an idle question.

Yvonne met Ulla's eyes across the table and lifted a brow. The assassin stared back at her, tight-lipped, staying silent.

"There was another assassin in the room. He escaped," Yvonne said, when everyone else had noticed the silence.

"An assassin?" Jaalam's brows lifted, and he tilted his head, indicating Ulla. "Like her?"

"I can hear you, goblin," Ulla said, voice sharper than it needed to be. "Yes. Someone from the school."

"You don't know who it was?" Jaalam asked, brows lifting in apparent surprise. He was being provocative, Yvonne thought. Something he had plenty of practice in.

"We didn't stop to exchange greetings," Ulla told him, shoulders tense.

"We should find him," Jaalam suggested, turning to Pieris.

"He was hired to do a job," Yvonne said, before Pieris could answer. "You know that assassins only kill under contract. Or in self-defence," she added, remembering the dead bodies in Lita's dining room. "We need the paymaster. I can't be sure, but I think we can guess who hired him."

Pieris' mouth set in a flat line. "The blood sorcerer."

She nodded, looking into her glass again, knowing that there were no answers there. She remembered the conversation with Pieris in the mid of night, not that long ago. The rending. When magic reached beyond the grave. It had almost destroyed the world before.

"There's more," Yvonne said, hesitating, and met Pieris' eyes. He nodded, once, agreeing with her. "Hiram used forbidden magic. And it's ..." her voice trailed off as she tried to find the right words. "There's a tear in the world," she finished.

"It's called the rending," Pieris said, voice so soft she had to strain to hear it.

"I've never heard of such a thing," Thort said, frowning. "The rending?" he shaped the words carefully, as though committing them to memory.

"A tear between this world and the next," Pieris clarified, still in that soft voice.

There was a heavy silence around the table.

"Hiram did that?" Guise asked into the quiet. Impossible to read his voice, or his expression.

"Yes. We need to find him and stop him," she said. It was so easy to say, except that she had no idea how to go about finding the blood sorcerer. And Guise needed more time to heal.

"Well, we knew we couldn't stay here forever," Brea commented, staring at Yvonne across the table. "I assume you have a plan?"

Yvonne felt the weight of everyone's gazes upon her, the expectation, and wondered when it had been decided that their future actions were in her hands. Still, she did have some kind of an answer for Brea.

"I've been trying to work out why Sarra settled here. She was in the King's Guard, and could have had any number of farms closer to the Royal City. Yet, she came here. It's good farmland. But there doesn't seem to be anything of note nearby."

"You think we're missing something?" Brea asked, eyes sharpening with interest.

"Yes. I'd like to look through Sarra's papers tomorrow." Her nose wrinkled slightly in distaste. There was a study on the ground floor of the farmhouse, a room full of books, ledgers and other papers. They had all avoided it until now. Yvonne had not wanted to intrude further on Sarra's privacy than being uninvited guests at her farm. Still, they needed answers. "And then, perhaps, ride out a little. See whether there's anything we've missed."

"There's nothing on the maps that I could see," Pieris told her. "And the birds didn't spot anything on the route we travelled."

"So, we can probably avoid that route, then," Yvonne concluded, exhaustion washing over her. "That still leaves plenty of ground to cover."

"Tomorrow," Guise said. "It's late."

"Tomorrow," she echoed. Tomorrow she would violate Sarra's privacy, searching through the soldier's personal papers to see if there were any explanations there.

Chapter Seventeen

She had made one last check of the horses, and the basic perimeter wards that she and Thort had set up, and was heading to her own bed, bones aching with tiredness. Reaching the top of the stairs, she heard a muttered curse word from Guise's room, opposite hers at the head of the staircase. Her brows lifted. She had never heard Guise swear before, let alone loudly enough to carry through a closed door.

She knocked quietly on the door.

"Guise, is everything alright?" Even as she said the words she wished she could take them back. He had been held and tortured, his fangs pulled. He was still healing from the physical wounds that he had been left with. She knew from bitter experience that the other wounds, the unseen ones, would take much longer to heal.

The door opened a little and he appeared, in his shirtsleeves, a towel draped around his shoulders and his head covered with something that made her blink.

"Is that shaving cream?" she asked, voice lifting in surprise.

"Come in," he said, and stepped back.

She stepped into the room and he closed the door behind her. She looked up at him and saw the faintest line of a razor cut on his scalp behind his ear.

"Are you trying to shave your hair off?" she guessed.

"I think I may be able to start growing it back, if it is all gone," he told her, sounding cross. He was holding a razor in one hand, the kind where the blade folded into the handle, brutally sharp and effective not just for shaving. He held it up. "The blade is defective."

She bit her lip, hiding a smile. She had never seen a bald goblin, or one with facial hair, and guessed that Guise had never had to use a razor before. Trying to shave his own head was an ambitious start.

"Shall I try?" she suggested.

He nodded, handing her the razor, careful to turn his hand so she could take the handle.

"Sit here," she said, pointing to the blanket chest at the end of the bed. "I can't reach otherwise," she added, when he hesitated.

He sat down, stiff and reluctant in his movements.

"If you would prefer, I can try and cut your hair so it's even," she suggested, not moving closer.

"I don't think that will work," he answered, not looking at her. There was a short pause, then he blew out a breath. "Thank you, mristrian."

"I haven't done anything yet," she told him, stepping up to his side and looking at the white shape of his head.

"Still, thank you."

It was said in a low tone, with a world of meaning behind it she could not guess at. She did not try, putting one hand on his shoulder for a moment in a silent acknowledgement, then turning her attention to his cream-covered head. Bits of his hair were long enough that they were poking through the thick layer of shaving cream he had applied.

"Where did you find the shaving cream? I didn't think goblins needed it."

"We don't. I found some in the dresser along with the razor. It's old."

"Possibly from Sarra's husband," she suggested, trying to decide where to start. "Stay still," she warned him, bringing the razor closer to his skull, "I don't want to cut you."

The razor and cream might have been old, but they were still effective, the blade slicing easily through the remnants of Guise's hair so that a short while later he was entirely bald, the towel around his shoulders covered with jagged bits of hair and cream where Yvonne had wiped the blade from time to time.

"All done," she told him, giving the razor a final wipe before folding the blade back into the handle. "How does it feel?" she asked, curious. When her hair had been shorn, it had grown back over time. She had never been entirely bald.

"Strange," he told her, putting a fingertip onto the bare surface of his skull. "Very strange. I prefer having hair."

"I think I prefer you with hair, too," she said, coming to stand in front of him, assessing. His eyebrows were intact, a defined arch of black against the pale grey of his skin, the bruising on his face faded so that it was nearly invisible, even the swelling around his mouth. His scalp was completely smooth, and she had an impulse to reach out and touch it, to see if it was as soft to touch as it looked. "Although I suppose I could get used to this. You look a bit like a pirate."

His mouth curved in a smile, gold flecks appearing in his eyes.

"I might need more colourful clothing," he said. A slight crease appeared between his brows. "And perhaps a gold tooth. Or an earring."

Her nose wrinkled in distaste before she could help herself.

"No gold tooth?" he queried, one brow lifting. "Or was it the earring you disliked?"

"They are your teeth and your ears," she told him, nose wrinkling again, trying to imagine him with either, and failing. Goblins rarely adorned their bodies in the same way as humans or other races did. They did not have tattoos or piercings or metal teeth. She could not imagine Guise with any of those things.

"It would scandalise my family," he said, speculation in his voice. But there was also a welcome undercurrent of laughter.

"May I?" she asked, lifting a hand, giving in to the impulse, but not wanting to intrude too much. He seemed vulnerable with his bare scalp.

He inclined his head, and she put her fingertips on the smooth expanse of his skin. It was as soft as it looked, warm under her fingers, and she stroked her hand back, behind his ear. He drew in a breath and tilted his head.

"Perhaps there are advantages to a bald head," he murmured, his eyes half-closed, bright gold showing between his lids.

"Sorry," she said, withdrawing her hand. He caught her wrist, holding her lightly, and pressed a kiss into her palm, sending a shock of warmth up her arm.

"No. Do not be sorry. It is quite pleasant," he told her, words muffled in the palm of her hand, breath warm against her skin.

She paused for a moment, absorbing his words, then dropped the razor onto the end of the bed and lifted her free hand, touching his scalp. He drew in a breath, air moving against her palm, and then lifted his head, tugging her forward so that she was standing closer to him, his eyes pure gold, warmth in them drawing her forward until their lips met.

The kiss was different without the weight of his fangs, bare skin under her fingers where there should be hair, and her standing taller than he was, for once. He moved, releasing her hand, wrapping his arm around her waist and drawing her closer.

She braced her hand on his shoulder to catch her balance, unthinking, and made a low sound of protest as her fingers slid in the remains of the shaving cream and bits of hair.

He released her at once, golden gaze on her face, looking for something. She was not sure what. She cleaned her hand on a corner of the towel, folding it and setting it aside, then leaning back towards him.

His lips curved up, showing white, even teeth. She had time to notice that his gums had healed, no sign now of the holes where his fangs had been, before he met her halfway with another kiss.

She had a moment of panic, unexpected and unwelcome, when he stood, arm around her waist, lifting her off her feet, her breath catching in her throat, heart skipping. He let her go again, his breathing rapid, eyes still shimmering with gold.

"Too much, perhaps," he said, half to himself, and she looked up, feeling unexpected tears prickle in her eyes. Her feet had lifted from the ground for a fraction of a second and old, old memories of fear and pain and helplessness had rushed in, no matter that this was Guise, who she knew would never hurt her. Confusion held her silent, words choking in her throat. He put his hand against her cheek, the rough texture of his skin anchoring her to the here and now, memories fading back to the past where they belonged. "Come," he said, taking a step back, along the side of the bed, "it is very late, and we need some rest."

She didn't want to leave him. Not with the gold in his eyes, and the warmth of his skin against hers. And realised that was not what he had meant.

She looked from the bed to him and her brows lifted. "Do you snore?" she asked, the first thing that came to her mind.

Flecks of green joined the gold in his eyes, lips curving up. "I do not believe so. Do you?"

"I don't know."

"Shall we find out?"

She woke to dawn light creeping through the window across the room, disorientated for a moment, not understanding where she was. Her weapons and boots were missing, but she was otherwise fully clothed.

There was a warm and heavy weight nearby, which sucked the breath out of her, panic rising, until she remembered where she was. Guise's room. At Sarra's farm. She had shaved his head, they had kissed, and she had panicked. And he had suggested they sleep.

They had managed, somehow, through the night, to find an accommodation on the bed so that she was lying with her back to him. She knew, without turning her head, that he was facing her, both of them tucked under a blanket, not touching.

It was the first time in her life that she had woken up with another adult beside her. The children had crept into her bed from time to time when they were small, waking from nightmares, needing the comfort. That had been strange enough. This was very different.

"You don't snore," she said, knowing he was awake.

A soft breath of air blew across her neck. A silent laugh.

"Neither do you," he answered.

They had a little while before anyone else would be up and awake. She was tempted to lie back down, go to sleep, but the texture of her clothes against her skin made her nose wrinkle. And Guise's presence beside her reminded her of something else she needed to tell him.

"I opened the parchment," she said, staring at the room's plain, whitewashed wall. "The one you gave me in the Royal City. I thought it might help to find you."

"No, it wouldn't help that," he answered. She was not looking at him, but had the distinct impression he was also not looking at her.

"Do you want it back?" she asked, her fingers remembering the smooth, cool surface of the metal disk.

"No," he said, sounding far more certain. "It is best in your care."

Which, naturally, made her more curious. She opened her mouth to ask, then shook her head slightly, feeling a wisp of hair against her face where it had escaped from her braid.

"I need to change," she said, sitting up in the bed, and looking over the side. Her boots and weapons were there, in easy reach.

When she was ready for the day again, she turned and stopped. Guise was still in the bed, sitting up with his back against the headboard, fully dressed, looking half-asleep.

That was not what stopped her, though.

"Your hair," she said.

He lifted a hand and brushed his head, touching the finger's width of black hair that had grown overnight, eyes widening.

"Well, that was quick," he said, running both hands over his scalp. "Is that better than bald?" he asked her, mischief in his face.

She resisted the urge to roll her eyes and left the room as quietly as she could, ducking into her own room with its unused bed, without seeing anyone else in the house, finding a silly smile on her face as she found a fresh set of clothes for the day ahead. Like a teenager sneaking back into her bedroom after a night's adventure. She muffled an unexpected laugh in her shirt as she took it off, catching the scent of shaving cream and Guise in the fabric and pausing to draw another breath in. An odd mix. Not unpleasant. She glanced out of the window and measured the height of the sun. No time for a bath before anyone else was up, so she settled for a cleansing spell, for her and for her clothes. There was work to do.

Chapter Eighteen

Yvonne's head ached with reading, from hours hunched over the ledgers that Sarra had kept, so meticulously, for the years that she had been here. The first writing in the books had been another hand, Yvonne assumed of Sarra's husband, now dead. Then the soldier had taken over, her handwriting difficult to read. There were records of sales and purchases of feed and livestock. It seemed that Sarra had recorded most of the events of the farm in brief notations, using her own form of code that made no sense to Yvonne's eyes, but which Guise had been able to decipher without too much effort, and a throwaway comment that it was a common code used by Valland soldiers, adding that it was far easier to work out than the code the agent had used for his notebook. Guise had not managed to read the agent's notes yet.

All of which made Yvonne wonder just how many codes Guise had knowledge of, and just how Guise had learned the Valland army's codes.

A soft sound of satisfaction from the other side of the room brought her head up from another notation of sheep sales, and she found Guise leaning forward in his chair, a smaller book held in his hands. From the finger's width that morning, his hair had grown more during the day, now perhaps two fingers' length around his head, some of the familiar silken sheen showing in the daylight.

"Found something?"

"Yes. Local legend."

Before Guise could go on, the door opened and Pieris burst in, closely followed by Jaalam, both of them looking like small boys who had just found a treasure trove of freshly baked cakes.

"I know why we're here!" Pieris announced.

"There's a barrow not far away." Guise and Pieris said at the same time.

Yvonne blinked, wondering if she had misheard them, and why that should be so exciting.

"A barrow?" she repeated slowly, wanting to make sure she had understood them.

"A burial mound," Guise clarified.

"Well, not exactly a mound. More like a tomb," Pieris said, excitement making his voice higher and faster than normal.

Before anyone could explain to her why that was so important, or exciting, Thort appeared in the doorway behind Jaalam.

"There's a rider on the way. Ulla says it's just one human. Brea and I are going to check the perimeter, just to be sure."

"Where's Lita?" Yvonne asked, setting the ledger aside and standing up. She already had her weapons and spell pouch with her, as normal.

"We've sent her to the kitchen," Thort said, turning as he spoke and disappearing back into the house, presumably to find his wife.

"We'll wait with Lita," Pieris suggested, giving Jaalam a gentle push to move him out of the room.

"And I will come with you, mristrian," Guise said, setting the book aside and standing up. He was far more fluid than he had been, even in the few days they had been here, although still not his usual effortless way of moving that she associated with goblins.

She didn't say anything, leading the way to the front of the house, with the best view of the path that led between the fields. It then led around the side of the house to the kitchen door, which was the entrance they most commonly used, out of sight to anyone approaching from the front of the house. Even so, the house looked occupied. A few of the windows upstairs were open to let the rooms air. There were horses in one of the fields nearest the house, and Lita had insisted on washing some of the sheets earlier, which were now hung on a rope strung between posts in one of the unused fields.

The front door had a narrow window to either side, and through the nearest one, Yvonne could see the lone rider making her way through the fields. Her horse looked a little weary, its head low, the rider looking from side to side as she rode.

"That's Sarra, isn't it?" she asked Guise, who was close behind her. His eyesight was sharper than hers.

"It is," he agreed.

"Well, we should go and say hello," she said, pulling the front door open before he could protest and making her way into the sunshine. She heard him close the door behind them so that no one could creep up behind them, and moved a few paces away from the house, aware of Guise moving with her.

They stood, shoulder to shoulder, waiting as Sarra's horse picked its way along the rest of the path, stopping a few paces away.

Sarra looked at them both, then glanced around.

"Farm looks good. Though you're overfeeding the sheep in the far field."

"That's Lita. She thinks they're beautiful, and can't resist their begging eyes," Yvonne answered easily.

"Lita. Now. I don't know that name."

"You surprise me."

"No, really. Him, I was expecting. And the goblin couple. Though I don't see them. And maybe one or more of the rest of the Hundred. But Lita's not a name I know." Sarra shifted her weight forward and slid off her horse, coming another step towards them, taking off the hat that had been protecting her from the autumn sun.

Yvonne drew in a sharp breath as she saw the soldier. Sarra had aged at least a decade, deep lines around her mouth and across her brow, shadows under her eyes, and more white at her temples.

"I am sorry about Victor," Yvonne said.

"Thank you. He was a good man. A good King." Sarra's voice was tight, as if her throat was closing, and she paused for a moment. "I know you didn't kill him. Despite all the evidence."

"Otherwise you would not be here. On your own."

That startled Sarra into a hard, short laugh, that sounded as if it hurt somewhere in her chest. "That's true." She stared at Yvonne for a moment, lips pressed together.

Yvonne waited for Sarra to decide whether or not to ask what was on her mind.

"The one thing I can't work out is why you were at the palace at all that night," Sarra said, after the silence had dragged on.

Yvonne's brows lifted in surprise. Of all the questions, she had not been expecting that. "Easily answered. I had a message. From Victor," Yvonne said. "I have it here," she added, realising that she had tucked it into the pocket of her trousers and forgotten about it. She pulled out the folded parchment with the Royal seal and handed it across to Sarra.

The soldier read the short message with far more attention than it needed, lines bracketing her mouth. "This isn't from Victor. Not his writing."

Yvonne drew in a sharp breath, realising that it had never occurred to her to question the message. "It was brought by a palace messenger, and has the King's seal," she pointed out to Sarra.

"I know," Sarra said, giving the parchment back. "But Victor's writing was worse than mine. That looks like Hiram's writing."

"Hiram," Yvonne repeated, showing the parchment to Guise, a silent watcher at her side. He cast a cursory glance over it.

"I would have considered it authentic," he told her. "There is nothing suspect."

"Well, if Hiram wrote it, then that's more evidence he was behind Victor's death," Yvonne said, mostly to Guise. He inclined his head. She tucked the parchment away again, turning back to Sarra to find the soldier pale, and even older in appearance than she had been.

"Why are you here?" Guise asked. A welcome change of subject, Yvonne thought.

"Needed to check on the farm," Sarra answered promptly.

Guise made a soft sound that perfectly conveyed his disbelief.

"You look worn out. Why don't we see to your horse and feed you, then you can tell us why you're here. The real reason," Yvonne added.

"Giving me orders on my own property?" Sarra asked, mouth tilted up in what looked like amusement.

Yvonne ignored her, leading the way around the side of the house, not surprised to find the kitchen door open and three faces peering out from just inside the doorway.

"I'll take the horse," Jaalam offered, stepping into the daylight.

Sarra's eyes widened, but she held her ground as the goblin lord prowled across the courtyard, taking her horse's reins from her with a small bow, leading the animal on towards the barn.

"That's not your own horse, is it?" Yvonne asked, staring after it. From what little she remembered, Sarra's horse had been of a much lighter build. This one looked like one of the big-boned horses used by cavalry, capable of carrying an armed man to battle.

"No. Had to leave her behind in the city. Silly mare is in foal," Sarra added, shaking her head in apparent disgust. "I've been trying to get a foal from her for two years, and now she decides to oblige."

"I'm sure the stables there will look after her," Yvonne said, sensing worry in Sarra's voice, moving towards the kitchen door. "That's Jaalam with your horse. This is Pieris. And Lita. This is Sarra. It's her farm."

"Ah. Lita. The one overfeeding my sheep," Sarra said.

"You keep them too thin," Lita answered, chin up. "Otherwise they wouldn't keep begging for food."

"Don't be fooled," Sarra answered. "They get just as much as they need. Too much feed and their wool's no good."

Lita sniffed, clearly not believing her, and turned back into the kitchen. "I'll put the kettle on."

Yvonne let Sarra go first into her own kitchen, and nearly ran into the back of her as the soldier stopped dead on the threshold.

"What have you done to my house?" she demanded.

Yvonne tried to stifle a laugh, and the soldier moved forward, only so she could turn around and glare.

"It needed colour," Lita answered, setting the kettle onto the hob. "And you had those beautiful wall hangings just going to waste in the linen cupboard."

"Did you ever think I might prefer the place plain? Or that you shouldn't be going through the linen cupboard?" Sarra demanded, hands on hips.

The kitchen, which had been plain and functional, now boasted a set of vividly-coloured wall hangings, textiles that Yvonne guessed had been given to Sarra and her husband long ago as gifts, and which had been in the linen cupboard. Lita had made changes elsewhere in the house, too, moving a few pieces of furniture, setting a vase of flowers in the hallway, but they spent most of their time here, in the kitchen, when they were all awake and in the house, so she had focused most of her attention here.

"We left your room alone," Yvonne said to Sarra, going to take a place at the end of the table, Guise settling beside her. Sarra was still on her feet, but Yvonne thought that was more a question of will than anything else. "Although we have spent the day in your study."

"Of course you have," Sarra said, lips thin, and took her place at the other end of the table, nearest the oven, and Lita.

Yvonne waited while Lita provided Sarra with a mug of tea and a plate of freshly baked scones, Pieris helping Lita pour tea for everyone else, leaving mugs out on the side, and more water on the boil for the others.

Sarra took note of the extra mugs but said nothing, drinking her tea and eating the scones.

When she was done, Yvonne set her own mug down.

"So, why are you here?" Returning to an out-of-the-way farm. A retired soldier, who was not really retired. A place where Hiram had sent his son. The answer was important. Guise and Pieris had edged close to an answer earlier. Yvonne wanted to hear it from Sarra, keeping her eyes on the soldier's face.

"It's my farm," Sarra answered, brows lifting. "Any reason I shouldn't be here?"

"Why are you here?" Yvonne asked for a third time. There was power in words, and in repetition, and she saw Sarra's shoulders slump.

"I told you I know you didn't kill the King."

Yvonne waited.

Sarra stared back at her, silent.

"You were asked to come here for a reason," Guise said, "when you retired."

Sarra's jaw set.

"There's a barrow nearby," Pieris added, a faint smile crossing his face as the soldier glared at him. "It's local legend, and not exactly a secret."

"It is supposed to be a secret," she answered, voice a low, furious hiss.

"This wasn't part of Valland originally," Pieris went on, and despite the circumstances, Yvonne had to resist the urge to roll her eyes. Pieris' love of learning was extraordinary, and he frequently forgot that not everyone shared his passion. "It was annexed some time ago."

"So, there was a battle here?" Yvonne asked. Her skin prickled as the implications of that sunk in. There were no prominent towns for quite a distance all around. No cities. No fortifications of any kind. Whatever had happened here, the Valland kings had decided to erase anything that could be used against them. And had also tried to eliminate the battle itself from history. She had never heard of a battle here. And did not know the name of the kingdom that had once occupied these lands.

"A long time ago," Sarra said, reluctantly. "Before the first Hunar and his brother destroyed half the world."

Yvonne's breath caught. That was a long time ago. But, more importantly, battles in those days had often been fought with magic on both sides. Before certain magic and practices were deemed forbidden. Perhaps even around the time that there had been a rending.

"Almost no one knows about it," Sarra said. "It was the closest that the Valland kings came to being defeated. They lost countless men. It's why there are no crops on this farm. If you dig deep enough, you come up with bones. Even now."

A shiver made its way down Yvonne's spine. The local area had a lot of crop farms, the fields carved into deep trenches and high mounds, to provide more growing space for the crops. She could all too easily imagine coming across bones when the soil needed to be turned over.

"So, the kings didn't want anyone remembering their defeat. But they didn't leave this land alone." Yvonne felt a chill wrap around her throat, even under the scarf she wore. "Sorcerers were killed here, weren't they?"

"Some said they were as powerful as the first Hunar and his brother. And even more deadly than the brother," Sarra answered, staring at the table surface.

"You're here to guard the dead."

"I was offered this farm to keep an eye on things. My husband thought it was fabulous. Away from the city. He never knew about the bones. Or the barrow."

"But you knew. And you reported any visitors back to the court." Yvonne stared at Sarra across the table as the woman lifted her head, every one of her years showing in her face. "And you knew what Joseph was looking for. Except you didn't tell him where to find it."

"He didn't know what he was looking for," Sarra answered, voice harsh. "And I didn't recognise him as Hiram's son." She shook her head, lips pressed together. "Hiram kept him away from the main court. Almost hidden."

"He didn't know about the barrow?" Yvonne asked.

"I don't know. He didn't ask," Sarra said. Yvonne remembered her first conversation with the soldier, in this kitchen, and the sense she had then that Sarra had been hiding something. And here it was. There was nothing hidden now.

"So, what was he here for?" Pieris asked. A reasonable question.

"I don't think he knew. He kept saying that his father had entrusted a task to him, and it would reveal itself to him when he was close enough."

Yvonne exchanged glances with Guise, seeing the tightness around his mouth.

"You know where the barrow is, though," Guise said. "And you will take us there."

"Not today, please," Sarra said. "Tomorrow."

"Tomorrow."

Chapter Nineteen

The place that Sarra led them to the next day, on foot across the fields, looked utterly harmless. None of them had spotted it from their previous patrols of the farm. A few large stones, too big to be easily moved, mixed in among mature trees, across the slightest mound of earth. There was no chill in the air. No scent of old blood. No echo of the screams that must have been part of the battle that had taken place.

Just the quiet autumn day. A few birds singing in the trees. The breeze rustling through the leaves overhead. The crunch of leaves and sticks underfoot as they followed Sarra to what looked like a haphazard arrangement of several stones.

"Apparently the entrance is through those stones," she told them. She had been stiff and distant all day, not looking all that refreshed from her night's sleep.

"Through the stones," Yvonne repeated, going forward with Guise. She could sense Pieris and Jaalam moving around them, looking for any clues that this might, indeed, be the barrow, that this was the final resting place of ancient sorcerers.

"Yes. I've never tried to find it."

"Really?"

"I was asked to keep watch over it. Not tangle with sorcerers' business."

Yvonne looked across the short distance to Sarra, seeing the older woman even more upright than normal in her posture, jaw set. Imperfectly trying to hide her fear.

It surprised Yvonne, even as she realised that it really shouldn't. Distrust of magic, and sorcerers, was deep-rooted in some places, and some people. And Sarra had lived and worked in a royal court alongside Circle Mages and would have a better idea than many people of what magic could do.

And she realised then the depth of Sarra's loyalty to her king. She had been appointed to watch this place on her retirement. A place where magic had been done. Where dead sorcerers were buried, and bones still turned up in the soil. Yvonne could almost imagine the conversation with the King, asking his loyal servant to undertake this task. Not the retirement she had been expecting. And yet, she had done her best. More than that, the farm was prospering under her management. It might be nothing more than a wish to stay busy. Yvonne did not think so.

"Victor was lucky to have you," she said softly, half to herself, and only realised she had spoken aloud when Sarra stiffened again.

"He was a good king," the soldier said, eyes too bright, face tight. A good king, and not long dead.

Yvonne turned away, to give the soldier some privacy, and found Guise crouching in the middle of the odd arrangement of stones, inspecting something in the earth.

"What have you found?" she asked, joining him.

"There are carvings on the stones." He pointed. Almost hidden by lichen, there were grooves etched into the stone.

"On all of them?"

"On the inner sides of these stones." He gestured to the stones around them. Great slabs of rock, tumbled into the earth, with carvings on the edges closest to them.

"This doesn't look like a doorway," Yvonne said, rising to her feet and turning on the spot, inspecting the stones around them. They looked like they had fallen, or tumbled at random, onto this spot, different sizes and shapes collected together, with no pattern that she could see.

"Yes." Guise rose to his feet as well, frowning at the nearest carvings. "Although, that looks like an old rune for 'open'."

Yvonne lifted a brow, wondering when in his life Guise had found time to study old human languages.

He was right, though.

"Open," she repeated, in the language of the Hundred.

The ground underneath them gave way, a rush of soil and roots and grass, and they tumbled down, feet first, into the earth.

Bits of root and stones caught her clothes, scratched her face even as she ducked her head into her elbow, trying to protect her eyes from the soil. Something caught in the scarf around her neck, half choking her. She scrabbled frantically, managing to untangle herself even as she continued to fall, thumping against something enormous and hard, then bumping against something softer, with a familiar feel to it. Guise.

They were falling together, tumbling down into the earth.

And then landed, with a shock that sent the breath out of her and left bruises where her sword hilt was shoved into her side.

She scrambled to her feet, sliding on the uneven, uncertain surface, and scrubbed a hand across her face, trying to clear some of the debris and soil away so she could see. Only to realise that it was pitch dark. There was no light here. Even looking up, the direction she had travelled, she could not see anything.

She called a light spell to being, sending miniature candles around her, and drew in a shocked breath, choking on the soil still in the air, coughing to clear her mouth and lungs, before looking again, aware of Guise on his feet beside her.

They were under the earth. A long way down. In what looked like a natural cavern of some sort, high enough that there was no danger of them bumping their heads.

And surrounded by bones.

Ancient dead, laid out in straight, stiff postures, wrapped in decaying cloth, a few bits of metal gleaming here and there showing that many of them had been buried with weapons.

"I think we have found the barrow," Guise commented, voice rasping more than usual. He coughed. Doubtless he had a lungful of earth, too. He put a hand to his side, grimacing as he did so.

"Are you hurt?"

"A little," he told her. "Ribs." Probably broken, she thought, staring at him for a moment, measuring the hitch in his breath. Goblins did not like to admit weakness. He must be in considerable pain.

"I have some healing spells," she said.

"One would be welcome, thank you," he said, and that, more than anything else, told her how much pain he was in.

The healing spell took moments to activate, and then he straightened, breathing more easily. She pressed her lips into a line. A little hurt indeed. There was no good discussing it, though. He would not change.

"I'm not sure how we get out," she said, tilting her head back to inspect the earth above them, and wishing she hadn't as a fresh shower of soil cascaded over them.

They were underground. In the earth. With no way out. Surrounded by dead.

Her throat closed up, vision wavering, heart too loud and too fast.

They needed to get out.

Needed to make their way through the press of soil above them. Needed to find air. There was no air. The air had gone.

"Mristrian." Guise's voice sounded a long way away. "We will find a way out. Barrows this size usually have two entrances."

The calmness in his voice worked through her panic, the meaning of his words following more slowly.

"You're right," she said, only then realising that she was huddled on the ground, knees drawn up to her chest. "I am sorry. I do not like underground spaces."

"They are certainly not pleasant," he agreed, holding out a hand. She took it without hesitation, feeling the warmth of his skin, and the casual strength he used to pull her to her feet. She kept her hand in his when she was standing. He had been in a number of underground spaces over the past few weeks. Chained. His blood taken by a crazed sorcerer. Beaten. His fangs drawn.

She took a step forward, moving closer, and tucked herself next to him, resting her head on his shoulder.

"I am sorry," she said again, not sure what she was apologising for. Her panic. His imprisonment. That they were in this burial chamber because she had said the activation word.

"There is no one I would rather be here with," he answered. It was typical of the old Guise, unexpected enough that she half-laughed, and looked up to find his eyes swirling to gold. He bent his head slightly and she met him halfway.

Kisses were still strange, and wondrous, and she could happily have lost herself for longer as his free arm came around her waist, holding her more closely.

Except that he let her go rather abruptly, stepping aside, leaving her confused until she heard a soft scraping noise from somewhere in the darkness around them.

"There's something else alive down here?" she hissed, hands going to her spell pouch and sword hilt.

"It seems so," he agreed, and cast his own light spell, to add to hers, and drawing his sword. He might not be at his full strength yet, but Guise was still formidable. If she must be trapped underground there was no one she would rather be with, either.

She kept pace with Guise as they made their way through the dark, moving out of that first earthen space and into a cavern of stone, some of it natural, some of it carved, tool marks still visible, making their way between the rows of dead, the ancient, empty eye sockets staring up to the ceiling. The light spells moved with them, casting the scene into shadows and sparks of light. There was one row of dead to either side, leaving a wide space in the middle, which led to a great slab of stone, almost waist-high, on which another corpse had been placed. The soft sounds were coming from beyond the slab of stone, a place still hidden in darkness.

There was someone there, kneeling at the base of the stone, digging into the dirt, shoulders hunched, a tangle of brown hair visible in the light from their spells, and a shuttered lantern on the ground next to him.

Yvonne's breath caught as she looked at him. Someone she had never seen or met before, but a spark of recognition lit. She had followed this man across the mountains around the Sisters' valley.

"Hello, Will," Yvonne said, her voice flat.

Chapter Twenty

The man stilled, then lifted his head, eyes widening in surprise. He must have been aware of their arrival, and the light, so it must be her identity he was surprised at. Or Guise's presence.

Guise and Will had known each other, a long time ago.

Yvonne stared at the man. The only person who had escaped the valley, in all the time the Sisters had held the Stone Walls. The newcomer who none of the other survivors had been able to describe. Who had searched for, and found, a way out of the valley long before the attackers had arrived. Who might be one of the few living heirs to the Valland throne. There was a lot of mystery and a lot of expectation surrounding this one man.

She glanced across to Guise, wondering what he was thinking, and feeling, seeing Will again. He was standing perfectly still, sword still out, eyes a mix of red and green.

Guise had made four promises in his life. Three of them had been to her. The first promise he had made, before he had met her, had been to the man crouching by the stone. And whatever that promise had been, Guise could not talk about it. Still, she had guessed enough of it to know that it had been a complicated promise, her curiosity thoroughly engaged as to what connection there could be between a lord of the Karoan'shae and the hidden heir to one of the most powerful kingdoms in the lands.

Seen in the light of miniature candles, Will was unremarkable. A pleasant face, topped with brown hair. Slender in build and tall, even crouched by the slabs. Nothing special to look at.

And yet. He had run from the attackers in the Stone Walls, across the supposedly impenetrable mountains around the valley, had outpaced wulfkin, had fooled the best trackers that Yvonne had ever met and, even more remarkably, had moved among the wulfkin and Rangers, offering them a drink or two, without them noticing him as the man they had been chasing.

He might not look remarkable. His appearance was a lie. She had never come across a human before who had the ability to hide so well it was as if he had vanished in plain sight.

He was still staring at her, ordinary face unreadable, and then he sighed slightly, rising to his feet.

"I suppose, if anyone was going to find this place, it would be you. Hunar."

"Why are you here?" she asked him. There were a dozen other questions she could ask him. That one seemed a good enough place to start.

"Hiram was trying to find this place," Will answered. Not an answer at all, Yvonne thought, eyes narrowing.

"He sent his son here. And did not tell Joseph what he was looking for. But you are here, and you know what you are looking for. What is it?"

"Are you always so blunt?" Will asked, mouth lifting in an unexpected smile. There was more than a bit of charm behind it, transforming his plain face into something beautiful.

But Yvonne had long since learned not to trust a charming smile, and simply lifted a brow, waiting for an answer.

"Do you know what this place is?" Will asked instead, the smile, and the charm, fading.

Yvonne swallowed her impatience. He was edging closer to telling her something useful.

"It's a barrow," she said. The plain, honest truth.

"Of sorts," he said. He reached down and lifted something. A smuggler's lamp, the candle mostly hidden, giving barely enough light to see by. He set the lamp on the end of the stone slab and lifted the side, so more light escaped, travelling as far as the nearest of the dead laid out to either side, their bodies and clothing having mostly rotted away. "What do you see?"

"Can't you just answer a question?" she asked, a snap in her voice. She could feel dirt under her clothes, lungs full of the scent of earth. They might be standing in a stone cavern now, but there was no natural light, and a great weight of soil above them.

"It looks like an honour guard," Guise said. Unexpected enough that Yvonne turned to him, and her eyes snagged on the body laid out on the stone slab. She had not paid it much attention, more interested in Will, but now looked at it. There was not much left but bones, clothing long since gone apart from a few scraps of cloth. Cloth that looked like plain linen. This person had not been buried with full honours, with their weapons, or their wealth. They had been wrapped in a linen shroud and placed here. But before he had been buried here, his body had been mutilated. She could see the clear division in his neck, and at his wrists. Head and hands cut off. Wrapped separately. There were still traces of linen around the bones.

Something stirred at the back of her mind. Something mentioned in passing in her studies with Elinor, or in the treasure trove of knowledge in the Lost City. An ancient custom. A long-ago superstition that held that the barrier between life and death was far thinner than anyone would like to believe.

"No," Yvonne said, a shiver working its way up her spine. "They are not here to honour him. They are here to guard him. To watch him into the afterlife."

The battle here had been a long time ago. Before the first Iunar and his brother had destroyed their lands. Perhaps as long ago as the first rending.

She shivered again, clenching her jaw to stop her teeth rattling together.

Buried with a guard into the afterlife, his body dismembered before he was left here. There was only one explanation.

"He was a criminal," she concluded, turning her gaze back to Will. He had not moved, still standing by the head of the stone slab, face solemn. "And not just any criminal, but someone who had done things so bad in life, the people of the time wanted him guarded even into death."

Will tilted his head, confirming her words.

"Why didn't they just burn him?" Guise asked, sounding genuinely curious. It was a good question.

Yvonne stepped forward, calling more light to her, and inspected the ancient bones laid out, hissing out a breath at what she saw. Dark marks on the pale bone. Marks not faded or blurred with time.

"Because he had grafted magic to his bones," she told Guise. "Look."

"Well, now we know what Joseph was here for," Guise said, eyes sparked with red as he looked at the old bones and the distinct markings. "But how did they kill him without triggering the magic?" He had spotted the mutilation of the body too. Of course he had.

"I wish Pieris were here," Yvonne muttered, circling the stone slab to get a better look at the bones. "He would know."

"I'm surprised he didn't follow us," Guise commented, turning to stare into the dark, as if he could make Pieris appear.

"I'm sure he's trying," Will commented, drawing Yvonne's attention again. That sounded like personal knowledge of Pieris, rather than a guess. The plain man was kneeling at the end of the stone slab again.

"What are you looking for?" Yvonne asked, coming to stand near him. Not too close. He might seem harmless. She did not trust that, though.

"Knowledge," Will answered, not looking up as he continued his work. He was using a small metal trowel, the sort Yvonne had seen bricklayers using, to carefully scrape away the earth from the base of the stone. Under his patient attention, lines were appearing on it. Some form of crude writing.

"The name of the dead, perhaps," Yvonne speculated, bringing her lights closer.

"Possibly," Will agreed, not pausing in his work.

"And how did you find out about this place?" she asked.

He tilted a glance across at her, and the hair on the back of her neck rose. Not harmless at all. There was a keen intelligence in that gaze, along with a hint of the ruthless determination that had seen him across the mountains around the Sisters' valley.

"I had the run of the king's records and library when I was younger. Sarra is not the first former soldier to guard this place," he told her.

The Valland king's records, and library, Yvonne realised, remembering the impressive collection of books on all manner of subjects that the Valland rulers had collected over the years. And the records which kept track of every bit of land that fell within the Valland kingdom.

Will's answer was more complete than she expected, and raised another half dozen questions in her mind.

"The records in the library were not very specific," he added. "But there was enough there to catch my interest. Hiram's, too. At least, I think that's how he knew to send Joseph here."

Yvonne stared down at Will's bent head for a moment, picking apart what he had said, and not said. He had spent time in the Valland palace when he was younger. And had known both Hiram and Joseph. And yet, no one had ever mentioned a Valland heir. Or anyone missing from the court. She wondered just how early in his life he had perfected the art of hiding in plain sight. And where he had learned it from. Not from any Circle Mage, that was certain.

She opened her mouth to ask another question and he slanted a glance back up at her.

"We can talk or we can work," he said. Her brows lifted. That had sounded close to a command. And in a tone that suggested he had issued a number of orders over the years, and been obeyed.

"It is possible to do both," Guise said, still standing. Keeping watch. In case there was anything else down here.

Yvonne's mouth curved as Will sent Guise an irritated look. Guise didn't notice.

"How long is it since you saw Guise?" she asked Will instead, drawing the small knife from her belt, crouching just out of reach of him and beginning to carefully scrape the dirt from the stone. Will was looking for knowledge, he had said. There might be something she could use, too.

There must have been a cave-in elsewhere in the cavern at some point over the years that the stone had been here. Whatever had happened had scattered earth across the dead on this side of the stone slab, coated the floor, leaving a thick layer of dirt at this side of the stone, a clear set of footprints emerging from the dark. Will was the only person who had been here since the soil had fallen.

"Years," Will answered, not looking at her. Or Guise. "Before he knew you, I think."

"Yes," Guise confirmed.

"And you know Ulla, too," Yvonne said, continuing to scrape away soil with the knife. There was definitely writing there, at the base of the stone.

"Yes," Will answered. "Does she know everything?" he asked Guise, speaking the goblin language. Yvonne kept her head turned away, not wanting to let him see she understood him.

"She is my bond partner," Guise answered in the same language, the words carrying layers of meaning in his native tongue that were lost entirely in the human common language. In the goblin tongue, the words carried twisted, intertwined layers of promises and meaning and magic.

"A human? Your mother must be pleased."

"Actually, she is. Delighted. My lady held her own admirably against the Karoan'shae."

"You took her to court?"

"At one of the palaces. And she brought herself," Guise added.

Yvonne could not help her smile, Guise's praise warming her through.

Will became still beside her and, when she looked up, he was staring at her with narrowed eyes and a set mouth.

"You understand goblin?" he asked, in that language.

"Of course. I could not have managed the Karoan'shae without it," Yvonne answered. "Your accent is a little strange, though. Out of practice?" she asked.

Guise laughed, a soft sound that warmed her again.

"I have not been in goblin lands for a while," Will admitted, still displeased. He glanced up at Guise. "You made a promise."

"I kept the promise," Guise answered, laughter fading.

"He did. He has," Yvonne confirmed.

"But you seem to know who I am," Will said, sitting back on his heels and glaring at her. "I've worked very hard not to be known."

She lifted a brow, sitting back as well. "There is a trail of death and mystery in your wake," she told him.

"Not my doing," he said, shrugging one shoulder. But he would not meet her eyes, staring instead at the lines he had uncovered.

"I did not say it was. It followed you. The Stone Walls are gone," she said, and could not help the catch of grief in her voice, the memory of Adira's cold hands in hers overwhelming for a moment. "You had plotted an escape route. You must have had some idea there was danger."

"I always have an escape route," he told her. "Always." He turned away from her, back to the stone and the careful scraping away of the dirt.

There was something underneath his tone. Something that made him seem more vulnerable, more real, than he had been. It drew an answering note of sympathy from her. She knew all about wanting to escape.

"So, you did not have any particular idea that there was danger when you went to the Stone Walls," she said, thinking aloud. "And planned your escape route just in case." She paused. That made sense. And it was a relief. He had not deliberately brought trouble with him to the Sisters. "And what about the sweet oblivion?" she asked. The drink that he had given to the Rangers and wulfkin who had been following him. A spy's trick, used to extract information and leave the informant with the worst hangover of their lives and no clear memory of who they had spoken to, or what they had said.

He would not look at her again, and she thought she saw a darker colour on his face. Hard to tell in the poor light.

"You wanted information," she guessed. "You could have just spoken to us."

"No," he said, still staring at the stone.

"She may help you," Guise said, unexpectedly. "If you ask the right questions."

"Hunar," Will said, as if tasting the word, drawing out its meaning. "You are not what I expected."

Before Yvonne could ask him what he meant, he leant forward, pulling his lantern closer. While they had been talking, they had uncovered a large part of the base of the stone, almost all the soil scraped away, revealing a series of letters. Ancient runes.

He muttered a curse that made her brows lift. Apparently he had spent time in the southern realms.

"I can't read it," he said, sounding defeated. He set his lantern down and reached into a pocket, producing a roll of parchment, settling back on the ground, beginning to copy the letters down.

Yvonne called more lights to her, and sent them around the base of the stone so that the full inscription was visible. Will might not know the language. She did. It was the ancient language used by the Hundred. The language that the first Hunar and his brother had used, and which was recorded in the library of the lost city.

She rose to her feet and made her way around the base of the stone. Some of the letters were still partially hidden by the gathered soil but she could read enough.

Here lies Asra, the destroyer of worlds. Four thousand souls died to stop him. Let his fate be a warning to all. The line must be held.

Chapter Twenty-One

Asra.

The name echoed in her mind, tantalisingly familiar.

Her lips shaped the word, trying to remember where she had heard it before, or seen it written.

The world around her changed, a swirl of light and dark, the ground tilting under her feet, making her feel sick and dizzy enough to fall to her knees, one hand on the bare soil in front of her, holding her upright, eyes refusing to make sense of what she was seeing.

The spinning continued and she clenched her jaw against nausea, trying to breathe lightly through her nose, willing it to stop.

Her fingers closed into a claw, grasping the thick grass under her palm, holding herself to the here and now.

Grass.

The fresh scent of green from the broken blades of grass cut through the nausea and the swirling light and dark, anchoring her.

The air against her face was heavy with the promise of rain, and carried less pleasant smells. The trace of freshly-spilled blood. Weapons oil. Beyond that was the familiar scent of horses and leather.

She opened her eyes, and flinched back at once, on instinct coming to her feet, unsteady, staggering a pace or two until she found her balance.

The cavern, the bones, the carved words were all gone. Instead, she was standing on the churned-up ground of a battlefield, the dead and dying scattered around, their clothing too marred by dirt and blood for her to tell what they were wearing.

Some of the dead were not human. At least, they did not appear to be. Twisted, blackened limbs splayed on the ground nearby, long fingers ending in blackened claws, slender, lethal-looking weapons lying discarded by the dead.

"Who are you?"

The voice was heavily accented, the words spoken in the ancient language of the Hundred.

She turned, staggering again as she was still off-balance, finding a group of armed men staring at her. They were dressed in a motley collection of clothing, and she would have thought them mercenaries, except that there were spell pouches at their belts, and the weapons pointing in her direction were far better quality than most mercenaries could afford.

In the midst of the group a half-naked man was kneeling, bound in chains that bit into his skin as he twisted against the hold, ragged dark hair covering his face.

"I am Yvonne," she said, carefully moving her hands away from her weapons.

"How did you come to be here?" another one of the group asked, a burly man with a heavy ruby pendant on his chest.

"I was in a cavern. With bones," she said, looking around her again.

There was a dark opening in the earth not far away, the entrance to something underground, surrounded by heavy stones, and a pair of stonemasons carving words into the stones, watched by another man wearing a spell pouch, his sword in its scabbard.

She blinked. The stones looked familiar.

The Firebird's wings moved inside her, her great eyes opening, looking around, the symbol at Yvonne's shoulder brightening with the bird's attention.

"You follow Jerresesh," one of the men in front of her said. The swords around her lowered, the men relaxing.

Jerresesh. The name of the Firebird. And the name of the Lost City, where the Firebird's temple had stood long before the first Hunar had lived there.

"Yes," Yvonne said, hand half-rising to the symbol at her shoulder.

No one in her time spoke the Firebird's name. Or the language that the men were using.

No one in her time.

Her knees gave out and she staggered another pace back, trying to stay upright, failing, falling to her knees, disorientated, heart thudding.

Not in her time.

She was in the past. From long before the first Hunar. Long before he and his brother had destroyed the lands they lived in.

And now she realised that, she could sense something wrong with the world around her. The twisted creatures on the ground were the least of it. The flat taste of blood was too strong in the air.

As if it had been waiting for her attention, the great, yawning void of the rending opened in her mind's eye. Stronger here than she had felt it before.

Here, though, it had an anchor.

Her eyes turned to the prisoner, swathed in chains, the tangled hair still covering his face.

As if he had been waiting for her attention, he grew still and lifted his head, staring at her through the knotted mass of hair.

"Come to savour your victory, Jerresesh?" he said, his voice too deep and too full of darkness to be coming from a human chest.

"Come to make sure you are dead, Asra," Yvonne said. At least, those were the words that came out of her mouth. The tone, and the voice, were not hers, the Firebird speaking through her, the flames filling her.

"It will not last," he answered, curling his lip. Where there should have been white, even teeth, there were blackened stumps.

Yvonne stared back at him, the Firebird using her eyes still, and saw something else looking back at her, and the Firebird, through the man's eyes. The waiting intelligence she had sensed in the void when she had seen it before. Whatever it was that had inhabited the rending. Here, present in the world, held in the form of this human.

"Be careful with him," she said, rising to her feet, steadier now. There was an enemy in front of her. And this time it was her own voice, and her own words. "He has grafted his own bones."

"We know," one of the men nearby said. He had the dark skin of someone from the southern lands, wearing an exotic array of colours favoured by Sir's court. He also had another pendant on his chest, a hefty sapphire, as big as the ruby the burly man was wearing. "How do you know?"

"I've met his kind before," she answered, keeping her attention on Asra. He might be captured. He might be chained. He might be kneeling among the others, apparently helpless. But he was too confident as he stared back at her, dark eyes partially hidden by hair. Too knowing.

"There are more?" the man with the ruby asked, his dismay clear.

"More bonded to the dark?" the man with the sapphire asked, jaw set in determination. "Where?"

Asra chuckled, the sound grating in her ears.

"There are no more here," Yvonne answered, somehow certain of it. Here, in this time, in this place, there was only Asra. The Firebird tilted her head, agreeing, and confirming. "What will you do with him?" she asked, the question drawn out of her, even though she had a fair idea. There was a barrow being built not that far away. And she had seen the skeleton laid out on the stone slab.

The men around her exchanged glances.

"We cannot kill him by normal means," the man with the ruby said. "And yet, we cannot let him live. Even bound."

Yvonne shivered, thinking about another magician drawn to the dark. The first Hunar's brother, who had been killed, or so the first Hundred thought. Taken from the Lost City to an anonymous spot by a mountain and buried so deep that the first Hundred thought he would never be found. Except he had been found.

And, in her own time and place, Asra's bones were in front of her, and someone had torn the barrier between life and death again, stirring the waiting dark.

"How did you catch him?" she asked.

"With too many dead," the man with the sapphire told her, glancing around.

Yvonne remembered the inscription on the stone. Four thousand dead. Looking around the battlefield, she could believe it. And yet, no trace of this battle had survived to her day. Kept quiet. Kept secret.

Between the men wearing pendants was another man, a warrior by his clothing, with pale skin and dark, close-cropped hair, jaw set.

"I don't like the plan," he said to the others.

"Someone must guard this place," the ruby-wearer said. "We need to keep him contained."

"All of you?" the warrior asked, voice tight.

Yvonne glanced around the group and her breath caught, realising that there were the same number here as in the barrow. Apart from the warrior.

"Claim this land. Keep watch over this space. Make sure your heirs do the same," the sapphire-wearer said.

Inside Yvonne's mind, the Firebird's head lifted, attention sharp, and a sense of warmth spread through Yvonne's chest. The Firebird approved.

The bringer of justice, who would rain fire on her enemies without hesitation. Approving the measures that this group of warrior-magicians had devised.

"We cannot lose your knowledge," the warrior protested. "There are too few skilled in magic as it is."

"We are not the only ones," the ruby-wearer said, voice reassuring. "And we must go. We have lingered too long."

The men holding the prisoner moved, bringing him more or less to his feet. When he was upright, Asra looked up, shaking the hair back from his face so that he stared back at Yvonne. A handsome face, marred by the sneer of his lips and the black of his eyes. His lips peeled back further into what might have been a smile, showing the remains of his teeth.

"I look forward to seeing you again. Yvonne."

The voice sent chills through her.

She opened her mouth to respond, not sure what she would say, even as he was dragged away by his captors, all the men following. All apart from the warrior. He stood, shoulders square, and watched the group walk through the stone opening the masons had made.

Yvonne shivered as she watched them go. They had not been dead when they went into the barrow. Guards for Asra, in this life and in his death.

She shivered again, and fell to her knees, the world spinning around her again.

Her last impression of the daylight world was the warrior, his back to her, standing alone, staring at the barrow as the entrance closed, stones appearing from nowhere to fill the hole.

Chapter Twenty-Two

She was lying on her back on a hard surface, breath harsh and rapid in her ears, indistinct shapes blurry above her.

"Mristrian, are you alright?"

Guise's voice. Guise.

She used him as an anchor and blinked. There. That particular collection of blurred shapes. That was his face. She blinked again, and he came into focus. His hair was still too short, barely a few fingers' widths around his head, not the fall of silk she had been expecting, and she had to blink yet again to make sure she was seeing properly.

"What happened?" she asked, the words sounding stupid in her own ears.

"You fell, and would not wake up," he said, holding out a hand. She put hers into it and let his strength draw her upright. Her legs were unsteady for a moment and she kept hold of him.

They were next to the stone slab in the barrow.

Will was standing by the end, staring at her, expression intent.

"What happened?" he asked her.

"I'm not sure. I was here. I read the inscription. Then –"

"You read the inscription?" he asked, taking a step closer, eyes bright. "What does it say?"

Yvonne looked at him for a moment, assessing the set of his jaw and the way his hands were curled into fists by his sides. The most emotion she had seen from him so far. She let go of Guise, moving a pace away and pointing to the letters at the bottom of the stone slab.

"Beginning here, it reads: *Here lies Asra, the destroyer of worlds. Four thousand souls died to stop him. Let his fate be a warning to all. The line must be held.*"

Her breath hitched at the end, remembering the last time she had read those words. Nothing happened this time. She was still standing by the stone slab, the ancient bones in front of her.

"Asra?" Guise asked.

"Is that all?" Will asked, before Guise could say anything more.

"Yes. That is all the writing that's there," she told him.

"That can't be right," Will said, crouching down by the letters again, using his trowel to dig into the ground. Or trying to. The ground was solid stone, unyielding. "There must be more."

"What were you expecting to find?" Yvonne asked, moving slightly so she was standing next to Guise. Will had come here for a reason. Perhaps the same reason that Hiram had sent his son to the farm above them.

"Something more," he answered, words a snap. "Four thousand dead and they didn't leave even one clue how to stop him? How they protected themselves?"

"Four thousand dead," Yvonne repeated. "Isn't that clue enough?"

"No," Will said, coming to his feet, shoulders square, jaw clenched as he glared at her, as if holding her responsible for the lack of information. "He tore apart the world, and they lived. I want to know how they did it."

Yvonne's breath caught. Finally. Something real. Something honest. From a man who did not like to be seen.

She glanced aside, not wanting him to read her expression, and her attention caught on a glint of red on the nearest body. Her eyes lifted, travelling along the row of dead. Eight on this side. Eight on the other. Sixteen. Sixteen warrior-magicians, who had captured and imprisoned Asra here. She moved away from the stone slab to the nearest body, with the glint of red, and stared at the faceless skull, the empty sockets seeming to stare back at her. In the rib cage, among the tattered remnants of once-fine robes, was the red she had seen. She bent forward, careful to avoid touching the bones, and lifted the pendant. A ruby pendant, the stone almost the same size as her palm, a flawless gem that sparked with centuries-old magic as she held it up.

"I met this man," she told Guise, almost forgetting Will for the moment. "After I read the inscription."

"He has been dead a long time," Guise commented, coming to stand at the other side of the skeleton.

"I know it seems impossible. But I did meet him." Yvonne heard her voice rise and wondered who she was trying to convince.

"I believe you, mristrian. I have met your grandfather, remember?"

His eyes were green flecked with gold and held her attention. Her grandfather, or the being that called himself that. The first Hunar. Believed to have been killed, many years before, by his brother. Neither of them had been quite as dead as people had thought. She would not have imagined it possible, if she had not seen it for herself. As had Guise.

"Never mind that," Will said, snatching the pendant from Yvonne's hand. It was held on a silver chain, untarnished despite the years, the links tearing Yvonne's skin as Will pulled it away. She hissed as the wounds bit, grabbing a clean cloth from her pocket and pressing it over the seeping blood.

Will did not notice, taking the pendant back to the light, holding it up next to his lantern, studying it.

"I wasn't even sure it was real," he said, so softly Yvonne knew he was speaking to himself, enraptured by the enormous gem he was holding.

"Is that what you were looking for?" Yvonne asked. "The pendant?"

"You don't know what this is, do you?" Will's mouth curved in a smile. Not a nice smile. It reminded her of a bully taunting a child.

Before she could answer, a far more welcome sound met her ears.

"Yvonne? Are you alright?"

"Pieris." She turned to find her fellow Hunar coming towards her out of the dark, the same path that she and Guise had taken, Jaalam beside him, both of them covered in earth.

"That was a most unpleasant experience," Jaalam commented, stopping at the other end of the stone slab. "Let us not repeat it."

Pieris lifted a brow at the goblin but said nothing, gaze turning to the bones laid out on the stone slab.

"Who was he?" he asked.

Trust Pieris to get to the heart of the matter, his eyes bright with a scholar's interest. Yvonne slightly shook her head.

"His name was Asra. Here, there's an inscription," she pointed out.

"Remarkable," Pieris said, tone almost reverential as he walked around the stone slab, reading the inscription.

It was only when Pieris had completed a full circuit of the slab that Yvonne realised something.

"Where did he go?" she asked Guise.

"Disappeared while we were distracted," Guise answered, mouth set in a hard line, eyes glinting with red as he looked into the dark.

Yvonne glanced down at the ground and saw two sets of footprints. Will's. One leading towards the slab, the other leading away.

"He's gone," she said, breath catching on a spike of irritation. He had managed to make his escape without alerting her. Even when she had been standing next to him, she had not been able to get a clear sense of him. A mystery. One she had no idea how to solve. And one that, she sensed, was important.

She scowled into the dark, at the trail of footprints. It would be impossible to catch him now. He had escaped, and outrun, wulfkin and Rangers before now. Still, there was some good news.

"At least we know there's a way out," she said.

"Who?" Jaalam asked. Pieris was still distracted by the stone and its inhabitant.

"The one calling himself Will," Yvonne answered, not sure if the promise Guise had made would allow him to answer. "He was here."

"He was?" Pieris looked up and straightened, eyes travelling around the dead to either side. "How did he find out about this place?"

"Apparently there are references in the Valland king's library," Yvonne said, voice dry.

"Did he get what he came for?" Jaalam asked. He was looking at the skeleton on the stone, eyes sharp. Definitely not the careless, spoiled lord of the Karoan'shae he had appeared to be when Yvonne had first met him. She definitely liked this side of him better.

"Yes," Yvonne said. "A pendant." She frowned, recent memories stirring. "There were two. He took the ruby one." The wounds on her hand stung, remembering the tear of metal links against her palm.

She moved past the stone slab to the other row of dead and found what she was looking for almost at once, the glint of brightness in the chest of another one of the dead. Another great jewel on a silver chain that had not tarnished over the years. She picked it up with her uninjured hand, and held it to the light.

"Remarkable. I have never seen a jewel that size. Or that perfect," Jaalam said, voice a hushed tone of reverence.

"It is remarkable," Pieris agreed, his gaze slightly unfocused. Using magic to enhance his sight, Yvonne guessed. "It is powerful," he added a moment later. "May I?"

He held out his hand and she handed over the pendant without hesitation. He took it by the chain as well, careful not to touch the stone.

"Remarkable," he said again.

"Pieris, can you study it later?" Jaalam asked, a softness to his tone making the words a suggestion rather than a command. "We are still buried underground."

Pieris blinked, staring at Jaalam for a moment, then his mouth curved up in a smile that transformed his face into a mischievous youngster.

"Of course." He pulled a clean cloth from one of his pockets, wrapped the gem and chain in it, and tucked it away. "How did you know it was there?" he asked Yvonne.

"Perhaps a story for when we are back in the daylight world?" she suggested, looking around. The atmosphere in the barrow had shifted somehow, a chill penetrating her clothes, brushing against her skin. "I am not sure the dead like being disturbed."

No one laughed at her, or called her foolish.

"Have we learned what we can?" Jaalam asked, a surprisingly practical question.

"Yes, I think so," Yvonne said, moving to follow Will's footsteps into the dark, calling the lights with her.

She glanced back as the others joined her, and shivered at the rows of dead, the shadows her companions made casting illusion of movement over the scene and the bones on the slab. Sixteen warrior-magicians who had sealed themselves in here to guard their prisoner. Safe and undisturbed for centuries. The empty eye sockets seemed to mock her as she left.

Chapter Twenty-Three

They followed the trail that Will had left, along the cavern floor where it changed from stone back to earth again, finding the source of the cave-in that had spread soil through the barrow to the base of the stone slab, a huge dip in the ceiling with ancient tree roots poking through, reminding Yvonne of the great weight of earth and trees above them.

Beyond the cave-in, Will appeared to have dug himself into the barrow, leaving a crude, narrow tunnel behind that started about knee-height from the cavern floor and led upward at a steep angle, towards the surface somewhere over their heads. The tunnel was barely wide enough for one person at a time to crawl through. For a moment, Yvonne was tempted to suggest that they find another way out, seeing the narrow, dark space, with no daylight visible. However, Jaalam and Pieris conferred in low tones before sending some magic ahead of them that provided a little bit of light and, Yvonne could see, held up the sides of the tunnel so they would not collapse on them as they went through.

Jaalam went in first, crawling ahead a little bit until just the soles of his boots were visible, and then reporting back that he could see daylight ahead. It wasn't safe for more than one person at a time, he said.

Guise sent Pieris next, saying he would go last. His tone did not allow for argument. Perhaps he found the underground as unsettling as she did.

She stood shoulder-to-shoulder with Guise and watched Pieris disappear into the dark tunnel, hearing his faint shout as he reached the end, calling her ahead.

"I will keep watch until you are safe, mristrian," Guise told her. Not unsettled by the underground at all, she realised. Wanting to make sure she was safe.

With that thought warming her, she made her way into the narrow maw of black, crawling on her hands and knees, feeling the ground brush her back. There was not enough air around her. She could not see. Could not sense anything apart from the press of soil, the scent of damp earth in her mouth and nose, hands coated with dirt.

A trail of fresh, cool air against her face drew a muffled sob. She was almost at the surface. Almost. Lifting her head, she could see the faint outline of someone at the tunnel mouth, waiting to pull her out. Pieris.

She dug her hands and her knees in, pushing forward, wanting to be out of this too-narrow space.

And flattened against the floor of the tunnel, unable to move further towards the air. One of her boots had caught on something. She kicked, trying to free herself, and whatever it was snaked further around her leg, creeping up towards her knee. And she could not move her other foot, either.

Trapped. Held motionless in the dark, the press of soil around her, with whatever-it-was closing around her legs. She scrabbled for her spell pouch, fingers finding a concussive spell.

"Yvonne?" Pieris called from above.

"I'm stuck," she said, voice too high. "Something grabbed me."

"Something?" That was Guise's voice, from beneath her. "What?"

"I don't know," she answered. Light. She needed light. She wriggled around so that she could see her legs and called a light spell.

And screamed.

Her legs were wrapped in what looked like spiders' legs, great, multi-jointed limbs that were as dark as the soil.

"Mristrian," Guise called from beneath her. "What is it?"

She tried kicking, wriggling away, and could not move, the limbs that held her tightening their grip and then, much worse, dragging her deeper into the soil, probably towards whatever body owned those legs.

She screamed again, and activated the concussive spell, the force of it aimed towards the thing that had hold of her.

The tunnel collapsed around her in a shower of earth and bits of stone and tree root, the weight of soil drowning out any other sounds or sensation.

She screamed again, fighting to move, arms pinned by the soil as securely as her legs had been. She tried kicking at the limbs holding her and found she could move her legs a little, wriggling away from whatever creature had crawled out of the dark.

Black. Soil. Lungs choked. No air no air no air.

No light.

Nothing.

She was going to die here. In the earth. Never see the light again. Never see her children again. Never see Guise again.

A sobbing sound. One she recognised, old memories surfacing. It was the sound of someone in distress with no hope of rescue. She had heard it often in the quarrel.

But there was no quarrel here. And no one else nearby. The sound came from her.

She tried to breathe in, choking as she drew in more soil, coughing, trying to clear her lungs. Breathing hurt.

Hurt was good. Hurt meant that she was still alive. And while she was still alive, she would not give up.

She was not the terrified girl from the quarrel. She had not been for a long time.

Moving slowly, trying to keep her breathing even, she managed to get a hand up, cleared the worst of the dirt from her mouth and nose, made a little bit of space. A tiny pocket of air. Just enough to fill her lungs without breathing in more soil. Just enough space to think a little and to realise that she was being held still only by the weight of soil.

Somewhere above her was the surface. Except she was not quite sure how far above it was, or how far she had moved.

Somewhere beneath her was the barrow with its watchful dead. And Guise. Who no longer had a way out of the ground, because she had panicked and used a concussive spell and collapsed the tunnel.

Another sob escaped before she clamped her mouth shut.

She might not know how far the ground was above her, but was quite sure that the concussive spell and struggle against the soil had pulled her further back down into the ground. Towards the dead. And Guise.

The soil at her feet was loose enough that she could burrow through it, using her elbows, knees, and feet for leverage, trying not to think that, instead of working her way down towards Guise and the relative safety of the barrow, she might be working instead towards the nest of whatever it was that had crawled through the soil to grab her.

After what felt like an eternity, soil fell away and her feet were dangling in space.

She gave another muffled sound, unable to help herself, and realised a new problem. There was open space below her, and she had no idea how deep it was.

"Mristrian?"

A familiar voice that had never been more welcome.

"Guise!" A fall of earth smothered her and she turned, shielding her head as best she could, coughing to clear the soil out of her mouth and throat.

Something grabbed hold of her legs, dangling in the air, and pulled.

Before she had time to kick or scream, she tumbled out of the earth and into Guise's arms.

He would have set her down but she clung to him, arms around his neck, and breathed into his shoulder. Goblins did not have much of a personal scent, and yet she would know him anywhere.

"Are you alright?" he asked, setting her down, eyes shaded with red and gold travelling her length, looking for injuries.

"Something grabbed hold of me."

"What?" he asked, gold fading, on alert at once, eyes travelling around the space.

There was light here. More than there had been. She recognised the magic as Guise's.

They were still in the barrow, near the cave-in, soil spilling across the floor and the nearest dead.

"It had lots of legs. Multi-jointed," she said, and had to pause and cough again.

"Did it bite? Sting you?" he asked, face grim.

"No. Just pulled. I panicked," she admitted, voice small. Used a concussive spell in the confines of an earthen tunnel, and almost drowned in earth as a result.

"You are alive, and unharmed," he told her. He was not calm, though, still looking around the cavern. "I thought I heard something. Before you screamed." That explained the light. Even goblin's eyes had limits.

"Do you know what it is?"

"Your description sounds like a dervish."

"This far north?" she asked, moving to stand back-to-back with him, hands going to her sword hilt and spell pouch, heart picking up pace again. Something she had never seen, only read about.

Ground-dwelling predators, living deep in the earth, dervish were usually only found at the borders of the goblin lands.

"They like magic," Guise said. "It might have found its way here."

"An old one, then?" Yvonne speculated, stomach tightening. The old ones were rare, as dervish were territorial and vicious with their own kind. Old ones were far more dangerous, though.

"Probably. Do you have fire spells?"

"Of course. Several."

"Fire works," Guise told her, shifting his weight to turn slowly in a circle, Yvonne keeping pace with him. Even with the extra light, his sight was far better than hers. As was his hearing. "There," he said a moment later, stopping in his progress.

Guise was facing the collapsed soil, leaving Yvonne staring at the rows of dead, the unmoving bones, and the raised slab with Asra's remains. She remembered the determined expressions of the sixteen warrior-magicians who had led him in here. They must have sealed themselves in, knowing they would never see the light again. Believing it was necessary to keep Asra confined and the world above them safe. And it had worked. For hundreds of years. Until another power-crazed sorcerer had experimented with blood magic and death magic and breached the line between life and death, rending the world again.

"It's coming," Guise said, breaking through her grim thoughts. "This way. There's only one. Stand with me, mristrian," he added, moving a few paces backwards.

Yvonne turned, standing shoulder-to-shoulder with Guise. He was facing outside the light, head tilted slightly, listening, the spelled edge of his sword gleaming in the light. Even as she tried to listen, and watch, into the dark, she noted a fine tremor in the light on the blade.

Guise was not at his best. Still recovering from the torture that Hiram had inflicted upon him.

"So, a dervish?" she said, keeping her voice calm, hoping Guise was too focused on the hidden predator to hear her thumping heart. "Well, if anyone can stop it, we can."

"So very true, mristrian," he said, a hint of a smile in the words, the light on his blade steadying.

There was no time for anything else as the creature spilled out of the dark. Far too many legs, all of them far too long and with far too many knees, or elbows, twisting in too many directions for Yvonne to count.

Guise held his ground. Of course he did. His blade flared with the spells written into it, slicing through the thread-like limbs that snaked towards him, not one of them getting past him to Yvonne.

She was frozen on the spot, throat closed, lump too big to swallow, seeing a thing of nightmares pouring towards her. As many limbs as Guise cut through, there seemed to be more taking their place.

Beyond the limbs, partly hidden in the dark, was a larger blot of dark, that must be the creature's body. Even as the limbs were moving, twisting all around in the rapid, random movements that had given the creature its name, the centre mass was still.

Yvonne pulled a pair of fire spells from her pouch and twisted them around her knife. Her new knife. She threw the knife, activating the spells when they reached the mass of limbs.

The creature shifted, moved, throwing up several of its limbs to catch the fire spells, the power and the magic fire burning out, sending acrid smoke into the air.

It could defend itself. Ice worked down her spine even as she drew another pair of fire spells, grabbing the knife from her boot. She needed to work out how to get the spells through the creature's defence. How how how? Guise was holding his own. Something else. Distraction. She drew another concussive spell, throwing that first, activating it so that it blew the reaching tentacles to one side, then threw the knife, activating the fire spells as the knife reached the creature, bursting into unnatural, brilliant magic fire.

The creature did not make a sound, the silence almost as terrifying as a scream would be, pulling back, wrapping its many limbs around its body. Protecting itself.

"It will put the fire out," Guise said, taking a step forward, slicing through another reaching leg. "More, mristrian."

"Yes." She pulled more fire spells from her pouch. "Knife," she said, and Guise put one in her hand, hilt first, without looking back.

The second wave of fire spells bit into the tangled mass of black, but not deeply enough. As Guise moved forward, a pair of limbs snaked out, trying to snag his legs. He swept his sword down, severing the ends, and kept going.

"More fire, mristrian," he said, even as he reached the tight knot of black and the many limbs that were writhing and twitching. Trying to protect the creature's body. Trying to put out the fire. Smother it, Yvonne realised.

She had another few fire spells, pulling them out of her pouch, following Guise towards the creature.

"Here, put these on your blade," she suggested. He did not look around, reaching one hand back to take the strips of parchment, winding them around the blade, then thrusting it forward, deep between the twisting limbs.

Yvonne activated the spells as his sword bit into the creature, then scrambled back, with Guise, as the knot of black erupted into white-hot flame.

She shielded her head with her arms as bits of burning creature rained down on her, the stench almost the worst smell she had ever encountered, moving further back, towards the stone slab, as the rain of fire continued.

"Definitely dead now," Guise said, satisfaction lacing his voice. "Well done, mristrian. That was a very old one. Very hard to kill."

"Indeed," Yvonne said, and coughed, smoke and stench choking her. She pulled a cleansing spell from her pouch and doused herself. Marginally better, although the air was still thick and foul with the rotten bits of corpse.

"Time to leave, I think," Guise said, putting his sword away.

"How? The tunnel is gone."

"If you will hold on to me, I think I can manage a way out," Guise told her, moving back towards the spilled soil and smouldering corpse.

"Really? Could you have done that sooner?" Yvonne asked, narrowing her eyes as she followed him. "Could Jaalam?"

"It requires a great deal of energy and focus," he told her. "Do you remember the finance offices in Willowton?"

She blinked, the apparent change in subject taking her by surprise, then she did remember. They had been following someone. And he had picked her up, gathered magic around him, and taken them down three storeys with barely a draft of wind and no jarring at the bottom.

"It's like that, only the other way," he told her.

"Do I need to hold on to you?" she asked.

"It would be easier," he said. Before she quite knew what he was doing, he had gathered her up, as carefully and effortlessly as he had in Willowton. She opened her mouth, then caught sight of the expression on his face. He was staring up at the ceiling with a single-minded focus she had rarely seen on his face.

All around she could feel the crackle of power gathering. Goblins so rarely used their magic in the open, it was easy to forget just how powerful they were. And Guise was no exception. He preferred to deal in secrets, trade information and use his sword.

Underneath the exquisite tailoring was a sorcerer, one who had been trained in using his power as long as he had been trained in using his sword.

He spoke a series of words she did not quite catch and the world around them shifted, power gathering, then lifting her from the ground, propelling them forward, straight into the earth above them.

The earth parted, shoved aside by an invisible force, and they rose, quickly at first, then more slowly, until the welcome scent and feel of fresh air caught her face.

They were on the surface. Only just.

Guise took one step to the side, staggered, and dropped her with no grace, falling to his knees.

Yvonne hit the ground with a thump that shook the breath out of her, and rolled to her knees, coughing as the fresh air bit into her smoke-filled lungs, eyes streaming with reaction.

"Guise, are you alright?" she managed to say between coughs.

"Yes," he said, lying on his back, staring up at the sky.

"What happened?" a familiar voice asked, face appearing beside her. Pieris.

"Dervish," she answered, and had to cough again.

"Here." Pieris handed her a flask. "It's Jaalam's, so it's probably not water," he warned, before she took a sip.

Forewarned, she took a cautious sip of the liquid and coughed again as it burned down her throat, warmth seeping through.

"Dervish?" Jaalam asked, surprise clear. "How did you get free? Those things usually take a dozen warriors to overcome."

"One Hunar and a goblin," Guise told his cousin, voice rasping. He was still lying on his back.

"Did it sting you?" Jaalam asked, surprise fading into concern.

"No."

"Then why are you lying down?"

"He used magic to get us out of the cavern," Yvonne said, managing to get to her feet, still holding Jaalam's flask. She staggered the few paces over to Guise's side, and held out the flask. "Here. It's Jaalam's."

"A rare honour," Guise said, taking the flask. She could not tell if he was being serious or not. He sat up, movement slow, and took a far less careful drink than she had, showing no reaction as the liquid burned down his throat. "Better. Thank you." He handed the flask up to Jaalam.

"Thank you," Yvonne said, crouching beside Guise, legs protesting the effort. "I think you saved my life again."

"I am not keeping score," he answered, gold shading into his eyes, mouth tilting in unexpected mischief.

"Of course not," she agreed, biting her lip to hide a smile.

"The ground's moving. We need to go," Jaalam said, urgency in his voice. He half-lifted Guise to his feet, and began dragging his cousin away from the bare soil, Yvonne and Pieris following.

Looking back, she saw a great patch of disturbed earth, where Will must have dug his tunnel, and where Guise had brought them out of the underground.

Jaalam hissed something at her, urging her forward, and she struggled to keep pace with him, moving among the ancient trees, away from the disturbed earth.

They seemed to pass some invisible boundary, a trace of old magic against her skin, and no sooner were they past that than there was an ominous rumbling sound beneath them, the ground shaking under their feet so that she staggered again, trying to keep her balance. When the shaking was over, there was a deep depression in the ground stretching out ahead of them where she guessed the barrow had been. She could all too easily imagine the scene underground, the soil and stone collapsed on the bodies, and had to lock her knees to remain upright. They had narrowly escaped being buried alive.

"I think it was waiting for us to leave," Pieris said. "Taking the stones must have triggered some kind of defence."

"That, or the dervish," Yvonne said, voice dry.

"I think it was the stones," Pieris said, quite serious.

It seemed utterly fanciful, and yet it also seemed to fit. And Yvonne knew that Pieris had studied history, and magic history, far more extensively than she ever would. She looked across at him and raised a brow. "Were such defences common?"

His eyes lit with enthusiasm and she almost regretted her question, sensing that he could talk about this subject for some time to come. Before he could answer, Jaalam put a hand on his shoulder.

"Perhaps this is a conversation to be had with some food and wine? We were down there for ."

Yvonne frowned, trying to work out what Jaalam meant, only to have her attention called away by the sound of rapid footsteps.

They all came on alert, even Guise, although he could barely stand, moving so that they were all back-to-back, weapons ready, she and Pieris with spells in their hands, waiting for whatever new enemy was approaching them.

Out of the darkness around them came two familiar figures. Brea and Thort.

They stopped, staring open-mouthed, as Yvonne and her companions put away their weapons.

"Where have you been?" Brea asked. "We've been searching everywhere for the past two days. None of us could get into the barrow."

"Two days?" Yvonne exchanged glances with Guise, and then turned her attention to Jaalam. "How did you know? It did not feel like two days."

"I have an excellent sense of time," Jaalam told her. It might have sounded like the arrogant brag of a spoiled Karoan'shae lord, but there was no bravado, just a simple statement of fact.

"He really does," Pieris said. "It can be incredibly irritating at times." They exchanged a look which told Yvonne that there was a very funny, and very personal, story that they were both remembering, and that neither of them wished to share.

"Where have you been?" Brea asked again.

"Among the dead," Guise answered. "We will tell you all about it, but we should move away from here. The ground has already collapsed once."

Brea did not look all that happy at having to wait more for answers, but followed Guise's suggestion, frown deepening as Jaalam moved to assist his cousin again. As they walked away from the depression in the ground, the ground shook again, the hollow growing so that some of the mature trees toppled over, roots lifting into the air, earth falling around them like rain.

Yvonne ran, not caring if she seemed cowardly, only realising after she had been running for a short while that everyone else was running with her. Putting as much distance between themselves and the shaking ground as possible, stumbling frequently as the ground shook again under their feet.

They reached the edge of what had been a copse of mature trees but which now looked like a great giant had walked through it, uprooting trees here and there, leaving them on their sides. Enough of the trees were still standing to form a protective ring around the barrow, so that it was hidden from casual view.

"I am really looking forward to the tale behind this," Brea said, a certain look in her eye suggesting that she may get violent if she did not get an explanation soon.

Chapter Twenty-Four

Lita, Ulla and Sarra met them on the way back to the farm house. Apparently those left behind on the surface had all been out searching for most of the day, and everyone wanted answers.

Thort refused to let anybody speak until they were back in the kitchen, glasses of wine in front of them. He moved to the worktop, gathering ingredients for a meal. Yvonne followed his movements with keen interest, realising just how hungry she was. Over a day spent underground. No wonder she was hungry. For the first time she could remember, Brea went to help her husband, gathering foodstuffs together, bringing a plate of cheese and bread and biscuits and fruit to the table while Thort continued to prepare a cooked meal.

"Don't look so surprised," Brea said. "I know how to use a knife."

Yvonne laughed, some bit of tension easing, and took a sip of the wine. Guise put a plate in front of her, piled with food. Sometime during the walk back from the barrow, he had taken a healing spell and looked far better. Able to stand on his own, at least. She thanked him.

Brea managed to wait until they had all had something to eat before she lifted a brow, the hard glint back in her eyes, fingers drumming on the tabletop.

"Well?" she asked. "You are all covered in earth. I'm assuming that the barrow let you in, and out again."

"Not quite," Yvonne said. She looked across at Guise, Pieris and Jaalam. "Shall I start?"

"Yes," Guise said, tension across his shoulders, "and do explain, as well, how you knew about the gems."

"Gems?" Lita asked, eyes brightening.

"In good time," Jaalam said, putting his hand across Pieris', stopping him from reaching for the sapphire which Pieris had hidden somewhere about his person.

Yvonne looked around the table. Some of her closest friends. People that she would trust with her life. And new allies.

"I told you before about the rending. That there's a tear in the world," she began. She saw Brea's frown, but the warrior held her peace, letting Yvonne speak. "When Hiram attacked the Stone Walls, or maybe before then, he broke something, or woke something up. That caused this tear. But, a very long time ago, before the Hundred existed, someone else did the same thing, or close to it. There was a battle here and a sorcerer was defeated at great cost."

"Four thousand dead," Pieris murmured, repeating the words from the stone slab.

"Yes. But that was not all. The remains of the sorcerer who started this are in the barrow. And he was guarded. Sixteen warrior-magicians. Somehow they managed to stop him, but thought he was dangerous even when they had killed him. When I read the inscription on his tomb I got a glimpse into the past and saw them. They had the sorcerer in chains. They were all still alive when they went into the barrow with him." Yvonne paused, her voice hoarse, and took a sip of wine, looking up around the table to find everybody, even Thort, watching her with intense, unwavering focus. No one interrupted. No one spoke, waiting for her to continue.

"When Guise and I went into the barrow, Will was already there."

"Will?" Lita asked, brow creasing. "The one who escaped the Stone Walls?"

"Yes," Yvonne confirmed, and shifted her gaze slightly to Ulla, sitting next to Lita. The assassin stared back at her, face expressionless. "He was looking for something," Yvonne added, and saw Ulla's jaw tense slightly.

"Did he find it?" Ulla asked, her voice flat.

"He thinks he did," Yvonne told her, holding her eyes, then glancing at Pieris. "When I saw the past, two of the warrior-magicians wore pendants. One a ruby. One a sapphire. Will took the ruby with him. I think he believes it will protect him."

"And you don't think so?" Brea asked, eyes sharp. Trust Brea to pick up on a potential enemy's weakness.

"No," Yvonne shook her head slightly. "I don't know how the man was stopped before. But I don't think they used the gems to do it."

Pieris reached into his pocket and laid the cloth package on the table, unfolding it to reveal the great sapphire and its untarnished chain.

"Oh, a memory stone," Thort said, standing behind Brea, brows lifting. "I haven't seen one of those for a long time."

"Memory stone?" Yvonne and Pieris asked at the same time.

"You tell them, I'll watch the food," Brea said, getting up and moving to the stove. "What?" she said, as everyone's eyes followed her. "I can tell when something is burning."

"The Karoan'shae have a few of these stones. Only a very few. They were used to store information," Thort explained, moving over to the stove to stand next to Brea, touching her hand with his, meeting her eyes. Whatever she saw in his face settled her anger and she left him to the cooking, coming back to the table.

"Information," Pieris repeated, drawing the word out in a reverential tone, staring at the gem on the table. "I've never heard of this technique. I wonder ..."

"Please be careful," Yvonne interrupted, before he could start experimenting. "The magicians I met were very powerful. They would have guarded their secrets."

"But, if Will has one of these stones, won't it have the information he wants?" Lita asked. As sharp with possible secrets as Brea was with weaknesses.

"I don't think so," Yvonne said, frowning. "I am not sure why, though."

"Something you saw or heard in the past, perhaps?" Guise suggested. He had been sitting quietly beside her, absorbing the conversation.

"I think they overwhelmed him with force," Yvonne said slowly, remembering the battlefield with the dead and the dying. The sixteen grim-faced warrior-magicians. "Four thousand dead. That's a lot. And he was not alone. There were creatures with him."

"You keep saying him. Who?" Brea asked. Wanting to know her enemy. Even a dead one.

"He was called Asra," Yvonne said, a chill working its way across her skin as she said his name. "And he was full of the same dark that Hiram had in him."

"Dark?" Brea prompted.

"There is something wrong with the world," Pieris reminded her, repeating Yvonne's earlier words. "Whatever Hiram did. Whatever Asra did. It's woken the dark."

It sounded as fanciful as the idea that the barrow would destroy itself when the stones were taken out of it, and yet no one laughed.

Silence fell across the table, broken by the soft sounds of Thort stirring whatever was in the pot he was tending.

"I don't understand," Lita said, deep crease between her brows. "Was Will looking for the dark? Or something to protect him?"

"He has been running a long time," Ulla said unexpectedly, not looking at anyone else.

"Most of his life, I suspect," Yvonne said, staring at Ulla's downturned face. "He ran from the Stone Walls," she added, turning to Lita. "I think if he had wanted to join with the dark, he would have waited for Hiram. I think Will has known about Hiram's, er, tastes for some time."

"And didn't warn anyone?" Lita asked, brows lifting.

An excellent question.

"He wouldn't," Ulla said, a shade of something in her voice that sounded like bitterness. "He looks after himself first. Always has."

Ulla looked up and met Guise's eyes across the table. Yvonne's brows lifted. There was a depth of anger, and hurt, in Ulla's face she had not expected. The three of them had a tangled and twisted past. Ulla, and Guise, and Will. Not for the first time, Yvonne wondered if the mess that had almost cost Ulla her blades had involved not just Guise but also Will. And the pair of them, the spoiled lord of the Karoan'shae and the assassin, had kept Will's name out of whatever tales they had told.

"Guise?" Brea asked, sending a very direct look across the table along with the firm tone of her voice.

"He can't tell you," Ulla said, one shoulder lifting in what might have been a careless shrug, except her body was too stiff.

"He made a promise. A long time ago," Yvonne said, voice soft.

"Promises," Brea said, nose wrinkling in distaste. "Well, we'll have to find out another way."

Yvonne found another unexpected laugh inside and let it out.

"And did you really say a dervish?" Jaalam asked.

"Where? Where is it? Has it spawned?" Brea asked, snapping from exasperated friend to warrior in a heartbeat.

"Dead," Guise told her. "An old one. Nesting near the barrow. No sign or trace of anything else."

"Cursed things," Brea said, settling back in her chair. "Once they're in the ground it takes years to get them out. You're sure there was only one?"

"As sure as I can be."

"I think Sarra might have noticed a dervish nest," Yvonne pointed out.

The old soldier, who had been sitting quietly and just observing everything around her, tilted her head. "No sign of anything underground," she confirmed. "Mind you, I didn't go near the barrow that often. Once in a while to check on things."

"You would have noticed a dervish," Yvonne said, quite certain, shivering as she remembered the far-too-many legs. The creatures liked to sting their prey, paralysing them, and then eat them alive. She shivered again.

"Food's ready," Thort announced.

Thort's cooking was excellent and, somehow, he had known to prepare a meal with no meat in it, a mix of pan-fried potatoes, other vegetables and eggs. Similar to a dish that Yvonne had cooked not that long ago, but tasting quite different thanks to the mix of spices Thort had used.

They ate in silence until every scrap was gone, although Yvonne could sense the questions brewing around the table. There were too many mysteries.

"What now?" Sarra asked when every plate was empty. She was looking at Yvonne.

Everyone else turned their attention to Yvonne and she felt the weight of those stares, and the expectation, pressing on her shoulders, pinning her to the chair.

"I'm not sure right now," she admitted, words slow. It wasn't just expectation pinning her to the chair. She was exhausted. "I'd like to know what Will is up to. But we also need to find Hiram and stop him." There, that felt right, the unfurling of a Hunar's promise a familiar sensation in her chest. "And we need to see if we can learn more about Asra and these stones," she added, tilting her head towards Pieris and the sapphire that he had stowed away again.

"You don't want to find Victor's killer?" Sarra asked, face pinched.

"Finding the killer won't help us," Yvonne answered, voice sharper than it needed to be. "He was killed by an assassin. I want to find the paymaster."

Sarra stared back at her, expression hard, lips closed.

"Most people seem to think I killed him," Yvonne added, not sure what she wanted from Sarra. More than that hard stare.

"No," Sarra contradicted, mouth in a flat line, then sighed. "Alright. Yes. A lot of people in the court think you killed him. There was so much evidence."

"We should ask Hiram about the King's death," Yvonne said, and had to cover her mouth as a huge yawn took her over.

"So, finding Hiram," Brea said, eyes sharpening. "I think we all have some questions for him."

"Do you know where he might be?" Thort asked Guise.

Yvonne's breath caught. A question that no one else had asked. And, now it had been spoken, something so obvious.

Guise lifted his head slightly, the ends of his too-short hair jagged points of dark in the candle-lit room. He held Thort's eyes for a moment, and all Yvonne could see was the tension in his jaw, the grip he had on the wine glass in front of him. It was not an easy question. To ask, or to answer.

"In the Royal City," Guise said at length, lifting his glass and finishing his wine in one swallow. "I think. I'm not sure."

"Something he said. Or didn't say," Yvonne speculated.

"He was not there all the time. The gaps were long enough for him to travel back and forth to the city. I think," Guise added, staring at his empty glass, cheeks darker than normal. Yvonne wanted to reach across and take his hand, holding herself still. He was not telling them everything.

"The Royal City. Well, I've always wondered how to break into it without being seen," Brea said.

From anyone else, it might have been humour, but from Brea, it was the simple truth.

"Perhaps Sarra can tell us," Thort suggested, and the goblin couple turned their bright, enquiring eyes to the soldier.

Sarra stared back at them, sides of her mouth pulled down, every year she carried showing on her face. A loyal soldier. Yvonne could imagine the conflict inside. Torn between her loyalty to the crown, and her wish to see Hiram found, and stopped.

"I know a way," Sarra said, after a long pause, words dragged out of her.

Not quite the truth. There was more than one way out. There must be more than one way in. Still, guided by a former member of the King's Guard, they should be able to get into the city undetected. There would be other challenges, Yvonne knew. Staying hidden. Finding Hiram. Perhaps even convincing the court that she had not killed the King. They could wait. They had the beginnings of a plan. Everything else could wait until morning.

Chapter Twenty-Five

Yvonne was amused to find that Sarra's way back into the city was very similar to the way she had left it, using one of the patches of false wall, this one with a slightly wider gap between the stones, letting the horses pass through more easily. It was the sort of route that Yvonne would expect a member of the King's Guard to know but, remembering the smugglers she had narrowly avoided on her way out of the city, she could not help wondering how many people were aware of the routes, and how close a watch the King's Guard, and the city's law keepers, kept on them.

"There's a building along here we can use," Ulla said, catching Yvonne's attention. The assassin had simply announced, the morning they set off from the farm, that she would find them a place to stay in the city. She had not said much more during the entire journey, taking part in the watches and chores as necessary, otherwise keeping herself apart from the others.

Yvonne did not know the assassin well, and yet had the sense that there was something troubling her. Perhaps being back in the Royal City. Perhaps the thought of tracking down a blood sorcerer. That alone was enough to make any sane person pause.

"Big enough for all of us and the horses?" Brea asked, curious.

"Yes," Ulla said, and took the lead of the group, not saying anything more.

The city was quiet in the small hours of the morning, almost all law-abiding folk in their beds. It wasn't quite early enough for the bakers to be going to work, and too late for the taverns to still be open. The only people they were likely to encounter were those up to no good. Or law keepers, keeping watch. Hopefully, they would be keeping each other busy.

Even so, Yvonne winced slightly at the noise they made. A large group, with horses laden with supplies. Anyone seeing them would definitely remember. They had stopped for more supplies on the way here, not knowing if they would be able to use the market places.

A few paces ahead, Ulla stopped in the shadows of a large, low building. Yvonne blinked in surprise, realising where they were. At one of the warehouses scattered through the city where wine and spirit merchants left their stock to mature in wooden barrels.

"What about the guards?" Brea asked, voicing Yvonne's immediate concern. Wines and spirits were valuable, and no merchant would leave their stock unguarded.

"We bought them long ago," Ulla said, dismissing Brea's concern with a wave of her hand. At the corner of her eye, Yvonne saw Sarra's brows lift to her hairline, and suspected that a careful review of warehouse guards would be carried out as soon as the soldier could manage it. "I'll just let them know we need the building for a few nights." The assassin then opened the nearest door, big enough for horses to pass through, and stepped inside.

Brea and Thort exchanged glances, then cast their gaze around their surroundings. The streets were deserted. But they should not linger.

A short time later, the door opened again and Ulla appeared, waving them in.

"There's no one else here," she said.

Inside the warehouse was surprisingly clean and dry, rows of barrels stretching into the distance, the horses' hooves echoing against the stone floor as Ulla led them along the aisle to the other end of the warehouse where there was what looked like an office, set apart from the rest of the building by half-height wooden walls, a desk and chair tucked inside, and a large, open space, part of it separated by another half-height row of wooden panels, straw on the floor, buckets of water ready and waiting, along with empty buckets that would take horse feed.

"The merchants let their caravans stay here sometimes," Ulla told them, leading her horse into the makeshift stable.

Yvonne shook her head slightly as she led Baldur into the stable. There was more than enough room for all the horses in the set-aside space. She could well imagine a merchant being happy to have his caravans stay here. There would be no fares from the city's taverns, and there would be someone to watch over his goods overnight, too.

On the other side of the warehouse from the stables was another half-height row of wooden panels, this time providing space for a row of travel cots. It was dry, and the blankets were clean. It was far from the worst place she had ever slept.

In the gap between the stables and sleeping area, the floor was bare. It probably held the wagons, when there were any, ready to leave through the high and wide doors at this end of the warehouse, heavy beams holding the doors shut for the moment. There was also a smaller door, big enough for a single horse to pass through, to one side.

"Apart from the door we came through and these ones, are there any other doors? Windows? Places where we could get in or out?" Brea asked.

"There's one side entrance, into the alley between this and the next building," Ulla answered, pointing down the rows of barrels. "You'll need a key to get in or out that way. The merchants like their goods to be secure," she added, a hint of humour in her voice which made Yvonne wonder how often Ulla had tried to find another way in or out of the building.

"Where do these doors lead?" Thort asked, tilting his head to the wagon doors.

"Another street, like the one we came in from. Mostly houses."

"Busy during the day, then," Brea concluded, exchanging glances with Thort. Uneasy. Too many potential eyes around them to make coming and going easy.

"We'll get disguises," Lita suggested. She had taken part in all the chores of the journey without complaint, but had noticeably brightened up as they came into the city. Back in her natural habitat, Yvonne thought. Buildings all around her, and the potential for intrigue behind every door.

"Disguises?" Jaalam's brows lifted. "You think you can hide me?"

"Well, perhaps not you," Lita said, eyes dulling a little. "But we can make Yvonne look less like, well, Yvonne."

"That's true," Yvonne said, remembering the change they had made in Willowton. Swapping clothes and adjusting their hairstyles had made them almost unrecognisable. She wondered what Lita would manage with a little more time, and resources, to work with.

"Very few people know me here," Pieris said, as Lita turned a speculating look to him. "As long as I can hide the Firebird's symbol, I should be able to pass."

"We'll need to stay in during daylight," Brea said, encompassing all the goblins in her gesture.

"I don't need a disguise," Ulla said, nose wrinkling in disgust. "No one sees me unless I want them to."

"Oh," Lita said, in a small voice that was quite unlike her normal manner, prompting a sympathetic echo in Yvonne's chest. The cloth merchant, so confident and capable in her normal life, was far out of place here.

"I will need a disguise," Sarra said, unexpectedly, nose wrinkling with as much disgust as Ulla had shown. "My face is too well known. And, no, I'm not staying indoors," she added, before Brea could voice that suggestion. "This is my city. I know it."

"Very well," Brea answered, with a clear lack of enthusiasm.

"We should get settled," Thort suggested, moving towards the sleeping area. A practical suggestion.

"We need some rest, too, and to set up watch," Brea added, following her husband.

Yvonne watched them work together, competent and familiar with each other, rearranging the sleeping area so that everyone had a space, then repurposing one of the cots into a make-shift larder, setting out their supplies, discussing how they were going to keep everyone fed and watered over their stay, however long it was.

As the beds were set up, most of the others drifted to their places, settling down for a few hours' rest. Even Lita had learned the benefit of sleeping when she could.

Yvonne paused for a moment near the rows of stacked barrels, feeling the depth of the warehouse behind her, the quiet of the space. She had a feeling that there would not be much quiet in the days to come.

Lita somehow persuaded Sarra to dye her hair an improbable shade of deep red, which softened the soldier's features and made her almost unrecognisable. Even more remarkable, she persuaded the former King's Guard into a dress, plain and serviceable but utterly different from anything Sarra had worn before, if her expression was anything to go by.

And the cloth merchant's efforts did not stop there. She had also found a dress for Yvonne, one that would allow her to keep her long dagger and spell pouch with her. With a simple cloth around her head, Lita declared that Yvonne looked quite different.

Yvonne was impressed, and said so. The changes made both her and Sarra into other people, who should be able to pass under the noses of the city's soldiers and law keepers. Lita ducked her head away from the compliment, colour high. The journey had been hard on her, Yvonne knew, more so than the rest of them, who were used to rough travel. And now the cloth merchant had been able to prove her worth.

Suitably disguised, they set off into the city the next day, Lita going with Sarra, Pieris and Yvonne heading in a different direction, leaving the goblins behind, Brea's commands ringing in their ears. They were to seek out information, listen and observe, and not get into trouble.

Yvonne exchanged a glance with Pieris as they made their way towards the nearest market place, unexpected mischief bubbling inside her. Brea's tone had reminded her of one she had used with Mariah and Joel when they were younger.

"I know," Pieris answered her, eyes bright with mischief of his own. "I cannot remember the last time I was so thoroughly put in my place."

There was no time to talk as they turned into a busier street, slowing their pace to mix with the rest of the people going about their business.

The normal bustle of a city morning was muted. Here and there Yvonne saw flashes of purple cloth, the colour of mourning in the Valland kingdom. Word of the King's death had spread. Of course it had. And his people were mourning.

Victor had been a good king, as far as kings went. Not perfect. But generally good. And his subjects had grown used to peace and prosperity under his rule.

The throne was vacant now. Victor had never named an heir, and there was no obvious or clear succession.

As she made her way around the market with Pieris, exchanging some of Guise's seemingly never-ending supply of coins for some fruit and fresh bread, she listened to the conversations around her. This market was mostly full of housekeepers and other household servants from some of the grander houses not far away. They were busy telling each other the snippets of conversation they had overheard from their masters and mistresses. How some of the nobility were vying for position, trying to claim a connection to the Valland family. Trying to prove their claim on the throne.

And also, from only one or two people, how the Palace was oddly quiet. The doors might look open, yet no one had gone in, or come out, for a day or two. The servants who would usually be out running errands were absent. The soldiers were still guarding the gates. Everything looked normal.

Except it wasn't.

A prickle ran across Yvonne's skin. They had come to the city looking for Hiram, expecting to find him hiding in the outskirts. What if they had misjudged him? What if he had settled himself into the strongest fortification this kingdom possessed?

It fit. It fit with his ambition. With his arrogance.

She and Pieris made their way along the nearest street of craftsmen. In this part of the city, close to some of the finer houses but not a particularly wealthy area, the trades focused on basic goods. Pottery. Clothing. The sorts of things that household servants might need.

The street had a similar atmosphere to the market. Subdued. People were worried, and tense, eyeing her and Pieris with suspicion at strange faces, rather than anticipation of a new customer.

There were fewer people than at the market, so she stopped at the apothecary's shop to buy a common mix of herbs used for everything from headaches to fever. It would explain their presence in the street, and the herbs would be useful. The apothecary was polite, but not warm, and they left the street, making their way back to the warehouse, making sure to take a long route so that no one could follow them.

Lita and Sarra were back just ahead of them, both grim-faced, with similar news. The city was in mourning. Everyone was on edge, wondering what would happen now that the King was dead.

And there was something wrong at the palace.

They were sitting on some of the spare cots, which Brea and Thort had arranged into a circle, in the space outside the sleeping area, the goblins tense at being indoors, the humans worn down from their day so far.

Yvonne tugged the headscarf off. She was used to the feel of cloth around her neck, not on her head, and it was irritating. She ran a hand through her hair, pushing it back from her face, and was conscious of a strong wish to lean against Guise, sitting next to her on the cot. She resisted the impulse. He would not object. The hesitation was all in her mind. The bond between them was a private matter, and she did not want to share it. Not even among this group.

And there was work to do.

There was no word of Hiram on the street. That was expected. But they all had a good idea, now, of where he might be.

They needed to get into the palace.

"It's impossible," Brea said, sounding more defeated than Yvonne could ever remember. "There was a prize, set by one of the previous stars, for anyone who could breach the palace and bring back proof. No one got it."

"Not impossible," Yvonne said, glancing at Ulla. "There were at least two assassins in the palace last time I was there."

"One person, maybe," Ulla said. She had ignored the arrangement of cots, settling instead on top of a pile of barrels, mostly hidden by shadows. "Not a group this size."

"There must be other ways in," Lita said, scowling at the assassin. "I'm sure the nobility don't use the front door all the time."

"I can try sending one of the birds in," Pieris suggested, grimacing slightly. "Although I haven't tried them in buildings before now."

"A bird would get noticed," Jaalam pointed out.

Nobility.

Yvonne's mind snagged on Lita's words. The cloth merchant was right, of course. The king's favoured friends and confidants would have another way in and out of the palace. A way that would have to be reasonably easy to access. She could not imagine the wealthy of the Royal City, or Circleside, creeping along the same tunnel that she and Ulla had used to escape.

"You have an idea?" Pieris asked.

The group's attention shifted to her.

"Remember Priss?" she asked them. Most of the people around her had been in the Forbidden Lands. "I met her the day the King died. She and her parents were in the market. Her mother offered me a favour of my choosing."

She turned to Guise and lifted a brow. He had a much better understanding of the mindset of nobility than she did.

"She might owe you her daughter's life," Guise said, "but she is also a loyal subject."

"Priss?" Sarra's brows lifted. "Priscilla? Hannah Grace's daughter, from Circleside? Your goblin is right, Lady Grace wouldn't let you in the palace."

"But?" Yvonne prompted, sensing something more.

"She might let us both in," Sarra concluded, unhappy. Doubtless it felt like a betrayal.

"Then we should ask her," Yvonne said, lifting her chin, holding Sarra's eyes. The soldier nodded once, lips pressed together. Not happy, but understanding the need for action.

Chapter Twenty-Six

The house reminded Yvonne strongly of the beautiful home that Lita had in Willowton, except this one was easily twice the size, and with three times the area of land and gardens. It was difficult to make out much detail in the dead of night. Well-tended gardens. Beautifully maintained fences. Candles set in glass jars around the house's main entrance, giving just enough light for someone to walk up or down the outside steps.

There were lights in the house, too. A few rooms lit, curtains open. The building was far enough away from its neighbours that no one could see in. There did not seem to be many people inside, which suited Yvonne's purposes.

She and Sarra rode their horses through the side gate, both of them covered in cloaks. There had been no time to change Sarra's hair back to its normal grey, but they were both in their own clothes again, easily recognised.

There was no one at the gate to challenge them, or on the narrow road that led to the house's back entrance. The road itself was well-maintained and it seemed a long distance from the gate to the house. Yvonne kept expecting a cry of alarm or discovery as they rode towards the house and heard nothing, fingers clenching around her sword hilt from time to time. The nobility that lived here had not kept their position by being careless.

At length, they reached the rear of the house and the servants' entrance.

Sarra had insisted, and Yvonne had not argued. They were in Circleside, and every householder within this small town wielded immense power and influence that stretched beyond Valland's borders. Some mean-spirited residents in the Royal City would say that the real power in Valland lay in this small collection of houses and their beautifully-maintained grounds.

Whatever the truth, the householders also held the secret of accessing the Valland palace without being seen. And it was that secret that had drawn Yvonne and Sarra to the house, and to the servants' door.

They left their horses in the shadows of the house, hidden in the darkness, and made their way to the servants' door, lit by a single candle in a niche on the wall.

As they approached, the door opened and a familiar figure came out, unexpected and welcome, blonde hair lifting as she ran full tilt into Yvonne and favoured her with a fierce hug.

"See," Priss said, turning back to the house, voice stern, "I told you she'd be here."

A taller figure appeared in the open doorway, dressed in similar clothes to Yvonne. A serviceable shirt and hard-wearing trousers. A far cry from the patched and repaired robes of a Circle Mage that she had first seen him wearing.

"You did indeed," Ewan answered, coming outside into the night. "Hunar Yvonne, it's good to see you again. Sarra. You look … well."

"You've changed your hair, Sarra. I like it," Priss said, voice bright.

Yvonne lifted a brow. They were standing outside the limited reach of the single candle by the door. Neither Priss nor Ewan, with their limited human sight, should be able to see Sarra's hair.

"We've been practising a spell to enhance our sight," Ewan said, perhaps reading the questions on Yvonne's face.

"In case I'm ever taken again," Priss said, in a matter-of-fact voice. "At least I will be able to see where I am."

"It is a very useful spell," Yvonne agreed, heart constricting. Priss was bright and brave, and thinking of things that no child her age should have to consider.

"And I have promised to teach her some other spells to leave a trail, so that, if she ever does get lost, we will be able to find her," Ewan added.

Yvonne could not read his expression in the dark, but his voice seemed forced, trying to match the matter-of-fact tone that Priss had managed.

"Ewan doesn't want me to think I might be taken again," Priss confided to Yvonne, slipping her smaller hand into Yvonne's fingers. "And I don't want to be taken. But it's better to be prepared, don't you think?"

Yvonne remembered Priss' mother staring after her daughter, and better understood the mixture of fear and pride.

"It's definitely helpful to be prepared. But, if you ever think you are going to be taken, you must try and tell someone. Ewan. Or me. Or anyone you trust."

"Of course," Priss said, and Yvonne had to be content with that.

"Have you come to see her parents?" Ewan asked.

"Yes," Sarra answered. "Although, I didn't realise you'd be here. You might know what we need."

"You should come and see Mama and Papa anyway," Priss said. "I told them you would be here and they're waiting for you."

Yvonne exchanged glances with Sarra, abruptly wary. Priss was delighted to see them, welcoming them to her home. Yvonne imagined that Priss' parents might have quite a different view.

Sarra's face, features difficult to make out in the poor light, was set in hard lines under her artificially red hair. Not liking the situation, either.

There was little choice, though. Even if there was danger, Yvonne did not want to insult Priss' parents by turning and leaving. So, she allowed Priss to lead the way into the house, Sarra behind her, Ewan bringing up the rear, the young Mage keeping pace with them as they went through the house.

The house was every bit as beautiful and grand on the inside as it had seemed from the outside, and reminded Yvonne even more forcibly of Lita's home with the startling simplicity of the interior. Everything was made with exquisite care, the floors spotlessly clean, the walls painted white, the better to display the paintings and tapestries that hung there.

It was also surprisingly empty. A house of this size, as well-maintained as it was, would need a considerable amount of effort to keep. But there were no servants. No other members of the household. Not even the shadows of one as they walked. Yvonne looked across at Sarra and saw the soldier taking stock of their surroundings, too, keeping her hands away from her weapons, but alert and aware.

"That's Great Grandfather Norman," Priss commented as they were passing one of the paintings. A burly man in armour standing with an enemy soldier under one boot. "He was not a nice man," she added, heading past the painting without looking up.

Yvonne cast a glance around the hallway with the portraits displayed. A family gathering. Priss' family, over the years. A lot of them seemed to be wearing weapons, and were portrayed defeating their enemies. Yvonne could not help wondering how many of them Priss would also describe as not nice and had to bite her lip to hide a smile. She might be young, but she was not stupid. Not at all.

Priss went through the next pair of doors that had been left standing open, and led them into a room that was almost homely by contrast to the rest of the house. Several different chairs were scattered around a magnificent fireplace that Baldur could easily have fit into, rugs laid across the wooden floor to deaden the sound of feet, the paintings on the walls replaced by tapestries showing idyllic country scenes.

In front of the fireplace, Priss' parents were waiting. Dressed for an evening at home, in the understated and expensive elegance that Yvonne remembered from her first meeting with them. Lord and Lady Grace. Hannah and Edmond, Yvonne remembered. They were standing together, holding hands, facing their visitors with square shoulders and lifted chins.

Anxious, not sure what to expect. Doubtless wondering if they were welcoming a king-killer into their house.

Yvonne took a step to the side and waited for Sarra to come alongside her.

The couple's eyes widened, shock setting aside the apprehension.

"Sarra. We did not expect you," Priss' mother said.

"Lady Grace," Sarra answered, making a brief bow. A gesture of civility. "I would not be here if it was not important."

"Of course," the lady answered, exchanging glances with her husband.

"We just did not expect to see you in such company," the lord said, chin up, face set. For a moment Yvonne saw a resemblance between him and Great Grandfather Norman. It was fleeting, though. This man, however powerful he was, had never had to fight his enemies with swords. "You know what she is accused of?"

"I told you," Priss said, before Sarra could speak, "Yvonne didn't do it. Hunar don't just kill people."

"We heard you," her father said, not taking his eyes off his visitors.

"But you didn't believe your daughter," Yvonne said. It was not what she had wanted to say. Not the polite thing to say. Not at all. But something about his dismissal of Priss' assurance had reminded her of the coolness from her own parents, through her own childhood. "Is she in the habit of lying?"

"No," Edmond answered, a hint of colour coming to his face. "In fact, quite the opposite. She is almost unbearably truthful."

"So, why do you think she is lying now? About this matter?"

"We found it hard to believe," his wife answered. "We have met with the General. He told us the evidence they had. That he had seen you."

"That is true. There is a lot of evidence. And the General did see me in the room where Victor died," Yvonne answered. "I got there too late. He was already dead. Someone used one of my knives to do it."

"The Hunar did not kill the King," Sarra told them, as blunt as ever. "Only an idiot would leave so much evidence behind. And the Hunar is not an idiot."

Yvonne had an unexpected impulse to laugh, wondering what descriptive words Sarra might use, if idiot was not accurate.

The couple in front of them exchanged glances, seemed to come to a mutual decision, and nodded, in unison.

"Come and sit down, then, and tell us how we might help you," Hannah said, moving to one of the chairs near the fire, her husband taking the one next to her.

Yvonne's brows lifted. That had seemed far too easy an acceptance. And then her eyes narrowed. They knew their daughter. They had shown themselves to be warm and affectionate parents. They had not known who to believe. The General, whose integrity was beyond doubt. Or their daughter, who told the truth with no finesse.

"I didn't get a chance to speak to the General," Yvonne said, taking a chair with a view of one of the sets of doors. Sarra's chair had a view of the other doors. "There was no time."

"Did you manage to escape on your own?" Priss asked, sitting forward on her chair. Her feet didn't touch the ground. She did not seem to care, confident and assured in her home. It might be an odd question, except that this girl had been kidnapped and held against her will.

"No. I had some help. A friend of Guise's," Yvonne answered, thinking that friend was too simple a word for whatever history Ulla and Guise had. But it was the best she could think of.

"Is Guise here too?" Priss asked, eyes bright. "And Grayling? And Sephenamin? And the others?"

"Guise is in the city," Yvonne told her, aware of the parents listening. "Grayling and Sephenamin are at home. In Fir Tree Crossing." As she spoke the words an unexpected wave of longing came over her. It felt like months since she had seen her children, or since she had passed an ordinary day tending to chores, or shared tea and biscuits with Grayling, exchanging news. She missed it. The house, and the town, might not feel like home to her, but some of her favourite people in the world were there, and she wanted to get back there and see them all again.

"So, who did kill Victor?" Edmond wanted to know.

"An assassin from Abar al Endell," Yvonne answered.

The lord and lady exchanged glances again, lips pressed together.

"We haven't had assassins at work here for some time," the lady said, face pale.

Yvonne was not as certain about that. The assassins were famed for being able to disappear in plain sight. But she understood the unease.

"That's not the worst of it," Sarra told the lady. "We think Hiram is in the palace. Hiding."

"Hiram?" the lady blinked. Whatever she had been imagining, that had taken her by surprise.

"He did not kill Victor himself," Yvonne added, "but he almost certainly organised it. I met the agent he used to try and arrange contracts with the assassins' school." She did not think it would be helpful to share the information that the contracts had been against the Hundred. Neither she nor Guise had been able to read the agent's notes, but Hiram was the most obvious suspect in arranging Victor's death.

Both Hannah and Edmond were pale now, and holding hands again, knuckles white.

"He has been in court as long as I can remember," Edmond said.

"I've never particularly liked him," Hannah added, glancing across to Priss, "and Priss has never trusted him."

"He was all wrong," Priss answered.

"I did not see it soon enough," Ewan said, in a soft voice, almost as if he hoped no one would hear him.

"But you did notice something," Yvonne told him. "And Priss is exceptionally gifted."

"We're so glad you came to teach her," Hannah said, managing a smile for Ewan.

Ewan blushed, ducking his head. Not used to the attention, perhaps. And, from the little she had seen of Hiram, Yvonne guessed he was also not used to praise.

Yvonne could imagine he was relieved, too. Out of the palace, away from Hiram's influence, and whatever had happened once the King was dead. Tutoring the daughter of one of the oldest families in Circleside was a worthy occupation for a junior Circle Mage. Extremely respectable, and not something that anyone in the palace would argue with. He had been safe here, and Priss had been learning.

"We need to look for Hiram," Sarra said, bringing the conversation back to their purpose.

Priss' parents stared back at her, both pale.

"You need to get into the palace," Edmond said. "And you don't want to be seen."

"Yes," Sarra confirmed.

"Isn't there a soldiers' entrance?" Hannah asked, brow wrinkling in confusion.

"There is. It's guarded. And very well known," Sarra told them.

"But there is another way in. One that a handful of people know about. And which we could use," Yvonne said.

"It's a secret," Edmond said, voice flat, mouth tight. "Trusted to a few families. No one has ever revealed it."

Outside their bloodlines, Yvonne knew. The secret was trusted to the nobility. Not to be used by ordinary folk. Ordinary folk like her or Sarra.

She clamped her mouth shut against saying anything unwise. Such as that previous Valland kings had been killed by the very people they trusted. That history showed that the nobility were, of all the people in the kingdom, the most likely to try and take over the throne.

"Victor is dead," Sarra reminded them, "and his killer is inside the palace."

"We've been listening in the city," Yvonne added. "The palace is closed. No one has been seen going in or coming out for some days."

"Hiram means to take the throne," Sarra added, face pinched, looking every one of her years. "We mean to stop him."

"How?" Hannah asked, lips thin, still gripping her husband's hand.

"We have resources," Yvonne answered, aware of the Firebird's symbol glowing at her shoulder.

Edmond and Hannah exchanged another of those glances, seeming to speak without words.

"They will help you," Priss said, with absolute confidence. "You just need to wait for them to make their minds up."

Yvonne bit her lip to hide a smile. A force to be reckoned with, indeed.

"You know you can't come with us?" Yvonne asked.

"I know," Priss said, nose wrinkling in disgust. "You'll say I'm too young. Which isn't fair."

"I will say that you are untrained, still," Yvonne said.

"Oh. That makes sense. I suppose. Will you take Ewan, though?"

Yvonne nodded. "If he will come with us."

"We can tell Ewan the way, and he can guide you. He knows the palace," Edmond said, a trace of relief in his voice. Yvonne could almost read the thoughts in his mind. Passing on the secret to someone almost in his household was far, far better than passing it to someone accused of killing their King.

"I know the palace, too. Far better than Ewan, I'd say. You can tell us both," Sarra said, as blunt as ever. "If you don't want to tell the Hunar, I'm sure she'll step outside."

"Gladly," Yvonne agreed, rising to her feet. "Perhaps Priss can introduce me to some more of her ancestors?"

"She doesn't like many of them," Priss' mother said, mouth curving in a fond smile as she looked at her daughter.

"They were a bad lot," Priss said, absolutely serious, and got out of the chair, heading for the door. "But if you want us out of the way, I suppose it's as good an idea as any."

Biting her lip again to hide another smile, Yvonne followed Priss out to the hallway and its array of splendid paintings.

Somewhat to her surprise, Priss did tell her some more of the stories behind the paintings, making Yvonne laugh with her descriptions of some of the more bloodthirsty of her ancestors. As well as Great Grandfather Norman, there were various uncles who had liked hunting four-legged things for sport, something which Priss clearly disagreed with. And a Great-Great-Great Grandfather, also Norman, who had killed one of the rivals for his wife's hand in marriage, and insisted on displaying the corpse at their wedding feast.

"Papa is the best of them," Priss said, coming to the end of the row. "Although I don't think any of this lot would approve of him. He much prefers reading and talking to fighting."

"He seems a good man," Yvonne agreed, feeling that something was needed. And he did. She looked back along the row of mighty warriors and killers and understood, a little more, why Edmond had turned out as he had. A form of rebellion against his family's history.

"Mama is much better with a sword than he is," Priss added. "She promised to teach me from my next birthday."

Yvonne felt her mouth curve in a smile again. She could imagine Hannah striking that bargain with her daughter. And could imagine that Priss had reminded her mother of the promise almost every day since then. Her smile faded as she thought about Priss' words earlier. About being prepared if she was ever taken again.

"Don't look sad, Hunar Yvonne," Priss said, tucking her hand into Yvonne's. "I need to learn how to use a sword as well as magic, so I can be a Hunar, too, when I'm old enough. I know I'm too young just now. And not trained yet."

"A Hunar's life is not easy," Yvonne heard herself saying. "It's a lot of travelling. A lot of hard work."

"Dundac didn't travel," Priss objected.

"No. Not much, I suppose. But he still did when he needed to," Yvonne said, heart constricting at the memories of Dundac. Laughing, full of life. And too still, discarded in an abandoned keep in the Forbidden Lands, drawn into a scheme for power and control by someone he would have trusted.

A quiet sound elsewhere in the house drew her attention. Almost like the gentle closing of a door. Someone who didn't want to be heard. Not yet. And she became aware, as she had been earlier, of how empty the house was.

"Priss, is there anyone else in the house?" she asked.

"No. Mama sent the servants away with my brothers when I told her you were coming. There's just the horses and George, who works in the stables. But he's in the stables."

"I think there's someone in the house," Yvonne told her, putting a hand on Priss' shoulder and guiding her back towards the sitting room.

"There shouldn't be," Priss said, turning her head to look, as if she could see whoever it was.

Yvonne opened the doors to the sitting room, attracting startled glances from the occupants.

"There's someone upstairs," she told them, as blunt as Sarra. "Priss said there should be no one else in the house?"

"I sent everyone away," Hannah said, rising to her feet, tension clear. "We have a property further out in the hills."

"It's fortified. Easier to guard," Edmond added. "We were going to join them. After."

After they had seen the Hunar.

"Are your horses ready?" Sarra asked.

"Of course," Hannah answered.

"Then let's go," the soldier prompted. "I have what we need," she told Yvonne.

"Shouldn't we stay, find out who's here?" Edmond asked.

"No," Yvonne said, before anyone else could speak. "Ewan, are you ready to travel?"

"Yes. Everything is in the stables," Ewan said.

Sounds over their heads drew everyone's attention. Footfalls on the floor above. More than one. And no longer trying to be quiet.

"Quickest way to the stables?" Yvonne asked.

"This way," Hannah said, starting forward.

"Let me lead," Sarra said, overtaking the lady. "Stay behind me and direct."

"Very well," the lady said.

Edmond took hold of Priss' hand and followed his wife. Yvonne waved Ewan ahead of her and brought up the rear, murmuring a spell to enhance her senses as she walked. She could still hear the footsteps overhead. Whoever it was hadn't found the stairs down to this floor yet. Or was planning something else.

"Do you have any weapons?" she asked Ewan, keeping her voice low, hoping that Priss wouldn't hear.

"Not with me. I have a sling and stones in my pack," he answered, turning to face her and almost tripping over his feet.

"Keep moving," she told him as Sarra led them down a narrow set of stairs. Servants' stairs, taking them down to the kitchens and the servants' entrance where their horses waited.

The footsteps overhead were gone. The silence was worse. She did not know where they were now.

She followed the others through the kitchens, unnaturally still and silent. Even the fire was banked, almost out. It was to the lord and lady's credit that they had sent their household away, out of danger. With their other children. But they had kept themselves and Priss here. Trusting their daughter. Waiting for the Hunar.

As Sarra reached the outside door, the footsteps sounded again. Rapid. Not far behind them.

"Get your horses," Yvonne called ahead. Baldur would come at her call, and she was sure Sarra's horse would, too.

Even as she stepped out into the night, a blur of movement behind drew her attention. A group of armed men were coming into the kitchen through another doorway. A half dozen at least. Perhaps more.

She slammed the outside door shut behind her, looking for something to bar the door. It was made of thick wood, muffling the sound of the oncoming attackers. She put her back to it, looking around. There was nothing there. But the door did have a metal handle and lock.

She pulled a fire spell out of her pouch and murmured a modification, setting the strip of parchment across the handle. The metal melted under the spell, setting into a single lump, holding the door closed.

"That won't hold them for long," she said, finding Ewan beside her, staring at the door handle. "Come on."

The others were ahead of them, running in a line, heading for the stable block. Yvonne called for Baldur even as Sarra whistled for her horse. The pair of horses came running out of the dark.

Breaking glass above them drew her attention and she looked up to find one of the upper windows of the house shattered, and an archer in the space.

"Go get your sling," she told Ewan, giving his shoulder a shove. He ran faster, outpacing the others. "Archer above," she called ahead, warning the others.

Hannah gave a cry of alarm, and ran faster.

Yvonne pulled a concussive spell from her pouch, twisting it around her knife, waiting for the first arrow.

Even with her sight and senses enhanced, she almost missed the blot of dark as the archer let their arrow fly. Yvonne threw her knife as hard as she could, and activated the concussive spell, knocking the arrow off target. Barely.

By then the others had reached the stables and Baldur was alongside her.

She pulled herself into his saddle from a full run, something which she had only practised before now, and wheeled him around, facing back towards the house. The archer was still in the window. Waiting for the others to come out of the stables. He had the advantage of height. And she caught a glimpse of a full quiver at his shoulder. He had more than enough arrows for all of them.

The sound of splintering wood told her that the attackers in the kitchen had found something to try and break the door.

"Is it safe to come out?" Sarra asked. She was sitting on her horse, just inside the shelter of the stable block, ducking her head to see through the doorway.

"No. Ewan, have you got your sling?"

"Here," Ewan answered.

Yvonne backed Baldur towards the stables, not wanting to take her eyes off the archer in the window.

"Come and stand here," she said, pointing to the side of her horse that was sheltered from the archer. "Can you hit that window from here?"

"I should be able to," he answered, a slight tremor in his voice suggesting he was not quite sure.

"Close by is fine. Here, wrap this around one of the stones." She handed him a concussive spell.

The stone flew, straight and true, and Yvonne activated the spell just before it reached the window, the impact knocking the archer back into the room, shattering the remaining glass in the window.

"Go now," she told the others, holding Baldur still. "You, too," she added to Ewan. The archer was gone. Temporarily, but gone for now. The rest of the attackers were not. They were working their way through the kitchen door, the sounds of wood splintering accompanied by swearing.

Hoof beats behind her and low-voiced commands from Sarra, urging the family to press their horses on, reassured her that they were underway. Not out of danger yet. Not by a long way. But it would be harder for attackers on foot to capture riders. And harder for the archer to aim the further away they got.

She twisted concussive and fire spells together, murmuring another change to the fire spells, and held them between her fingers, waiting.

Baldur moved sideways at her command and she risked a glance over her shoulder, seeing the group disappearing into the house's grounds, Ewan on a small, pale-coloured pony bringing up the rear.

When she turned back towards the house, the attackers were running towards her. She threw the first twist of spells in front of her, then another, the concussive spell knocking the attackers back, the fire rising in a wall of flame, blocking their path.

Baldur whirled at her command, galloping after the others, ears back. He did not like to run from a fight. But Yvonne knew there were more important things than winning every battle. There was a family to keep safe, who had no doubt been targeted because of their connection to her.

The others were through the boundary gate when she caught up with them, joined now by an elderly man with weathered skin, his horse calm under him. George, who worked in the stables, Yvonne guessed, turning her attention to the gate. It was a great metal structure set into a high stone wall. Yvonne pulled one of her last fire spells out of her pouch and set it onto the metal, melting the lock closed behind them. It would not hold the followers for long. But it would delay them a little.

Then they were off again, Ewan's pony struggling to keep up with the others. An elderly creature, Yvonne could not imagine that it had been required to do much running, and certainly not keep up with warhorses, Sarra's mount snorting with impatience as she held it back to a steady canter.

They were moving through the lesser-used streets of Circleside, the streets that the servants and tradespeople used, snaking behind other properties just as large and well-maintained as the one they had left. The other properties were all populated, though, many of them with armed guards visible at doorways, doubtless wondering what had happened at the neighbouring house.

"Riders ahead," Sarra called, voice sharp. Worried, Yvonne thought. And no wonder. They had pursuers on foot behind them. The last thing they needed was mounted attackers in front of them, too.

She looked ahead, enhanced sight showing her the small group heading towards them, and almost laughed with relief.

"Friends," she told Sarra, realising that the warrior couldn't make out the details in the dark.

"What are they doing here?" Sarra demanded a moment later, recognising the riders heading towards them.

By that time the rest of Yvonne's group had seen them. Brea, Thort, Guise, Jaalam, Pieris and Lita, riding along the road to meet them, Lita tucked into the middle of the group. The only one missing was Ulla, but Yvonne suspected that the assassin was close by.

"It seems you've been having fun without us," Brea said when they were in earshot. She sounded cheerful. "How many are following?"

"Half a dozen. Maybe more."

"A poor showing," Brea commented.

"Barely worth the effort," Thort agreed.

"They managed to get into the house without raising alarm," Yvonne said, voice dry, seeing the worried looks that Priss' parents were exchanging.

"Ah. Perhaps they are worth the effort." From the keen looks from all the goblins, they were eager to find out.

Chapter Twenty-Seven

"There's an archer," Yvonne warned, as Brea, Thort, Guise and Jaalam flowed past her, heading back towards the house.

"Are any of you hurt?" Pieris asked, calling her attention as the goblins rode on into the night.

"What?" Edmond asked, startled, then shook his head. "No. Just shaken. We were not expecting anyone to attack our home."

"We should keep riding," Sarra said.

"What about the goblins?" Hannah asked.

"They'll catch us up," Sarra said, waving the lord and lady on up the road. "Particularly if we're travelling at the pony's pace," she added, sending a glare at the elderly pony Ewan was riding.

"Prince has served me well," Ewan said, patting the pony's neck, chin lifting in defence of his mount.

"I don't doubt it," Sarra said, riding alongside him for a moment. "Probably since you were barely able to walk."

"Will you lead us?" Yvonne asked, before Ewan could come to the defence of his pony again. Sarra lifted a brow, but pressed her horse forward, to the head of the group.

"You must be the Circle Mage, Ewan," Pieris said, taking Sarra's place. "It's good to meet you. I'm Pieris. This is Lita."

"Pieris? Another Hunar?" Ewan asked, eyes widening. Some people could pass their entire lives without meeting a single Hunar. And Ewan had now met three.

"Even so."

"Priss talks about you from time to time," Ewan said as they continued to ride forward.

"She talks about everything," Pieris said in a dry tone that drew a smile from Yvonne.

Yvonne held Baldur back for a moment. With Sarra in front and Pieris riding close to Ewan and Lita, she took the rear of the group, trusting Baldur to find his way forward while she kept glancing back over her shoulder, mentally reviewing the spells she had left. She had taken to carrying more concussive spells and fire spells. Even so, the supply was limited.

They rode out of Circleside, passing by the last boundary and into open country, rolling hills all around them, the road still well-maintained, rising into the hills. Yvonne had never travelled this route, relying on her memory of the maps she had studied to provide some guidance. This road continued for a while, winding through the higher ground then falling into a valley beyond, full of fertile land and farms. The Grace family were not the only ones with property along this route. It would be an obvious spot for any would-be attackers to hunt them.

As they rode higher into the hills, she turned back once more and drew Baldur to a halt involuntarily, staring beyond Circleside.

"What is it?" Pieris asked, then gave a low, shocked sound. That stopped the rest of the group as well, everyone turning to look at the Royal City.

The Royal City was burning. A great swathe of it was engulfed in flames that lit the night sky, carrying clearly to their spot, high on the hill above Circleside.

"Is that the palace?" Ewan asked, trying to see.

"No," Yvonne said, voice flat, able to see better thanks to the spell still working on her senses. "It's the warehouse district. Where we were staying."

"Just as well we followed you, then," Pieris said, face grim, lit by the distant flames when Yvonne turned to him. "Don't ask how she knew, but Ulla said we should come after you. Then she vanished."

"Of course she did," Yvonne said, almost under her breath. She knew that the assassin was no enemy. She was not precisely a friend, though.

"We need to go," Sarra said. She had brought her horse back along the road, stopping beside Baldur.

"Not yet. We need to see the family safe. Make sure there are no more attackers lurking. Then we can go," Yvonne said.

Sarra opened her mouth, looking like she wanted to argue, then shut her jaw with an audible snap, inclining her head once in agreement, turning her horse and riding back to the head of the group, urging everyone to follow her.

As they rode on, Yvonne could hear murmurs between the lord and lady. Too quiet for her to hear what they had to say, but the tone was clear. Dismay. Alarm. Distress.

Yvonne focused on her breathing for a while, trying to settle the uneasy feeling in her stomach. Someone had set a fire in the Royal City big enough to be seen even from this distance. Someone had known where she, and the rest of her group, had been staying. The spot between her shoulder blades prickled with unease. She had thought they were hunting Hiram. It seemed he might be hunting them.

Priss was quiet, riding alongside the stable hand. Too quiet. Yvonne wanted to offer some words of reassurance but nothing came to mind. Priss had experienced too much, and had seen too much, to be fooled, or soothed, by a word or two. And Yvonne would not lie to her, even to help her be calm.

They had been riding for a while when hoofbeats behind them drew her attention. Baldur stopped at her word, turning to face whoever was coming along the road behind them. He was showing no signs of alarm and as the riders drew near, Yvonne saw why. The four goblins were catching up to them. Not a scratch or injury among them.

"They won't be following us," Brea said briefly, riding past with Thort to take over the lead of the group. Jaalam moved to ride with Pieris, leaving Guise to ride with Yvonne.

Turning Baldur to move alongside Guise's horse was familiar from their journeys together, the horses moving in even strides, well matched.

"Someone found the warehouse," Guise commented. The goblins all had far better night sight than she did, even with the spell.

"Pieris said Ulla warned you."

"She did. I did not ask how she knew."

"Of course not," Yvonne said, an unexpected laugh bursting out. "Because then you would have to return the favour."

"How well you understand me, mristrian," Guise said.

She glanced across to find his eyes bright with green mischief, smile playing at his mouth. She shook her head slightly, turning her attention back to the night around them.

"Are we taking Priss home?" he asked a moment later.

"To the family's other property, yes."

"Do you think there will be more armed men waiting?" Guise asked, sounding almost as eager as Brea for a fight. She found herself smiling, tension easing into lightness. He sounded completely himself, as if there had been no capture and no torture.

"Probably," Yvonne said, and then sighed. "It's the obvious place to look."

"I wonder how Hiram knew to attack Priss' house?" Guise speculated. He might be talking with her, but he was also paying attention to their surroundings.

"I was wondering that, too. I would guess that he had Ewan followed."

"The young Mage. That pony is older than I am," Guise added.

"He probably cannot afford better," Yvonne told him, an edge to her voice. Guise had never wanted for anything. Not anything material, anyway. Clothes. Horses. Weapons. An endless supply of coins. He placed almost no value in objects, and as much as he might like his horse, if he needed to, he knew he could get another one, equally well bred and well trained. From time to time he seemed to forget that not everyone had those resources.

"Mristrian," he said. She glanced across to find he had put his hand on his heart and made a small bow. A gesture of contrition.

The sharpness faded and she felt guilty for a moment. Guise might not value material things. He did value the few friendships he had. And the bond he had with her. She opened her mouth, thinking she might try to explain her irritation, and closed it again. She was not sure she could explain it herself.

"We'll get him a new horse soon enough," she said instead. Not what she had meant to say, either. Now that the words were out, they felt right. After all, Elinor had supplied the younger Yvonne with her weapons and horse, albeit as a gift from Renard.

Her mind snagged on that, and she wondered if Renard had any horses in training that might suit another apprentice Hunar. Ewan would need a horse now. And Priss, if she was still determined to follow a Hunar's path, would need one in a few years, too. She had a feeling that Ewan would be far more impressed with a new horse than Priss would.

Guise made a soft sound that might have been a cut-off laugh. "He is coming with us, then?"

"Perhaps. I haven't asked him yet."

Guise made another of those soft sounds but said nothing.

They rode in silence as the first signs of dawn appeared on the horizon, showing the valley ahead of them in growing light as they made their way down the gently sloping sides.

Yvonne's heart cracked, seeing the valley in the morning light. It was so peaceful, full of farms with crops growing, healthy livestock grazing. A place of prosperity and abundance. Like the Sisters' valley had been. It was a place that looked like no harm would ever happen here. That there could be no possibility of war, or conflict. No armed men waiting to meet them.

Except that her mind knew that was not the case, and she rode forward with Guise, leaving Pieris and Jaalam to bring up the rear of the group, passing Priss and exchanging a solemn nod. Priss was pale-faced, dark smudges under her eyes. This had been another great adventure until now. But she was a child. Exhausted. At the end of her strength.

Even as Yvonne thought that, Edmond moved alongside his daughter's horse and pulled her out of her saddle, settling her in front of him, one arm around her waist. She could fall asleep safely there.

Brea, Thort and Sarra were riding in a row at the front of the group, Sarra's horse breathing heavily. It had been a long day.

"It's the second road to the right," Brea said, as Yvonne and Guise settled in behind the front three. "Everyone should still be asleep."

"Any sign of trouble?" Yvonne asked. The land around them looked peaceful and quiet in the early dawn. But Brea had sharper senses, and a warrior's way of looking at the world.

"There have been horses along here recently," Sarra said, unexpectedly. "Not just the family's."

"Similar size of hoof prints, and riding in straight lines," Thort added.

"Soldiers," Yvonne concluded, a knot tightening in her stomach. Here, in the Valland kingdom, that was likely to mean the king's soldiers. Well-trained.

She had fought them before, in their search for the person responsible for the fall of the Stone Walls. An ambush out of nowhere, the soldiers out of uniform, presenting a formidable opposition for the much larger group she had been part of. Even then, there had been serious injuries among the Rangers.

"I can't fight Valland soldiers," Sarra said, voice tight.

"If they are Valland soldiers, you should not have to," Brea agreed. Too easily, Yvonne thought, and wondered if Sarra realised that she was riding between an exceptionally dangerous couple. From the sideways glance Sarra sent to Brea, it seemed the soldier was well aware of her situation.

They were still riding at a fair pace, all the horses breathing hard now, even Baldur, his neck dark with sweat.

"Is it much further?" Yvonne asked.

"Just past this next copse of trees," Brea said, not looking back.

There was a stand of trees near the road, screening whatever was behind them from view. Yvonne spared a long, hard look at the trees. An ideal place for an ambush.

No one attacked them. No arrows flew. No cries of alarm sounded. Just the low call of a bird.

"That's a signal," Sarra said, reluctance clear. "We use it."

Valland soldiers, that meant.

"Arms," Brea called over her shoulder. She and Thort moved a fraction ahead, pushing Sarra behind them. Guise and Yvonne separated a little, letting Sarra's horse come back between them as the soldier reined in a little. Not wanting to be first. Not wanting to ride with hostile intent towards her own comrades.

"What is it?" Hannah called from the back of the group.

"Soldiers ahead," Sarra told her, riding behind Yvonne. "Waiting for us."

"Soldiers?" Hannah's voice rose in pitch. Surprise. Fear.

"Stay back a little," Brea recommended, sparing a glance over her shoulder, her grey skin shadowed in the morning light, eyes bright green with prominent flecks of red. "Let us see what they want."

They were round the other side of the trees now, fields of livestock to either side, the cows lifting their heads, mildly curious as the riders passed them.

And in front of them was a farmhouse. Modest, for this family. About the same size as her own house, Yvonne was amused to see, with a collection of outbuildings around it.

And a group of soldiers in front of it, on foot, waiting in formation.

No possibility to avoid the soldiers. No chance that they had not been seen.

"Our people," Hannah said, voice catching.

"Our sons," Edmond said.

Yvonne lifted her chin slightly, looking at the soldiers. There was no sign of battle that she could see. No sign of blood. Just the company of soldiers, waiting in front of the farmhouse.

And a familiar figure in their midst, striding out from the others to meet them. The General.

She remembered her first sight of him, on the front steps of the Valland palace, straight-backed and tight-faced, unyielding. She knew him better now. Loyal to his core, he would have been shattered by Victor's death. And determined to see his King's killer brought to justice.

He had seen her next to Victor's corpse. Had found her knife, and the Firebird's symbol, and the scrap of cloth as he had been meant to. He had doubtless also seen the torn shirt left in her hotel room.

More than enough evidence to condemn her.

And yet, he was coming towards them with his hands free, palms held out to either side, showing he had no weapons to hand.

And none of the soldiers behind him had their weapons drawn, either.

"Disarm," Brea commanded, putting her own sword away, reading the same cues that Yvonne was. The General was not here to fight them. Not yet.

Chapter Twenty-Eight

"Hunar Yvonne," the General called when they were still several paces apart. Just within bow-shot for a skilled archer. "I would speak with you."

He stopped in the middle of the road that led between the fields, out of easy reach of his soldiers, and out of easy reach of the goblins, too.

Brea drew the group to a halt and stayed on her horse, watching the humans in front of her. Yvonne guessed that there would still be red in her eyes.

Yvonne slid off Baldur's back, wincing slightly as she met the ground. It felt like it had been a long day and she was stiff and sore. The cots in the warehouse had provided a place to sleep but had been about as comfortable as sleeping on the ground.

"What are you doing?" Brea asked, brow lifting as Yvonne paused by her shoulder.

"I am going to talk with him. It would be good if you stayed here, I think."

Brea made a low sound of disgust that did not need any translation.

Yvonne walked forward to meet the General, somehow not surprised to find Guise with her. He was walking half a pace behind her until she paused and turned slightly, waiting for him to catch up.

"The General looks older," she commented when they were side-by-side, walking again.

"He is not in good health. There is something unclean around him. Do not touch him, mristrian." She found herself thinking, again, that he was back to his normal self. Arrogant. Assured. At another time, she might have questioned the command in his tone. For now, she was grateful for the warning.

"I won't," she promised, and came to a halt a few paces away from the General.

He did not look well. He looked as if he had aged a decade at least in the time since Yvonne had seen him, face full of lines, purple smudges under his eyes, which were bloodshot. Lips pressed together in a firm line to try and disguise the faint tremor that ran through him.

Yvonne murmured another spell to enhance her sight and almost recoiled at what she saw. Guise's nose had picked up the scent of something corrupt. It was far worse than that.

With her sight enhanced, there were dark coils of corruption twisting around the General, spreading from his heart along his arms, to his fingers. Oddly, the corruption had not reached his head. Not yet.

"You did not kill Victor," the General said, voice shaking. He was trying to speak with his jaw clenched shut.

Yvonne met his eyes and her breath left her. He knew. Whatever it was that had been done. Whatever foulness had been put into him. He knew. He was standing, as proud and straight as he could.

"There's something you want to tell me," she said, voice soft. There was a pain in her chest. A lifetime of loyal service to the Valland crown, and this man did not deserve this end. To see his King slaughtered, and to have forbidden magic done to him.

"He's in the palace. He's trying to assert control. I've got most of the soldiers out on patrols and training exercises," the General said, words coming in odd fits and starts as he fought to contain whatever it was that had a hold of him. "I couldn't stop him. He turned up when we were laying Victor out for burial. Insisted that there would be no funeral. Not yet. And he's been taking over. Bit by bit."

"What did he do to you?" she asked.

"I can't tell you. Doesn't matter. Dead walking," the General said, his whole body trembling with effort. Not just effort. The corruption was coiling around him more tightly, blackened strands sneaking their way up his neck. "Death magic on my bones. Can't kill me. Can't knock me out."

Yvonne tilted her head, remembering the men who had been looking after Guise. She had knocked them out, left them tied up. Hiram must have found them.

"Sarra," the General called, the sudden strength in his voice startling her. The words carried through the still morning, back to the soldiers behind him, and to the group in front of him. "I nominate you as my successor and command that all loyal soldiers follow you as they have followed me."

"What are you talking about, old fool?" Sarra demanded.

Rather than answering, the General drew the long dagger from his belt and drew it across his exposed throat, slicing it open.

Yvonne heard a cry of denial and anguish behind her, then she was lifted bodily off her feet, Guise's arm around her, dragging her out of the way of the spray of blood. Black, corrupted blood that flew into the air, seeding it with a stench she would never forget.

The General's body was on the ground, lifeless, before the foul blood had fallen.

Yvonne and Guise had their swords drawn, not moving from their spot.

There was a cry of outrage from somewhere among the waiting soldiers, and movement forward.

"Stay back," Yvonne called. They did not listen. "Sarra, tell them to stay back. There might be a death curse."

Sarra did not question her, simply yelled sharp orders across Yvonne and Guise's heads, which had the effect of stilling the soldiers.

Yvonne held her ground, focus on the General's body and the corrupted blood seeping into the ground.

Nothing.

No movement.

"No death curse?" she asked, brows lifting.

"He took his own life," Guise answered. He was still on alert beside her, ready to act.

"He did." Yvonne reached into her spell pouch and pulled out cleansing spells, casting them on the ground to deal with the corrupted blood nearest to her, then taking a step forward, closer to the General's body. Nothing. The body remained still.

The trail of corruption had faded, the worst of it bled out on the ground around them.

She scattered more cleansing spells, moving around the body with slow, careful steps, Guise with her, until the ground all around the General was clean, free of taint.

"There's still death magic in his bones," she observed, putting her sword away and crouching, still a few paces from the body, to see better. "It's not active."

"How did he know killing himself would stop the death curse?" Pieris asked. He was standing a few paces away, Sarra beside him. The soldier's face was showing her age again, eyes bright with unshed tears.

"Hiram may have told him," Yvonne speculated. "It would be quite like him. Giving the General a choice."

"He would have hated it," Sarra said, her voice hoarse. "He believed that we should face up to our fears, not run away from them into death."

A common enough view, Yvonne thought. And Hiram had lived among the Valland court long enough to know the General's views. And had given him this choice that was no choice at all.

"We can't leave him like this," she told Sarra, glancing up again. "The death magic could still be dangerous."

"You need to burn him," Sarra said, voice cracking. "I know. Let me tell them first," she said, moving in a careful half-circle around the body then continuing on to the soldiers waiting.

"He almost lost," Yvonne murmured, looking back at the General, his face twisted in fury. The corruption had been snaking around his neck, perilously close to taking him over completely. Only his iron will had held it back long enough to allow him to act. To take his own life. Stop the death curse.

"Hiram is more dangerous than I thought," Pieris commented, crouching at the General's other side. "This is incredibly subtle work," he explained.

Yvonne enhanced her sight again, and saw what Pieris meant. As well as the corruption, lines of spellworking crossed the General's body. Intricate work. Done by the hand of a master, with no hesitation.

"He's been practising," she said, lip curling. "The last magic I saw from him wasn't this finely detailed."

"He's been drinking goblin blood," Pieris said absently, still focused on the spells. Then he stiffened slightly, and tilted his head. "Sorry, Guise."

"It's true," Guise answered. He was standing nearby, hands tucked behind his back, his shortened hair lifting slightly in the morning breeze. "He will be enjoying this time. He will feel more powerful. And then he will go mad." His tone was matter-of-fact, as if it was quite unimportant, and he was wearing one of the masks he was so good at.

"He was already quite mad," Yvonne said, rising to her feet and moving to stand next to Guise. Not touching, just there.

Footsteps behind them signalled Sarra's return. The soldier came to stand nearby, at parade rest.

"Do what you must," she said. She had been crying. And doubtless would shed more tears later. The General had been a fixture at the Valland court for a very long time.

Yvonne exchanged glances with Pieris and they each drew fire spells from their pouches, Yvonne twisting some cleansing spells in with hers. They laid the spells on the body, stepped back and activated them.

The General's body vanished into fire and ash, tiny glowing embers floating in the breeze, gradually falling to earth, leaving only a patch of scorched ground where the body had been. Another victim of Hiram's ambition.

Even with the ashes of one of Valland's most prominent citizens on the road, and soldiers around their property, Priss' parents were gracious hosts. Sarra wanted to return to the city at once. Hannah insisted that everyone must stay for refreshments and some rest. It would take the better part of the day to get back to the city, she reasoned, and they had been travelling all night.

Sarra was grudging in her acceptance. Understanding the need for some rest. Not liking it.

With Baldur resting, supplied with water and feed, Yvonne settled on a stone bench that backed against the house's wall, welcoming the short respite and the morning sun. Guise was settled beside her, both of them watching Sarra as she moved among the soldiers, checking equipment, exchanging a word or two here and there. She knew most of them, Yvonne realised, and wondered how many of the men that the General had brought were King's Guard.

"She's Regent now," Guise said, breaking the comfortable silence.

"What?"

"If there's no ruler on the throne, the leader of the armies is Regent."

"So, the General was the Regent? And now Sarra is." Yvonne turned back to look at Sarra. "She won't like that."

"I don't imagine she does."

"But she will do her duty," Yvonne said, blowing out a breath and shifting her position slightly so that her shoulder rested against Guise's. Even though it was daylight, and public, no one was paying them much attention. He was solid and real, helping her stay in the here and now. "He'll be waiting for us," she said.

"I know."

"Any ideas?"

"Cut off his head and burn him," Guise said promptly.

Yvonne spluttered a laugh. It was not funny, and yet it was. "So easily?"

"I have faith in you, mristrian."

She looked up to find his eyes tinged with gold, warmth spreading through her at his expression. He was not someone who trusted easily.

Running footsteps drew her attention away. Priss was coming around the side of the house at full tilt. Yvonne straightened away from Guise, waiting for Priss.

"Mama says you'll be leaving soon."

"That's right."

"Will you stop the bad man?"

"That is my intent," Yvonne confirmed.

"Good," Priss said, standing still and serious in front of her in the morning sun.

"You need to stay here. With your parents. And keep learning."

Priss stared back at her, the serious expression on her face, then nodded once.

"Stay safe," Priss answered, coming forward to favour Yvonne with another fierce hug, her eyes bright when she pulled back. She nodded to Sarra, who was on her way over, before turning and running back along the side of the house.

"Is she really going to be a Hunar when she's grown?" Sarra asked.

"Perhaps," Yvonne said, then laughed softly. "I think she will do whatever she sets her mind to."

"I'm not sure the world is quite ready for Priss as Hunar," Sarra commented.

Yvonne laughed again. She could see Priss in her mind's eye, grown up and as confident as ever, still speaking bluntly and truthfully to everyone she met. The world might not be ready. Priss would not care.

"We're ready to leave," Sarra said. "There's a shorter route across country. We'll be at the city before dark."

"Then let's go," Yvonne said, standing, Guise with her. Ready to face their enemy.

Chapter Twenty-Nine

The Royal City was surrounded by open land, giving almost no cover for anyone trying to approach. They came within sight of its walls as the sun was fading, and Pieris and Yvonne cast invisibility spells over the group, the effort making Yvonne light-headed as she settled on Baldur's back. The soldiers were uncomfortable with the deception, even if they understood the need. None of them could be sure who was watching, and where their allegiance lay.

Seen in the fading light, the damage done by the fires of the night before was clear. A large part of the city still smouldered, thick trails of smoke rising into the darkening sky. Yvonne was too far away to see much detail, having the impression of ruined buildings. She could only hope that Hiram's fury had not caused too much damage. Or death.

As the invisibility spells had been put in place, the soldiers had also muffled the metal bits of their horses' harnesses, even as Yvonne and her companions did the same. The horses made no sounds, seeming to understand the need for quiet, even at this distance.

Then they crossed the open space between them and the city, darkness providing some additional cover as they moved, the spot between Yvonne's shoulder blades prickling, expecting discovery at any moment. The walls of the Royal City were always patrolled. Always guarded. A few smugglers, or a single Hunar, might be able to escape. An entire company of soldiers, even covered by an invisibility spell, should not be able to make their way into the city undetected.

Sarra took the lead, dismounting as they came to the steep, rocky hillside that led to the walls above, making her way up the slope, seeming to follow a path that Yvonne could not trace. Yvonne, with Guise, Pieris and Jaalam, were a few paces behind Sarra, everyone else in single file behind them, Brea and Thort taking charge of the rear.

The walls ahead of them, larger as they approached, seemed absolutely solid. Sarra did not pause, leading them a little way along a narrow path alongside the walls to a point where the wall seemed to turn in on itself, nothing visible but deep shadows.

Sarra walked into the shadows, the others following.

When she reached there, Yvonne found the same arrangement of solid stone and narrow passageways as she had encountered before. It was a tight fit for Baldur, her young horse following her without complaint, ears flicking back and forth when she glanced back to check on him, until they were through the wall and into the city.

Sarra had brought them near to the burned area. Yvonne could smell the smoke.

They were in a narrow gap between buildings that looked like warehouses. Sarra left her horse and made her way to the end of the buildings, gesturing Yvonne to follow. Yvonne exchanged glances with Guise, coming to a swift, silent agreement with him, Pieris and Jaalam, which saw her and Guise joining Sarra on foot, leaving the other pair to keep watch with the horses as more of Sarra's soldiers filed through the gap, filling up the narrow alleyway.

She forgot all about the others, even Guise, as she took in the scene ahead of them.

The warehouses to either side were intact, undamaged. Nothing else that she could see was in one piece.

The fires that had been set had ravaged the area. Across the street in front of them, the cobbles partly scorched by fire, were the charred remains of what had once been tall, solid buildings. The walls had crumbled under the heat of the fire, stones and bricks tumbling to the ground in ragged heaps, the occasional bit of wall still standing, corners where two walls were braced against each other. The great wooden beams that had held up the roof tiles were gone, bits of charred wood visible among the piles of bricks and stone.

The destruction stretched ahead as far as Yvonne could see. Unending and overwhelming.

"He likes to make a point, doesn't he?" Sarra muttered. "The warehouse we used was several buildings down, in that direction." She pointed.

Hiram. He had destroyed not only the warehouse they had used for refuge, but everything around it. A display of power, perhaps. A display of temper, more likely.

"How did he find out where we were?" Yvonne asked.

"The warehouse was owned by the crown," Sarra answered, voice flat. "And the Circle Mages kept an eye on crown buildings."

"You might have mentioned this sooner," Guise said, in a mild tone that did not fool Yvonne. Or Sarra, she suspected.

"And give you all of our secrets?" Sarra said, a snap in her voice. "Not likely."

"Hiram could have found us at any time," Yvonne said. "It would have been good information to have."

"I suppose." It was as close to an apology as they were likely to get, the soldier still fiercely loyal to her kingdom.

"At least we were all out before the fires started," Yvonne said.

"What about your assassin friend?" Sarra asked.

"She's fine," Guise answered, before Yvonne could. "She'll show herself soon enough."

"I was waiting for you to stop gossiping like old women," Ulla's voice said from the shadows nearby. Yvonne blinked, but, even with the enhancement spell, still could not see the assassin. "There are no soldiers or other watchers around just now. Come with me."

"There are a few more of us now," Yvonne said.

"I know. Come with me," the assassin answered, impatience in her tone.

Yvonne exchanged glances with Guise, who shrugged slightly, more used to Ulla's abrupt manner.

"I'll get the others," Sarra said, and turned back into the alleyway.

Yvonne stepped out of the shelter of the buildings, skin prickling with unease, aware of how vulnerable they were, crossing into empty space. There were no obvious places around them to hide for an ambush, with all the burning. That did not mean much. Hiram was a powerful sorcerer and doubtless knew invisibility spells of his own.

"Are we being watched?" she asked aloud, not sure who the question was directed to.

"I think so," Guise answered.

"No," Ulla said at the same time, voice flat. She was tucked into the shadows nearby, under a slight overhang from the building. "I made sure of it."

"Stay where you are," Guise said, tilting his head. "There is something."

Yvonne couldn't hear anything, or see anything, but that did not mean much. Guise's senses were far more acute than hers, even with the spell to enhance them. She trusted his sharper senses, though, and her own instinct that something was wrong.

"Problem?" Brea's voice asked from just behind her. She managed not to make a sound, or jump, at the goblin's unexpected approach.

"Yes. Something's wrong," Guise said, although he did not sound quite his normal self. Not sure. Perhaps not trusting his senses.

"Yvonne?" Brea asked, making Yvonne's brows lift. She could not remember the last time the goblin warrior had asked for her impressions to support Guise's. She turned her head slightly, and realised why Brea had asked her question. Guise was staring into the distance with an abstracted frown, far less focused than he normally was.

"Yes. Something is definitely wrong," Yvonne said.

"Good," Brea said, teeth bared in a grin as Yvonne glanced across at her, brows lifted. "It's been a long time since I had a decent fight."

"I thought there was fighting back at Circleside?" Yvonne said, before she could help herself.

"Barely," Brea answered, a distinct sneer in her voice. "The archer was good but the rest of them barely knew one end of a sword from the other."

"How did you survive living in Kelton for so long?" Yvonne asked, the question out before she could consider that it might be rude.

Brea grinned, a flash of white teeth in the darkness. "With some difficulty."

"Practice, she called it," Thort said, standing behind his wife. "I'm sure I still have bruises."

"I don't remember you complaining at the time," Brea said, her eyes full of gold as she looked back at her husband. Yvonne looked away, with the sense that she was intruding on something private between the two of them.

"When did you get to be so frightened?" Ulla's voice asked from the shadows. "We don't have all night, you know."

"If you want to go first, by all means. It will let us know where they're hiding," Brea said in a bright, conversational tone.

Ulla made a low sound in her throat but did not move.

"Problem?" Sarra's voice sounded behind them and Yvonne choked on an unexpected laugh, hearing Brea's question echoed by the soldier. She half-listened as Brea explained, in typically blunt fashion, most of her attention on their surroundings. Whoever was waiting for them must be well hidden as even her enhanced senses could not pick them up or work out where they were. But she was certain there were people out there, waiting for them.

Sarra did not waste time on questions, calling behind her and issuing terse orders that had a pair of soldiers climbing up the side of the building. They did not have any ropes or other equipment that Yvonne could see, simply flowing up, into the dark above.

A moment later a low whistle sounded. And then another. Sarra looked even more grim than she had before, if that was possible.

"Both roads out are blocked," she said. "Someone knew we were coming here." Her eyes travelled to the darkness where Ulla was still invisible.

Ulla made another low, disgusted sound.

"You said that the Circle Mages kept an eye on the buildings," Yvonne said, the hair rising across her body as a horrible suspicion took hold. "Anything else?"

Sarra stared back at her, expression flat and fixed, lips pressed together.

"We carry the king's tokens," she said, words forced out of her. "All the King's Guard."

"You mean the king's tokens that are made by the Circle Mages? With magic in them?" Yvonne asked, with forced patience.

"So he just had to follow those," Brea concluded, shaking her head. "We're lucky they didn't just cut us down as we came through the wall one by one."

"He was part of the court. He lived with us for years. Decades. With no hint of ..." Sarra's voice cracked and she closed her mouth, shaking her head, then turning back into the alleyway, barking orders for all the soldiers to remove the king's tokens from their uniforms and horses.

A ripple of protest followed her command, but the soldiers complied. Yvonne looked back to see Sarra gathering all the tokens into a cloth sack, even calling for the soldiers on the roof above to throw theirs down.

"They are not used to looking for traitors so close to home," she murmured, aware of Brea bristling with irritation nearby.

"Innocents. They would not survive a day in the Karoan'shae," Brea said.

"Very few humans would," Yvonne said.

"You did."

"I had all of you, and the protection of the star," Yvonne answered. She had rarely been left alone in the Karoan'shae. Either Guise was with her, or one or more of Guise's trusted friends.

"We didn't do much," Brea said. She sounded disappointed. Spoiling for a fight. Yvonne wondered how many would-be attackers were waiting in the darkness around them, and had a moment's sympathy for them. An angry goblin warrior was a formidable opponent, even for an entire company of soldiers.

Movement behind her signalled Sarra's return. The soldier was on her horse, the company of soldiers gathering behind her, settled on their own horses in the narrow confines of the alley, grim faced, the gleam of metal showing they had their weapons out. Yvonne saw a few more climbing the walls, bows strapped to their backs along with quivers full of arrows.

"Get ready," Sarra ordered. "We'll draw them with us. You get to the palace."

"A bad plan," Brea said at once. "We should not split up."

"This is my city," Sarra answered, sounding as fierce as any goblin. She was wearing a set, stubborn expression that would not permit argument. "You'll only slow us down."

"We can run as fast as your horses," Brea said, lip curling back as her fangs descended, pinpricks of red in her eyes gleaming in the dark.

"Fine."

Before Yvonne could think to say that she could not run as fast as the horses, the soldiers were away. Out of the mouth of the alleyway, gathering in a solid group in the space, then wheeling in one direction. A predetermined move. All of them heading away from the direction of the palace.

They had not gone more than half a dozen strides before attackers poured out of the shadows of the ruined buildings, from all directions, swarming towards Sarra and her soldiers.

"Hold!" Sarra yelled, over the oncoming tread of boots. "We are on the King's business." She held up a golden crown, one that Yvonne recognised. It was the symbol of the King's Guard. A recognition of a lifetime of service and loyalty.

"There's no king," someone shouted back from the oncoming crowd.

Mercenaries. Mostly. But, among the mercenaries, some soldiers. Their uniforms ripped, torn in places as if they had all been in a fight. Struggling against captors. And in the darkness, their eyes reflected traces of red. A colour that should not appear in any human's eyes.

"They're blood bound," Pieris whispered in shock, just behind her. "He's powerful if he can manage that on so many people."

"Just the soldiers, though," Yvonne said.

"I assume the mercenaries are being paid," Brea said, voice dry.

There was no time for more conversation. The mercenaries and blood-bound soldiers surged forward, weapons raised, against Sarra and her company of soldiers.

Arrows flew from the rooftops, thinning out a few of the attackers. Not enough, though. Nowhere near enough.

"How did he get that many mercenaries?" Yvonne muttered, hand going to her spell pouch.

"Money?" Brea suggested, baring her teeth. "Who cares. The humans can't hold for long."

With that, the goblin warrior strode forward, Thort with her, both of them bearing weapons, and joined in the fighting.

Yvonne put her back against the nearest wall, concussive spell in one hand, looking for an opportunity to use it.

Sarra's group was entirely surrounded, two and three attackers deep, the soldiers holding rank, fighting with the smooth efficiency of well-trained soldiers, moving as one unit, the archers on the roof continuing to rain arrows down, taking out a few of the attackers. The General had chosen his soldiers well, Yvonne thought. And trained them well, too. They were standing their ground, not yielding. Impressive against the attack they were facing.

And then Brea and Thort attacked from the rear, the pair moving in harmony, cutting a swathe through the attackers in smooth, graceful moves that had the mercenaries and blood-bound soldiers turning on them, confused. They had come prepared to deal with human soldiers, it seemed, not furious goblins. And they were not prepared to deal with an assault from two sides, either. Unlike the soldiers, who adapted quickly at Sarra's commands.

Two goblins, and a company of well-organised soldiers. More than enough for the mercenaries and blood-bound soldiers.

"Go!" Brea yelled, over the sound of fighting. "We'll catch up to you."

The two goblins made the difference. Yvonne could see that. There were still more attackers than soldiers, but there would not be for long.

"Mristrian," Guise said. She turned, finding him holding out Baldur's reins. "We should not delay."

Hiram.

Who would be waiting for them. Doubtless keeping an eye on what was happening here. And aware that the mercenaries and blood-bound soldiers would not hold them for long.

"Ewan knows the way," Pieris added.

Everyone else was on their horse, ready to go, even Ewan. Yvonne released the concussive spell she had been holding on to, tucking it back into her spell pouch, got on Baldur's back, and followed the others. Away from the fighting. Away from the joyful, savage laugh as Brea whipped her sword around. Away from the low orders that Sarra was giving, in a calm voice that carried across the open space. Away from the flying arrows.

She did not like running away. At all. And yet, sometimes it was necessary. There was a greater enemy ahead.

Chapter Thirty

Ewan was at the head of their small group, Jaalam riding beside him, Pieris immediately behind him.

The streets were absolutely deserted. Perhaps no surprise, given the hour. And yet, the quiet had a quality to it Yvonne had not felt before. Not in this place. The residents of the Royal City were used to peace. Used to feeling safe within the city's walls. However much of an illusion that safety was, it was something they had taken for granted.

And now, a huge part of the city smouldered. Burned by a madman.

And the residents were terrified.

The fear was present in the air as a bitter, flat taste in her mouth, cutting through the lingering scent of fresh baking, of the horses that had passed through the streets during the day, the flowers planted here and there, and even the lingering taste of smoke from the burned buildings.

The fear was so strong it made her wonder what Hiram had done. How he had created such terror. Too many possibilities crowded her mind. She had too many memories of what Hiram was capable of already, part of her did not want to know what he had done here.

Ahead of her, Pieris was riding with his shoulders hunched, doubtless tasting the same thing in the air. Then she realised he had one hand on his chest, a faint glow beneath his fingers that was not from the Firebird's symbol.

"What is it?" she asked, moving Baldur alongside Pieris' horse.

He glanced across at her, face drawn, lines of strain around his mouth and eyes, and did not answer.

"It's the stone, isn't it? You put the pendant on?" she hissed. That seemed a rash move, and quite unlike the normally cautious Hunar.

"Information," he said, the word forced out. "Too much information."

"Memory stones are not meant to be accessed all at once," Guise said. He was riding behind them, and all Yvonne could be sure of was the sharpness in his voice. "Even goblins are careful not to do that."

"I didn't," Pieris said. "Asked question."

"Then try a different question," Yvonne said. "More detailed."

"Like what?"

"I don't know. How about asking the stone if it knows the spells required to blood bind more than one person to service, and how we can break that spell?"

"Try," Pieris said, and closed his eyes for a moment, lips moving. He gave a gasp of relief a moment later, opening his eyes again, the glow fading under his fingers. "Better. There is a spell. Two possibilities, actually. One is voluntary."

"I doubt anyone volunteered," Guise said, voice dry.

"True," Yvonne agreed. "The other one?"

Pieris inclined his head, half-closing his eyes, and then recited the spell, as if reading from a parchment.

The lines of the spell appeared in Yvonne's mind, clear and stark, imprinting on her memory. Blood magic. Forbidden magic. And requiring a great deal of power.

"He's had some help," she concluded, voice flat, after she had reviewed the spell. "Even with some blood, that requires a lot of power."

The bulk of the palace rose in front of them, square and uncompromising, and she shivered. The palace was not full. Yet it had held dozens of people. From kitchen maids to messengers to soldiers to any guests the Steward deemed worthy of the honour. More than enough to power Hiram's ambition. Assuming he would be prepared to kill them all.

Memories of the valley behind the Stone Walls rose in her mind. The burning buildings. The scattered bodies. It had required absolute determination and ruthlessness to plan and then carry out that attack.

If Hiram was capable of that kind of slaughter, he would be capable of killing the palace residents.

"I wonder how many are still alive," Pieris said, looking ahead, as if reading her mind.

"We'll find out soon enough," Yvonne answered, glancing across at him again. He looked better than before. He still did not look well. "Are you able to fight?"

"Of course."

"Keep that stone hidden. Hiram probably knows about them."

Pieris' face tightened again, but he drew the pendant out from under his shirt front, tucking it into a small leather pouch, then putting it into his spell pouch. "Satisfied?"

"It will have to do. We just have to hope he can't feel it, somehow."

Guise made a low sound of agreement behind them, then Ewan and Jaalam turned off the road they had been following, into one of the many gardens around the palace, drawing everyone's attention forward.

"This is the way into the palace?" Guise murmured. "Through a hedge?"

"I doubt this is directly into the palace," Yvonne murmured back. "We're still some distance away."

"A hidden path," Guise concluded. Yvonne was tempted to turn and look at him to confirm that his eyes had brightened with interest. Secrets.

"This garden is favoured by the nobility," Ulla commented. She had been riding in silence ahead of Pieris, Lita next to her.

"A good place for their secret entrance, then," Yvonne answered, watching as Ewan did, indeed, ride through the hedge in front of them. The tall, evergreen plants had been grown so that their branches intertwined, forming an effective barrier that seemed to have no gaps. Close up, almost as Baldur's nose touched the leaves, it was clear that this hedge was constructed like the walls around the city, with closely-spaced layers.

"This must be guarded," Yvonne said, following Pieris through, Guise bringing up the rear.

"I would think so," Guise agreed.

"Will Brea and Thort be able to find us?" she thought to ask, turning to look back at him.

"They are almost here," he answered, stopping his horse and twisting in his saddle. "Two riders, moving quickly."

Moments later, Yvonne caught a glimpse of the goblin couple through the narrow gaps in the hedge. They were making good ground, heading unerringly for the gap, and Guise. She would be in their way very soon, she realised, and moved Baldur on.

The other side of the hedge was what seemed to be a private garden, full of delicately scented flowers and narrow walkways, designed for one or two people to walk comfortably. It was not designed for armed people on horseback.

As Guise's horse emerged from the hedge, Brea was behind him, Thort following.

"Sarra is tidying up," Brea said, sounding almost cheerful. "She said she'll follow when she can. Might be a while."

"You didn't want to stay?" Yvonne asked, before she could help herself.

"Tidy up?" Brea said, nose wrinkling. "And miss learning a secret way into the palace?"

Yvonne shook her head slightly, smiling, as she turned to the others. They were gathered in a group, waiting.

Ewan was frowning slightly, looking around the garden.

"Lost your way?" Jaalam asked.

"Just trying to make sense of the directions I was given," the Mage answered. "Can anyone see a sundial?"

"There," Jaalam said, with no hesitation.

"How can you see that?" Ewan asked, peering into the dark.

"Goblins are superior," Jaalam answered, sounding like an insufferably arrogant Karoan'shae lord.

"Really?" Ewan asked, with seemingly genuine interest. It prompted a snort of laughter from Pieris, which he unconvincingly turned into a cough when Jaalam glanced in his direction.

"Which way, Ewan?" Yvonne asked, before Pieris and Jaalam could start to argue.

"This way," he said, turning his horse. "According to the directions, we should be able to take the horses all the way through."

"Let me go first," Jaalam suggested, seeing the narrow, dark opening ahead of them.

"Because you are superior?" Ewan asked, in the same innocent tone as before. This time, Yvonne laughed as well as Pieris.

"He has better night vision, anyway," she said, lifting her brows as Jaalam glared at her. "What? It's true. Goblin night vision is far better than a human's."

Jaalam's eyes were brilliant green, but he turned and made his way into the dark, narrow opening that Ewan had pointed out, Ewan following him.

It was indeed a secret path. Bordered on one side by the garden, and on the other by the palace walls, that turned slightly at the end of the garden, leading into a tunnel that burrowed its way through the palace walls, reminding Yvonne again of just how mighty the walls were. Nearly twice Baldur's length.

The tunnel had been carved out of the stone, the horses' footfalls echoing off the walls and ceiling, the tunnel itself rising, still high enough to accommodate a horse and rider, snaking upwards until Yvonne thought they were almost at the same level as the palace entrance.

Even as she thought that, Jaalam made a low noise at the front of the group.

"Door ahead," he called back, his words reverberating around the tunnel.

Yvonne resisted the urge to cover her ears with her hands. Jaalam's voice carried, rippling back on itself in an uncomfortable wave, growing louder instead of quieting as a normal echo would.

Magic.

Whoever had built this tunnel had been well aware that it made the palace vulnerable, and had set magic into its walls so that any speech would echo, the sound growing louder.

Jaalam seemed to come to the same conclusion, sliding off his horse and making his way to the door ahead, wrestling with the latch as his words grew louder and more painful against the stone, the horses tossing their heads, Ewan's horse backing up into Lita's horse, which snorted in disgust, the horse's sound adding to the twisted echo of Jaalam's words.

Brea and Thort were on their feet, silently running through the horses to Jaalam, helping him with the door that seemed to be resisting all efforts to get it open.

Baldur shifted sideways, shaking his head so vigorously his whole body shuddered.

The noise was so loud it must be carrying outside the tunnel. Yvonne looked back the way they had come, expecting to see soldiers at any moment, but there were none. Just Guise, the reins of Brea and Thort's horses looped around one arm, his own horse showing its displeasure with white around its eyes, backing into the side of the tunnel.

A fresh breeze of air told her that the door was open.

The horses surged forward with no need of asking, the sound of their hooves on stone lost amid the deafening echo of Jaalam's voice.

They came out of the tunnel to a dark, narrow space, and the bare edge of soldiers' weapons. Brea and Thort were ahead of Jaalam in a heartbeat, their own weapons out.

Yvonne slid off Baldur's back, shaking her head to try and clear her ears. She could not hear anything over the roar of her own heartbeat and the continuing echo of Jaalam's voice.

The goblin lord had staggered to one side, blood trickling from his ears. The noise must be far worse for the goblins' sensitive hearing.

Brea and Thort were moving with their usual grace and deadly efficiency, the clash of steel on steel unheard in Yvonne's ears.

The echo was still going on, making it impossible to think clearly.

She had no prepared spells to counter it. But a cleansing spell might help. Could not hurt. It was the most gentle magic she had. So, she drew a cleansing spell from her pouch and threw it into the tunnel, activating it with a word she could not hear.

The sound cut off immediately, leaving her with just the roar of her pulse in her ears.

Still, it was an improvement. She drew her own sword and staggered forward, legs not willing to work properly after the enormity of the sound.

Brea and Thort did not need any help, though. They had the soldiers mostly disarmed and unconscious, stripping their uniform jackets off, tearing them into strips as makeshift ropes.

Yvonne sheathed her sword, needing two attempts to do so, her hands shaking as badly as her legs.

Jaalam was still slumped against the wall, Pieris with him, the other Hunar with his hands over the goblin's ears, slips of parchment in his fingers. Healing spells.

Lita and Ulla were half-collapsed a short distance from Jaalam, breathing hard.

Ewan was huddled on the ground, hands over his head, rocking back and forth.

And Guise was standing with the horses, eyes sparking red, but holding himself still and under control.

Yvonne went forward to Ewan, putting a hand on his shoulder. He jumped to his feet, startled, face pale, traces of tears down his face. There was blood at his ears, too. Yvonne pulled a healing spell from her pouch and pressed it to his forehead, activating it. He shivered, calming, more tears flowing.

"I'm sorry," he said, the words faint and distorted to Yvonne's ears. "Lady Grace said to be quiet. She didn't say anything about the trap."

"We're alive," Yvonne told him, pressing a hand to his shoulder for a moment. "Just breathe. Take some water. Food." They did not have time to rest. Hiram was waiting. But practical tasks like eating or drinking would steady the younger Mage.

Ewan made his way to his horse to get the supplies as she made her way to where Thort was tying up the last of their attackers. He was paler than normal, mouth in a tight line.

"That was unpleasant," he said as she joined him.

"You didn't kill any of them," she commented.

"No. They are not blood-bound. Just soldiers doing their job."

"There will be more along soon, I'm sure," Brea added, grimacing as she put a hand to her ear. "Nasty stuff."

"Yes," Yvonne agreed, looking back at the open mouth of the tunnel. It was a spell designed to incapacitate or kill whoever set it off. A trap, as Ewan had said. Not triggered by the horses' hooves. Triggered by speech. "I didn't think any Circle Mages had that skill."

Something about the quality of silence around her drew her attention back to Brea and Thort. They were both wearing the sort of expressionless masks that Guise was so fond of.

"What?" Yvonne asked.

"It's not human magic," Thort told her, speaking goblin as he walked along the row of captive soldiers, checking their ties.

"I didn't think that was allowed," Yvonne said, speaking the same language, unable to hide her surprise. Human and goblin magics did not mix. At least, that was the common wisdom. Pieris and Jaalam had proved, with Pieris' map and the messenger birds, that it was possible.

"Not a mix," Brea clarified. "No human set those spells."

"There were rumours that one of the former kings of Valland had a goblin lover," Thort said, satisfied that all the soldiers would stay bound. "It's the sort of trap a goblin might set to stop anyone following them."

"Do you think the kings knew about it?" Yvonne asked, brows lifting as she went with them back to the horses. Her legs were steadier, hands no longer shaking, but she could still feel the after-effect of the spell working through her, gradually fading.

"They must have known. They did tell the nobility to be quiet," Thort said.

The others were looking a little recovered, too. Ewan had regained some colour. Lita and Ulla were standing on their own feet, and Pieris and Jaalam were sharing a packet of food, keeping an eye on the soldiers that Thort and Brea had tied up.

Guise was the only one who seemed unchanged. There were still red sparks in his eyes, and he had not moved away from the horses, standing next to his own mount, a tight grip on the reins. Yvonne made her way across, stopping by Baldur's side to fetch some food for herself and give her horse a head scratch in response to his demand, his nose shoved into her chest.

"Are you alright?" she asked in as quiet a voice as she could manage, still speaking goblin.

He blinked, and looked down at her, the red still in his eyes. The rest of his eyes were a flat, dull green. A shade she had never seen before.

"I am functional, mristrian, I assure you," he answered, sounding distant.

Something was wrong. And he did not want to talk about it. One more thing to worry about. Her skin prickled. Following the direction of his gaze, she saw the palace rising above them. Somewhere in there was the blood sorcerer who had burned the Royal City, blood-bound some of the kingdom's soldiers, and kept Guise as a prisoner for some time.

"Cut off his head and burn him," she said, returning to the human language, repeating Guise's words.

That surprised a half-laugh out of him, brightness returning to his eyes, the red fading.

"I like that plan," Jaalam said. "Simple. Direct."

"We just need to find him first," Pieris added, staring at the building that rose above them.

"Well, we're not going to do that standing here," Lita said, lifting her chin. She took her horse's reins and began walking forward. "I assume it's this way?"

They made their way through a narrow opening in the heavy walls that surrounded the palace building, finding themselves in what must be one of the lesser courtyards, around the back of the building. There were no windows that Yvonne could see, so no risk of a casual glance outside catching sight of them, and the long wall of the palace had two doors, plain wood, firmly closed against the night. Kitchens, Yvonne would guess, or some other kind of service entrance. Not big enough for their horses to get through.

Against the outer walls, across from the doors, there was a long, low barn-like structure that proved empty, a series of hooks hanging from the ceiling and the heavy scent of herbs in the air telling Yvonne it was usually used for some kind of preservation. There was more than enough room for the horses, who seemed happy enough to be left to doze after their hard day.

Their riders were not so lucky. There was more to be done before they could rest. They left the drying shed as a group, making their way across the narrow courtyard, Ewan leading them to the nearest of the wooden doors. It yielded without a sound to his touch, leading into darkness.

Brea went in first, sword drawn, and beckoned them to follow her a moment later.

They were in some kind of entrance room, pegs arranged around the walls, a few cloaks hanging here and there, boots set in racks underneath them. From the quality of the cloaks and boots, Yvonne guessed they belonged to palace servants, perhaps those who lived in the city.

There was no one around as they left the entranceway into a long, wide corridor that seemed to stretch the entire length of the building. Further along one side of the corridor was an open door casting the faint light from candles, the sound of people moving about and the scent of cooking. Kitchens. Yvonne thought about the solid wall, with the lack of windows or vents to allow heat and smoke to escape, and did not envy the kitchen workers.

Closer to her, stairs led up. Probably to the main floor of the palace.

Ewan took the lead, Brea shadowing him, taking them up the first set of stairs, the plain walls and bare floors giving way to the more elaborate interior that Yvonne remembered from her previous visits to the palace. The Valland kings had acquired wealth over their years in power, and liked to display it.

It was only as they arrived on the main floor, that Yvonne realised she had no idea where to start looking for Hiram, or how they might find him.

The palace's main floor was a maze of inter-connected rooms that she still could not navigate easily, even after several visits. The room they were in was relatively plain, in comparison to the ones closer to the king. A room for relaxation and leisure, soft chairs paired with little tables scattered around the space. She was quite sure she had never been in this room before, and had almost tripped over one of the tables already.

Behind the walls there would be servants' passages, and for a moment Yvonne wondered if they should try and search the palace through there. Then she remembered her last time in the servants' passages, how narrow they were, and how easy it would be to stage an ambush or a trap.

"Where to start?" she said, keeping her voice low.

"Room to room," Brea murmured, voice pitched as low as possible. "And we stay together." This last with a direct look at Ulla, the assassin still with them. Ulla inclined her head slightly, not saying anything. It might be agreement.

Brea's plan was sensible, and prudent, and it would take them half a lifetime, Yvonne though, exhaustion taking hold. The palace was enormous.

"I can find him," Guise said, his voice flat, eyes returned to the dull green she had seen before. He would not meet her gaze, or anyone else's, lowering his eyes. It was so unlike his normal manner that Yvonne took a step towards him, not sure what to do.

"Tell us where," Thort said, voice more gentle than it needed to be.

Even in the poor light, Yvonne saw the wash of colour across Guise's face. Shame. Not something she had seen from him before.

"This way," Guise said, and started walking.

Yvonne matched his stride, staying with him, letting the others fall in behind them, stomach twisting in unease. Something was wrong. Badly wrong.

"Does he know we're here?" she asked Guise.

"He'll know I am here," Guise answered, not looking at her. She sucked in a harsh breath, shock checking her stride. She remembered his expression when he had suggested that they go to the Royal City to look for Hiram. It had seemed a guess. Even though she had known there was something he was not telling her. And here it was.

"Did the blood taking form a connection?" she asked. It was probably a harsh question. Perhaps even rude. And she did not care. She wanted to shout at him for keeping the information from her.

"Something like that. Yes," he answered, and glanced down at her, his eyes the mix of red and dull green she had noticed before. "I do not know if I am safe," he said, so quietly she almost missed the words.

Her spike of anger vanished. She had an impulse to stop and hug him. He sounded vulnerable. Something she would never have thought possible.

"You are Guise," she told him. "You have never hurt me. You will never hurt me."

He looked down at her, gold shimmering in his eyes for a heartbeat, then shook his head.

"I am not safe," he said again, voice a harsh whisper she could barely hear.

"We will not let you hurt her," Brea said from behind them, voice firm. Yvonne glanced back, only then realising that they had all stopped walking.

The rest of the group were facing them, facing Guise, expressions ranging from confusion on Ewan's face, to the determination on Brea's.

Yvonne opened her mouth, not sure what she wanted to say.

"Thank you," Guise said. She looked back at him to find that his shoulders had straightened, and his eyes had brightened.

Not a threat from Brea. A promise. A reassurance.

"Company coming," Thort murmured, drawing everyone's attention.

Yvonne could not hear anything at first, even with her senses enhanced. That did not mean much.

"There's an armoury nearby," Ewan said, turning full circle in the middle of the room they were in. Ewan, who had lived here, knew exactly where he was. "Yes. This way." He set off at a rapid pace, passing Yvonne and Guise and then turning down the next opening, everyone else following in his wake.

The armoury sat alongside a plain, unadorned room, and was protected by a heavy wooden door, bound with iron and a pair of locks that gleamed with magic in Yvonne's sight. Pieris and Jaalam made quick work of the locks with spells that teased Yvonne's senses as a mix of Hunar and goblin magic.

The door opened and Pieris sent light spells inside, showing a small room with shelves and racks along every wall, covered with weapons. Crossbows and bolts. Bows and quivers full of arrows. Swords. Battle axes. War hammers. Long daggers, knives and throwing knives.

To everyone's surprise, Lita headed for the bows and crossbows, slinging a pair of quivers across her shoulders and moving along the row of weapons, testing a few before she found one that suited, then grabbing a crossbow, settling the quiver of bolts at her hip.

"What?" she said, seeing everyone staring at her while they took weapons of their own. "I know how to shoot." Yvonne remembered the crossbow bolt that Lita had used in her office, in Willowton, and opened her mouth to ask just how accurate Lita was normally.

"You might have mentioned this before," Ulla said in a tone that could cut glass, before Yvonne could say anything.

"I didn't?" Lita said, eyebrows lifting. She seemed genuine in her surprise.

Ewan also took a bow and arrows, and a crossbow with a quiver of bolts.

"Good," Brea said, eyes gleaming. "The two of you stay in the middle and try not to shoot any of us."

Lita's brows lifted again, along with her chin, mouth setting in a hard line. Ewan looked sick.

"They're almost here," Thort said. He had selected another sword and a war hammer, slung across his back, and then stationed himself at the door, listening. "Ready?" he glanced back to his wife.

Brea smiled, her fangs showing, and moved to join her husband, a pair of borrowed swords in her hands. "How many?" she asked.

"Ten. Perhaps more."

"Hardly a fair fight," Brea said, sounding disappointed.

"A little practice, then," Thort answered. He was staring into the dark outside the door, so Yvonne could not see his expression. He sounded quite serious.

"Are all goblins so bloodthirsty?" Ewan asked Yvonne, in what he probably thought was a whisper.

"Most of them, yes," she answered, speaking in her normal voice.

"We do like a good fight," Jaalam agreed.

Yvonne could hear the footsteps now. It sounded like a good number of boots moving together, drawing closer.

"Move," Brea directed, waving them all out of the armoury, then closing the door behind them. "Can you seal the door?" she asked Pieris.

He moved to do as she asked without comment, a spark of magic half-blinding Yvonne for a few moments.

As her vision was clearing the boot steps grew louder still, a gleam of light growing at one end of the corridor. The inside of the palace was still dark in the early morning. Whoever was moving towards them had brought their own light.

"Hiram is that way," Guise told her. "Not far."

"The audience chamber is that way," Ewan added. He had an arrow ready on the bow string, pointed at the ground. Not willing to raise weapons against the palace's defenders. Not yet, anyway.

"That would fit," Yvonne said. She had taken a few more throwing daggers from the collection in the armoury, nothing more. She always seemed to run out of daggers. "He would enjoy sitting on the throne," she added, half to herself.

There was no more time to consider that. People had appeared in the open doorway to the room, carrying torches with them. Mercenaries, Yvonne saw at once. Around a dozen of them, she thought, as they saw her group.

"Stand firm," Brea said, voice quiet. Yvonne glanced around to find Lita and Ewan shoulder to shoulder, both of them pale, their weapons ready but still pointed to the ground. Ulla had disappeared somewhere in the shadows. Pieris and Jaalam were standing shoulder to shoulder, Pieris with a scrap of parchment in his fingers that she recognised as a prepared spell. Jaalam's fangs were out, eyes a mix of bright green and red.

"Intruders," the mercenary in the lead said, lips curling back to show yellowing teeth. He was old, for a mercenary, his short, patchy beard and close-cropped hair almost entirely white, a sharp contrast to his weathered skin. "You're not welcome here," he told them, throwing the torch he carried on the floor in front of him. There was no rug, or any furniture, in this room to burn. Still, Yvonne flinched slightly at the damage done to the old, polished floorboards. "Let's show them how we treat visitors," he said, speaking over his shoulder to the rest of his company.

The mercenaries spread out. Most of them were seasoned veterans, Yvonne saw, apprehension crawling down her spine. Experienced in fighting, many of them bearing scars to prove it. They carried their weapons with casual confidence, moving forward as a single group. Used to working together, too. A dozen of them. Against her smaller group, with Lita and Ewan already trembling.

"Now," Brea said. Arrows flew from Lita and Ewan, striking home, into an arm and a shoulder, much to Yvonne's surprise. And the mercenaries'. They checked in their forward momentum. "Again," Brea said. Another pair of arrows flew, hitting home again, one landing in a mercenary's shoulder, the other into another's leg.

The mercenaries surged forward. Brea waved Ewan and Lita back, against the wall, and met the oncoming attackers with bared fangs and bared steel, Thort beside her.

Yvonne found herself next to Pieris, both of them holding spells ready in one hand, a sword in the other.

There was nothing for them to do.

Brea, Thort and Jaalam cut through the dozen mercenaries with ease, sending bodies, torches and weapons scattering around the room. The fight was over almost before it had started.

"Well, that was a nice warm up," Brea said. She was looking around the room with eyes full of green and red, her sword still ready. "I wonder if there are more of them?"

"Let us hope so," Thort answered, eyes as bright as his wife's. "This way?" he asked Guise.

"Yes."

Guise had kept himself still and out of the way during the fighting. Not safe, he had said. He had not even drawn his sword.

There was no time to worry.

Hiram was waiting.

Chapter Thirty-One

They made it to the last room before the audience chamber without meeting any more mercenaries, much to Brea's obvious disappointment.

There had been some changes since Yvonne was last in this room. The Valland kings had not wanted their guests to be too comfortable while they were waiting, and not provided many chairs. Certainly not as many as were laid out now, lit by torches set in the walls and a few lanterns scattered on the floor.

The room was filthy. There were plates and tankards scattered around, with crumbs and half-eaten food, the smell of something rotten lingering in the air, untidiness that the Steward would never have tolerated. And finally, the biggest change, the room was full of mercenaries. Some of them were sleeping, rolled up in blankets on the floor. Some of them were more alert, glancing up from their card games, idle conversation or beer as the door opened.

However filthy the room was, the sight of armed people coming through the door drew an immediate reaction. The mercenaries who were awake were on their feet, weapons raised, a few sending up cries of alarm which woke the ones who had been sleeping.

"Finally," Brea said, a savage edge to her voice. "Go ahead," she said to Yvonne, waving her hand. "We'll hold them off."

Yvonne shook her head slightly, saying nothing. The goblin warriors were heavily outnumbered. Brea did not care. The longer they delayed, and the more noise they made, the more time Hiram would have to prepare for them. She had to keep moving. With Brea drawing most of the mercenaries' attention, there was a clear path to the next pair of doors, leading to the audience chamber, and she moved towards them, Guise with her.

"He knows I'm here," Guise said, voice flat. It sounded almost ordinary, where his voice would normally sing in her senses. He was pale, lips pressed together, his eyes the dull green and red that she had seen too often since they came to the palace.

"Let's not disappoint him," she said, in her most cheerful tone, and pushed open the doors, ignoring the twist in her stomach and the crawl of apprehension along her skin. It was a foolish idea, confronting a blood sorcerer when she was worn out and did not know his resources. It was far from her first foolish idea, she told herself sternly, and kept walking.

The audience chamber had also been transformed. The great, high ceiling overhead was dulled with what looked like smoke, the vast expanse of windows that had looked over the city covered with the same grey substance. Blocking out the light. Blocking out the view of the city for the most part.

The floor was untouched, gleaming and perfect, stretching ahead of her to the raised dais with the modest throne of the Valland kings.

At least, there had been a modest throne there the last time she had been in this room.

The piece of furniture that sat on the dais now was anything but modest. It towered halfway to the ceiling, soaring overhead, a fanciful affair of gold leaf and other things.

"Are those feathers?" Yvonne asked, incredulous, looking at the throne. There were great fronds of what looked like display feathers sticking out from the sides, roughly where the occupant's head would be. Doubtless to give him the impression of an aura. "Purple feathers?" She lifted her brows and turned to Guise. "I am not imagining them, am I?"

"No, mristrian," Guise said. "They are a quite startling colour."

The dry tone was almost his typical manner. Almost. There was still strain at the edge of his voice and she knew, without looking, that there would be red in his eyes.

"Guidrishinnal, how delightful to see you again. And looking so much better since our last encounter."

Yvonne had been so distracted by the improbable purple feathers that she had entirely missed the fact that the throne was occupied. She had a feeling it would annoy the sorcerer to be told that, and did so.

"Hello, Hiram," she said, in as cheerful a voice as she could manage. "I didn't see you there. Those feathers are quite distracting."

The blood sorcerer sitting on the throne, in the midst of all those vivid purple feathers, bared his teeth at her.

"And you are looking much better since I last saw you, while we are passing out compliments," Yvonne said and heard a muffled sound from Guise that sounded like a choked laugh. "Mind you, last time I saw you, you were mostly dead. Somewhere over there, wasn't it?"

She turned her head slightly, careful to keep the sorcerer within her sight, and looked across the gleaming, unblemished floor to the spot where, not that long ago, Hiram had been lying in a pool of his own blood, his head almost severed thanks to her sword.

She turned back to him as he made a low sound somewhere between a growl and a snarl. He did look better. Outwardly, he looked like many Valland males. Dark hair swept back from a high forehead and a face that, apparently, many women considered handsome. The bared teeth had been white. His whole appearance was fairly ordinary, returned to the disguise he had worn when she had first met him, hiding in plain sight among the Valland court as its most senior Circle Mage. Clad in splendid robes, the staff of his office in one hand, he looked as benign as a Mage could. Almost human, in fact, except her skin was crawling and the enhancement to her sight and her senses told her there was nothing human about him. It was probably not a good idea to antagonise him. And yet, she could not stop the words coming from her mouth. Besides which, in her experience, people tended to make mistakes when they were angry. Particularly arrogant madmen.

"Did you make that throne yourself?" she asked, continuing her conversational tone. "Gold leaf and purple feathers? I'm sure there's a children's tale with a throne like that in it. Is that where you got the idea from?"

"Is this him?" Pieris asked from somewhere behind her.

Behind him, she could hear the sound of fighting in the outer room, the mercenaries putting up a decent fight. Brea would be pleased.

"I read that story, too, about the throne," Jaalam said, in his most helpful tone. "The king was quite mad by the end of it, wasn't he?"

Hiram's lips curled back from his teeth, which seemed too long and too bright to be human. He muttered a word and flicked his staff, and the doors behind them slammed shut on the sound of fighting.

"You cannot escape now," he said, satisfaction in his tone. He rose to his feet and stepped down from the dais, perhaps to avoid any more comments on his throne, taking a few steps towards them before halting. The distance was nicely calculated, Yvonne saw, nothing casual about it. He was too far away to reach with a thrown spell, or the edge of a sword.

"Is that supposed to be frightening?" Jaalam asked Pieris, in a stage whisper that echoed off the ceiling.

The sound rippled oddly around the room, in a wave that reminded Yvonne of the tunnel and its sound trap. She looked up, seeing nothing but the smoke. Or what she had thought was smoke, moving in ripples and random swirls. It seemed more substantial than mere smoke.

"Oh, do be quiet," Hiram said, and made another gesture with his staff, sending a concussive blow into Jaalam that swept the goblin off his feet, sliding across the polished floor until he struck the wall with a thud that made Yvonne wince. Pieris went after his partner, face tight. Impossible to tell whether he was annoyed with Jaalam or Hiram.

The smoke had rippled down the walls, too, Yvonne saw, in sinuous curls. She was so distracted in trying to work out what Hiram had used to coat the ceiling with that she almost missed his next words.

"Kill her."

Yvonne snapped her attention back to the sorcerer, wondering who he had been speaking to. Apart from him, there were two goblins and two Hunar in the room. No one else.

A hissed breath beside her and she realised that Hiram had been speaking to Guise. Giving him an order.

"No," Guise said, jaw clenched. He was holding himself absolutely still.

"I command it," Hiram said, voice soft and silky. "You know you cannot disobey me."

"You think Guise is going to do what you want?" Yvonne asked, brow lifting, before turning to Guise. "Hasn't this been tried before? Some power-hungry madman trying to get you to kill me?"

He looked down at her, eyes flat and dull, filled with red, his jaw clenched, a tremor running through him.

Whatever Hiram had done to him, it was powerful enough to hold a goblin in its thrall.

But Hiram had underestimated his target. Guise had grown up among the Karoan'shae, where self-control was prized. Even with the magic pulling him, Guise was managing to stay still, to not move. Not reach for his sword.

"I command you. Draw your sword." The sorcerer was having to exert himself more, Yvonne realised, the veil of humanity he wore slipping away. There were traces of blackened veins across his face. "Now."

Guise drew his sword. The slowest Yvonne had ever seen him move, fighting every single motion, no grace or fluidity at all. He lifted the blade into an attack position and turned to face her, the too-short strands of hair around his face sticking to his skin. She could not remember the last time she had seen him sweat with effort, telling her how hard he was struggling with Hiram's commands.

She met his eyes. There was nothing but red in them. Any sane person would run.

She stayed where she was, ignoring Hiram.

Guise would not hurt her. Yvonne knew that. It was one of the absolute certainties of her life. And not even Hiram could take that from her. Or from Guise. Even with the blood sorcerer's command working through him, he was holding himself still, keeping her safe. She wished she could help.

And then realised that there was something she could do.

"Mrista," she said. The male equivalent of the word he used for her. My lord. And, because it was in the goblin language, it was layered with other meaning. Most strongly, it was a claim of possession. A statement of something like ownership. The word rang through her, clear and bright, no hesitation or doubt in her. They belonged to each other.

His lips parted, intake of breath clear in the quiet room. The point of the sword dipped, the blade clattering to the floor, dropped and discarded.

His eyes cleared, the dull, lifeless red replaced with swirling gold, and he moved. One long step towards her, hands cupping her face, head lowering until his lips were against hers. And she forgot about everything else as Guise kissed her, winding her arms around his neck to draw him closer.

The world spun around her, ground disappearing from under her feet, and everything tilted.

Not the kiss, she realised. Guise had slid his arms around her waist, lifted her off her feet, moving her, then setting her down, breaking the kiss, stepping in front of her so that she had an excellent view of his shoulder.

She blinked, mind and senses trying to catch up with each other, and her skin prickled with the heavy static of magic in the air. Hiram.

Guise had sensed the threat before she had.

"What trickery is this?" Hiram asked, voice low. "I ordered you to do something." He was losing more of his human appearance, the blackened veins in his face growing, stark contrast to his pale skin, lips shading to grey, teeth no longer the unnatural, blinding white they had been.

"I had a prior claim," Yvonne told him, moving to stand next to Guise, shoulder to shoulder. "Except that you wouldn't understand that. You only see people as things to be used."

Guise laced his fingers through hers, warmth creeping up her arm, and she felt colour rise in her face, the show of affection unsettling her more than the kiss, which had taken her by surprise.

"You could take notes," Pieris said, from somewhere behind her. Speaking to Jaalam, she knew, just from the tone of his voice.

"Oh, I am, believe me," Jaalam answered in a low, rich tone that made Yvonne's colour rise again, sensing something private between the pair.

"Pathetic. All of you," Hiram said, lips curling back from blackened teeth, lifting his staff. It hurt Yvonne's eyes to look at it. It had grown more corrupt since she had last seen it, like its master.

"You wouldn't understand," Yvonne said again, freeing herself from Guise and taking a step to the side. Enough so that she could draw her sword without slicing into him.

"He really is quite ugly," Pieris commented, moving to stand beside her, Jaalam beside him.

No one had their weapons drawn. Not yet. Guise's sword was still on the floor beside him.

"Is this it?" Hiram asked. "The four of you? To try and stop me?"

Yvonne's knees buckled and she had to stagger back to stay upright, the weight of exhaustion and despair pressing on her. Who was she to think that she could defeat the creature in front of her? He was steeped in blood magic and power, the single most powerful being she had ever seen in her life. And ruthless with it. There would be no mercy. None. Better to just turn and leave, run while she still could.

Her feet shifted, moving her a fraction further backwards, and she forced herself to be still. She would not run. She had come here for a reason, even if she could not remember what that was just now. But she would not run. Not now. Not from Hiram. Not from this room.

"A charm spell," she murmured. Not the first time Hiram had tried that. "You really don't have much imagination, do you?" she said, pulling a cleansing spell from her pouch and throwing it into the air in front of her, activating it.

The weight that had been trying to shove her to the floor lifted, along with the lingering despair.

Hiram was still standing straight, confident, his staff beside him. Too confident.

The magic he had used on them so far had been little more than a normal Circle Mage could manage. A touch more power in the spells, but the spells themselves were nothing special.

A bit like his ridiculous throne, they had been meant to intimidate and impress.

Even as she thought that, she realised that she could no longer see his throne. She blinked, wondering if the spell she had used to enhance her senses had faded. It was still too early for daylight, but she should be able to see around the room.

Hiram was clear to her sight, but everything around him was shrouded in smoke. The same smoke that had been coiling along the ceiling and down the walls, now trailing towards him in sinuous ripples.

Magic. Some kind of magic that she had never seen before.

"What is that?" she asked Pieris.

"I don't know," he answered, voice clipped. "I've never seen anything like it."

"Ignorant sheep," Hiram said, blackened teeth bared in another snarl.

"Why don't you enlighten us?" Yvonne asked, not really expecting an answer. Out of the corner of her eye, she saw Pieris' hand move to his pouch, where he had put the sapphire pendant, and took a half-step forward, drawing Hiram's attention to her, away from Pieris. She hoped.

"You lack the intelligence to understand," he sneered, waving a hand through the smoke that was curling around him, obscuring the robes he wore.

"Death dust," Pieris said, sounding shaken. He had his hand curled in a fist by his side, gleam of blue light between his fingers.

"Now, what do you have there?" Hiram asked, eyes narrowing. He swept his staff forward, carrying smoke with it.

Yvonne shoved Pieris out of the way of the magic, which caught her on the shoulder instead, pulling her towards the blood sorcerer.

"You have stolen from me," Hiram said, flicking his staff again, releasing Yvonne from the magic and sending her stumbling onto the floor.

"Really?" she asked, crouched on the floor, staring up at him and the clouds around him. "I have not taken anything that was yours."

"Death dust," Pieris said, from somewhere behind her. "Made from the dead. It is death magic."

Yvonne's eyes widened as she looked around the room, at the great clouds of smoke, the coils around Hiram.

"How many dead?" she asked him, throat tight. "How many had to die to create this?"

"Beautiful, isn't it?" Hiram said, running his fingers through the smoke around him. The smoke twitched, as if wanting to move away, then stilled.

Yvonne looked again at the smoke. The coils around him were moving faster than those in the rest of the room. The smoke was drifting down from the ceiling, curling around Hiram, then spinning away. As if it was drawn to him, but repelled by him at the same time.

She got back to her feet, Guise coming to stand with her, ahead of Pieris and Jaalam.

"The essence of the dead," she said, voice flat, heart a heavy weight in her chest. "You are using the dead as well as blood for your power."

Hiram smiled back at her, showing his blackened teeth, dark veins on his forehead standing out.

"Why?" Yvonne asked, the question pulled from her. She sounded bewildered, even to her own ears, looking around at the gathered smoke, the pull of it towards Hiram, drawn towards him, and the rush to get away. It suggested that the smoke was not simply smoke. It retained something of the people it had once been. Some part of the smoke understood what Hiram was. Just how dangerous he was.

"Because this should all be mine. I should serve no one," Hiram answered, an edge to his voice that was no longer human, or pretending to be.

"You think we should serve you?" Yvonne asked, lip curling. "Worship you?"

"You do not have a choice. I am more powerful than any of you."

She stared back at him, at the darkness looking out from his eyes, then at the twisted bit of filth that was the staff he held. The beautifully crafted robes, stitched with gold thread.

He believed it. He believed that all this should be his. The power. The right to sit in the ridiculous throne. The right to draw on other people's blood, and death, to fuel his power.

Inside her chest the Firebird's wings stirred and the bird's shriek cut across her ears, the tone of outrage clear.

"You have no right to this," she told him, straightening her shoulders. "No one has the right to use other people like that."

"Really?" he asked, smirk pulling his mouth. He lifted his free hand and a coil of smoke curled around his fingers. "See how they are drawn to me. All the voices."

Yvonne saw the smoke making itself as thin as possible to curl around his fingers and then speed away, up to the ceiling, as far away as it could get.

"I do see," she said, shoulders still square, hand going to her spell pouch. "Will you surrender them?"

Hiram's mouth curved, an unpleasant smile.

"You cannot make me."

"I would not be so sure," Guise murmured. He might be standing still beside her. He was still paying attention, ready to act.

"You think you can defeat me?" Hiram sneered.

"A little man with big ambitions?" Yvonne answered. "It will not be the first time."

He raised his staff, dark power gathering around it that she could not look at, not directly.

She threw a concussive spell at him, wrapped around one of the knives taken from the palace armoury.

The spell exploded above his head, sending the trails of death dust swirling away from him, clear space left around him. He took a step back, off balance for a moment, then sneered again.

"You missed."

"I did not," she answered, wrapping another concussive spell around another knife, and throwing that one. Away from Hiram. Towards the great expanse of windows, covered by the smoke, desperately seeking to move away from the sorcerer.

The glass shattered, jagged pieces clattering onto the polished wooden floor, a rush of cool morning air sweeping in even as the great cloud of smoke sped out, rising into the air, thinning as it went.

She turned back to Hiram to find him staring out the window.

"Impossible. They cannot escape me."

"They were not yours to control or command."

"Not quite so powerful now," Jaalam said from somewhere behind Yvonne. She resisted the urge to roll her eyes. Goblins. Always spoiling for a fight.

"I do not need them," Hiram declared, lifting his staff again, the tip of it pointing towards the ceiling.

It drew Yvonne's eyes up and she could see, finally, what the smoke had been hiding. Too many long, dark limbs tangled together, too many eyes staring down.

"What in the worlds are those?" Pieris asked, voice faint.

"Dervish," Jaalam answered, grim. "Back to the wall, now."

"What –" Pieris said, sound cut off, replaced by the sound of boots against the floor.

Yvonne was moving, too, Guise with her, back towards the wall, eyes following the sinuous movement of the creatures on the ceiling. She remembered all too well the feeling of the creature's limbs around her legs. The panic of the underground space. And that had been one creature. There were at least three full grown adults above them.

"Get the doors open," she said to the other three, stopping a pace or two from the wall, concentration on the creatures ahead of her. She scrabbled through the spells in her pouch. A few concussive spells. A few fire spells. More cleansing spells than one person should ever need. Not enough to defeat the three dervish that were unwrapping themselves from each other, moving towards Hiram's staff.

"Stand back," Pieris warned, voice flat, and she moved quickly away from the doors. Not a moment too soon as they exploded in a shower of wooden splinters. Pieris must have used almost every concussive spell he had.

Brea and Thort were first through the doors, swords drawn. They took one look around the seemingly empty chamber, their eyes going unhesitatingly upward to the dervish that were still poised on the roof.

Brea paled. Yvonne had not known that goblins could go that particular colour. She took a sharp breath in, then barked orders across her shoulder.

The room flooded with soldiers, Sarra among them. All of them bearing the signs of battle. Weapons out, blades coated with blood, a few makeshift bandages tied around arms and heads.

There were archers among the group. Sarra's orders followed Brea's, arranging her soldiers in a tight formation, blade carriers in front of the archers, everyone's attention on the creatures above.

None of the humans had seen a dervish before, Yvonne was quite sure. But they would have heard about them. Legends whispered around campfires in the dead of night. Tales told in taverns over far too many beers.

For a moment, there was stillness. The humans staring up at nightmares. The nightmares staring back. Even though they were soldiers, she could see the tension in the bodies facing into the room. The square shoulders. The slight quiver along the length of a blade betraying a trembling hand. The slightest sound of a boot against the floor. Someone's foot moving back, wanting to be away from the things on the ceiling.

Towards the back of the group, Lita and Ewan were standing, bows ready, visibly trembling. Holding their ground, but only just.

One of the creatures overhead bared its fangs at the soldiers in a silent warning.

Yvonne heard the sound of more boots moving, and looked down from the ceiling to see Hiram standing underneath the creatures, a faint smile of satisfaction on his face.

He thought he had won.

He had read the fear in the humans. Despite the full company of soldiers, they were no match for three dervish. And the soldiers knew it. And Hiram knew it.

He thought he had won.

Yvonne's mouth was full of the bitter taste of fear. She swallowed, and took a careful, deliberate step forward, making sure her boots struck the ground loud enough to carry. Shoulders back, standing upright, chin lifted, she stared across the room to her enemy.

"Hiram, you have broken the laws of magic," she said, her voice even and clear despite the knot in her stomach and the foul taste in her mouth. "You have used death magic. You have taken lives. You attacked the Stone Walls." She paused, Adira's face rising in her memory. Not as she had last seen her, her body broken, her life slipping away, but years before, when Adira had faced down a group of mercenaries who had thought the Sisters would be an easy target. Adira had turned them away with nothing more than her presence and her voice.

The knot in her stomach eased, replaced with warmth. She could almost feel Adira and Elinor at each side. In her chest the wings of the Firebird fluttered and the bird's scream echoed through her ears.

"What now. Are you going to offer me my life if I repent?" Hiram asked, mocking tone clear. Except it was not quite right. Not quite as self-assured as he had been.

The Firebird lifted her head, the eye that Yvonne could see in her mind staring, unblinking, at Hiram. At her enemy.

Somewhere behind her, Yvonne could hear the sound of something heavy moving across the floor. There would be nothing there if she turned, she knew. But the great bear was there. The spirit the Sisters had lived with for so long, still wounded and grieving, making a small sound of pain as she looked ahead, seeing the one who had planned the attack ahead of her.

Yvonne turned her head slightly. At the edge of her sight she could see the bear and the Firebird.

"Leave Hiram to me," she told them, taking another few deliberate steps forward until she was at the edge of the line of soldiers, Guise her shadow. "Brea, Sarra, you will need to deal with them," she said, tilting her head slightly to indicate the dervish, still holding themselves unnaturally still high above. "I think you will have some help," she added, glancing back over her shoulder to where the Firebird hovered, wings outstretched, next to the spirit bear standing on her hind legs.

"With pleasure," Brea said, fangs bared, eyes full of red.

The humans were not as eager to fight.

Then the great bear made a low sound and moved forward, through the soldiers, who straightened as she passed through them, their own shoulders squaring, the nervousness fading as the great bear moved ahead of them, becoming more solid so that by the time she stood in front of the line of soldiers, she appeared flesh and blood, standing on her hind legs, staring up at the ceiling into the eyes of her enemy.

The dervish moved. So quickly that if Yvonne had not been watching, she might have missed it. The creatures simply fell from the ceiling into the room below, their mass of legs unfurling as they fell, spreading out, so it was almost impossible to tell which limb belonged to which creature.

Arrows flew. Some striking home, some clattering to the floor. The bear roared and swiped at the nearest dervish with her great claws, tearing through the limbs she caught, scattering bits of dark across the floor along with the creature's blood.

Perhaps it was the bear. Perhaps it was seeing that the creatures could actually be wounded. Whatever the reason, the soldiers swarmed forward, the air full of battle.

"Now," Yvonne said to Guise, grabbing spells from her pouch as she made her way through the chaos.

Hiram was still near his throne, watching the fighting with a hard, intent look. He had not expected anything to be able to stand up to the dervish, she realised. And even with the great bear's help, the fighting was still fierce. He was trying to decide if he might lose, she thought, as impossible as that had seemed to him a short while ago. And deciding what to do.

She did not want to wait and find out what other terrible magic he might have ready to use.

"Call them off," she said.

He turned to her, lips peeling back, skin splitting to reveal the corruption beneath his skin, and raised his staff, the twisted thing painful to look at.

Guise flowed past her, sword out. One swift stroke, and he had severed Hiram's hand from his arm, the fingers still clutching the staff as it fell to the floor.

"You can't kill me," Hiram said, staring in shock at the staff and hand lying on the floor.

"He did not kill you," Yvonne said. She was close enough to him that she could smell the corruption of his breath, feel the heat coming off his skin, the sweet smell of decay that was twisted into his robes.

"And you think you can?" he said, teeth bared.

For her answer, she put her hand on his chest, a trio of spells held there. Fire. Cleansing. Unravelling. She spoke the activation words, holding the spells to his chest.

The spells bloomed under her fingers, the heat of fire scorching through to her bones, even with its main power directed forward. The cleansing and unravelling danced among the fire, covering every part of him.

Hiram, blood sorcerer and former Circle Mage, simply ceased to be under the force of her magic. The unclean magic he had used to hold his body together disintegrated, tearing itself apart, a wordless scream of fury and pain ringing in her ears as the corruption vanished, burned out of the daylight world, the force of magic scattering bits and pieces of ash into the air around him, across the floor and over Yvonne.

The ashes swirled in the heat of the fire spell, floating in the air in front of her. She was coated with the stuff, her hand still held in front of her, palm out, where Hiram's chest had been, her skin crawling from the contact with the blood sorcerer. He was gone. Absolutely gone. Reduced to the little bits and pieces swirling in the air. Not one fragment of him bigger than her smallest fingernail.

Before she could move or react, warmth curled around her wrist, tantalisingly familiar, and tugged her forward. Or tried to. She held her ground, but could not pull her hand back.

"Little sister." A voice she had heard before. In the ashes of Hiram's son, when she had killed him and unleashed the death curse he had grafted into his bones. "We see you."

It was trying to pull her forward, still. Trying to draw her in. Towards the great void she could sense ahead of her, centred on the pile of Hiram's ashes.

"Come. Join us."

"No," she said, voice less certain than it should be.

"Join us," the dark suggested again, pulling gently. The warmth was creeping up her arm, invisible fingers sliding across her skin under the shirt sleeve.

"No," she said, more firmly, and set her heels to the floor, pulling back.

A moment later and a shower of familiar magic washed over her. Pieris' cleansing spell.

It did not chase away all of the dark, but was enough to loosen its hold. Enough that she could take a step back, away from the ash, her hand still held in front of her, sooty marks around her wrist where it had held her.

"Mristrian?" Guise asked.

"Mrista," she answered, without thinking, holding out her other hand. He laced his fingers through hers.

"You cannot escape me now," Guise said, eyes bright with green and gold.

"I don't want to," she told him plainly.

He lifted a hand, cupped the side of her face, his skin warm and slightly rough, fingers shifting in a pattern only he knew the meaning of.

"You claimed me," he said, voice full of wonder.

"Well, it seemed fair," she said, heat rising in her face. She had not really thought too much about it. The goblin word rang in her mind again. Mrista. A staking of possession.

"I have been yours for a long time," he told her, voice low, not meant to carry to anyone else.

She met his eyes, seeing the depth of feeling there, and felt her mouth curve upwards.

"Does that include your wine collection?" she asked.

"Everything," he said, without hesitation.

"Everything?" she asked, brows lifting, mischief taking hold. "So. The wine. The clothes. The –"

She didn't get a chance to finish her list as he kissed her, as thoroughly as he had before, and she forgot all about the carnage around them, the other people in the room, the ruined windows, forgot about anything else apart from Guise.

Chapter Thirty-Two

Two days later, Yvonne walked into the audience chamber that was, finally, free of all traces of Hiram's presence. All the dead had been removed, including the remains of the dervish. The mercenaries, and the dervish, had been burned the day before. The funeral rites for the soldiers had taken place that morning. The few mercenaries who had survived had been gathered together and were now being escorted out of the kingdom by Valland soldiers.

The palace had been searched, from the underground treasury to the rooftops, and every trace of Hiram and the unclean magic he had practised had been removed and destroyed, including jars of body parts and a collection of bones similar to the ones Yvonne had found near Guise. Hiram had believed in practising his craft, that much was clear. Yvonne thought it would be a long while before she wanted to eat any meat again.

Hiram had managed to seed his magic into almost every part of the building. She was exhausted, a niggling headache telling her she had pushed her magic too far, the turmoil in her stomach telling her that, even if she did not want to, she needed to stop, rest and eat something.

Before then, there was a conversation she needed to have. What she hoped would be one bright moment in an otherwise grim day.

The young Mage, Ewan, was standing in the middle of the audience chamber. He was still dressed in plain, ordinary clothes, very like her own. A shirt that had seen better days, trousers and boots. Even though he was near the middle of the chamber, he was staring out at the city below.

The room was spotlessly clean, and bitterly cold. There had been no time to repair the windows that Yvonne had broken, freeing the death dust. And this high above the city, the slight breeze that drifted in through the windows carried the promise of winter with it.

"I keep wondering if I missed something. If I could have done something," Ewan said as she came to stand near him. He did not look at her, staring out at the afternoon light, the Royal City apparently peaceful, apart from the great stretch of burned buildings.

"You think you could have stopped a blood sorcerer?" Yvonne asked.

"You did," Ewan answered, then shook his head, bright spots of colour in his cheeks. "Sorry. I didn't mean ... I just think I could have done something."

"I didn't stop him on my own," Yvonne reminded him. "There were quite a few other people around. And the Firebird. And the great bear." She let the words sink in, watching the colour fade in his face, his shoulders ease a little, and turned to look out at the city. Her human hearing could not catch the sounds, but she could imagine the city slowly returning to normal. Craftsmen and women getting back to work. Markets full of goods. Taverns full of conversation and beer.

"What will you do now?" she asked Ewan. It was not the real question she wanted to ask him, but the most direct way she could think of to ask him about his future.

He hesitated long enough that she turned to look at him. He had colour in his face that had not been there a moment before, and had clasped his hands together.

"I want to learn. To do what you do," he said, the words coming out in a rush.

"You recognised the magic, didn't you?" she asked.

"Yes. It felt ... clean, somehow. And like something I knew, but I don't know where from."

"It's the magic of the Hundred," Yvonne told him, keeping her voice as calm and low as possible. "And you have it inside you, too."

"I do?" His brows lifted to his hairline.

"Yes. It's a birthright. And, yes, you can learn to use it."

"Can I learn to be a Hunar?" he blurted out. And that was the question. The real question, that he had been holding on to. "I mean, I know I'm probably too old to train. And I'm not nearly as powerful as you. Or Pieris. But I'd like to learn. I really would."

Yvonne smiled, and laughed softly, brightness blooming in her chest, the grimness of the day fading.

"You are not too old. And your power will grow in time. Yes, you can learn to be a Hunar. We can teach you."

"We?" he said, and then followed her gaze. Pieris was a short distance away.

"I followed Yvonne. I suspected she was coming to talk to you," Pieris said, the symbol at his shoulder glowing faintly in the daylight. "And I think you will make an excellent Hunar, in time," he added, to Ewan.

"When do I start?" Ewan asked.

"You already have," Yvonne told him, unable to stop another smile. He had the right instincts. The desire to help. And the magic of the Hundred running through him. "You'll need to travel with us."

"The training can take a long time," Pieris added. "And the life is not an easy one."

"But is it worth it?" Ewan asked.

"Oh, yes," Pieris and Yvonne said together.

Ewan grinned, and then swayed slightly on his feet.

"When was the last time you ate?" Yvonne asked.

"Food? I don't know. Perhaps this morning?" he answered, brow wrinkling.

"The others are gathering for a meal downstairs," Pieris told them. "Thort has taken over the kitchens. He promises a feast to remember."

"He is an excellent cook," Yvonne said, turning to follow Pieris out of the room. She hesitated when Ewan did not follow them.

"I can come with you?" he asked, sounding as young as Priss.

"Yes. We'll be leaving soon. Perhaps tomorrow. Perhaps the day after." Yvonne shook her head slightly. Now that Hiram was gone, she wanted to see her children. "You'll need to gather your things, and you should bring your pony, too. I had to retire my old horse not that long ago, and he would love some company."

"Really? I can bring Prince? Oh, thank you."

Yvonne shook her head slightly, conscious of Pieris' quiet laugh beside her.

"Were we ever so young and eager?" she asked him.

"I don't remember," he answered, then laughed again. "Young, certainly. A few months of training, and he'll be less eager."

"Oh, yes. The weapons practice," Yvonne said, shaking her head again as she remembered being almost too sore and worn out to move.

"Weapons?" Ewan asked, following them out of the room. He still sounded eager.

Yvonne and Pieris exchanged a glance and laughed again.

Thort had somehow taken over the great kitchens of the palace, and the servants' dining room, which was dominated by a long table and a series of plain, wooden chairs. Enough for all of them to settle on.

Guise had, predictably, found some wine, and there were bottles scattered around the table amid the many dishes of food Thort had prepared.

Yvonne sat next to Guise, food settled in her stomach, half a glass of wine taking the edge off her headache, and looked around at her companions. Old friends, and new. Lita and Ulla, bickering in a good-natured fashion at the other side of the table. Ewan settled next to Sarra, wide-eyed, listening for all he was worth to the conversations around him. Pieris and Jaalam, the lines on Pieris' face eased again, the sadness he had carried in his eyes gone. Brea and Thort, relaxed after what even Brea had to admit had been a worthy fight.

In a lull in conversation, Sarra, not far away from Yvonne around the table, set her wine glass down and sighed. "I know you'll be moving on soon," the soldier said. "I will miss you."

Yvonne felt an answering echo in her own chest. She liked the old soldier.

"You'll be kept busy," Brea commented. It might have sounded heartless, but it was a warrior's sympathy, roughly expressed.

"I know. We've had people at the door all day. I've no idea what to say to them," Sarra said, grimacing. The palace had been closed for the past few days but the people of the Royal City were used to easy access to the palace, and the doors could not stay closed forever.

Yvonne looked at the older woman, measured the weight of her words and the catch in her voice.

"I thought the Steward was still alive?" she asked. In fact, she knew he was. He had been thrown into one of the palace's cells and left, seemingly forgotten. He had been absent for the past couple of days, recovering from lack of food or water.

"Yes. I'm sure I saw him walking about today," Ewan said.

"Then, I would suggest that you let the Steward answer questions," Yvonne said to Sarra.

Sarra's shoulders straightened, and the shadows across her face lightened into a smile that held unexpected mischief.

"I knew I liked you, Hunar," the soldier said. She lifted her glass and made a silent toast, smiling as she set the glass down. "Any other ideas?" she asked the table.

That was invitation enough for Jaalam, who came up with a half dozen ridiculous suggestions for dealing with rude enquiries that had everyone at the table laughing for a while longer. Lita joined the debate, her sharp mind and love of intrigue equalling Jaalam's.

Under the table, Yvonne linked her fingers through Guise's, and laughed along with everyone else. They were alive. Their enemy was dead. She had found a new apprentice Hunar. And she would soon see her children again. It was a rare moment of peace in a Hunar's life. One to savour.

THANK YOU

Thank you very much for reading *The Searching*, The Hundred - Book 5.

It would be great, if you have five minutes, if you could leave an honest review at the store you got it from. Reviews are really helpful for other readers to decide whether the book is for them, and also help me get visibility for my books - thank you.

Yvonne's story concludes in *The Rising*, The Hundred - Book 6, also available at Amazon:

If you want to know what I'm working on and when the next book will be available, you can contact me and sign up for my newsletter at the website: www.taellaneth.com.

CHARACTER LIST

NOTE: TO AVOID SPOILERS, some names may have been omitted, and some details left out.

Adira - human, senior head Sister in the Stone Walls
Annabelle - human, one of the Hundred
Baldur - Yvonne's horse
Brea - goblin, wife to Thort and mother to Jesset
Dora - human, law keeper in Fir Tree Crossing
Dundac - human, one of the Hundred
Edmond - human, Priss' father and Hannah's husband
Elinor – human, deceased at start, formerly of the Hundred
Ella - wulfkin, in Sephenamin's range
Firon - human, one of the Hundred
Frida - human, dressmaker, from Fir Tree Crossing
Grayling- human, head of law keepers at Fir Tree Crossing
Guise - goblin
Hannah - human, Priss' mother and Edmond's wife
Helgiarast - goblin, star of the Karoan'shae, Guise's mother
Idal - human, apprentice Hunar
Jaalam - goblin, one of the Karoan'shae
Jesset - goblin, Brea and Thort's daughter
Joel - wulfkin, one of Yvonne's wards and Mariah's brother
Kraig – human, senior law keeper, reporting to Grayling

Lothar - Yvonne's horse

Mariah - wulfkin, one of Yvonne's wards and Joel's sister

Mica - human, one of the Hundred

Modig - mixed heritage, former hotel manager in Three Falls

Pieris - human, one of the Hundred

Pridthan - goblin, Helgiarast's older son

Rebecca - human, from Hogsmarthen

Renard - wulfkin, famous horse trainer

Roa - human, one of the girls taken by the ancient enemy

Sephenamin – wulfkin, cerro in Fir Tree Crossing, owns The Tavern

Sillman - human, one of the Hundred

Suanna - human, one of the Hundred

Thort - goblin, Brea's husband, Jesset's father

Varati - goblin, one of the Karoan'shae

Yvonne - human, one of the Hundred, legal guardian of Mariah and Joel

PLACES

Abar al Endell – southernmost city, at the edge of the desert, near the Forbidden Lands

Coll Castle - part of Kingdom of Valland

Fir Tree Crossing - busy trading town on the Great River

Forbidden Lands - desert territory beyond Abar al Endell

Hogsmarthen - closest city to the Sisters in the Stone Walls, on the Great River (upriver from Fir Tree Crossing)

Kelton - artists' town on the Great River between Hogsmarthen and Fir Tree Crossing

Royal City - home of the Valland Kings, furthest upriver on the Great River

Silverton - small trading town upriver from Fir Tree Crossing

Stone Walls - home of the Sisters in the Stone Walls, a high-sided mountain valley not far from Hogsmarthen

Three Falls - city state near Valland

Valland - largest Kingdom in the lands, holds the Royal City, a lot of the Great River and Coll Castle

Willowton - Elinor's home town

ALSO BY THE AUTHOR

(as at February 2024)

The Hundred series (complete)
The Gathering, Book 1
The Sundering, Book 2
The Reckoning, Book 3
The Rending, Book 4
The Searching, Book 5
The Rising, Book 6

Fractured Conclave
A Usual Suspect, Book 1 – expected to release early May 2024

Ageless Mysteries (complete)
Deadly Night, Book 1
False Dawn, Book 2
Morning Trap, Book 3
Assassin's Noon, Book 4
Flightless Afternoon, Book 5
Ascension Day, Book 6

The Grey Gates (complete)
Outcast, Book 1

Called, Book 2
Hunted, Book 3
Forged, Book 4
Chosen, Book 5

The Taellaneth series (complete)
Concealed, Book 1
Revealed, Book 2
Betrayed, Book 3
Tainted, Book 4
Cloaked, Book 5

Taellaneth Box Set (all five books in one e-book)
Taellaneth Complete Series (Books 1–5)

ABOUT THE AUTHOR

Vanessa Nelson is a fantasy author who lives in Scotland, United Kingdom and spends her days juggling the demands of two spoiled cats, two giant dogs and her fictional characters.

As far as the cats are concerned, they should always come first. The older dog lets her know when he isn't getting enough attention by chewing up the house. The younger dog's favourite method of getting her attention is a gentle nudge with his head. At least, he would say it's gentle.

You can find out more information online at the following places:

Website: www.taellaneth.com

Facebook: www.facebook.com/taellaneth

Printed in Great Britain
by Amazon